I would like to thank my children, Jenny, Josh and Logan for their much greater than expected interest as well as providing names sakes for characters. I should take this moment to mention that any likeness are pure chance and that whilst names have been used likeness's have mostly not!

I would also like to thank my two closest and eldest friends in Simon and Adam for having read and provided feedback along the way. Especially Simon who must have received an alarming numbers of drafts and alterations!

Whilst their names have not been used it should be noted that this book is intended as the first in a trilogy..... So watch this space gentleman.

PROLOGUE

Morpheus stood alone atop the rocky cliffs overlooking the raging sea. He watched in awe as the dark and powerful army below him marched in unison, traveling towards their destination in Midjun. The lands of Midjun were barren, but the sea was alive, with waves crashing against the sharp rocks below, creating an ever-changing pattern of foam and bubbles.

He watched in admiration, but also with a sense of dread, as the soldiers moved like a massive machine. He knew that this was just the start of something far bigger, and he wondered what dangers or destruction would soon be unleashed upon these lands.

The sun was beginning to set and Morpheus felt an even greater urgency to move on. He needed to figure out the best way to stay ahead of the looming threat that was coming closer and closer with each passing moment.

The Jinn had stepped out from his dark fortress in Maredrom and into the howling wind. The trees near his stronghold were bent in half with their massive arms reaching up as if to grab him and drag him down to their murky muddy pools as he walked by. He held his head down and kept moving, slowly, steadily towards the land of Lemuri, and more importantly Lemuri Falls themselves. The journey was treacherous and dangerous, but he knew that there was no other way for him to achieve his goal. He had been working on this dream for over a century and now it was finally coming to fruition. Morpheus knew that he could not allow this to be true. The Jinn achieving control over the Lemuri falls would spell the end. The end of peace, the end of right, indeed the end for the humanity that lay above and all life within the realms around.

The Lemuri falls were a pathway into the dreams of all life, within which they contained a bridge to not only Earth but all of the other realms within the known universe. The long falls poured into the pools at the base and flowed outwards through underground rivers in all directions. One of these led to the land of Sofpavel where trees with translucent leaves made a roof over the streams, and flowers that flickered like candles lined the river banks. These lands maintained the balance of good and provided the realms with great dreams and wonders and fuelled the life force that they so heavily depended on. This was where the people named the Lemurians lived. They were ruled over by Morpheus, a Great warrior and much revered by all. The Lemurians' home of

Sofpavel with its green, lush fields, amazing mountains, and sheer beauty were a sight to behold. Through the Lemuri falls flowed dreaming orbs, colourful balls of light that held within them the hopes and wishes and fantasies of every soul out there in the wider beyond. Once these orbs reached Lemuri they made their way through those underground channels and flowed up the majestic falls and off into the void, making their way to the various realms.

On the other side of this however lay Maredrom. The energy there was dark and evil, and it would create nightmares with a power that could not be matched by any other source. Torches flickered in the night, driven by a wind that never stopped blowing. Broken trees with branches looming like the long fingers of a frail old man lined the banks of a riverbed, the water long since gone. The fortress looked decrepit, as though it were on its last legs; its walls crumbling, its towers leaning to one side. Crumbling dead trees line the ground like dry bones. Dark energy flowed from here all over the world, creating misery and suffering wherever it touched down – this was where the nightmares began and evil was rooted. The unfortunate, necessary balance.

The land was occupied by strange and terrifying creatures all veering from left to right, staggering with little purpose or aim. Under instruction from a dark lord they can become quite a force, a singular moving swarm consuming all in their path, but without, simply lost, wandering souls. A mist covered the plains, and to either side of the road roamed packs of these undead-soldier corpses that attacked anything that moved. Corpses and skeletons with mottled flesh and feasting flies, these were of little danger to strangers. However, the Men and women clad in armour made from bones who clanked together and loped along near the edge of what was once a lush forest, each with their swords raised high were another matter. A few small fires burned here and there, but had done little to diminish the cloud of smog that hung over everything like a veil. This was hell as real as it ever could be. The dark orbs flowed from here to create the nightmares and evil that exist throughout the realm, flowing through the one remaining river, this river flowed strong with raging, ferocious torrents and along their path travelled directly underneath the castle which was inhabited by whichever dark lord lay claim to these lands at the time.

Morpheus took a deep breath, the fresh air of Midjun in the distance travelled across the seas, filling his lungs. He had been travelling for a few days, and he was tired but determined to keep going. His long locks of hair were wet and matted against his face entwined with his long wiry beard. The journey had lasted longer than he had planned, poor weather conditions had held them up but he refused to let it end here. Instead, he pushed his stallion on, sheathing his sword against a nearby tree while keeping one hand on the reins so they could step forward at a moment's notice. Under the setting sun his stallion's black coat shimmered with highlights as it panted heavily from its exertion but seemed restless and eager to proceed.

Morpheus's Nyx soldiers stood tall and proud, their helmets shimmering in the setting sun as they marched solemnly across the final stretches of Sofpavel towards the awaiting Armada. They shone like polished silver in the late afternoon sun and twinkled like stars flickering on and off with every move they made. Dust rose from the earth that kicked up and swirled around their feet as they tread forward. Their steps were sure, but their faces were narrow with worry, they had seen many battles but never quite like this.

They towered over the land, in their glinting silver breastplates and sharpened spears, a vengeful presence ready for battle. Their gazes swept across the terrain with binoculars, surveying the impending battlefield beyond Midjun, already swarming with enemy forces outnumbering them at least twenty-fold. Resolutely, they prepared to march into the fight.

The soldiers marched solemnly onto the awaiting ships, their movements solemn and still. The sea churned wildly, creating a tempestuous pattern of whitecaps and bubbles as the waves bashed against each other without mercy.

Far down beneath the waves they could see the orbs making their way down towards Lemuri amongst the fish and sea creatures that called these waters their home. Morpheus watched on in pride as his fleet began its journey towards what they hoped was their final destination of Midjun, the island lay centrally, between themselves in Sofpavel and the lands of Maredrom. It had never been occupied by any other than the watchmen of the tower and was a relatively barren land, void of shrubbery or any particular scenic areas to speak of.

The voyage seemed to last an eternity as they sailed through unusually turbulent waters and fierce gales, struggling to make it through the relatively short distance unscathed. But eventually the awaiting land came into clear view on the horizon. As they approached shore they were met with guarded optimism.

Morpheus led his exhausted troops ashore and gave them time to rest before assembling for battle. He inspected each warrior carefully, ensuring that everyone was ready for what lay ahead of them. As he looked upon these brave warriors, he felt a great sense of pride swell within him - these were his people.

Morpheus and his Nyx soldiers stood ready for battle, their armour gleaming in the now fading sun and spears held firmly in hand. Each one had pledged their loyalty to Morpheus long before they set off, and now they were here—on the threshold of a battle that would decide the fate of every living being. The opposing army had begun to eagerly move towards them the second they made land, any respite they thought they may have would not be that long lived.

The island was under siege by a well-known force of which was being led by the powerful Jinn – a being who had grown more powerful than had been imagined whilst ruling over the lands of Maredrom. He led the dark forces in a way that had never been done before, they were usually unpleasant and dangerous if interacted with but had always until now stayed to their own, unable to forge any real threat. They were a necessary side in this balance but one that had always known its place and obediently stayed to it. The Nyx had no idea how sinister a plan the Jinn may have devised and therefore moved cautiously forward as they took on each new challenge presented to them. They knew he was a dark lord like none before and an extremely intelligent and ambitious one at that. He had no intention of knowing his place and if he did, he did not plan to remain there.

Morpheus was conscious of the extreme consequences that would ensue should the entirety of Erobus be subjugated by the sinister lord. He and his forefathers had been guarding against this potential result for millennia, never accepting it to be a genuine prospect. Yet here they stood, confronting their greatest fear: that the darkness might reign supreme. The Jinn had undeniably become overwhelming. In what manner precisely however, Morpheus had no knowledge. One thing that could not be denied however, is that he had attained power enough to make the unimaginable achievable.

The Jinn stomped a long swath across Midjun until he reached the war-torn battleground. He trekked for days, yet remained undetected by the towering keepers of the watchtower that guarded the way to Lemuri. Through some extraordinary feat, he marshalled an entire battalion from Maredrom in secrecy, and finally arrived at his planned destination.

The three hundred-story tower stands tall and proud against the harsh landscape. The outside is made of strong stone, encasing the technology within. Its windows are small, but the top floors have a balcony for viewing the entirety of Erobus. It is visible from far away and is a reminder of the protection Morpheus and his ancestors have worked hard to provide. Its location beside the narrow pathway leading to Lemuri gives it an additional layer of protection, providing a guardian for the great falls.

Morpheus had taken the lead as they disembarked from the ships, mounted on his horse and galloping towards the red glow that now illuminated Maredrom ahead of them, bright and alluring in the far distance. His Nyx soldiers followed closely behind, with swords drawn and now appearing orange as they glint from the reflections of the low-lying sun. Most of these knights had never left their homeland before, or even set foot into Midjun; it was largely forbidden territory given the need to protect Lemuri so strongly.

The Nyx soldiers fearlessly charged upon the nearing enemy and attacked the Koschei forces, the mass of undead warriors knew not of fear and moved rapidly like a wave of locusts, as they finally met towards the middle of the island. As their blades clashed and they shouted with rage, the Nyx fought with the constant reminder of how the outcome of this battle could have catastrophic consequences for everyone if they did not win burned deep within their minds. With that thought in mind, each one was determined to fight to the death in order to ensure victory. Despite the uneven numbers the Nyx were much more uniformed and disciplined, much more equipped and well suited for the battle.

Morpheus pushed through his forces and moved to the forefront of the battle lines, of which were made up of some of his more hardened and experienced soldiers. The scent of the battle filled these lands with a smell they were not accustomed to, death and destruction was an unknown entity for Midjun, a land only accustomed to the solace of absence.

The two sides were always foes, but the cold war kept hostilities in check. These days, their mistrust was so palpable you could cut it with a knife. Over the past few decades, the sides had been fighting more as tensions grew, the two sides having grown a greater mutual disdain for one another, fuelled by occurrences that are too numerous and complex to recount here.

Morpheus generally had other foes to also contend with, any creatures making their way into lands they should not be were usually easy to vanquish back to their own place. As were any forces planning on stepping out of line and causing potential unrest through the realms.

He glanced at Hypnos, who had served as his General for a decade and who was older than he. Those ageless eyes betrayed that victory here was not a foregone conclusion, even though Morpheus struggled to hide it behind brave words that invoked the gods of war. Here, in this desert where they had not seen action for so long, the presence of the enemy would make or break them.

The Nyx had to stay rooted in place if they were to prevent the Jinn from taking control of Erobus, these lands to the North of here the key to everything, he had to do all he could to ensure that they stay secure.

Hypnos looked forward and did as his leader instructed, he stood at an impressive seven-foot-tall, his broad shoulders and muscular frame amplified by the dark grey gothic armour that seemed to absorb the light of the moon. His wingspan was approximately five feet wide, a deep ebony hue with small flecks of silver that sparkled in the night sky. His face was stoic, yet his sky-blue eyes glowed with life. His view snapped towards Morpheus as he charged forward. With sword raised high, Hypnos shouted an incantation that echoed throughout the battlefield, beating against Morpheus's ears like the clanging of iron he once heard in his own dream's eons ago.

The remaining soldiers of the Nyx forces responded with vigour, their fast-depleting numbers continuing on as buoyant and determined as could be. This small force continued pushing back the dark cloud of evil Koschei forces that seemed to have a never-ending wave of soldiers. The Koschei had been joined by the other tamed beasts of their land creating a fearsome looking brood of foes, a dark cloud emanated from the Jinn who had moved from within the centre of it all and had now become visible on the front lines of the battlefield, his imposing presence looming large, the large pointed horns on his tar black helmet penetrated far higher than the heads of even the tallest of enemy.

Morpheus's eyes widened in surprise as the Jinn's presence seemed to become more powerful with each passing moment as he absorbed and drew in the dark orbs and the nightmares that lay within. The figure of the Jinn shimmered and rippled, becoming larger, while his black armour grew duller and greyer with each orb he consumed. How was it possible? He had found a way to harness their energy and use it against them, but how?

Even from so far away, Morpheus could feel the cool breath of his dark magic as it spread out and threatened to snatch up everything in sight. He knew he had to act if he wanted to prevent the darkness from overthrowing all of Erobus and destroying all of the realms. He clutched his sword and stared down at the tiny lights moving at a snail's pace across the islands floor. Erobus itself felt as though it was willing Morpheus on.

Morpheus shouted further orders for Hypnos and his loyal Nyx army to press forward, although this time he seemed much less certain in his tone as to if this was the correct move. Despite their continued heavy losses and exhaustion, they managed to break through the Koschei forces and begin their advance towards the Jinn himself who had slunk back within the mix ever so slightly seemingly aware that his opponent had no intentions of slinking away. The other Nyx soldiers followed suit and began their march forward pushing through, determined not to fail in this fight against evil.

Morpheus squinted. A slight frown crossed his face, and he returned to gazing at the sea. "We are at war," he said quietly. The news was not a surprise, but neither was it welcome. The fact that the war had been bought so close-the plains of Sofpavel barely forty miles distant-put Morpheus in a quandary. He had great faith in his army and his generals as a whole in dealing with any potential invasion of Midjun and most definitely their lands of Sofpavel. However, this was an invasion that should never have been able to happen. It wasn't just that his opponent should never have been strong or bold enough to dare; they should never have found out ways to access Lemuri and they should not be so aware of the magical tree that held the key existed.

The noise and chaos of battle was all around him, incalculable numbers of warriors battling endlessly. Arrows whistled through the air and quarterstaffs clashed with the clank of metal on metal. Warriors called out to their allies to rally against the enemy – though it was difficult to tell friend from foe amidst the sea of steel. Amidst all this turmoil, he moved toward his own, purposeful goal. He knew that if he failed to act now, everything might fall apart. The Jinn's army would conquer Midjun and gain unprecedented access to the falls. It seemed as though The Jinn had all but won already. He needed to be here to lay claim to the falls for himself in whatever way he could. In his mind, this could well be the endgame: a pitched final battle where lives are lost on both sides until only one side remains.

His power had grown to a point where the distinction between him and the elder dark forces was almost invisible. His heavy steps echoed in the empty chambers of his palace, but he could feel their presence in every brick, every plank of wood, in the very air around him. He knew he had become the most powerful being Maredrom had ever seen and all those who walked before him were willing him to victory.

The horns on the Jinn's helmet glowed as if they were straining against a magnetic field, shedding light that was otherwise absent from his body. Streams of blue electricity crackled along their edges, spilling down his armour and into his hands.

How he had grown quite so strong was still mostly a mystery. They knew he had been absorbing dark energy, but how and from where? They knew dark magic was involved but again, this was not something that any being had the knowledge of which to conjure, not for millennia anyhow. But the Jinn had seemingly found a way to gain access to this knowledge. It was known this was not his first attempt on Lemuri and he had been trying for some time to gain access. He had discovered a passageway through the dark mountain ranges at the far end of Maredrom. The paths were a maze and if somehow you found your way through, of which he did a being is said to block your way through. This is rumoured to have happened to The Jinn although no other being has managed to find their way to this point to clarify if what he stated was true. He kept knowledge of the locations and directions to himself, always fearful of someone attempting to rise against him, however improbable this seemed.

As the sun began to set, the two armies stood facing each other, ready for the final showdown. The Jinn now stood at the front of his army upon a pile of broken earth and decaying trees. The trunk at the base of the tree had been exposed, grass had grown over the wound and held it in place like a bandage. The tree had died a long time ago and clung to its grassy saviour to maintain any signs of having once been. His horns were glowing with an eerie light causing the Nyx to squint as they peered in his direction, while Morpheus stood tall with his sword drawn, ready to face his opponent. The air was thick with tension, and both sides knew that this battle appeared to be drawing towards a conclusion.

Morpheus pushed forward into the fight, keeping his focus on the enemy ahead. Dark clouds and thunder billowed from Maredrom; it was an unthinkable sight. With every step closer, he felt the evil emanating from the island, growing thicker like a black cloud releasing more and more ash from its depths.

Morpheus watched Hypnos and his army of Nyx warriors disappear into the masses as they became surrounded and immeasurably outnumbered. Looking ahead, he saw a red mist hovering in the air as the Jinn slashed through his soldiers as smoothly as through butter. His axe was awash with fresh blood, releasing its hold on its edges as it continuously swung back and forth drenching everything around it. He swung his axe again, this time in a wide arc directly in front of his body, a blast of dark energy shot forward, cutting through the air like a hurricane. The soldiers were thrown back, their bodies torn apart by the sheer force of the blast.

Morpheus could see a glint of silver as a sword swung in his direction. He barely flinched as he removed his, defending himself with a single block. Morpheus stood a giant of a man at almost 8 feet tall and his sword was in proportion. The blow to the incoming weapon as it struck his own sent the opposing warrior reeling. Morpheus continued to create himself a pathway, the strength of his stead forcing all aside and his swaying blade dealing with those it did not as he fought towards the Jinn.

Morpheus could virtually feel his scarlet eyes piercing through the armour that enveloped his head as he approached, with the horde of undead becoming more concentrated with each step.

A malicious grin slithered across the Jinn's face.

Morpheus's forces were fast growing thin and they both knew it. It was clear to both of them that a victory for the Jinn was in sight; Morpheus would hold firm alone if necessary, however they both knew his defeat was seemingly inevitable. The Nyx remaining were dwindling rapidly. Even the mighty Hypnos had been taken down by a shower of arrows, which had left his wings too damaged for flight. He may not be able to take off, yet he still intended to fight until the bitter end, just like his leader.

They had battled shoulder to shoulder for millennia, forming a connection and kinship beyond any other bond; it was more akin to a fraternal bond.

They have rarely had to fight meaningfully, their sheer presence alone within the cosmos usually providing the protection required to maintain order. The Jinn however was feeling proud of his accomplishments up to this point and had grown more daring, stronger and wiser. He had never been able to reach this point before; he had never been so successful and he was sure he was going to win the battle, if not the war. Before, he would have stayed away from someone like Morpheus directly on the field of battle, uncertain about winning, or even holding his own against him. But now, he decided to stand his ground.

He had always had the power to stand up to his opponent just like any other, but had been too smart to be drawn into battles he knew he could not win. With the bloodied axe resting by his side, he raised it and pointed towards his enemy, he taunted him, almost as if Morpheus did not wish to fight the battle himself, which truth be told was partially true. Morpheus would much rather there be no fight at all. He beckoned his adversary forward, challenging him to enter the fray.

Morpheus charged forward, all between them seeming to have vanished, the Jinn peers to his left and then to his right, and with a nod signals to his commanders who all obediently part ways and reveal their secret weapon. Morpheus slows his charge, the expression on his face changing as he can scarcely believe what he witnesses emerge. He comes to a complete stop in shock and despair, dismounting his horse and dropping his mighty sword at his feet, a tear rolls down his face as he falls to his knees. Hypnos witnessing from afar is shocked by this scene; he watches with concern as the Jinn taunts Morpheus with a vile chuckle.

"For all of your strength and famed wise vision, you were still blind to what was before you," the Jinn jeers in his dark almost whisper of a deep voice.

Morpheus looked on in disbelief as he stared at the figure standing boldly, unashamedly before him. His brother, Probetor, had turned his back and now stood to fight against him. The shock of betrayal ran deep as he realized this man he had trusted with his every thought and action was now joining his greatest adversary. His heart began seething with rage as he contemplated the cost of such a treacherous act from a brother who had been absent for so long.

The Jinn's eyes glinted with glee as he watched the reaction of Morpheus, feeling an immense sense of satisfaction at having taken the wind out of the great leader's sails. Probetor had been a part of the Nyx army since time immemorial and was viewed as one of their strongest, smartest warriors - or so everyone thought. He had often fought side by side with both Morpheus and Hypnos, his magical gift had always been a huge asset to their army. Now however, he had chosen to align himself with the Jinn's darkness and use his strength for evil instead of good.

Morpheus's golden gaze hardened with resolve as he realized the truth. His brother, Probetor, had abandoned their principles and had chosen to side with the Jinn in this fight. He took a deep breath, steeling himself against his doubt and fear. "Up, sire," shouted a nearby soldier, urging him to continue. He nodded grimly, thrusting his sword into the ground and pulling himself to his feet.

Morpheus was aware of how much his brother could help the Jinn. Probetor was a master at deception and sorcery. He had an encyclopaedic knowledge of Erobus and the realms within it, as well as knowing many of the secrets that connected them all. This is no doubt how the Jinn acquired most of his knowledge of the passageways he had been attempting to use. Probetor watched over Earth, he was to ensure that nothing became out of hand, watch and inform on anything of concern. However, he had grown fond of watching the humans, wished to become one and became infatuated. He broke the rules that forbade direct interactions and found a way to use magic to visit the human world, and so he was exiled. But Morpheus did not regret his choice; Every person must choose which path they wish to walk. Rumours suggested he fell in love during his sentence and refused to return home when the time came for his sentence to end. So why would he submit himself to the service of the Dark Lord now if this was true?

Jinn's mocking laughter filled the air as Morpheus watched, his brother's eyes now empty and black. He had been taken over, lost to Jinn's power. Despair gave way to a boiling anger in Morpheus; he knew he must act to destroy the Jinn if the realms were to be saved, but there was no helping his brother at this point.

His brother could hold the key to all the Jinn's hopes and plans. He was trying to increase his people, control the whole known cosmos, and rule over every soul.

If need be, he would be required to stop his brother also. Morpheus wrenched his sword from the cloying ground, brandishing it in both hands. The steel sang as he twirled it around, stars raining down to light the sky of night. With a war cry Morpheus charged forward, slamming his blade against the Jinn's defence. Sparks flew as their weapons clashed and the Jinn planted his feet firmly, beginning to overpower Morpheus with each blow. A frenzied assault began as the Jinn summoned aid to join him in combat, bearing down on Morpheus who was struggling to keep up.

Morpheus was pushed back again and again; Hypnos and the Nyx were unable to provide enough aid against the Jinn's army as they struggled to approach through the blanket of enemy soldiers smothering them.

Knowing that his army couldn't match the multitudes of powerful enemies, Morpheus looked up to Hypnos despairingly, telling him to pull back their troops, he would save all he could. This was an unprecedented move for the leader, but knowing that they'd have to leave their home undefended if they stayed to fight any longer and that they would be unable to mount any further defence's, Hypnos did as he was told and shouted for a retreat, ordering his most elite remaining soldiers to the tower in an attempt to at least provide a last standing defence for Lemuri's pathway should they fail.

Hypnos observed his troops retreating with trepidation, noticing the injuries they had incurred in battle. He then noticed that Morpheus had turned back to fight and did not plan to flee and join the retreat. In the distance, he could make out Morpheus, unwavering in the face of danger. As if feeling Hypnos' gaze, Morpheus looked towards him and smiled. He knew that those injured and retreating would return safely to Sofpavel, and he now understood what he needed to do to stop the enemy's progression. He had one final play remaining of which he hoped with all he had would work, despite having desperately wished to not have had to use.

He swung his sword with a powerful arc, pushing the Jinn and Probetor away. Lifting it high above his head he brings it down with a mighty crash into the ground. The deafening sound echoes through the air and instantly splits the earth below them for some distance into the surrounding area, sending the broken remains of nearby trees crumbling to the ground under the impact as Hypnos feels the vibrations under foot like an earthquake tearing through the area.

The Nyx swiftly shuffled to their waiting ships, scrambling onto them with haste. The shimmering vessels served as beacons of hope, dazzling the menacing undead and providing the Nyx with a fighting chance to escape. Their glimmering hulls granted a safe haven as they stampeded away from the oncoming terror.

Morpheus leaned on his mighty sword and briefly closed his eyes, gathering the strength he would require. The final blow was a heavy one, but he felt more determined than ever to finish this. He knew the assistance he needed to do so was not readily available. The message travelled with the speed of light back to Sofpavel and across its lands. Freyja sat patiently in her chair deep in the castle of Sofpavel, awaiting news of what she hoped would be Morpheus's return. Suddenly the wind shifted around her, so cold it pierced her furs, leggings, and robes and brought tears to her eyes. She froze as a message arrived from Morpheus: "Freyja," it whispered into her ears in a voice akin to thunder rumbling over distant hills. "I need your help."

Freyja had told Morpheus of a powerful spell she could conjure, in case he ever found himself in a dangerous situation such as this. She hated even mentioning it, as it would come with dire consequences and could potentially kill them both. But when pressed for more information from an obviously desperate friend, Freyja reluctantly explained the unbearable pain, but dramatic benefit that accompanied using her most potent magic.

She rises to her feet and says goodbye to the people around her before beginning to chant an ancient spell. With her hands pointed towards the sky, tears rolling down her cheeks, she utters a mighty prayer and grinds her teeth as the powerful energy courses through her body.

The air around her crackles and boils with inky blue mist, radiating the force of her spell. Tears streak down her cheeks like rivulets of sorrow, knowing the tragedy that awaited her ally. She clenches her teeth, agony wracking her body as the power surges through her veins like a maelstrom.

At last, the spell is complete and Freyja releases a thunderous scream of pure energy. A massive explosion of blue light bursts outward from where she stands, as the light cracks over Hypnos head like a thousand lightning bolts striking at once he momentarily winces from the blazing light above him. It crashes into the raised blade held high aloft the head of Morpheus. He buckles momentarily under the enormous power and weight, then he staggers back as if pushed by an invisible force.

The Jinn and his brother look on in terror as their plans for domination hang in the balance. As the dust settles, they can make out Morpheus still standing with his sword held high above him like a beacon of hope amidst all of the destruction they have caused.

Morpheus drew the sword back once more and swung it down in a scythe-like arc, crashing into the earth below with such force that it sends the Jinn to his knees. The Probetor, unnoticed, took his opportunity amidst the chaos and slipped away into the night. Freyja's spell took hold of the sword guiding it through the air and pointing towards the Jinn, Morpheus struggles to maintain hold of the blade, the heat and energy burning up along the handle causing the flesh on his hands to begin to burn. He slams the blade into the ground with a mighty strike, and it instantly begins to devour The Jinn's soul and essence like a hungry beast. With each moment it drains away more of his life force, until finally the dark army falls like broken wind-up toys scattered across the ground, unable to fight back against the might of its captor. As the blade finalises the absorption and the Jinn becomes locked inside its cold metal prison Morpheus releases his grip sending the blade crashing to the ground, now blackened from the darkness within and smouldering from the heat. Morpheus glances up at the sky, admiring its beauty once last time before collapsing, exhausted. Though he is frustrated at his brother's successful escape, he knows that the main objective has been accomplished.

He desperately stretches out his arms, grasping at thin air as he tries to reach the sword. His body is wracked with pain - every breath feels like poison and every movement a struggle against death itself. Hypnos, having seen his soldiers onto the ships, now stands by Morpheus' side in deep agony as he gazes upon his leader's fading eyes. As Morpheus softly whispers for him to take the sword, Hypnos tremblingly lifts it from the ground and immediately cries out in pain - it feels like molten iron against his skin. He clasps Morpheus' hand tightly as tears stream down his face; feeling the grip loosen with each passing second - knowing that soon all would be silent. The greatness of Morpheus sacrifice could not be a burden with yet he felt he should suffer. The Jinn is now locked away forever within the sword and they are triumphant however losing his leader, his friend was too much. With a broken heart and defeated mind, Hypnos looks around at the scattered debris; recognizing victory but profoundly understanding defeat.

1. Holiday dreams

'AL, AL' Josh yells from across the room, 'what do you think?'

Josh leaned forward toward Alec, hoping to glean some insight into the question. Alec shifted in his seat, not quite sure what to say. He knew he had not been paying attention, and he had no intention of getting it wrong.

He felt Josh's gaze upon him, his friend seemed briefly agitated but compassionate. Alec considered a lie, but then thought better of it. Josh had always been able to see through any lie of Alec's, not that it was something he attempted often. How could he yet again attempt to explain his lack of attentiveness? Alec tiredly surveyed the dimly lit room hoping to see some clue as to the question that had just been thrown his way. He sat back in the lounge chair that he often called home and tried to look intently as if he did indeed have the answer but was giving it, some thought before speaking. He hesitated, searching for the right words, but when nothing came to mind, he took a deep breath and decided to be honest.

"Well," Alec said sheepishly, "I don't know what to tell you. you'll be surprised to hear I was not paying attention, sorry."

Josh leaned forward; his eyebrows furrowed in perturbation as he watched Alec's face. Slowly, he nodded, his own features softening in understanding. The two had been friends since they were just seven years old, meeting for the first time on the playground at school when they were strangely introduced on a surprise play date invitation despite Josh having been new and Alec not having spoken to him. They instantly felt a great connection and had plenty in common. Both of Alecs parents were had passed when he was young and he was being raised by his grandparents on his mother's side whilst Josh had been adopted from a young age.

The fact that neither of them had their real parents to turn to seemed to help their friendship thrive, since they were both subjected to the same emotionally draining situation.

Even back then, it had been difficult to gain Alec's attention- Josh could hardly count the number of times he'd found his friend tuned out and daydreaming about something else entirely. They were both in their early-twenties now, but some things never changed. The fact that Alec hadn't been fully listening on this occasion was nothing new nor surprising.

Josh smiled and continued to explain his idea as if Alec had indeed provided him with some kind of reflection.

"We should totally take that trip," Josh said, eyes aglow with enthusiasm. "Think of all the places we can explore - far away from Jenny and all the worries of life! We can find somewhere with amazing food and a place where we can just chill out and forget about everything." He tapped the table with his fingers as he spoke, his excitement palpable.

Alec smiled at his friend's excitement and also with amusement listening to the contents of the essential ingredients for said trip.

They had been planning on getting away for around 6 months now. Around the time that Alec found himself newly single after Jenny unceremoniously ended their relationship in front of all of their colleagues at the Morning Gazette. After around 3 years together she had decided to move on and did not seem to show any reluctance in doing so with haste. Alec was conflicted by his feelings and Josh had found himself collecting the pieces and constantly acting as a source of distraction.

Alec had been feeling lost ever since the break-up, his mind constantly drifting to thoughts of Jenny and what he could have done differently. How long had he been a bachelor again? About a year? It felt like it although he couldn't pinpoint exactly when he'd gotten lonely, or how. They had both been fascinated with each other in college. Both had studied journalism and their shared goal was to be big time news reporters. Alec had a flair for research and found everything fascinating, he equally enjoyed sharing his discoveries and found journalism a fantastic outlet for this.

Josh had never been keen on her but Alec had always put this down to a slither of jealousy on his friend's part who may well have felt put out by any attention he may have felt diverted that way. Alec and Josh had still always spent a lot of time together, which hadn't changed at all despite how Josh may have felt.

Jenny was always trying hard to push Alec out of his daydreaming ways, always trying to make him concentrate harder and often discussed them leaving to go to some mysterious place she knew in a country she had never actually disclosed, always stating that there was plenty there to research and help him focus. Josh hadn't minded this at all; sometimes he found it hard to follow where Alec's wandering mind went. He thought it fascinating how his friend could drift off into such great detail about something that may have piqued his interest, sometimes something not even real, but equally found this a source of great frustration.

Yet, as he desperately sought to keep him focused, his disdain for Jenny intensified with each passing day. He couldn't decipher the source of such loathing; however, he assumed it must have been due to her incessant nitpicking.

Whilst he had shared some of her wishes, he would never have pressurised his friend to change who he was, it was he was sure part of the reason he was such an interesting person to know after all. Each day, she pushed a little on Alec's tendency to drift off.

"Get back to reality!" she'd say when he would let some detail (the sun glinting off the raindrops in puddles for example) of the larger world zoom into his mind. She always seemed pushy in this respect and was obviously trying quite hard to change him in many ways, as well as always discussing the possibility of going to a faraway place which also annoyed Josh greatly. She seemed to equally dislike Josh and he believed she wished to move far away from him, regularly commenting on his untrustworthiness. He often thought this warring between them was quite possibly the catalyst that ended the relationship and for this he did have a small amount of guilt, his friend cared for her regardless. Alec dug deeper into journalism after she left, he had found a flair for copyediting and would spot misspellings or misuse of hyphens from hundreds of feet away, although he was still an avid fan of the research elements of his role, he found himself forcing into the more mundane.

But now, as Alec sat there with his friend, after a fair amount of time had passed since his heartbreak, he felt a glimmer of hope. Maybe this trip was just what he needed to forget about Jenny and hit that big reset button. Heading into an adventure unknown, a new chapter in his life being signalled as such perhaps, who knows.

Alec's face cleared. "Great!" he said, smiling. "How about a rather Latin-based holiday, or even just south of France? I hear they have great food and should certainly tick your boxes."

Josh perked up again. "Really?" he asked, his voice eager and bright. "Any place in particular?"

Alec grinned. "C'est toi qui décide," he said playfully, inviting Josh to decide for himself, although secretly he had some trepidation as to where Josh may choose, he could often be a little random and may well throw out a Timbuktu from nowhere!

"Great," he said. "I was thinking of a beach vacation, somewhere with crystal clear waters and white sandy beaches. We've had enough action for a while just the relaxation would be nice. Certainly could tick this easily enough within those areas? What do you think?"

Alec nodded, picturing himself lying on a beach, drink in hand, feeling the sun on his skin.

"That sounds perfect," he said.

He recalled the last time the two of them went away as this was not an unusual event. Whilst looking to relax on this occasion they were often seeking out a little adventure with their trips. This had at times bordered closer to trouble however! Alec's grandparents often concerned as to where their trouble may end up.

Josh turned back to his laptop and began searching for vacation packages. Alec watched him, feeling a sense of relief, or perhaps even excitement building inside him. This was exactly what he needed right now, a chance to escape and forget about his growing list of predicaments. They had been rather stuck in their loops for a while. the mundane reality of work and life in general had dragged for a while. Everything seemingly mediocre of late, something Alec often became frustrated with.

As Josh typed away, Alec's mind started to wander. He couldn't shake off other issues also of which he hoped would be aided by this trip, the dark dreams that had been haunting him for the past few weeks had been growing in intensity and frequency.

Since he was a child, vivid nightmares had plagued him mercilessly. They were often so intense; he swore he could feel the icy fingers of death clawing at his soul. He would wake up in the middle of the night with sweat-soaked sheets, gasping for breath and feeling as though he was being dragged to other worlds entirely.

The darkness seemed to take on a life of its own, stalking his every waking moment with its malevolent presence. Yet somehow, amid the chaos and confusion of these terrifying dreams, he found something exhilarating about experiencing such unbridled fear. It was as if they held some secret key that unlocked an ominous door leading to new and fantastical dimensions. His grandmother had often told him stories of his mother and how she had told fantastical tales to Alec of a world beyond theirs where dreams were formed. An amazing place that with incredible creatures and a beauty to behold around every corner. His father had vanished one day when Alec was young. He had always been told he had passed away and although this had not been confirmed it was now seen as fact. The day of his funeral was a strange affair under the circumstances, one that Alec could just about still remember. His mother shortly after had unfortunately passed away leaving his grandparents to raise him, they always had taken this in their stride despite the clear sadness that they must have felt in losing a child. He did not hold many memories of his mother either but again his grandparents were good at keeping the memory alive and he knew that she had loved him a great deal.

Every night recently however, his dreams had changed from the fantastical ones he had always had whether good or bad he was at least accustomed, he would now be transported to a world of chaos and destruction, where he found himself in the middle of a pending warzone on a strange, barren island. The more he tried to fight to get away, the more it seemed like he was losing his mind and it only served to plunge him deeper into this strange world. Alec was not a fighter. He would always shy away in fact. Whenever trouble may have been brewing, he would always find a way to excuse himself or simply vanish. He was not a coward, however never saw a need to fight.

Although he had a preternatural ability to detect when danger was lurking. Josh made light of it, teasing Alec about an uncanny crystal ball at his disposal. But it was true nonetheless; Alec always got a palpable feeling of foreboding whenever issues were looming and it had saved them from a few dire predicaments in the past!

He shook himself from his thoughts, why he had to remind himself of dreams he did not enjoy so often baffled him, and returned to concentrating on what Josh was trying to say, he did not want to miss it again!

Alec suddenly snapping back to reality fortunately heard Josh asked him a question.

"Hey Alec, you okay? You seemed miles away just then?"

Alec smiled weakly and shook his head. "Yeah, I'm fine," he said softly. He looked at Josh and sighed. "It's just these dreams I've been having," he confessed, feeling a little embarrassed to suffer from things that did not usually seem to bother the masses

Josh nodded in understanding and leaned over toward Alec.

"It's okay mate," he said reassuringly. "You're probably getting stressed from all the recent things that have been happening - it could just be your mind trying to cope with it all. You know how you have always suffered from things like that." Josh continued, " I say suffering but i always found it quite cool, it's like that lucid dreaming stuff."

He paused for a moment before continuing further in an almost whisper, "And you know if this is about Jenny...you can talk about her if you want too, I just don't think it's good for you." Alec sighed to himself, there were a lot of issues haunting him of late, Jenny yes but he found that through various investigations and writings he was left with many questions along the way, he was not one to let thoughts dissipate and had an awful tendency to dwell.

"So, I found this great deal for a place on the southern French coast," Josh said excitedly moving the conversation away in an attempt to bring Alec back to a happier place, "We'd get our own private villa right on the beach with all meals included."

Alec smiled appreciating Josh's diversion tactics as images of white sandy beaches and some peace and quiet filled his mind. It sounded perfect and exactly what they both needed - a chance to escape their current lives for a short period and return fresh, ready to start a new. At least he felt like he would be able to relax for the first time in months.

As Alec pondered on thoughts of sandy beaches and azure waters, he began to develop one of his uneasy feelings. He disregarded it as simply the thoughts of his dreams; however, all of a sudden there was a flash of lightning that illuminated the room, startling Alec out of his thoughts. He looked out of the window but saw only clear skies. The wind had picked up, and he heard a distant rumble of thunder in the distance. It had been a pleasant day, warm and without clouds, and now heading into the evening with the sun setting it hadn't shown any signs of turning.

He glanced at Josh who was still looking at something intently on his laptop, seemingly unaware of what was happening outside. Unnerved, Alec got up and walked to the back door. He opened it and stepped onto the patio, letting out a breath he hadn't realized he was holding when he saw nothing but darkness. He put his head back through the rear door where he had clear view of Josh still sat staring at the screen before him.

"Did you see that?" he asked Josh.

"See what?" Josh replied curiously.

Alec shook his head, feeling oddly uneasy for something so inconsequential. Maybe he was hallucinating.

"Never mind," he said, trying to push the feeling aside. He stepped back outside onto the weathered, wooden porch of the cottage; it had been old when the house was built and the years hadn't been kind to it. Alec recalled falling onto it not long ago and coming away with numerous splinters, a situation he had found happening over and over since he was young. He looked up and saw a single star twinkling in the night sky and instantly relaxed. He had always found comfort in looking at stars; they reminded him that even in darkest times there was still beauty to be found. As he thought this, rain started to softly drip from the sky, maybe this incredibly pleasant day held some rain in it after all.

He pulled up a rickety chair by the now propped-open door and began to converse with Josh. Despite having to raise his voice slightly, Alec found the idea of a storm brewing oddly soothing. The smell of the rain now lightly dropping onto the ground filled his nostrils and ears, tantalizing him as he continued to plan their trip. However, even as they discussed their itinerary, Alec couldn't shake off the feeling that something was off. It was like a sixth sense that kept nagging at the back of his mind – an unshakable sense of foreboding that twisted his gut into knots. Every gust of wind felt ominous. It felt like a premonition of some unknown danger lurking just beyond the horizon. The air seemed to hum with a sense of foreboding as they talked, and even the soft pitter patter of the water on the surrounding dry ground failed to calm Alec's growing unease.

As they spoke and the weather continued, Alec stood and took a few small steps forwards to peer up at the sky that had been sheltered from view by the overhanging porch. The sky was overcast, heavy with rainclouds that roiled and churned overhead like a living thing.

Unexpectedly, his thoughts were interrupted by another streak of lightning that lit up the night sky followed by an explosive crash of thunder that seemed to shake the ground beneath him. The lightning flashed in jagged lines across the horizon, illuminating the landscape with brief flashes of brilliant light. He turned once more to Josh who again had apparently not noticed. He barely had time to think about what he saw before his head jolted with a sharp pain that caused him to stop in his tracks. He cringed, trying to shake it off, but the throbbing only got worse. It felt like something was trying to break out from inside of his skull.

"Al, are you okay?" Josh asked, noticing the discomfort on Alec's face. Sure, Alec thought, this he now notices.

Alec shook his head, trying to clear the pain as it throbbed. "Yeah, I'm fine," he said, although he wasn't entirely sure himself if this was true.

He rubbed his temples, trying to massage away the throbbing sensation. The world swam in front of him, and he was having difficulty focusing on any one thing. His mind felt foggy – like he had been drinking, except he hadn't, although at this point, he wished that was the cause.

As he slumped, breathing in the chilly air and kneading his aching head, vivid snippets of his nightmares surged to the top of his consciousness. He glimpsed the face that had been menacing his sleep now with more clarity than ever before.

There was always the same surrounding dark mist, the usual feelings of fear and trepidation but also strangely of reassurance and hope. He could usually only just make out the figure that stood in front of him, a tall strong looking man with eyes as blue as a Caribbean Sea. There was always the strong voice that came from him, although the words always seemed a blur and he could never hear what the figure was trying to tell him. It felt like he was looking right at Alec, or at least towards him, almost as if he could see him.

Josh looked over at Alec nervously, "We should probably get you checked out, these headaches of yours have been really intense lately" he said, concerned.

Alec nodded in agreement but the pain in his head exacerbated and continued to persist, showing no sign of letting up without some intervention. He needed to shut his eyes for a while and decided it would be best to head inside and up to his bed for a quick lie down. As he walked by, Josh gave a knowing nod and reengaged with the task he was working on. One thing was always certain: Josh would enthusiastically throw himself into sourcing the perfect break.

As Alec lay down, the pain slowly slunk into his bones and eased down to a steady throb. His body felt heavy and unsteady as he shifted in bed. A sense of relief washed over him like the tide coming back out, leaving only soft sediment behind. The rain tapped against the window pane like a gentle lullaby while he let himself drift off to sleep. His mind was still racing. This place in his dreams had a strange effect on him.

Alec had almost managed to drift off into an uneasy sleep when he found himself interrupted, startled by a loud deep echo that reverberated in his chest and mind.

His eyelids snapped open and he jolted up, frantically darting his eyes around the room in search of the interruption. The voice reverberated, causing him to lunge forward in shock. Someone was here! He whirled around his bedroom, desperately attempting to locate the source of this unfamiliar sound. A figure loomed near the base of his bed, the same one that had haunted his dreams with azure eyes and a desolate expression, illuminated by a brilliant light.

"Alec," the strange figure repeated, its voice commanding and authoritative. "You are needed, I will be coming for you soon. You have been chosen for the task that lay ahead."

The man stepped forward, and Alec felt like he was standing in an icy abyss. Every muscle in his body locked up as if encased in a block of solid fear. The man's mere presence seemed to fill the air with an unimaginable heat, radiating from some otherworldly power that overpowered all human comprehension.

"Chosen for what?" he demanded, his voice quaking trying to sound confident but only hearing fear in his voice. At this point he had noticed the silence outside, no rain was currently beating onto his window pane and there was only silence outside of this interaction, he could not help also but wonder if Josh downstairs could hear the current going ons.

"To save your world, all worlds" the voice replied, however even the voice speaking seemed unconvinced by this statement.

Alec attempted to understand the words, but they were incomprehensible to him. What was this enigmatic being trying to convey?

"What....What, what" he repeated, feeling utterly lost. "This makes no sense, I don't understand."

The voice whispered, "Neither do we. Just wait and the route will present itself to you. We will find a way to get you through to us tonight, we are not here to harm you, please remember this." With that as soon as he had appeared he was gone, the light and his presence vanished as if a light switch was flipped off.

Alec remained there for a few moments, looking around at the empty room. His mind was still spinning from what had just happened, and he couldn't make sense of it. The dread lingered in his heart, even though the mysterious presence had gone for now, it was clear that he did not intend to stay that way. Despite this, the pain in his head had gone and all seemed mute and still. Even the rain outside had ceased for now.

What on earth had just happened? Was he haunted?! Illogical as this seemed it disturbingly seemed like the most logical answer. He felt that something paranormal was happening to him, something beyond his control. And he couldn't get rid of the notion that this was only the start.

2) The gateway

Alec lingered for an instant, his mind whirring. Had what he just experienced been a mere delusion, or reality as strange as it may be? Was he ill and experiencing hallucinations? Could this have just been an incredibly realistic dream, or was it real? He felt the air swish around him and smelled the scent of the place - no doubt existed in his mind. But how could this all have happened?

His eyes followed a drop of sweat as it rolled over his arm and soaked into his bed sheet. Alec finally found the ability to function again.

He leapt out of bed with a new found sense of urgency and ran down the stairs, all the while struggling as his legs felt like giant lead weights dragging along behind him. His confusion caused his mind to have a hard time keeping up with the world around him; everything moved at half speed, the steps creaked loudly and felt incredibly heavy under foot.

He dragged his feet forward, one in front of the other until he painstakingly reached the base of the stairs. He looked over at Josh still sitting at the table fully engrossed in the task at hand, the faint glow from the laptop illuminating his face against the dim backdrop outside as night had by this point set in.

Josh looked up at him as his feet clumsily turned on the floor and he struggled to stay upright. He leaned back against the wall for a second and reached for the nearby side table to steady himself as it rocked under its thin wooden legs. His fingers scrawled across the wood as he grappled for anything to hold. Josh could see he was visibly shaken however he seemed much more confused and anxious than scared. Regardless his wide eyes and apparent unsteadiness caused Josh to be a little bewildered.

"What happened?" Josh questioned with alarm having paused his activities and stood to his feet.

Alec paused for a moment trying hard to compose himself and gather his thoughts, maybe this was just an extension of his dreams he thought again, struggling to grasp what was currently real and what was not. Surely not he concluded, this was now all too real. He had been tired lately and his head had been hurting. As he thought this, he also noticed how strangely this pain had passed, maybe even the pain itself was confused by the events!

Alec looked over at Josh who was still there awaiting an answer. Josh threw his hands out in front of him complete with a raise of the shoulders as if gesturing him along with the answer.

"Well, I don't actually know, just the strangest things are happening," Alec said, gesturing with his hands as if to emphasize the words.

"It seems like I fell asleep for a minute, or maybe something startled me awake—I don't know." He felt relieved to be speaking about it aloud, even if the explanation sounded every bit as crazy as the event itself, he was aware that he was making no sense at all and it was apparent that this was so as he watched Josh's face contort in front of him.

"I could see him right in front of me," Alec continued. "He was talking about saving the world and some other stuff." Alec sounded exacerbated. He could see the look of confusion creeping deeper and deeper over Josh's face as he unveiled his story.

"Who's 'he', Alec are you ok? Is your head that bad that you're hallucinating?" Josh began, not sure where to begin with his questioning.

"I... I don't even know," Alec stammered, the feeling of disquietude overwhelming him as if someone was listening to his every word.

"It was like a voice in my head. And then I saw him. He said I'm wanted, to save the world.," he continued, not believing what he was saying himself—even as it left his lips. Josh knew Alec wasn't one to fabricate tales but he could discern the increasing bewilderment in his friend's eyes. Would he go mad?

Josh raised an eyebrow, his look of disbelief and worry evident in the lines creasing his forehead.

"Save the world? That does sound a bit far-fetched, don't you think?" Alec felt any confidence he had previously had in this experience being genuine wavering beneath Josh's concerned gaze. Perhaps he was just fooling himself, wishing for something impossible to be true. He reluctantly nodded in agreement, another wave of doubt washing over him.

Still, he couldn't shake the feeling something remarkable had happened. His surroundings were now quiet and reality began to creep back in, but he knew within himself, deep down, that what he had said was true and not imagined it all.

"But why me?" he said aloud now beginning to question the nature of the message rather than its reality, "Why would I be chosen for something like that?"

Josh shrugged his shoulders. "I don't know. But maybe it's just your mind playing tricks on you. You've been under a lot of stress lately with everything that's been going on with the whole Jenny scenario and stuff. Maybe you're just stressed out. Let's face it, dreams rarely provide anything to be taken that literally."

Alec considered Josh's words noting he understandably felt it was nothing more than a dream. Understandably so Alec thought. He had begun to look at Alec with eyes that seemed to show pity now rather than concern, almost as if he thought he were going crazy. But perhaps Josh was right, perhaps he was just imagining things?

The feeling of it all was so real and so intense, so tangible; everything about him felt as if he had physically been there during the event. He was sure he could still smell the smoke and see the outline of the figure.

Alec tried to focus on his thoughts, but he couldn't help feeling like there was some force drawing him in. The figure seemed so familiar yet distant, and the more Alec thought at it the more confused he became. He felt a strange connection between them, as if something was propelling him towards the figure even though he knew nothing about it.

He walked over to the window having begun to regain his composure and looked out at the darkened sky. The clouds had grown thicker and more ominous looking since he had left the porch, almost like they were coming to life.

He felt the spring storm that had been building earlier would soon release its fury. A soft drizzle of rain began to flow once more and fell against leaves and concrete sounding like footsteps, many footsteps. Not yet though, he thought, it's almost time. He looked out over the city with great pride and great sorrow as the rain made everything seem older, but also simpler. It seemed like there were fewer people on the streets now, it was beginning to drag on into the evening now.

The air seemed to hum with a strange, unseen energy. His skin prickled as if something was drawing ever closer. He felt a wave of shock rush over him, mingling with a low rumbling fear. What was happening? Curiosity gnawed at his bones, demanding an answer.

"Something's not right," Alec muttered under his breath.

"What do you mean?" Josh asked, looking over to him. Their eyes met in speculation.

"I don't know," Alec replied, anxiety creeping into his voice.

Without warning, a loud crack of thunder crashed through the room, interrupting their conversation. They both jolted upright in surprise, that almost seemed to have been inside the room they stood. The lights flickered on and off repeatedly, then winked out completely until they came back on again, flashing.

Josh flinched and almost uttered a strained cry as he looked around. What the hell was that?

Alec felt a cold shiver run down his spine. He looked around trying to gauge where it had come from before noticing that a rumble of thunder had begun to show outside once more off in the distance. The lights flickered once more before turning off, the room plunged back into darkness as the rain once again beat down on the window pane once again.

A chill ran down Alec's spine as the hairs on his neck stood on end. He could practically smell danger in the air, like an animal sensing its prey due to some mysterious intuition. Instinctively, he knew it would be foolish to ignore these warning signs.

Josh jumped and felt for the light switch, only to discover that there was no electricity flowing to it. He began to run around the house using his phone light, desperately searching for any other form of light he could find or use but he soon realised there was none.

He stumbled back to Alec's side, still unable to comprehend what was happening. His face aghast and his voice trembling with fear, he implored Alec, "What is happening?!"

Alec felt the air shudder with a tangible force as the thunder claps grew ever more frequent and intense, so powerful that even the walls of his home seemed to tremble in its wake. Abruptly, out of the abyss of silence a voice pierced through the atmosphere - deep, commanding and authoritative.

"Alec," it fiercely bellowed. "The time has come. The darkness is upon us. You must fulfil your destiny or all will be lost."

Alec felt his heart thumping in his ribcage as the voice resonated with clarity, confirming that what he had experienced was real. Panic flooded through him, and Alec knew he needed help. He tossed a desperate glance towards his friend Josh, hoping for rescue, only to see shock and disbelief mirrored on his face. In the same moment of realization, they both accepted that either Alec hadn't gone mad - or they'd gone mad together.

"Josh," Alec said, desperation rising in his voice. "We have to find a way out of here."

Josh nodded, his face set in grim determination as they started heading towards the doorway. "Agreed, and by the way I can definitely hear things now!"

But as they did, the storm grew even angrier - lightning flickered like sparks of electricity around them, illuminating an even darker reality than what had been inside only moments before. The thunderous crackles of the storm shook the foundations of Alec's home, threatening to tear down walls and windows in its wake.

Alec spun around to confront the front of the room as from the corner of his eye he noticed a disturbance rumbling within the dim light. A gigantic swirling maelstrom of energy, a conglomeration of turbulent clouds and crackling lightning, loomed in the middle of the room. It kept swelling as objects were drawn in like dust motes into a gravitational vortex. The mesmerizing suction was irresistible.

As Alec watched, he realised that it was drawing items from all over the room. Paintings and rugs began disintegrating into dust as they floated towards the cloud. Wooden tables splintered into chunks and plummeted through the air towards the burgeoning sphere. He felt lightheaded all of a sudden and looked down at his shoes realising they too were being pulled towards it as he tried in vain to take a few steps backwards.

The ground shook beneath their feet, sending tremors reverberating up through their legs and into their stomachs. They felt themselves being dragged towards the thundering, rolling mass that had formed, a cyclone of whirling sound and motion. As they were pulled closer, the noise grew louder and more intense, resonating off the walls in a deafening roar that threatened to swallow them whole. The surge of air pushed against their backs like an invisible hand, and they both found themselves reaching out and clutching at thin air just hoping for something to hold in order to stop themselves from moving. The world spun around them, blurring into a dizzying mess of colours and sounds.

The two were overwhelmed with confusion and fear at the sight before them, a chaotic storm raging with a menacing intensity.

A booming crack of thunder shook the heavens, and a commanding voice thundered from the depths of the storm:

"You must embrace your destiny," it declared. "Do not doubt me, she has revealed to me that you must come now, I am here for you, and I will bring you with me!"

Alec's heart pounded violently in his chest. Who was this mysterious 'she' and what was this ominous voice speaking of? He looked towards Josh and saw that he too wore an expression of consternation, there was no doubt in their minds now about the reality of the situation. With a silent exchange of glances, they both knew without words what had to be done; taking a deep breath in unison, they walked into the unknown knowing it was in inescapable outcome.

The kaleidoscope of colours and cacophony of sounds that assailed their senses as they ventured into the vortex was unlike anything either had ever experienced. Everywhere around them, luminous streaks of light glimmered and fluttered, while a deep rumbling thunder vibrated through their ears. Whirlpools of glowing energy spun in a hypnotic dance, carrying them further into the unknown. Time seemed to stand still as they rode the waves of energy, soaring through a timeless void before landing on a beautiful emerald green field.

As they lay bewildered on the ground, Alec felt his eyes slowly adjust to the harsh glare from the sun, having been in the dark for a while and then thrust into such brightness caused an even further assault on his senses. He squinted as he held a hand in front of his face trying to focus on who was in front of him. A familiar heat came to his cheeks from the blazing sun as he began to see the familiar silhouette of a person standing in front of him. Through the glare of sunlight, he could make out the figures standing in front of him and moving around them: a woman with long flowing silver hair knelt down in front of them and then extended her hands towards Alec, smiling warmly.

"Welcome," she said softly as Alec blinked to push away the dazzle from the light beams shining off her hair like tiny stars in the night sky. His heart filled with warmth at her words; it was almost like talking with an old friend, such a sense of friendliness and familiarity ran through her words. He looked up at Josh and saw that similar feelings did not seem to be washing through his companion.

Josh stood up first and helped Alec to his feet. He rubbed at his wrists and glanced around, taking in the view around them.

A mountainous skyline silhouetted the golden-orange horizon, its hills painted in emerald hues of short trees. Majestically laid out before them the vast grassland seemed to stretch for eternity, delicate reeds swaying in unison with a calming breeze. The rolling hills and deep forests blended into the distant haze, leaving an incredible tapestry of jagged landscapes that meandered off into infinity.

Some strange yet wonderous looking creatures could be seen moving around through the tall grasses and flying in the skies above. They seemed similar to creatures Alec would know well but quite different. To their right Alec could see some form of structures made out of wood and stone which appeared to be walls surrounding some sort of building or courtyard within a small village setting.

"Who are you?" Alec asked, his voice hovering barely above a whisper.

As he spoke, Alec became aware that there was someone very large standing just behind the silhouette of this beautiful woman. Their large body cast a long shadow over her, making it seem as though she were eclipsed by the sun. He could tell that the figure was male, and that he was wearing some kind of armour; bits of silver glinted in the rays of light shining on him through the branches above. It wasn't until the man turned slightly that Alec to his surprise caught a glimpse of wings protruding from each of his shoulders like those of a giant swan.

What kind of entity had arrived? Were they gods or sprites or local rulers? The peculiar occurrences were beyond comprehension, but he wasn't so fixated on who it was. He wanted to understand why he had been summoned here.

She looked into his eyes as if she could see into his soul. Her lips curled in a beautiful smile, showing a set of perfect white teeth beneath her red lips.

"I am Freyja, I am a protector and some say a ruler here in Sofpavel. To be direct, you have been chosen to fulfil a great destiny, one that will determine the fate of the world, not just ours but yours also." She took a breath in between her sentences as if there was time for him to absorb each piece of information.

Freyja leaned forward and compassionately took Alec's hands in hers. "I know this is hard to believe, but it is all true. You must hold inside you something special and I think that maybe you are going to be able to do something when the time comes." She stroked his fingers with her thumbs as if they were friends chatting and then leaned back again. Alec felt a sense of disbelief wash over him. How could he, a simple man with no special abilities, be chosen to save the world? Surely there were many better options!

"What is this destiny?" Josh asked, having now found his voice.

Freyja looked at Josh for a second, her friendly blue eyes turning a little sterner. The light ice-blue summer dress which Freyja wore danced mesmerisingly in the soft wind coming down from the mountain peaks. Her pale skin glowed in the warm sunlight that lit up her face and cast shadows under her eyes and around her carefully decorated necklace. She had an air of a queen about her, but she also looked like a woman who was bored by all of this talking and impatient to move; if she were a child, her feet would be tapping impatiently with petulance.

Josh noticed this, and he shifted his feet as he turned his eyes away; with delicate gestures Freyja brushed some hair out of her face before answering. Her tone was well-mannered, but her face showed no signs of amusement.

"I will explain more to you Alec when we arrive back at the castle," she said casually. "You however, should not have come here." She gestured towards Josh. It was then that she turned to look at the tall figure behind her of which Alec could now see much clearer; he stood strongly with his arms crossed over his chest, looking at nothing in particular like a schoolboy preparing to be scolded.

His appearance was threatening whilst equally soothing, a strange combination of pure strength and relaxing peace. Freyja spoke again: "You should not have let him pass through without my permission," she told him bluntly.

If he had been human Alec was sure this giant of a being would be tomato red, yet even though he wasn't he still managed to blush with embarrassment.

It was quite the sight, and he couldn't help but almost let out an awkward laugh at his error whilst saying "magic is not my forte Freyja apologies, you were after all in control of the spell..." That's when Alec took notice of the voice and realised, that this was the voice from his dreams, the one that had appeared in his room. Alec couldn't believe it! With this He turned to face Josh who looked back at him with curiosity.

Freyja sensing discomfort continued "...This is Hypnos, and yes he is the one who has been reaching out to you, I have been sending him to your dreams, not an easy task I must say!"

Alec felt a chill run down his spine as he heard her words. He was being sent to my dreams? How is that even possible? This isn't possible! None of this makes any sense at all. Creatures of which were unknown to him, magic, and even a man with wings able to teleport to his room! He looked at Josh again hoping for something, but he seemed just as bewildered as Alec was. He attempted to ease the tension by shrugging his shoulders at Alec, but he began to feel like an intruder, unwelcome in this strange land and this made him even more reluctant to now get involved.

Freyja continued explaining that she has extraordinary ability due to her ancestry of witches and sorcerers combined with the choices of the Lemuri falls spirits. The land is a nexus of trapped time which oversees and maintains balance throughout the realms. The spirits chose Freyja to receive their visions because it had sensed something in her, awaking gifts it deemed necessary for survival. Those gifts include magical abilities like clairvoyance and the power to know and see things beyond herself. She also gartered great respect and admiration from her fellow people, Hypnos most of all who had been serving with her for a long time and held her in the highest esteem. He was the leader of Sofpavel's armies and as such held the highest military title throughout the realms.

He, like all Erobians, was limited in his movements and travels. The rules stated that each race must remain within its realm, most other realms without even having acknowledgment of other realms besides their own. Hence, he could not enter any earthly land, nor any others for the matter, as it was a strict rule held amongst Erobians.

Alec was certain that something momentous lay ahead, for why would they have gone to such great lengths otherwise? Surely though he was not the person they required but how could such advance beings make an error? He posed the question to Freyja – what role did he play in this grand scheme of things? She simply smiled tenderly and replied that all would be revealed back at the castle. There was much to divulge.

As they set off on their journey to the castle, Alec couldn't help but feel a sense of unease. The world around him was so different from anything he had ever known, and the idea of being chosen for some great destiny made him feel like he was in over his head. Freyja seemed to sense his apprehension, and she reached out to him tenderly.

"Don't worry, Alec," she said softly. "You were chosen for a reason and Lemuri would not expect more from you than you are capable."

Alec looked at her, feeling a mix of emotions. He wasn't sure he was ready for this, but at the same time, he felt a sense of duty to help. He had always been one to help others, and he couldn't ignore the request however confusing it may well be at this moment in time. He found Freyja comforting and decided to lay his trust in her regardless of his trepidations.

He nodded and took a deep breath as if understanding already the task in hand. Freyja smiled in return and patted him on the shoulder. With a deep breath, they all continued on their way towards the castle.

As they marched, Freyja stayed beside Alec, trying to calm him with her conversational banter. Meanwhile, Hypnos led the way with a sense of command, growling and huffing out short bursts of rage at every interruption in their journey. Some curious locals looked on as they passed, wondering who these outsiders were as some of their youngsters played alongside. Alec noticed that they were all slightly different than those he had seen before, with changes both big and small. Just like the creatures that populated this world; they were both familiar in appearance and foreign at the same time. Overwhelmed by curiosity, one of the younger locals walked up to Josh and stared hard at him for a brief moment before running away laughing, Josh tried not to take offence to this realising to them he was possibly quite odd looking in himself.

They reached the edge of the tall grassed fields and headed into the woods, Josh had dropped off the pace a little and was lagging behind however nobody other than the curious child seemed at all interested in him, encouraging him to awkwardly catch up with the others once again. The trees loomed like giants, closing in around them as they walked as if leaning over to peer down on the travellers themselves. They seemed alive and he was sure he could feel them turn and look upon the group with each one that they passed. A chill breeze left a blanket of foreboding across the forest, and the rustling leaves seemed to whisper some ancient secret. Alec felt as if he was being watched from all sides, but when he looked there was nothing to be seen.

The Main Road was wide and cobbled, smoothed by the passage of many feet and hooves. They passed a small village along the way and chatted with some of its inhabitants.

They pressed forward until looming in the distance was an enormous castle, jutting up and standing sentry atop a small mound encircled by the below city's surrounding buildings.

The vast, ancient structure had once been an outpost of the full moon coven during its reign over humanity, and it continued to operate as their fortress until relatively recently when Freyja, a founding member originally, decided it best disbanded unsure if it was heading in the right direction and in the best interests of the people. The walls were surrounded and protected by thickets of trees all running parallel.

Freyja marked the changing scenery and peculiarities that flew by, as if their dialogue was a typical part of an ordinary day.

It was obvious they were working hard to keep the focus away from Alec's destiny, although everyone knew it would inevitably overshadow them all eventually....

3) setting the stage

As they neared the castle, Alec couldn't help but feel a sense of awe at the sight before him. It was a grand structure, built from white stone that glimmered in the sunlight. The walls were adorned with intricate carvings and there was a moat surrounding the castle that was filled with crystal clear water. The stone shined so bright that he almost had to squint as the sun reflected off in his direction.

As they walked through the exterior walls leading up to the castle itself, the stones of the walls towered high above them, casting deep shadows that seemed to pulse and move with each footstep. The large heavy iron gates lay in an open position, their thick black metal gleaming dully in the sun. Two guards keeping watch sat perched atop massive horses, breathing out puffs of steam into the chilled air as they scanned the surroundings with cold eyes. It was a formidable sight, one that felt both secure and oppressive at once. However, they were not on horses at all. Instead, they rode giant beasts with 6 legs and thick grey wings tucked against their backs. Freyja saw the look of surprise on Alec's face as he gazed upon the magnificent creatures.

"These are the Celeris horses—direct descendants of the great Pegasus himself." She proclaimed proudly. "We only in recent times managed to begin riding them, we discovered they could not be tamed, only reasoned with." She said this with a smile as if it were a joke she had always found amusing.

"The soldiers with them are our Nyx fighters," she continued, looking at Hypnos as he carried on marching steadily through, acknowledging each of his men as he passed. He did not break his stride, but nodded curtly to random soldiers who threw their fists into the air and cried out a greeting. The recruits threw up their spear-like flags and shook them like pennants in honour of their High General as he passed through.

As they entered the castle, Alec was greeted by the warm glow of torches and the sound of music playing in the distance. The air was thick with the scent of burning incense, and the walls were decorated with tapestries depicting various scenes from Erobian history.

They walked through a series of rooms lit with candelabras, their flames casting dancing shadows into each of the far-flung corners. Freyja led them through the castle's halls, explaining that they were in the castle of light, the western wing of the great fortress and where the rulers of Erobus resided having done so since the beginning of time. The eastern wing was failing into disrepair since the coven had departed and would soon be maintained for the soldiers' quarters.

Freyja led them to a grand hall, where sitting centrally an incredibly grand table was set with a feast fit for kings. A towering tree of gold and crystal held place of honour at the end of the table and weighed down with trinkets that shimmered in the candlelight. Up above it stood a showering of stars made from silver and gold discs. The candles trembled as Alec caught a whiff of the delicious aromas emanating from the food that adorned the table. Freyja gestured for them to sit, and they began to eat it only having just occurred to Alec how hungry he suddenly was. The food was perfect and plentiful, it would have taken an expert eye to see where one dish ended and another began. There were tiny little fish of which Alec did not recognise stuffed inside each other's mouths, and what seemed like roast pigs carved in patterns of stars, woven together into constellations. The attention to detail and appearance was incredible.

Reaching out to serve herself some more food, Freyja looked across the table and smiled warmly at Alec, and he found this comforted him greatly.

Once they had all finished eating, Freyja led them to a private chamber where they could talk in more detail and privacy, the walk down the corridor became increasingly more tense and Alec recognised that they were about to move away from the overly enthusiastic hospitality. As they entered the room, Alec couldn't help but be awestruck by the wonderful array of various magical artifacts that adorned the walls. There were books filled with spells, potions, and incantations from all around the world, hers and others. He was sure he had seen one or two in the museum just down the road from his house, but then again, he could have been mistaken.

There were also beautiful paintings of the land and surrounding landscape, as well as the various warriors who had helped to shape the world as they knew it today. Freyja showed Alec some of the artifacts and explained a few of the ones that seemed to have caught his eye in greater detail. These were mostly trinkets and small items from history, a couple of oddities also from throughout her times. Freyja's gaze stopped upon a large wooden box at the end of the room. Its stained, heavy oak seemed to have been through much wear and tear, as it was held together by rusty dark metal joints and latch, though it was the plainest looking item with the room it was clear to Alec it held some importance. The sun shone through one of the dormer windows and illuminated the dust that had gathered over time on the surrounding items, however not on the box itself Alec noted. Freyja ran her hand over its surface before turning around to look at Alec with a heavy sigh.

"This is the reason you are here, or more importantly the contents within are the reason." She said gesturing to the box. She looked towards Josh, who had stopped just inside the doorway. "Josh," she said. "Would you mind leaving for a second? I wish to talk to Alec alone." Josh hesitated, looking at Alec and then back towards Freyja. Alec nodded to Josh, highlighting that it was fine.

Josh felt less sure and was preparing to protest instantly, however at that moment, the Nyxian guard cleared his throat behind Josh, and he realized that Freyja wasn't asking—she was telling him to leave. Josh did not realise but he could count himself fortunate, after all, on most days she would not generally have been so polite about it given her clear feelings towards him.

He could think of no response other than the verbal one: "Yes." With that Josh walked past them through the door and headed back down the long hallway to where Hypnos had waited with the remaining entourage.

"Alec", Freyja continued turning her attention back to the matter at hand. "You are here for a reason that is not yet clear to me, however it is to do with what is in this box and the potential greater consequences around it", As Freyja spoke, she opened the heavy lid of the box to reveal its contents.

Alec looked on in confusion, other than for a few metal clasps and a clear case it was empty. "There should be more there to see" Freyja continued sensing Alec's confusion.

"This case contained the Angurvagal, it was the blade wielded by Morpheus, the last king of Erobus and the saviour of all life as we know it." She paused again as she reflected on her many great memories of her old friend. Although neither her nor Hypnos appeared it, they were both now well over 5,000 years in age and the two of the eldest living beings on Erobus to their knowledge by at least three of those thousand, and a lot of time had passed since Morpheus fell.

Erobians boasted a lifespan much longer than their Earthly counterparts, yet Freyja and Hypnos were endowed with almost eternal life as the current guardians of Erobus. Despite this advantage, they could still perish like any mortal being, except not by old age alone. Luckily, their appearance remained nearly unaltered over time! It was a point that Freya emphasized to Hypnos repeatedly.

Alec stood listening, he did not know who Morpheus was nor the importance of this sword, however he could see its importance to Freyja and gave her the time to speak listening intently and politely. Freyja continued as she looked at the empty space with sorrow and frustration.

"The blade had originally belonged to the Chronos, he was the first ruler of Erobus" she explained, as she kept her hand hovering over the empty space almost as if expecting it to spring to life or the blade to reappear. "It was forged in the molten flows below Lemuri. It had been handed down from leader to leader, leaders became gods and gods started to fall", Freyja paused for a breath before stating the next sentence "Morpheus, he fell, or rather jumped onto his sword, the last heroic act by the great god."

Freyja continued, entirely engrossed in retelling the story, it was rare she was able to share these things with anyone who was not a child learning their history in school, "Morpheus knew he must make the ultimate sacrifice to save the world from destruction. All life, including those on Earth, would have been wiped out had he not found a way to vanquish his foe. But his adversary was too powerful to be killed straight away. The fragile balance of life and death also meant that there were always forces at work seeking to tip the scales between the two. He used his sword to imprison the Jinn in order to restore harmony."

Freyja said the Jinn's name with almost a whisper, Alec could sense a hatred and felt a more aggressive nature in her tone for the first time, the distain she still felt for him evidently ran deep. "The blade was placed here in Sofpavel for safe keeping, knowing that if anyone were to find it and free him from his prison that a dreaded terror would consume the land.

This ancient case and the sacred box within had been protected by powerful spells for nearly 1,000 years preventing any being from coming near, the room itself guarded at all costs with relentless dedication. Even touching the sword would be fatal for most because of the immense power held within. The doors themselves are tall and heavy, fortified with unyielding strength while the castle grounds seethe with protective magic, ready to ward off any intruders."

Freyja paused again, this time in heavy thought. " I sensed the air shift and my blood ran cold, it was as though the protection spells were nothing more than a thin sheet of paper - someone had breached them with ease. I scrambled to raise the alarm but it was too late, the coveted Sword of Runes had been stolen with breathtaking skill and force. Not even the faintest trace of the culprit could be found - whoever this thief was, their power must have been greater than anything I'd ever imagined to have achieved such a feat so effortlessly."

Freyja said her words slowly as if giving Alec time to take them all in, but also as a warning of what may come next.

Alec struggled to take in all of the information that was being unloaded onto him but he realised just how serious a situation he had found himself in. He eventually managed to speak through all of his thought process however in order to ask one pertinent question, "So what am I here for?" whilst staring at Freyja for an answer.

Freyja's piercing gaze shifted over to Alec having been transfixed on the box this whole time, her words echoing with the power of a thousand voices.

Her expression was stern and serious as she thoughtfully answered his question - "The Lemuri Falls is the gateway between Erobus and other worlds, an impenetrable veil that protects us from the dangers of the unknown. The Orbs flow through this passage, manipulating our dreams and creating the scenarios that control the realms. We call these dream Orbs and they flow to Lemuri from the rivers of Sofpavel as well as the one in Maredrom. These create dreams within our minds when we sleep, fantasize or try to imagine the right way forward. Some call them angels and demons. Our ideas are often of our own making however the Orbs show us how to achieve them and promote balance in the world. We have free will but the Orbs provide us with guidance, should we choose to take it."

Alec was still trying to wrap his head around this concept and its implications. Was it possible that all of greatness throughout the ages came from something like this? Is this really how the great thinkers had arrived at their brilliance over the centuries. His mind began to drift to the opposite extreme—all the pain and suffering in the world. A feeling of dread started to form in Alec's gut.

"What about all that is bad?" he asked hesitantly.

Freyja looked up at Alec and nodded solemnly, "There are Orbs for that also," she stated. "They are the ones that flow to Lemuri from Maredrom, they work in exactly the same way, but these are bad, where those are good. The two combined is the balance that I refer to. The necessary balance that we so struggle to maintain. Unfortunately, some sides do not respect the balance and wish for dominance. They want all out power."

As Freyja spoke Alec continued struggling to take in all of the information. He continued to glance around himself at the other items as if something would make him click and scream eureka. This all sounds like a biblical fantasy land! There is nothing he could offer in this scenario and remained baffled as to why he was here, the answer to this was less clear than it had been before.

She moved up to Alec and placed her hand in his. His muscles relaxed at the tenderness of her touch, and an inexplicable calm spread through him. Could this be some type of spell she had cast over him?

She then brought him over to stand before a large tapestry that portrayed all of the great leaders that had gone before them. It stretched from ceiling to floor and had been stitched together from various pieces of material, obviously many years of work had gone into it and Alec had been marvelling at the amazing piece when he first came into the room.

Freyja's finger traced a path along the richly woven tapestry, her nail catching on knotted threads and fine embroidery. The colours were vibrant and alive, depicting rolling hills and steep mountains, cool streams and vast oceans. "This here," she said, pointing towards the lower end of the tapestry, "this represents our history. It also shows all of Erobus."

Alec leaned in closer to examine the map as Freyja continued her tour, clearly marking out the lands she had spoken of. Sofpavel to the west with its deep ravines and winding rivers, its beautiful rivers and lush grass clear to see. Maredrom to the East, rocky and dark.

"Who inhabits these lands?" Alec asked, pointing to Midjun.

"Nobody," Freyja responded with a shake of her head. "These are the middle lands; this is where the majority of battles occur. These lands hold the key to the passageway towards Lemuri." Her eyes roamed over the expanse of territory before lighting on a large tower depicted in Midjun just prior to the entrance of the passageway. "This tower is where we guard the lands from," she explained further, "It reaches incredibly high and from its peak you can see over everything."

The tower was depicted with such stunning accuracy that Alec could almost see individual stones making up its walls. It was as if he was looking upon an artist's rendition of a real structure, rather than a mere embroidery on cloth.

As she turned her gaze back to the tapestry, Alec's eyes followed hers. An epic tale of war and power unfolded before them, with Chronos himself perched at the top, ruling over all. Strange lands, mythical beasts, and great leaders were depicted in vivid detail - but it was Morpheus who caught their attention. The god of dreams fought valiantly in a fierce battle, eventually showing a scene where he fought alongside Hypnos. But something was off; a dark figure lurked in the shadows of the circle encompassing the warriors, its name unspoken.

"Who is that?" Alec questioned.

"That is Morpheus brother, Probetor. His brother was a strange character but ultimately one who was very good and held the principles of Sofpavel in high regard. He was once a valuable soldier and loyal to Sofpavel. However, he made some misjudgements which ended in his banishment to earth. Somehow, he was turned by the Jinn, the entity locked in the sword I mentioned earlier" Alec nodded, it was a story he would not be forgetting any time soon. "Probetor turned on Morpheus" Freyja's voice trailed off ever so slightly as she recalled the events that led to Probetor's fall "he escaped when the Jinn was defeated. We believe he has been hiding all this time but we have no idea what he has been doing, we do however fear he may be behind the blade being taken. He is a being of dark magic, very clever and very capable, we fear just how capable he may actually be. We have not seen him for a long time and there is nothing to say he has returned; however, he is the most logical culprit in this crisis." Freyja looked down briefly visibly a little upset as she recalled the events that had taken place all those years ago, "He was good, I will never know what enabled the Jinn to turn him, his time on earth maybe? Maybe we should not have banished him there. Maybe it was our faults"

Alec felt a chill run down his spine as he contemplated the true nature of this being of dark magic. He remained silent, his mind racing with thoughts of danger and betrayal. Could he trust anyone in this world of twisted magic and political style intrigue? He certainly hoped so and he felt that so far, he had no reason to distrust the people of Sofpavel. The question did still remain though of what he was doing here exactly, a question that seemed to be taking a long time to answer.

Freyja looked up at Alec, explaining what had been over recent history he could see was emotionally challenging for her. She had of course been there and witnessed the vast destructive nature of it all. She had seen her friends fall and some die and she watched those around her also suffer as a consequence.

Freyja began to explain, her voice carrying a hint of wonderment, "My ancestors were magical folk, and legend says they were there when the Lemuri Falls first appeared. Some even said to have been born of the falls themselves. The falls contain powerful spirits that I can communicate with, it's an ancient gift passed down through the generations of my family, and I'm the last one alive who can do it. It's hard to explain, even after all this time; they are mysterious forces, and they can give me glimpses of what's coming or what is needed, however they do often do this in riddles it must be said." Alec listened intently; his eyes wide as he tried to absorb what Freyja was telling him. Even she didn't understand the full scope of it after centuries of study, how could he ever be expected to grasp it?

She paused for a brief second, looking at him as if she were about to impart a great secret. "They're the ones who told me to bring you here," she said matter-of-factly. "They are the reason you are here, the voices from Lemuri. When the blade went missing, they told me we needed you, that you are, or at least hold within you, the key to ending all of this. No reason why, just that it is you." their voices still echoed in her head. They had told her that he would help end this all the instant that the blade went missing. No reason why, just that it was to be so.

Alec was shell shocked and could not believe what he was hearing. He was to end all of this? The question he had repeatedly asked himself he heard himself whimper out loud, "But how? These are gods we are talking about."

Freyja's face was serious, yet kind as she spoke. "I don't know," she said softly to him. "I wish I did. I can see you have a good heart, Alec. I can see it in your soul that you are strong willed." She paused for a moment, searching his face for understanding and acceptance of her words. "There is something else about you," she continued. "Something that the falls have always known about you. There is more inside you than other people, but what? I do not know and I cannot answer your question."

Alec sat back, stunned. He had no idea what to say to Freyja's revelations or kind words, rarely had he be spoken of so highly. "However, be warned that this is a dangerous path," she continued, growing sterner with each word, as if directness was the only way to convey how dire things were. "You have always been watched over, and I would imagine also always hunted to some degree. " Freyja then sighed before continuing, "This brings us to Josh." The words hung in the air before him, making it harder to breath. At last, he found his voice. "What about Josh?" he asked Freyja, who shook her head and replied, "He should not be here, he was not meant to travel with you and knows far too much at this point." Alec was surprised again by her mention of his friend. He had almost forgotten about him amongst all of the revelations he had confronted. "His travelling here was an accident" she continued "we also can see very little about him which concerns me greatly, we need to send him home whilst you remain here"

Alec mulled over her words, comprehending what she was asking of him but needing his companion to stay too. Everyone was insisting that he had to be on this mission, though the idea left him unenthusiastic.

"I need him here with me," Alec declared forcefully, "if you send him away then I'm leaving as well," Boldness filled him at the sound of his own voice, however the intense stare Freyja gave him right after caused the feeling to dissipate quickly.

Her voice bordered on a plea as she attempted to drive home the gravity of the task that lay before them. Though not his intention, Alec felt like he was being scolded for not taking this plight seriously enough.

"Josh and I have been friends since childhood and always enabled each other to achieve the best we can, I need him with me if I am going to help you, I do understand the importance and that is why I wish for you to have the best of me, not the worst." he said firmly.

Alec knew he had been chosen for all of this for a reason whether he believed they were correct or not, yet he could not do it alone if he was to try and help. He needed his friend to accompany him if they were to have any hope of succeeding. Freyja pursed her lips, her eyes flickering with understanding and doubt. She knew that Alec would not be swayed easily, that his determination would not falter even if they tried to force Josh to leave. Finally, after what felt like an eternity, she took a deep sigh and admitted defeat in this battle.

"Very well," she said slowly, her gaze gradually moving away. "But he must understand the gravity of this situation. He must follow our lead and obey every command, without question or hesitation, he is not to prove an obstacle." Alec nodded, grateful for the opportunity to keep Josh by his side. He knew that he would have to speak to his friend and explain everything to him before they continued.

Freyja stood up from her chair, her eyes scanning the room as she gathered her thoughts.

"Now, we must return to the others and start preparing, we will also show you where you may stay and see if we can discover what you can do to aide in this fight. There is much to be done, and time is not on our side." She paused again before continuing. "There also must be a good reason the falls have called for you, no human has ever been here and getting you here took a lot of energy and work, from the falls as well as myself.

Leaving themselves temporarily weaker is a strange decision, we need to see what it is that lies in you." Alec nodded, feeling a sense of urgency as well as trepidation bubbling up within him. He knew that they had a long journey ahead of them, filled with danger at every turn. He also continued to wonder if the falls had made an error, he knew of no reason why they would want him, especially with the degree of importance they seem to have put on his presence.

As they made their way back to rejoin the rest of the group, Alec couldn't help but feel a sense of dread settling over him. He knew that the stakes were high and that failure was not an option, this much had become clear. However, was he really a simple average man, about to fight in a battle he failed to understand. One that may even end his life. Alec stared at the ground whilst taking the short walk back to the hall and tried to keep his mind on what had already been said. He had already decided, if nothing else he would at least do whatever it took to help them succeed.

4) Revelations

Once they reached the grand hall, they were greeted by the patiently waiting group, Josh looking a little perturbed was still unhappy about being asked to leave and seemingly feeling uncomfortable surrounded by the large soldiers sitting around him.

Alec and Josh were shown to their quarters by one of Hypnos men, whilst Alec knew that these men were there for their own protection, he could not help but feel a little nervous in their presence. They were giants of men, not as big as Hypnos himself but not too far away. Alec himself could not have been much further from them in appearance. Alec is a contrast to the other men in the room. He stands no taller than five feet ten inches, and he has darker features standout out against them. His hair is dark, his eyes are a rich chocolate brown, and his skin is tanned from either the sun or his ancestry. This was the complete opposite of these fair-haired giants of men. As they settled down and began to have a second to absorb all that was happening, Alec couldn't shake the feeling of unease that lingered within him.

Even though he appreciated being safe inside the walls of the castle he knew it was a temporary setting, he knew that safety was an illusion like everything else. He did however, now having slowly absorbed some of the plethora of information he had been provided, almost feel a real sense of purpose and understanding for this strange world of which he had not appreciated up till now. He knew that what lay ahead was daunting, and the weight of expectation they seem to be placing upon him weighed heavy on his shoulders. He wondered how he could possibly be the key to ending all of this, and what it was that the falls saw in him that they felt was so special but he felt a small glimmer of pride in the possibility that maybe, just maybe, he was important. He also could not help but doubt they were right. Can they be wrong given what he has been told?

Josh, on the other hand, seemed unfazed by it all even if he had been a little put out previously.

"Dude, can you believe this place?" he exclaimed as he looked around the room.

The room itself was magnificent, with four-poster beds each with incredible wood carvings lining the walls from floor to ceiling. A large dining hearth sat in the direct centre, and a simple rug lay beneath it. Two corridors extended beyond this room; they could tell one led to a study while the other led to a washroom.

He wasn't sure exactly where it went so he wandered toward the study where he found a small room, dimly lit with a small table and chairs, a few books and some games, thousands of years' worth of royal portraitures lined the curtained walls from floor to ceiling. Maybe this had previously been used by a child he thought.

Alec recognised some of the creatures amongst the wooden carvings back in their own room as ones from old fairy-tales and mythology stories that his grandmother used to read him, flying horses and fire birds were prevalent along the intricate designs and two creatures they thought very highly of.

"I mean, we're in another realm! This is unbelievable!" Josh continued to gain traction in his enthusiasm—his voice rising and words tumbling over one another—as he explained himself. "I mean, sure they appear to not like me much but this is crazy, right?"

Alec sat down slowly in a velvet cushioned chair near the open full-length window at the far side of the room as the sunlight shone through onto his face and the birds sang outside, he couldn't help but smile at Josh's enthusiasm and forgot for a second what they had actually entered into. He was grateful to have his friend by his side, even if the situation was dire. However, Josh had a good heart and Alec was concerned that in a realm with so much potential danger and clear animosity towards his presence that his friend could become an easy target.

"Yeah, it's pretty crazy," Alec replied, trying to sound as enthusiastic as Josh but not quite feeling it. "But we need to take this seriously, Josh.

This is a serious situation and I am struggling to comprehend just how dangerous it could be. Plus, I have been told to warn you, it's not a disliking of you but you are here by error. I had to beg for you to stay so you really have to just keep your head down and do as they say."

Josh's expression turned serious as he nodded in agreement. "I know, it's ok. I'm with you all the way, and don't worry I'll behave I promise. Sorry I was getting a little carried away. So, what is the score anyway? What is this even all about? Who are these people and what on Earth have you got to do with it?!"

Alec's chest rose and fell as he took a deep breath, the air filling his lungs like a balloon. He began to explain everything that Freyja had told him: the importance of the sword first forged in ancient times, its power still sharp after all these centuries, and all about Morpheus and his brother's alliance with the one they called The Jinn. Alec spoke of their plan for domination, their lust for power so great it threatened to spill over into every realm. He warned of the potential consequences for all realms, including Earth should they fail. Alec's voice grew tense as he recounted the dire warnings from Freyja.

As he spoke, Josh's eyes widened with each passing moment, a mix of fear and disbelief etched across his face. Alec paused, his eyes searching Josh's face for any sign of understanding.

"Holy shit," Josh muttered under his breath as Alec finished his explanation. "So, we're basically fighting for the fate of the world? Or well you are, no pressure then."

"Yeah, something like that," he said with a wry smile. "But we'll do it together right? We'll follow Freyja's lead, and we'll make sure we succeed."

"Do we have any idea who has it?" Josh enquired disregarding the question.

Alec shook his head. "No, but they suspect it's someone in this realm, they suspect Probetor, Morpheus brother. They.... WE, have to find it before it's too late." Alec said, his mind racing with the weight of the responsibility that lay ahead.

Josh nodded in agreement, "You can count on me. Let's do this, I guess?"

The upward infliction as he tailed off that sentence made Alec smile. It summarised in that one spoken sentence how he himself felt, acting and speaking boldly with nothing to enforce any reasoning behind it.

As they spoke there was a stern knock from the heavy wooden door behind them. Alec and Josh looked at each other briefly with Josh simply stating, "Well it is not me they are likely to be knocking for is it!"

The velvet upholstery of the chair was plush to the touch, feeling almost like a cloud with its soft, downy material and Alec was quite enjoying how it felt. The sound of the knock was loud and jarring against the peaceful atmosphere, breaking the concentration of Alec and Josh and their discussion. Josh's quip made Alec smile ruefully once more, as he removed his hand from the chair and stood up with a sigh. It had been a while since he had felt so comfortable, and with the conversation winding down, he may have even dozed off if it hadn't been for the knock. Alec opened the door to find a Nyx soldier standing there, his unflappable expression giving nothing away.

"Freyja requests your presence," the soldier stated, his voice deep and commanding. Alec nodded, feeling a sense of urgency in the soldier's tone. He could only imagine what Freyja needed to tell him now.

As he made his way through the castle, Alec could feel the eyes of the Nyx soldiers following his every move as he passed them. He could sense their unease, their tension as they guarded the castle from potential threats all feeling as uncertain about him as he did himself.

It was a heavy burden to bear, and Alec knew that he needed to earn their trust if he was to succeed in his mission. Alec felt his heart rate increase as he stepped through the corridors, and he was followed closely behind by Josh.

The halls were dimly lit as they entered the corridors now deeper into the castles setting, the only light coming from flickering torches and the occasional beam of light filtering in through the high windows.

The air was heavy with the scent of musty old books and stale candles that lined the walls. He wondered what time it was here, and then again on Earth - did time difference work the same way as this would surely be a different time zone here!? The silence was pierced by the sound of dripping water, echoing throughout the corridors like a haunting melody.

Alec shuddered as he realized just how deep and dark this place went, clearly, they had been heading down for some time and the windows had stopped appearing, were they now underground?

Finally, they reached a large chamber at the end of a long hallway. The floor and walls were made of plain white stone, but a pool of water softly shone in the centre of the room with a faint blue glow emanating from beneath its clear water. The surface reflected the dim light from torches that burned from sconces on the wall. Alec could feel a sense of power radiating from the pool itself, and he had a sense that it was connected to the Falls themselves. He could tell by the glimmering water and the way others respectfully stood around it that something magical lie within there.

Alec's heart skipped a beat as he waited for Freyja to speak as all stood in silence waiting as she laid out some items in front of her, she stood across the water looking at him awaiting all to cease moving entirely before continuing. He could sense the gravity of the situation just from the look on her face but had no clue as to what would be happening next. As he gazed into the water now below him, he felt as though it was almost speaking to him, he felt he could hear its voice in his head, reaching out and begging him to enter.

Freyja's voice was a thunderclap in the silent room as she spoke, her words vibrating off the walls and echoing with importance.

"The sword has been seen!" she announced gleefully. "As if ripped from the pages of a legendary saga, we have been graced with an unmistakable sign from fate, appearing unexpectedly in near Midjun. Too faint for our eye to see, only fortunate enough that those from the watchtower saw it and revealed it to us. A spark ignited as we realized what course it was taking: Maredrom! Scouts have already been sent to search the area and trace the movements of whatever mysterious entity we had seen, but now it is time for each of us to reflect on ourselves and step up in this momentous occasion. We could be facing a confrontation that would decide the fate of all who lived here and beyond. If our suspicions are true and this was Maredrom's doing, war could come very soon." She stopped, her gaze sweeping around the tense faces in the room, Alec was a little shocked hearing Freyja talk like this, her generally soft demeanour had changed dramatically in a way he had not seen till now.

"Alec, I had not intended to do anything further with yourself till sunrise but I need to see if you do indeed hold anything worthy for us, we need to take the next step now."

Alec's mind raced as he tried to process what he had just heard and what Freyja intended for him to do next, there was not long to wait for his answer "Step forward," the soldier said, motioning towards the pool. He looked down again at the waters, it still persisted with its magical whisper as he wondered to the purpose of this, was it a rite of passage?

Alec dips a toe tentatively into the pond, a shimmer radiates outwardly like fireflies dancing with joy at the incoming company. He steps forward further slowly lowering himself into the pool feeling a chill as the cool water laps at his feet. The pool crackled with a strange energy that seemed to emanate from its depths and he could not help but feel a twinge of fear and trepidation mixed in amongst excitement and wonder. His body began to glow with a golden light that shimmered and pulsed in brilliant hues as he immersed himself further into the water, his skin glowing a blueish tint which slowly enveloped his body till all you could see was a blue outline within this golden light. His eyes began emitting a bright white light and his back arched as he looked towards the sky struggling to take on the power that was now coursing through him. His hands stretched out far to his sides as the waters lifeforce ran through his soul and he felt as though they had entered every atom within his body.

The sensation was overwhelmingly strange, a torrent of energy surging through his body, making him quake and quiver as it blasted outward from within. His skin crackled with the might of the electricity like a detonation of heat, filling him with an overwhelming force and vigour. Alec at this moment had no dominion over his own frame and he couldn't make out anything clearly as his vision hazed amidst the luminosity enveloping him.

He dropped to his knees in the shallow waters no longer able to stand, the water was now level with his chin and a stumble further would see him thoroughly submerged, despite now splashing around his mouth and nostrils he was unable to move his face away and regain control, the fear of potentially drowning adding to his growing list of concerns in the present situation.

Without warning images began to flash in front of his closed eyelids; other worlds full of creatures he knew and some he did not, seeming close enough that he could almost reach out and touch them through the dazzling light show.

Just then he caught a shimmer in the distance, he realised what he could see, Morpheus blackened sword. It was being carried across a baren land by a man he had not seen before in a dark cloak making his way with purpose on horseback. The stead appeared to almost be a mist; the body nor head very visible almost as if the dust kicked up by its mighty hoofs had blanketed the beast in dust from the dry ground below. The rider ground to an abrupt halt, almost as if they had sensed the presence of Alec watching them. The hood was raised and a long dark beard protruded from the gap like a sinister snake. Two eyes stared out, piercing though the darkness and settling onto Alec's own gaze. Without warning a quiet low voice hissed out a name - "Alec?" - like a ghostly whisper on the wind. In a flash, Alec felt like he had been thrust onto the back of a motorcycle and shot off into the night, noticing the distant shape of the figure giving chase before fading away into oblivion.

As the visions stopped the incredible sensations did not, his body crackled with energy, and he looked down at his hand to see tendrils of light draping over his skin. They pulsed and glowed in a brilliant array of colours now, racing over his arms and up across his body until Alec's whole body hummed alive with magic.

Josh looked on, firstly with fascination but this soon grew to fear, fear for his friend who seemed to be suffering terribly, "stop" he involuntarily heard himself shout "you're killing him!"

Freyja glared over at Josh and simply raised a single finger to her lips, she knew he would be ok, but Josh looked back at Alec the concern etched across his face. He felt the urge to jump in and pull him out but he knew that he would be unable to with the soldiers guarding the area, and even if he could what would the consequences be then and would these waters simply kill him off also?

As his thoughts ran away with him, he watched on beginning to look for ways to jump in and save him as Alec continued to suffer, however the light radiating from his body was slowly ebbing away and his shouts were lessening. His breaths became more measured, and his fists unclenched as he slowly regained control of his bodily senses. He swayed slightly, but steadied himself on his feet again until the glow had vanished and he had returned to a near normal state.

As Alec came through, he looked over at Josh, the relief was clear in his eyes as his friend breathed a huge sigh of relief, he then cast his eyes back over to Freyja. He looked quizzically into her eyes and she lifted her head to respond to the questions she could see in his eyes.

"I'm sorry" she started with, clearly meaning it in the most apologetic tone of voice he had ever heard.

"If I had told you what to prepare for, it may not have worked. These waters show us a person's true colours and enables the one submerged to see something of importance, if the person is not pure of heart or holds an ulterior motive the waters will darken and take the necessary steps." She nodded toward the water around him. The golden tinge seemed to glow against his skin.

"This is good then?" he asked uncertainly.

"It is certainly not bad," she responded. His chest swelled with relief; he was beginning to prepare for the soldiers to lynch him and throw him back to Earth having discovered their error.

The water he noticed had risen, forming a pool around him. It sparkled in places like white silk on a golden sunbeam, but before he could appreciate the beauty, it settled back into place like rain pattering down onto the forest floor.

He looked around whilst composing himself, he could see that the others in the room looked a little more at ease now seemingly reassured realising that he was the person the falls wished for and that he equally was not a spy or any other bad entity in disguise. He had not known however there was as much scrutiny and doubt as there obviously had been. He also noticed murmuring around him, there were glances between the few soldiers around him which was incredibly odd from generally such serious, well-disciplined and quiet folk. They had till now reminded him of giant versions of the queen's guards as they March around their London home with the incredible discipline they possessed. Freyja raised her hand noticing the disturbance and all went silent, "do we have a question?" she asked aloud to the open forum.

One of the soldiers plucked up the courage to ask what they were all wondering "Apologies Freyja, the waters, they were golden?"

"Indeed, they were" Freyja said, "indeed they were." The soldier looked towards Freyja again as if to follow up but Hypnos glared towards him instantly snapping him back into his standing beefeater stance. Alec looked at Freyja, still trying to process everything that had just happened. He couldn't shake the feeling that there was something significant about the golden colour of the water given the questioning, but he couldn't quite put his finger on it. He decided to ask Freyja directly, the soldiers seemed curious so why should he not be.

"What does it mean that the water was golden?" he asked, his voice laced with curiosity.

Freyja paused for a moment, as if considering her response carefully. "It means that you are indeed destined for greatness, Alec," she said finally, her voice ringing out across the room. "You possess a pureness of heart and a strength of character that is rare in this world. The waters have deemed you worthy of our trust and our respect and as such you will have it."

Alec felt a thrill of excitement run through him at her words. He had always wanted to do something important, to matter, to know he had done something that would make a difference in the world. He had never until this point thought that he would be the one to find the sword or help these people to victory and he had always thought that if he succeeded in making a difference anywhere that it would be on his own world! Now it seemed like anything was possible and he began to believe there actually was something within him. As the excitement settled in it soon subsided as he began to feel the weight on his shoulders. The responsibility of being deemed worthy by the waters was not something he had anticipated. He looked over at Josh, who was watching him with a mix of pride and concern as well as a continued good dash of confusion.

Freyja seemed to sense Alec's unease. "Do not worry, Alec. We will guide you and help you to harness your power for the greater good, whatever those powers may prove to be. We can teach you how to use anything within your-self."

Alec felt reassured by her words, but he couldn't shake the feeling that there was more at play here than just finding a sword. He had seen things in his vision, things that he couldn't explain. The man on the horse, the creatures in the other worlds...there was more to this than just a simple quest for a magical weapon regardless of what it may hold within.

"Freyja," he said, his voice serious. "I saw something during all of that, I had what seemed like a dream or a vision. A man on a horse, carrying the sword. It seemed like he could see me, sense me, he even said my name and seemed to give chase as the vision came to an end. Do you know who he is or what it meant?"

Freyja's expression turned grave. "What did this man look like," she said softly.

"It was difficult to make out his face," Alec replied, his voice tinged with fear at her reaction. "His horse seemed more like a phantom than an animal; made of swirling mist and fog. He wore a dark cloak and had long, black hair that he pushed away from his face. He spoke my name as if he knew me."

Hypnos' jaw tightened, the first sign of emotion that Alec had ever seen on his stern features. "Surely it cannot be," he muttered to Freyja. She looked away briefly and leaned against a nearby boulder, her body tense with trepidation. The group knew that whatever had appeared before Alec would be anything but harmless.

Alec felt a chill run down his spine as he saw Freyja and Hypnos exchange fearful glances, his stomach turning to a churning cauldron of anxiousness. He knew that whatever the horseman represented, their task would be far from an easy ride in finding him and retrieving the sword.

"Freyja," he said again, his voice urgent. "What's going on? Who was that man?"

Freyja straightened up; her expression grim. "Alec, that man is Probetor, it appears he lives and that my fears are true." As these words left her mouth it seemed as if the whole world stood still.

She had given Alec a cursory explanation of the key players in Erobian history, and it seemed that this being was the impetus behind why achieving balance had been so difficult when those great sacrifices were made.

The brother of Morpheus, the trickster of Erobus who had spent his days on Earth until joining up with the Jinn and disappearing into the unknown during his capture.

Alec felt a sense of dread settle even deeper in the pit of his stomach. Probetor sounded like a formidable opponent, someone who had been preparing for this for a long, long time if he was still around. How could he, a simple mortal, hope to stand against him, golden water or not. The room fell silent, the weight of this revelation weighed heavy on them all.

"This is a dark and worrying time for us all Alec" Freyja continued, "I need you both to go back to your rooms for now please, I need to meet and discuss with you Hypnos, everyone else you can leave please."

Alec's heart sank as he processed the news. Freyja did not want to hear what he had said but definitely needed to know. He hesitated before voicing a question, afraid of what the answer might reveal.

"Freyja, how did he know my name? How did he see me?" he asked knowing Freyja was not certain of the answers herself.

"I don't really know, but I can guess at several possibilities." She paused for a few moments to gather her thoughts, not wanting to upset Alec any further—if that were possible. "His dark magic goes beyond my own capability, and I cannot explain the nature of what he could have done or seen." As if sensing Alec's doubts about this explanation, she clarified, "I'm afraid it isn't just you they've been watching all these years." After another pause, she continued: "Now we must get back before we are all too tired for tomorrow."

A guard stepped forward and escorted them back to their room.

"He is a being much of much higher magical ability than us Freyja, and if you recall Morpheus did not kill him. He knew how to traverse between us and Earth under darkness and despite his changing sides, he is still of royal lineage. "

Hypnos responded, "How did he know the boy though? If he is noticeable to Probetor he must be someone of importance."

Freyja shook her head showing she did not know the answer to this question and wondered this herself. She believed in Lemuri and believed he must be someone due to having been requested but who he is remained a mystery to her.

"Also, are we to discuss the golden water? The men clearly noted it themselves." he continued. Freyja looked up at Hypnos and sighed heavily knowing this question was as unavoidable as it was unwanted at this moment.

"Well, it shows the falls were justified in their choosing but it does leave as many questions as it does answers. However, I feel this may not be the important question to answer right now." She said whilst starting to walk around the waters looking deeply into them as if hoping for further answers.

"But Freyja" Hypnos responded in disagreement, "the colour signifies he is not simply human, he is at the least a demi-god!" Freyja looked up sternly at Hypnos.

"And that information is not to leave this room! You are to ensure your soldiers present today fully understand this fact also. It does indeed mean this yes, but he does not need to know that yet, it would be of no benefit. That being said I do wish to know who his father is."

Freyja glanced again at the water below, the gold now all but gone. As she looked, she moved closer bending down in order to reach out, caressing the waters with a puzzled look upon her face, thoughtfully gazing into the crystal-clear movements of the settling water.

Hypnos crept up to her side, almost nuzzling her arm as he studied the surface of the water. He zoomed in on her dainty hand and squinted his eyes, searching for what was causing her distress. Suddenly, he could make out small black specks within the dissipating golden liquid; a few dark flecks were scattered across the glittering impurities.

"Surely a little darkness is to be expected?" he questioned "Darkness is bound to the human condition after all," Freyja nodded, not in agreement but acknowledgment of his words.

"This is true" she replied "However that is not what i believe this to be, this is not just the human condition within him," and with that she stood and walked swiftly towards the exit "come" she said to Hypnos turning back towards him before heading out of the doorway and into the hallway beyond, "we have much to do." Freyja stared at the water once more as she left, watching as it cleared. It was done; Lemuri was unlocking its secrets and would pass them on to Freyja as and when it believed required before all was done.

"I feel something is troubling you further?" Hypnos's questioned as they departed. She looked back at him, eyes sparking with a glimmer of curiosity whilst her face had etchings of concern within the lines that ran across it.

"Yes," she said thoughtfully "There is something I've yet to see, some things are still well hidden from me, i can feel that much of the picture is not visible to me." He waited for her to go on, but she let out a sigh and turned away from the spring. "Come," she said. "We have much to do." and with that she left. Hypnos glanced again at the water; it was all but clear again. He wondered for a second what Freyja may not be telling him, or what these waters and indeed Lemuri had, or had not been telling her, before himself leaving the room and following Freyja to see what she planned on next.

5) A tyrants love

Alec and Josh re-entered their room in silence, dumbstruck by the recent events. The Nyx guard left rapidly and without saying a word quickly departed back down the hallway which they had just come from, leaving the door open behind himself. Josh stood centrally in the room, his head cocked to one side and his eyes wide, as he looked at Alec in disbelief and concern. He angled his body with his back towards the door before stepping slowly backwards towards it with his eyes riveted on Alec.

He controlled his breathing as if he were in a sparring match, taking slow, deep breaths through his nose and exhaling out of his mouth. He paused for an instant, took a few more steps backward towards the door that separated them from the remainder of Erobus, stretching out his hand behind him to push it closed. The large wooden door fit back neatly into its tight frame with a soft crack like an animal's tail swishing a warning to predators. Josh licked his lips and looked at Alec.

"Dude," he said, "what was that?"

Alec looked back and wished to respond, but he didn't know what to say—he wasn't sure himself. He felt a chill run down his spine as the weight of what Freyja had revealed to them was still heavy on his mind. "I don't know," he finally replied. "It's like everything just got even more complicated without any understanding of why."

Josh walked over to his bed and sat down heavily; his eyes still fixed on Alec with each step that he took. "So, let me get this straight," he said, his voice barely above a whisper. "We're up against some ancient, powerful being who's been watching you for who knows how long, and we have no clue how to stop him or where he is or even really who he is?"

Alec nodded, sinking down onto his own bed. "Yeah, pretty much."

They both sat in silence for a few moments, each lost in their own thoughts. Alec's mind was racing, trying to come up with a plan of action. He couldn't just sit back and let Probetor do whatever he was planning, he needed to help them as they wished however he still was none the wiser as to what he was able to do in order to assist them.

Finally, Josh spoke up again. "So, what now?"

Alec looked up at him, determination in his eyes. "Now, we start preparing to help," he said confidently. "We have to be ready for whatever comes our way. We'll await to see what Freyja is planning I guess and for someone to tell us what we can do."

Josh looked uncertain, "Are you sure we can trust Freyja? We know nothing of any of these people," he asked.

Alec looked up questioningly but did not answer. He put it down to Josh seeming to dislike her, possibly due to her reluctance to allow him to stay there. Besides this he was also a little lost within his own thoughts. Josh could see this and left the question alone.

As he rolled over realising how tired he was, he dropped off into a light sleep of which Alec was a little grateful for, he wanted the peace to be able to try and think clearly. Alec lay in his bed and tried to make sense of it all as Josh began to lightly snore, but it was like trying to put together a puzzle with missing pieces. He couldn't shake the feeling that there was something more important in all of this that he was missing, something that would help them make sense of everything that was happening. His eyes started to become heavy as he stared up at the ceiling, his mind racing with thoughts of Probetor and what he was capable of. He couldn't shake the feeling of dread that settled in the pit of his stomach.

As he closed his eyes, he heard a faint whisper in his ear. It was a voice he didn't recognize, but it was familiar in a way that made his skin crawl.

"I'm watching you, Alec," the voice said. "And I always will be."

Alec jolted upright in his bed, his heart pounding. His eyes darted around the darkened room, searching for the intruder that he was certain must be creeping towards him. He turned towards where Josh lay and saw his friend still face down asleep, a small pool of saliva had gathered under his chin where his mouth lay open, the day had taken its toll on him. He settled back down realising that no-one was there and wondered whether it had been a dream or if it actually happened? Although now he questioned dreams themselves more than he had ever done before; they were real right? Or at least connected to some form of reality in this world. He still didn't understand any of the rules around this.

Alec lay back down with a heavy sigh, trying to force himself to relax as he realised he was alone other than his sleeping friend. But it was impossible. The voice in his head wouldn't let him. He closed his eyes and took a deep breath, trying to push it out of his mind. But it was no use, it was solidly in there and had set up home quite happily.

He sat up once again, his heart was still racing in his chest. He couldn't stay in this room any further. He had to get out, get some air. He quietly slipped out of his bed, careful not to wake Josh, and made his way towards the door. As he reached for the handle, he paused. He didn't want to risk running into any of the Nyx guards. He had no idea what they might do if they caught him wandering around in the middle of the night. He was certainly not a prisoner in his eyes but was he allowed to wander? Whilst soft in the approach they have been very strict so far. Alec hesitated for a moment longer before making his decision. He didn't know where he was going or what he was looking for, but he knew he couldn't stay here. He slipped out of the room and started walking down the dark hallway.

As he trudged along, night had now descended and the moonlight gleamed through the windows on a crystal-clear night. He couldn't shake the feeling that he was being spied upon as he marched down the passageway listening to the reverberation of his own strides ruminating yet again how the Nyx sauntered so silently.

He persisted in glancing over his shoulder, but he knew that there was no one there. He twisted back once more to contemplate the path in front of him to find Freyja standing there in the corridor gazing at him. She was surveying him with an expression of solicitude on her face.

"Alec," she murmured, "Are you okay?"

Alec stopped, surprised to see her there. "Yeah, I'm fine," he said, rubbing his eyes tiredly as if trying to give the appearance of sleepwalking. Alec frowned, still feeling uneasy. "I heard a voice," he said. "It felt as though someone was watching me."

Freyja's eyes narrowed, a look of concern crossing her face. "Whoever it was, they're not here now," she said reassuringly. "You're safe."

Alec nodded, still feeling uneasy. "What do we do now?" he asked.

Freyja smiled a glint of mischief appearing in her eyes as she sensed Alecs feelings that he may be being disobedient simply by walking the castles hallways.

"You know you are allowed to wander around and you are free to use the facilities as you please." She stared at him for a moment, as though she were contemplating something. Her voice was casual, but the air was warm and resonant, like an excellent singer's. She continued, "we have archery and sword fighting training in the woods just behind the castle gardens most days if you're interested. I can show you where everything is, or you can explore on your own when I'm not around." There was a pause between that sentence and the next, though he wondered whether it was for dramatic effect or because she had to think about what she was going to say before saying it, "now though it is night, if you cannot sleep, I have a suggestion" she said whilst turning to walk away down the corridor, "follow me".

A soft, musical light seemed to emanate from Freyja's body as she glided through the corridors and Alec could not help but notice her steps equally seemed to make no sound. He had noticed before that she had a trait that could lend itself to an almost ethereal presence, one of old-world charm and grace, yet she also seemed quite beautiful in modern terms. The halls were decorated with incredibly intricately carved wooden doors, each one designed differently from the others and each one clinging to its own complete story within the wood grain. He marvelled at such artwork and wondered how many great artists had contributed to the culture of this place over the years to achieve such a masterpiece. Eventually they came to a standstill outside one of these magnificent doors. As Freyja pushed it open Alec could not believe his eyes. Rows of shelving full with fascinating looking old books lay in front of him as far as his eyes could see. They had mostly withered and many seemed bound in old brown worn leather. Freyja ushered Alec to step through the doors as she followed closely behind.

"Many of these books explain our history, as well as yours and that of all the other realms. There are documents of all the influential beings that have been and gone throughout the many years of existence and details and stories, some more accurate than others explaining how the realms became and how each has been managed and functioned. Each had its own design and purpose in the beginning, unfortunately most of those purposes are no longer remembered or acted upon."

Alec swept his gaze around the towering shelves holding books and scrolls in enormous quantities, the moonlight was shining through the high windows, cut within the ancient stone walls. The dust in those uppermost shelves had gathered over years of storage. Alec walked between the shelves, his fingers brushing over the spines of the books. He wanted to explore every one of them and learn everything he could about this world and the others. The titles were fascinating, some in languages he didn't recognize, while others were familiar but seemed to have vastly different meanings.

As he walked amongst the endless supply of historical documents, he found himself drawn to a particular book. It was old and worn, the pages yellowed and dog-eared, but it seemed to call to him. He reached out and ran his fingers over the cover, feeling a strange energy emanating from within its pages. He hesitated for a moment before reaching for it, slowly pulling it from the shelf and rolling it over in his hands.

Freyja watched him closely, her eyes following his every movement. He could feel her presence behind him, at time she became so close that he could feel her warm breath on the back of his neck. He opened the book and instantly became fascinated by the strange language as the words on the page were in a language not only foreign but one that he did not even recognize, but as he read, the meaning began to reveal itself to him thanks largely to the intricate and detailed pictures that accompanied every page.

The book was filled with dark magic, spells and incantations that could unleash dangerously unimaginable power in the wrong hands.

Alec felt a thrill of excitement mixed with fear at the realisation of the power within the pages as he read on. The book seemed to speak to him, urging him to explore the depths of the unknown as it made much more sense as he read on than it should have done given the strange language and workings that would equally be foreign to him. The book described the worst of the dark beings as almost invincible when they have access to certain amenities, their powers becoming unmatched by any known force under certain circumstances.

The Jinn, Probetor and others were named as such being who could achieve this level. He felt a shiver run down his spine as he realized just how dangerous their situation was, more particularly and somewhat selfishly he thought, especially for a stranger like himself, especially just a mere mortal. Freyja placed a hand on his shoulder, pulling him from his thoughts.

"Don't worry," she said softly. "We will figure this out together, please trust that I am here to assist you on this path in any way that I can, it is clear we need you every much as bit as you would need us to help."

Alec nodded, grateful for her reassuring presence as well as her words. He continued to peruse the book, his mind whirring with thoughts of how they could defeat these unstoppable creatures when and if the time came, whilst secretly hoping that said time would never materialise. As he turned a page, his eyes fell upon a passage that made his blood run cold.

"The dark beings are said to have the power to possess the body of others" he read aloud. "Once they are in control, they are almost impossible to remove should the being possessed not have the internal tools required, of which few will have."

Alec's heart pounded in his chest as he realized they can possess the bodies of those not strong enough to reject them.

He read on further, in particular about Probetor who was of greatest interest to him given his presence in his visions.

As he delved deeper into the tales, he failed to notice that Freyja had gone, she must have slipped out whilst he was enthralled in the depths of the pages.

The pages came thick and fast, thick and broad with yellowing edges and they were filled with spider web veins of colour, popping from the page to catch the light. The book went on and explained how Morpheus had banished Probetor to Earth due to his dealings with the humans and his tendency to fabricate reasons to travel there, eventually not providing reasons at all. Travel was only permitted for emergency prevention, the means of doing so only known by few and never easy to accomplish. He had become fascinated with Earth and humans and was punished for this. He was equally punished for falling in love with a human which especially as royalty was frowned upon.

It was clear he was no longer welcome back for a period of time being made to serve his time in the place he seemed so eager to stay, and as a result ironically became desperate to return home. Alec felt some empathy for Probetor, he himself was quite often taken by things that he should possibly not be as interested in, and being punished for intrigue seemed extremely unfair. The relationship between Probetor and the human he supposedly fell in love with itself was never explored in detail, it seemed they did not know much on the subject except for that matter; however, she must have been special indeed for it to have all been worthwhile. From the scarce information provided Alec interpreted that they had become bound together, her world and his mashing together until they could not tell one from another anymore.

There were in fact empty pages, this story of his time on Earth was yet to complete and the space had been left in order to do so. The book goes on to explain how the Jinn sensed that there was a god like Erobian, one from Sofpavel, banished to Earth, angry and feeling defeated at being punished for his emotional connection to this one person. He took advantage of this and found a way to exploit him, slowly manipulating him and turning him against all he had previously believed. He found a weakness, exploited it and took full advantage.

Freyja had often wondered what had happened to this woman, she must have meant a lot to Probetor for him to be banished from his home and turn on all he had ever known, giving up his rights to the throne and leaving behind all he had known. She wished the book went into more detail about her and the relationship between them herself, it was clear that she must have been something special for him to go through all of this trouble. Freyja knew deep down there was still time to continue Probetor's story, even if she had thought it long finished, she could feel it in her bones.

She leaned over Alec and closed the book, carefully placing it back on the shelf behind him, her hand lingering for a period on the book as she left it in its original place. Alec took a deep breath, feeling a sense of sadness at the tragic seeming love story that had unfolded before him on those pages.

He looked at Freyja who was still standing by his side, her eyes filled with compassion and understanding as she if all of this was new to her, he could see an element of guilt in her eyes and he knew that she must have played her part within his banishment. She was of course all too familiar with the stories Alec was reading having not only been there at the time but having also studied these books herself and re-read her own history numerous times, the ending always remaining the same much to her disappointment. Without speaking a word, she reached out and placed her hand in his, squeezing gently before pulling away. Alec smiled sadly as he realized that Probetor had not been able to find true happiness despite all of his efforts, possibly the only thing he truly wished for from all of his efforts.

If anything, Probetor was as much a victim as he was an aggressor. Certainly, now he may well be the greatest oppressor of peace but once he had merely been in love. Alec contemplated how despite its sorrowfulness this information could be employed to help them vanquish these dark creatures forever.

Alec turned to Freyja and felt his throat tighten. He opened his mouth to speak, but she beat him to it, her words coming faster than he could process them. "It is good to see these things Alec," she said softly, her voice barely above a whisper.

"This knowledge can certainly be powerful. However, keep in mind that this is merely just that, knowledge. It can be manipulated, changed, and the outcome is yet to be determined. Use it to your advantage and never forget that the future is up to you. Believe in yourself and continuously strive for greatness, because you can write your own story!"

Her eyes were like two deep pools of wisdom and experience, their bright blue depths holding more secrets and knowledge than he could ever hope to possess. Alec pondered her words for a moment, feeling lost in thought as the weight of her message sunk in. He did not believe in fate, noting that these comments suggested Freyja did not either, but lately he was less and less sure what was worthy of his belief and what was not.

Finally, after a long pause, he spoke, his voice low and serious.

"Thank you" he said simply. "I will keep it in mind." Alec knew that Freyja was right - nothing was set in stone. The world was always changing, always shifting, and it was up to each individual to decide how they would react to those changes.

Freyja nodded and then smiled softly at him encouraging him to sit, her face lighting up as she began to tell Alec stories of Morpheus and even how the Jinn came to be, the history of Erobus and the customs that to Alec seemed so strange and foreign. As she spoke, Alec was mesmerized by her words.

He felt as though he was getting an even deeper glimpse into a world so different from his own - a world filled with wonder and beauty that he had never known before but found so fascinating. Freyja seemed to understand the power of this knowledge and how it could be used for good or ill, having utilised it for many years, teaching Alec about the importance of understanding one's enemy before making any rash decisions was an important lesson for him to learn. By the time Freyja had finished speaking, Alec felt like he had learned another language - one filled with wisdom and insight that only those who have seen what darkness truly has to offer can understand. She turned to him before finalising what had seemed like the greatest lesson of his life,

"This information is not of a nature to be shared. Some of the things I told you are not even known by many Erobians. I can see it in you, even if I do not know yet what 'it' fully is. I do feel Lemuri knows completely however and will impart this onto me when the time comes, either that or it will become apparent all on its own."

He looked so deeply and intently into the empty table that stood before him, his eyes focused on a single point that was maddening to look at. His grip tensed even more as he rose up, but it didn't matter. He could feel the cool night air beginning to break away and reveal that the sun was not far from appearing over the horizon. The sounds of the first birds outside were beginning also, but he didn't care about them either. For within the room, there was everything that he needed. He took a moment to glance back and look upon Freyja who had patiently guided him along this path till now.

She smiled back at him warmly before saying goodbye and turning to leave the room "stay if you wish and read further, I do suggest some rest however. That rising sun is not far away now, you'll need your rest," with this she left carrying with her the remaining secrets that she still had yet to reveal, as well as those she wished to remain hidden.

Alec nodded and knew that she was right - he needed some rest, but he wanted to continue exploring Erobus, discovering more of its customs and history, he was captivated by the mysteries it held. He opened the book Freyja had gifted him and began to read. As his eyes moved over the pages, he felt as though he was being transported through time into a world of mystery and intrigue. He read stories of ancient battles between powerful sorcerers, tales of legendary beasts that roamed the land long ago as well as the stories of those that still do to this day, descriptions of a people who are said to have had magical powers so vast that they could alter reality itself. Every page held something new for Alec - secrets that made him feel excited yet nervous at the same time.

Finally, when dawn began to break in earnest, Alec closed the book with a satisfied sigh and slid it back onto its shelf. He had learned such an incredible amount about Erobus during his exploration tonight - it felt like an entire lifetime condensed into just one night!

With a tired but contented smile, he stood and made his way back to his room. He had done enough exploring for one night - now it was time to get some rest before the others began to wake but he intended to return when the time was right. He snuck in quietly, careful not to make too much noise, and settled into bed. His mind was buzzing with all of the knowledge gained tonight, but even so it didn't take him long to fall asleep as exhaustion soon overcame him.

6) Troubled friends

Alec blinked away the grogginess and frantically scanned the room. Josh was nowhere to be found. The bed lay vacant, its sheets crumpled from what seemed like a whirlwind of activity. Alec stomped anxiously around the space, attempting to decipher what had just occurred. Josh wouldn't normally depart like this—given his hesitance towards Erobus and how they treated him, it was astonishing that he had ventured off alone.

However, Josh always enjoyed discovering new places as much as he himself did, so he guessed it made sense that he would wish to explore if he was now a little more comfortable with their surroundings. Given the holiday they had been longing for was apparently in a perilous position of not happening he may well wish to treat this as such.

There was a sudden knock at the door, making Alec's heart skip a beat as it echoed through the silence. He approached the large door cautiously given that he was not expecting any company. However, he was aware that at this point he had no real knowledge of what the time may be, especially as clocks did not appear to exist here, he mused. He approached the wooden door feeling the sounds of creaks beneath his feet as he moved.

He placed a hand strongly on the handle, peering through the keyhole before opening it up to reveal Hypnos, standing tall and as imposing looking as always on the other side. His polished armour clattered with each step he took towards Alec, causing Alec to step backwards in return. Although he knew Hypnos was on his side, he still felt ever so slightly nervous of him.

"Good morning, Sir Alec" Hypnos said addressing him in the gentlest of tones that Alec had heard from him to date, which did go some way towards lowering his own nervousness.

"We would like you to join us in the great hall later this morning, we have news and strategy to discuss. We are aiming to gather there when the sun is at its peak and I will send you an escort prior so please ensure you are ready,"

This description of time as 'the sun at its peak' amused Alec, it was all very medieval sounding and made him think of the incorrectly romanticized times that accompanied them. Alec nodded in acknowledgment of the instruction, he noticed he had been stood at attention, as if he were being addressed by an officer, which whilst technically he guessed he was he felt a little foolish. As Hypnos turned to leave Alec quickly called out.

"Have you seen Josh at all this morning by any chance?" Alec questioned "He was not here when I woke up?"

Hypnos turned back to face Alec, his towering figure seeming to fill the tight space of the corridor which seemed much smaller than Alec had recalled it the previous night. He shook his head in response to the question and spoke in a low, gravelly tone. "He went out early this morning I was informed. The guards said he wanted to wander through the woods on his own. They offered him guide and security personnel but he foolishly declined, this is his right." Hypnos looked rather annoyed at this point as if insulted by Josh having done so, " you should both be perfectly safe here, however, in these uncertain times and given your lack of knowledge of Sofpavel you would be wise to advise him to accept in future, as well as you yourself if you really are of as much importance as we are led to believe."

He felt in Hypnos voice that he was more demanding than requesting the allowance of escorts to accompany them on their travels. He nodded to him obediently as he left to assure him that his instruction was understood fully.

Alec looks out the window and sees a breathtaking sight. The sky is open and inviting, the sun shining brightly in the blue sky. The countryside stretches for miles, full of lush green forests and deep valleys. He sees vast expanses, undiscovered and full of secrets, waiting to be explored. He had however only been given permission for a few hours of venturing, and even then, it would be advantageous for him to be learning combat skills or aiding the others in their training, they do seem to be expecting him to fight it would appear in some shape or form so actually being able to do so would help!

Despite the dangers, Alec was irresistibly drawn to venturing out with Josh. They had often explored new places together. He knew Hypnos would object and that Freyja might have some understanding of his yearning for a journey, especially since she had granted him permission to wander last night, even seeming to cheer him on. Yet his fascination had been greater than his fear, and Alec sprinted off after Josh, eager to find unknown realms and creatures; who knew what bizarre things could be hidden in these lands.

The tall grass of the hillside rippled in the wind as Alec walks eagerly towards the woodlands. He was grateful not to be noticed by any guards on his way through the castle, he would have felt obliged to accept the entourage wishing to accompany him.

The creaking of the trees mingled with the chirps and laughter of a multitude of unfamiliar birds as he stepped through the first few fluttering trees at the outline of the vast stretch of forest. A cool breeze blew in from the west, carrying with it the smell of fresh rain and pines. It was still early and everything was alive.

The light filtering through the leaves created a dappled pattern on the ground, while thin wisps of mist curl around the trunks of the ancient oaks that have long stood tall shoulder to shoulder.

The castle walls loomed over him as he glanced back. He felt he had walked quite a distance, yet it was still easily visible in the horizon. He noticed a few Nyx guards patrolling atop the tall walls that were fortified with its protection. One particular guard intently gazing at him, perhaps instructed to do so. It was evident he was being watched.

He was mesmerized by the magnificence of his locale as he plunged further into the woods when an uncanny fog began to settle all around him. Alec stepped boldly onward, anticipating the same thicketed forest and swaying shadows, however instead he discovered himself standing in a foreign place with an even more powerful atmosphere of sorcery, the forest that had enveloped him melted away and a lambent halo descended on him.

A cracking sound, which Alec initially mistook for Josh's presence, echoed through the air above him. When he looked up in anticipation, wary due to the recent events of the day, he was shocked by what he saw before him: a magnificent entity was heading down towards him with its wings spread wide, flames dancing off of each feather like a thousand stars. It surveyed Alec intently, and its eyes shone brighter than any midday sun. Alec felt his bones quiver in awe as he took in the sight before him, the legendary Phoenix. Everything about this majestic animal spoke of wisdom and authority stemming from its origin: born from the molten lava and cooled waters of Lemuri during its creation—whose every move held within it all the wisdom of its birthplace, its every move seeming to contain the rhythm of the falls in their majesty and grace. Alec had read about these creatures of Erobus the previous night, none could have prepared him for this one's intense power and beauty.

As Alec beheld the majestic creature before him, his limbs trembled with veneration. It seemed so much greater than any creature he had ever encountered, powerful enough to rival the gods themselves. He felt the amazement swell inside of him like a tempestuous sea, its power so overwhelming that he was transfixed in its force.

Then, slowly fading into earshot, Alec heard a voice within his mind – as though hundreds of voices sang in unison, soft and yet domineering at once: "I am here for you, Alec," it said. "Your father's blood and your mother's heart run deep within you; you are chosen for a purpose greater than yourself; you can use both sides of this coin to your advantage." Alec looked at the great bird knowing the voice had come from this source but not understanding how this was possible.

The Phoenix appeared to almost smile at Alec through its eyes before it rose majestically into the air, wings reflecting the crimson hues of the setting sun.

As Alec watched it disappear into the horizon, he felt something stirring inside him, like a seed coming to life beneath fertile soil. He didn't know what this meant or how it would impact his life, but he knew that something extraordinary had just happened to him. The bird spoke of his father; however, he could not believe he had just heard that correctly, his father? He did not even know who that was, how is he relevant to all of this? How does the Phoenix also know about his mother? As the Phoenix left his sight Alec heard the words "at the moment you most need, I will be there, I will be watching you, as i always have."

Alec sat for what turned into hours beneath the trees, trying to understand the phoenix's words and exactly what they meant. They were seemingly heavier than any he'd been given before, but more importantly, he knew this gift was imperative for him to follow his calling. The knowledge that his parents had something to do with this left confusion, the Phoenix did not provide any context after all but it did leave him wondering, was his own lineage from this place and not from Earth as he had believed?

The sun crept through the canopy above to shine reflections from the leaves high above onto his face once more. Below the halo of light that shone so beautifully through to him, Alec remained sat under the trees looking up into them in contemplation. He felt a sense of peace settle over him as he watched the twinkling lights dart across the sky and once again the birds rang through as he heard their brilliant song fill the air around him.

As Alec dragged himself to his feet, ignited by the idea of learning more about his parents, he remembered why he had set off into the woods in the first place. A new-found determination surged through his veins as he stood upright.

He had come searching for Josh, to explore with him and take the opportunity to speak with him away from all of the listening ears of the castle. He peered around himself at the immense forests ahead realizing just how far he could have travelled in the time he had spent sitting there, equally how much further Josh may have travelled himself.

Alec lugged forward through the forest, picking up his pace to make up for lost time. As silence enveloped him and the sound of bird song seemed to fade into the background, an intense feeling of anticipation lingered in the air and he knew that every second counted as his internal alarm system alerted him to something not being quite right. Suddenly an animal shot from behind a tree not too far from where Alec trod, darting to another and disappeared into nothingness. A rabbit? He thought, before discarding the notion — it had been much larger than a rabbit, however he knew not how large they may well be here. An unexpected noise disturbed the still atmosphere again and a dark silhouette more clearly darted between trees on Alec's right-hand side, it was definitely no rabbit.

His heart rate increased drastically as adrenaline surged throughout his body — was it possibly Josh? He did like a prank after all and may be trying to scare him. He stepped closer, endeavouring to figure out exactly what it had been. Then he heard a faint rustling sound off to his left this time and swivelled towards it but nothing appeared to be there.

He ran towards the direction of the figure wondering if doing so was the best idea, but it vanished from sight before he arrived. The world around him was darkening as the canopy overhead drowned out the light coming from the sun above as it grew thicker and thicker the deeper he found himself going, all he could hear was the sound of branches hitting against each other from his left and right as he pushed his way through the thickening woodlands. His feet splashed through small puddles as he leapt over fallen logs, until he caught a glimpse of something white moving quickly between the trees up ahead.

The rustling soon grew louder, and Alec knew that whatever it was, it was close.

Finally, after what felt like hours of running, he burst into a clearing, the thorny overhanging branches scratched at his face as he winced back in pain, briefly looking back at the inanimate object as if it were to blame for not moving. He had forgotten how bright the sun had been that day as he entered the clearing, the sun temporarily blinding him as he left the shelter of the overhanging forest.

As his vision adjusted, he spotted a form sprawled on the ground in the middle of the clearing. It didn't take him long to realize that it was Josh, prostrate and unresponsive.

Alec rushed over to his friend's side noticing his injuries as he approached.

"What happened to you?" Alec whispered, trying not to jolt Josh too much whilst rolling him onto his back, gently propping his head up within his arms.

Josh groaned, his eyes fluttering open. "I don't know," he mumbled, trying to sit up, "I was just walking and then everything went black, it feels like I've been hit by a train."

Alec grabbed Josh's arm and pulled him up from the ground. His face was contorted in pain, and he could barely stand on his own.

Alec looked at him with concern surveying for any obvious damage. He noticed that his own chest was heaving heavily, he had held his breath in anticipation seeing his injured friend, however he still had not caught his breath after running through the woods and now required some deep heavy breathing to catch up.

"Okay," he said softly. "Let's give it a second."

They both stood in silence for a moment, Alec watching Josh closely as he tried to steady himself and stand on his own two feet, not quite managing and returning to the leaning post that was Alec. But as they stood there, Alec couldn't shake the feeling that something was not right. He looked around the clearing, trying to spot any signs of what he had previously seen moving around within the woodlands, it had seemed fairly large so may have been what attacked Josh.

The clearing before them had an unearthly quality, with trees knotted like gnarled hands and thick vines looping around their trunks. The air was dank and still, only the occasional crack of a branch or rustle of leaves breaking the silence. It was like nothing Alec had ever seen before, and his body was screaming at him alerting him to the clear present danger, the unease crept up his spine through the surrounding atmosphere that was looming over the pair. Alec was worryingly aware that out here somewhere, they had company.

Momentarily, he caught a brief sight of movement out of the corner of his eye. He whirled around, his gaze frantically darting between the trees as he searched for the source of movement he thought he had seen, frustrated at the continuing ability of whatever this was to remain undetected. He could have sworn there was something there just moments ago - what was going on? Had he imagined it? Was his mind playing tricks on him? Fear and confusion warred inside him.

"Alec, what is it?" Josh asked, his voice barely above a whisper and still croaking with pain.

"I don't know," Alec replied, still scanning the area frantically for any signs of movement. "I thought I saw something; I know I've seen something."

As they stood there, almost appearing to be waiting for the mysterious danger to reveal itself, Alec could feel the hairs on the back of his neck standing on end. He knew they needed to get out of there, and fast. If there is indeed something there, even if not malevolent it had an unhealthy interest in the pair.

"Come on," he said, taking Josh's arm and leading him towards the edge of the clearing. "We need to find some help." Josh looked up towards him, through his discomfort he allowed himself a wry smile and exclamation,

"Great, a famous Alec feeling by any chance?" He mockingly asked even though he knew that historically there was a lot to them.

They begin to stumble forwards one step after another, Alec leading the way while Josh leaned heavily on him for support. As they slowly moved, Alec's mind raced with possibilities.

Had they stumbled upon some sort of dangerous creature? Are they being hunted? Or was there someone else out here with them, some of the young previously seen playing mischievously in the surrounding grounds now teasing them, trying to be scary perhaps. Alec did not have much belief in this theory unfortunately, however he felt it one well worth trying to convince himself of.

Alec's fearful expression drew his brows together and his mouth tightened into a frown.

As Josh leaned into him, he felt his own knees begin to buckle beneath the weight. But despite this, he remained steady enough to keep them both upright.

The rustling in the surrounding tree lines and shrubbery intensified, and now broke free from its restraints to run freely through the shallow grassy field around them. It clattered steadily closer making its presence known, like an approaching army; trunks swayed hard against each other almost drumming out a rhythm of fear.

Josh leant entirely on Alec at this point still suffering from whatever had happened, he raised his drooping head to look his friend in the eyes. As Alec looked back at Josh in brief intervals, between his scanning of the wooded outline and his fear, he realised his friend was looking increasingly concerned. He looked down again at Josh with the realisation that he needed some comfort and reassurance.

"It's ok Josh, we'll get out of here, we've been in plenty of sticky situations before, right?" He tried to comfortingly inform his friend; however, his voice was betraying his words as he spoke with much more uncertainty than he was attempting to portray. As Josh had mocked, he knew he had had one of his feelings, and this time it was on overdrive so he was concerned and was certainly not doubting it. If ever he had wanted his feelings to be wrong it was now. "Maybe this is just a giant group of herding squirrels we have yet to be informed of!" he nervously joked.

Josh sniggered at this comment, he always had appreciated Alec's habit of trying to lighten the mood but knew through his voice and the look of his face that this was not a feeling that he genuinely believed.

Josh's grip on Alec's forearm tightened and he took a deep breath before continuing. He knew there was no turning back now, that soon all of this would be beyond his control if he didn't act fast. With the weight of the world upon him, he had to make some revelations to Alec, as well as tell him what was going on.

"NO, stop," Josh said, a little louder than before but still not raising his voice enough to draw too much attention.

Alec did as he was told but kept staring at Josh's face, trying to figure out what was happening. It wasn't just that Josh looked different—something had changed in him. He had known something for a long time but hadn't wanted to believe it before now.

"I'm sorry," Josh continued, lowering his head and looking down at the ground. His tone remained low and even, but conveyed a great agony instead of its usual purposeful resolve. "Just remember that whatever I tell you is real, and something I should have perhaps shared with you long ago."

7) Old flames

Alec's intrigue was now peaked to a point he had almost forgotten about any pending dangers, Josh's injury or indeed the fact they were no longer even on Earth.

"Josh what are you talking about? And is now really the time?" Alec questioned trying to draw attention back to the issue at hand. He could see through the surrounding thicket that although the sound had lessened there appeared to be shadows lining the areas around them, a good number of them as well, he hoped at this point it indeed was a large brood of giant squirrels! He looked down at Josh as if pushing him to reveal more information but in as fast an amount of time as possible.

"My name, is not Josh, it is JoFrey, however, that being said, I'll only ever go as Josh now, it has been such a long time since I was called by my birth name!"

Alec looked at Josh with disbelief, almost as if he felt he was choosing an awfully bad moment to be telling a terrible a joke. Josh could sense this and saw it in his eyes, he grabbed hold of Alec with both hands as if to try and reinsert his point.

"Listen, I will explain more when we make it out of this but for now you need to listen. I believe we are surrounded by Koschei forces; we need to find a way out of this and the best way may well be to make ourselves safe until help arrives, they must have been seen entering Sofpavel and I am amazed they made it this far!"

Alec listened with confusion and was still struggling to believe that his friend of all these years could possibly be anyone other than who he knew him to be. All these years, the stories and indeed the very real friendship, in fact Josh was more a brother to Alec than anybody, especially in the absence of any real siblings.

He had no real time to think on this too much however, as the cracking from the surrounding areas exposed a breach, causing both to pause as he they sight of three silhouettes emerging from the undergrowth.

Their appearance was extremely alarming to even the strongest minded of people. He could make out their half-decayed figures, cloaked in silver armour that had long since corroded with age. The leather straps holding the pieces flimsily together oozed a putrid green mould, and their faces were an amalgamation of flesh and bone. In the hands of these creatures, Alec saw shields and swords, glinting menacingly in the light.

As they lumbered forward, he felt his stomach drop—these creatures looked more like competent zombies than anything else, and it terrified him to the core. They ventured towards them and reached a point about halfway between the cover of the trees behind and the point in which they both now stood. They stopped and just stood there, locked in place, waiting for something to happen.

"Don't move," Josh whispered over the noise of wood creaking to Alec's right and the groaning noises from the Koschei forces in front.

The Koschei lowered their weapons down towards the floor and waited for any sign that they should attack.

They had a bloodthirsty look about them and Alec did not believe that they were showing any restraint from the goodness of their own hearts.

Josh reached into his inside coat pocket and revealed a small glowing ball, no larger than a marble and seemingly relatively innocuous other than the light that shone from its surface. The light illuminated the patterns carved into its surface, which looked for all the world like some ancient scripture from an extinct language. He rolled it between his fingers and lowered himself to his knees, still holding himself in pain but managing to at least heft himself into a kneeling position. He placed the ball onto the floor before moving back away from it, silently tapping three times on top of it with his index finger. A low buzzing sound emanated from the ball as it started to vibrate and before Alec knew it, it had expanded into a large blue sphere that created a barrier around them.

Alec looked on upon the blue thin energy shield that now cocooned them, protected them, although by how much he had no idea. He reached out and thoughtfully touched the protective layer. The silvery shield tickled his fingertips just like a stream of water as it flows over smooth rocks. However, he could feel nothing other than a strange force preventing his hand from penetrating through to the other side.

"Josh" Alec started absolutely bewildered by all he that had just transpired, "Who the hell are you?" Josh stood himself back up looking over towards the Koschei, they remained where they stood, unflinching and almost seeming uninterested in anything that they may be doing.

"I am a messenger of your mother's Alec." Josh sighed. "I'm sorry I never told you, I swore I would not until the time was right, if the time was ever right." The information he was readying to offload weighed heavily on him, and Alec could see it seemingly falling from his hunching figure like leaves off an autumn tree.

Josh's voice was low and even, yet intense as he began offloading information. He spoke of a distant realm - Alerion - his own home, and how Alec's father had been an Erobian God. He had told Alecs mother wonderful tales of Erobus and taught her all about the realms and how they worked.

He had described them all as a tree, with Erobus being the roots and all of the others being the fruit the tree would bare, she was as fascinated with it all as he was with Earth. Josh watched Alec carefully as he spoke, noting the chaos that played across his face.

The silence hung heavy in the air between each brief pause as they both stood in stillness, aware of the enemy soldiers keeping watch nearby and being reminded by the faint grunts that could be heard every time Josh came up for air. He felt compelled to finish his tale, seemingly having been longing to do this for some time, but time was running out and danger lurked close by.

"Your parents relationship deteriorated however, not through fault of his own, he as many others have in the past, had his attention diverted by The Jinn when he witnessed the hardships inflicted upon him from the rulers of Erobus. His tribulations overflowed into his relationship with your mother no matter how hard he strived to contain it. Maredrom has allured many Sofpavelians, furthermore having recruited from everywhere across the realms. The Jinn's influence spread far and wide and the ambition to rule was overpowering, resulting in informants and adversaries everywhere. It is also why the Koschei army swelled so vast and why not everyone is undead. Much of this you could have surely read about. This was why Morpheus realized he had to make such a penance, why The Jinn's force became so insurmountable and why the necessity to stymie him was so dire. Whilst he could not traverse between the realms with ease, he could guarantee that Morpheus had enemies coming from all realms simply by transmitting his message and propaganda. There is usually combat to an extent but none like The Jinn initiated, none like they are possibly devolving back to now, and indeed none that had ever crossed from realm to realm."

Josh knelt down and ran his finger along the glowing sphere, as he did it partially separated and out shone a holographic beam displaying an intricate map of all the realms. The map included all of the mystical realms and Alec was amazed by the intricacy of its details and could see its clear likeness to that of a tree, with paths branching out from each realm in to one another. He could see how Maredrom's influence had spread as parts turned black on the map like a storyline revealing the true extent of the damage that had been caused, drowning out any opposing forces in its wake.

"Erobus, and specifically here in Sofpavel they had been granted a power beyond those of other realms" continued Josh, "but the price was paid in blood and iron. The Jinn, the main enemy of peace though the ages, possessed a wisdom and strength that eluded all others. A sacrifice was needed be made in order for the Jinn to gain the control he wanted. He needed a demi-god, of Sofpavelian blood. Your mother had seen this future and did everything she could to protect you from it, as what they wanted Alec, was you, the singular living demi-god at the time."

Alec was horrified and overwhelmed by what Josh was telling him. He put his hand up as if to indicate that he could not hear more. Josh knew however, that as he had started, he now must finish. Or at least make good progress towards letting Alec know who he was and an indication as to why he was here. Whatever events transpired over the next few minutes may be dire, he needed to know now.

"Your father," Josh continued, "he also did what he had to, to protect you, he gave himself to the dark lord and turned against what he believed, yes partially through his pain at being punished in the way he had and due to clever manipulation on The Jinn's part, but largely as he believed, arrogantly, that he could protect you from within and bring them down winning back favour in Sofpavel. But he was over powered, completely unprepared for how much dark magic the Jinn now had access to, and as such he turned to the dark himself."

Alec paused, a look of horror and realisation filling his face, the colour draining away as he recoiled shaking his head. The story that Josh was reciting to him sounded very familiar, it sounded like a much kinder explanation than the ones he had read within the Sofpavel library the previous night, the god living on Earth, in love with a human, who turns to the dark side amidst all the feelings of betrayal. He looked at Josh, he had paused in his story telling, he had seen the realisation hit Alec like a bullet train and believed he may now know who he is and why it is that he may well be a big player in this unfolding drama. He nodded his head whilst lowering himself back to the ground in a seated position. He was still dazed and in some pain from what had happened and coming clean with all of this information was extremely draining.

Alec almost lunged at Josh, balling his fists as he screamed.

"Are you trying to tell me, that my father, is Probetor!?" He took a step back from the realisation and fell to the forest floor in shock. Josh's expression narrowed and a deep sadness darkened his face. He had never seen what appeared to be anger emanate from his friend, even if for a brief moment and it upset him deeply to know he had been the cause of it. He moved to touch Alec's shoulder but stopped at the last moment.

He answered, with clear regret in his voice, simply "Yes."

Alec dropped his head into his hands and shook. The world had been turned inside out in just one day, no in one moment; he was shocked and disturbed by the information he had just learned. He looked up suddenly, "But, but how, it makes no sense, for starters the stories of them are thousands of years old, that would make me ridiculously old?!"

Josh grinned, noting Alec's surprise at the age difference, entertained by Alec's ability to remember and point out glaring holes and inconsistencies even while under so much mental strain. He knew there was still a lot more to this story, but he wondered how much time they had before something needed to be done about their current situation. They were safe within their sphere, yet trapped in it as well; they couldn't move with it, and so were sitting targets, just waiting for whatever the soldiers' appeared to be waiting for.

" Your mother found solace on my planet, Alerion, where time moves at a much more sluggish rate compared to Earth — it's synchronized with Erobus. That is why when you have a dream that appears short-lived, you can awaken to the entire night gone. The dream orbs contain times from Erobus — due to the immense dilatation between us, staying in Alerion or Erobus for years may equate to mere hours passed in Earth. If we linger here for a few weeks, when we go back to Earth it will be mere seconds after our departure. So, whilst you've aged 23 years on Earth, simultaneously your mother has lived through thousands of years in Alerion. Does that make sense? It is something you will never become accustomed to; you thought jet lag was bad right?"

Josh tried hard to insert a little joke hoping it would relieve Alec's clear tension, it clearly did not and with a frown Josh continued.

"Your parents were otherworldly beings, even if your mother did originate from Earth. They were able to traverse other realms, ones that humans can only dream of. Your mother was a prodigious human and had extensive knowledge of the realms beyond any human's understanding before becoming Alerion. During her pregnancy with you, she spent most of her time in Alerion, returning to Earth just for a few months after your birth thanks to the help of an Alerion elder, one of a few who have ever been able to move between the realms, she took me with her, hired me to be your guardian. I age physically much slower than you whilst on my home planet, so when you saw me as they young child you befriended, I was actually in reality more the age of your mother. My time on Earth meant I needed to age at your pace and this was a sacrifice I willingly made. Once she had secured your safety, she hastily abandoned you with your grandparents. She dared not bring you back to Alerion as it was perilous and almost inconceivable to access Earth from there. In fact, a nearly inconceivable journey from anywhere as Earth is the most obscure realm to traverse given its unfamiliarity, she knew you were shielded there and if she stayed guarded on another realm could deceive the surveillance and keep it on herself instead of you. Though she kept a close watch on you from afar, she felt it was insufficient; she realised you were always in imminent peril and strove to preserve you, one of the reasons I was placed with you. In the end, she became an Alerion herself, dwelling in a place where time flowed differently than here on Earth. While mere days trickled by for you, years ambled past for her, forming a predicament where observing you mature was agonisingly slow for her."

All of a sudden, two figures appeared from the heart of the woods.

They were flanked on either side by a troop of Koschei soldiers and adorned in hooded cloaks as dark as night with eyes that glowed an eerie purple hue. Alec was bedazzled by their presence while Josh seemed to be expecting them; his pallor taking a shift for the paler. A deep echoing voice came from one of the figures, almost as if it originated from all directions simultaneously. The figures advanced towards them with a menacingly slow pace, the broken trees bowed in reverence and the surrounding grasses lay still as if frozen in time. As they made their approach towards the sphere, Alec prayed fervently that it could not be penetrated.

"It's so nice to see you again, Alec", the voice said in a deep, echoing yet feminine voice with a sinister tone behind it, "I had wondered how to get you here for some time, and then in the end they bring you for me, how kind and stupid of them."

Alec felt a chill run through his body as he looked at the figure in front of him. She stood stubbornly, exuding an arrogant air and seemed to take great pleasure in knowing he was here.

Josh surveyed the stranger with an overpowering animosity, his scowl intensifying as he recognized them. Alec could make out their concealed features under the hood and observed a malicious smile growing wider on their face as they glanced at Josh.

Alec recognized the voice, even though it was different. A realization hit him—the person he was hearing was someone he knew well, although not like this. She had been appearing in his nightmares recently for other reasons, and images of their past started flashing through his mind. It all became clear to him: the name on the tip of his tongue was Jenny, his ex-girlfriend. The one he had felt so strongly about, whom they had planned a holiday to forget. But there she stood before them, with an intent that seemed much different from when they were together.

Josh after a long pause spoke, his voice shaking with anger confirming Alec's thoughts "Jenny...what are you doing here?" His heart raced with anger as he realised now why he had always had such an intense hatred for her; she was from Maredrom, he knew he had sensed something dark in her through all the years she was on the scene, for a place so hard to reach there seemed a remarkable number of beings that had been able to inhabit Earth.

Jenny smiled a bemused smirk, her eyes gleaming now with a sinister intent enjoying having revealed herself after all this time. She laughed mockingly at Josh's question, and spoke in an icy tone

"Well Josh, it looks like I'm here to collect Alec, thank you so much for playing delivery boy, you were not always as useless as I had thought".

Alec could not believe what was happening, it seemed like something out of a movie, to have his ex-girlfriend materialise as a bad person is an old twist that maybe he should have predicted. Jenny signalled to the troops around, the original three had now been joined by many more as they began to prepare for an onslaught, Alec did not pause to count but he guessed there must be at least twenty now standing there. He looked towards Josh with eyes begging for the answers on how to get out of this hoping he had a secret or two to reveal that may solve this problem that lay in front of them.

Josh seemed to sense this as he turned to him and began to answer the question without having been asked. "Alec this dome will only hold us safe for so long, and I have no other tricks I can use, I do not know what to do right now but if an opening becomes free, you run, do not look back, run, and make noise, the soldiers at the castle will hear you, how they do not know there are intruders on their land already I do not know. I was counting on them to arrive before a situation like this arose."

Josh's words made Alec feel more nervous than ever, but he nodded in agreement and readied himself for what was to come, not that he at this point had the faintest idea of what that may be nor did he wish to flee and leave his friend behind, regardless of who he may really be. However, as if on cue, the Koschei began their attack on the dome, their formless shadows merging into one against the blue hue shining from the protective shield that they were so currently dependant on. With every blow they dealt to the dome it seemed like a thunderstorm was raging around them, each strike causing a flash of light as it strongly repelled the incoming blades. As they continued their relentless assault Josh could not help but wonder how they would escape this situation and Alec could not see any possible opening happening from which to pitch an escape attempt of his own.

As they desperately thought of a way to avoid what seemed their inevitable fate, they heard the rustling of leaves in the distance as it grew louder, morphing into the cacophonous rhythm of galloping horses' hooves. Hope wrapped around them as they realized that help was indeed on the way. A plume of dust rose in the distance, signalling the approach of Hypnos and his elite guard from the castle.

They quickly reached the protective dome and instantly engaged with the Koschei troops, driving them back from the protective barrier that had stood so well against the attackers. Alec had never seen such a sight before and his fear gave way to a sense of almost excitement as he watched what those charged with protecting him could do.

Jenny retreated defiantly, secure in the belief that her soldier could still free them from the dome. And as she took a few steps further into the shadows, accompanied by her mysterious ally, she knew that there was no chance of combatting this force any longer. A vile oath escaped her lips as they fled into the depths of the woods for safety. Alec spied her amidst the throng and wondered who the cloaked figure was that stood protectively behind Jenny, never uttering a sound, seemingly observing her every move. Their gazes locked across the divide and he saw her one last time before she vanished in a cloud of smoke, leaving her mocking laughter reverberating in his memory.

Alec now turned his attention toward the shadow that had formed above him and watched in awe as Hypnos took the air, landing just in front of them before strongly ordering his men forward in pursuit of the assailants. He gave orders to those still standing as well as the few who were wounded to return to the castle walls before turning to face both Alec and Josh.

His eyes expressed both fury and frustration, but also a subdued concern that was very controlled. Alec waited for him to say something, anything, because he suspected that under normal circumstances there would have been a tirade waiting for him. It would be prime 'I told you so' territory for most but Alec had the impression this was not Hypnos way.

"Lower the barrier" he sternly said to Josh. Josh instantly obliged, tapping the side of the ball in formation causing the barrier to instantly close back down in on itself and the glowing inscriptions across the ball to fade. As the barrier fell, Alec was felt Hypnos' presence looming over them. The towering warrior – his face a tense mask of dark brows and sharp cheekbones – was standing with one arm folded across his chest and the other resting on the handle of his sheathed sword. Although he intimidated Alec, Hypnos was decidedly a positive force to have as an ally. Despite his own frustrations, he desperately wanted their safety.

"I told you that it's dangerous to be out here," he said, his voice softening. "If it's true that you are as important as they say...if you're so important, we can't let anything happen to you. If needs be I will place you under house arrest!"

Hypnos shook his head conveying a sense of disappointment that made them both feel like children and hoped that they understood, certainly at least hoped that they now realised the dangers that exist around them.

"Come" he said, "we must return to the castle, you have been gone for some time and we are overdue on our discussions, I do not like poor punctuality, please take note!" Alec nodded a little sheepishly, he had recalled that Hypnos had informed him that he only had a few hours.

Hypnos turned to a couple of nearby Nyx and instructed them to assist Josh back for medical care, " it would appear we need a different type of discussion with you" Hypnos said, Josh no longer however looked concerned by their companions here, in fact he seemed to have unexpectedly grown an air of confidence, of strength. Alec did not know quite what to make of this, it was all alien compared to what he knew of his friend, however he knew that he would find out soon enough.

8) Off come the gloves

As Alec strode back into the castle courtyard, a whirlwind of emotions and questions rushed through his mind. The last few days had been an intense journey of self-discovery, and he was eager to reach its end.

Josh, who had been carried back to the castle by Hypnos' men, was taken away for medical care and no doubt was preparing himself for quite a grilling. Alec looked down at him as he laid in the makeshift stretcher travelling beside him and laid a hand affectionately on his arm. He couldn't bear to speak for fear that he would start trembling again.

"Thank you," Alec said softly. As he watched them leave for the medical room, his stomach twisting with emotion—he still cared deeply for this man he'd known for years, but now couldn't help but feel wary of what Josh's true identity might be, it was hard not to shake the knowledge that he is a different person to the one he believed he was and this damaged his trust levels in a way he hoped it would not.

All those years hiding his true identity were so impressive, it was almost inhuman, it was inhuman he guessed. Alec was now left with Hypnos, who gave him a small, uncharacteristic smile as they headed out. The remaining soldiers with them either went to seek their own medical treatment or went off on their daily tasks. The warrior seemed to sense Alec's confusion, concern and general bewilderment, as he turned to face him and spoke in a quiet yet firm voice in an attempt to be reassuring,

"Alec, you have demonstrated tremendous bravery and tenacity today — something I had unjustly not anticipated from you. You must learn to rely on yourself and be careful in selecting your friends — that is the way these occurrences will make sense and how you will thrive. I remain unimpressed that you left without a bodyguard after I ardently warned against it, yet you rendered impressive aid to an injured comrade and, despite being doubtless afraid, did all that was within your capabilities. Loyalty is a characteristic I highly esteem."

Alec nodded, unsure of how else to respond, it was the first time Hypnos had spoken to him without an order or general strictness coming through in his words, even some compliments being implemented was of huge comfort. Hypnos paused before continuing "Now, would you like to talk of what happened today, I am sure you have many questions of which, if I can, will help to answer."

Alec again nodded, he had many questions and felt that Hypnos may know many of the answers. The slight trepidation he had previously had around the man had fallen away, he seemed to have earned some respect and this was something that Alec also wanted strongly to build upon. Whilst more confused and scared than he had been at any point up till now he felt just as staunch and determined about helping in this battle and more importantly for him, learning more about his true identity.

Alec's questions came out in a confused jumble, and as Hypnos prepared to suppress a gentle laugh at his new comrade's lack of eloquence, he thought better of it. He could sense Alec's internal conflict and growing frustration with the mystery that now surrounded himself and his family.

"Neither one of them makes any sense to me right now; I don't know what else in my life is real anymore. My father has always been more or less a mystery, but now my mother? Who am I supposed to be from here on out? Who are Josh and Jenny as well, all the years of lies and hidden secrets, do they know each other well then? Did they know about each other when we were all together on Earth? What in my life is true at this point?"

Hypnos remained silent, listening intently and feeling acutely the unrest radiating from Alec. How best to answer this he did not know but he was happy to provide any insight he could.

"Who you are Alec is not determined by who your mother, father or friends are, nor what they do. Who you are is determined by you and who you chose to be. I feel many of your answers have been provided in recent history, I have no doubt that they also possibly are leaving as many questions as they did answers, however, the identities of these people should be becoming clear. What they expect from you does not matter. It is what you expect of you that does."

Alec looked up to Hypnos, he had not expected this warrior to become a mentor as well as a protector, certainly not in this capacity, perhaps as an example of how to go to war but not from a morality angle that was for sure. He very much appreciated this new side he was seeing however.

"Did you know my parents?" Alec questioned already partially knowing the answer. "Josh told me, he told me that Probetor is my father," his words whilst saying this almost turned into a whisper, the slight shame he felt in saying that aloud as he uncomfortably scuffed his feet across the floor and kept his head hanging low were clear to see.

"Hmmm" Hypnos responded thoughtfully, whilst he had known from the water illuminations that Lemuri had shown that Alec had the blood of a god within him neither he nor Freyja knew for sure who that may have been and they would have both suspected it to be, but hoped that it was not Probetor. However, who else could it really have been? Hypnos now looked downwards and shook his head, it was obvious, the limitations on who could have gone to Earth and have a child were unbelievably small, it was obvious, maybe they had not wished to acknowledge the truth that had stared them so directly in the face in that moment.

He felt the need to break the silence and stepped forward towards Alec, placing a hand on his shoulder. Alec was gobsmacked at first at the magnitude of the hand, he could not recall ever having seen such a sizeable paw!

"Your father is Probetor - it stands to reason this is correct. But he is more complicated than that, not a person who has been wicked all his life, and of course not born that way. You may ponder what kind of individual that makes you, but don't forget that you didn't come into the world like that either and your different choices have shown you are not like him. He chose one route while you took another. These decisions could have any number of motivations behind them. Jenny would have been sent to sway you, and sway you did not, despite your feelings towards her."

Hypnos spoke softly, his voice reverberating with knowledge and wisdom that seemed to fill the room around them both.

As they spoke Freyja entered the room, she had of course been all too aware of what had transpired but found herself surprised at the heart to heart that she had walked into. She walked up to Alec and stood directly in front of him. Long white hair hung down her back in a thick braid as she glanced up at Hypnos knowingly and sympathetically for Alec's plight. He stepped away and sat himself down into a chair near the door as she adapted the story-telling stance that she had been so accustomed to over many years of teaching the history of the interwoven realms.

"I feel that Hypnos and Josh may have filled the blanks for you, however i will now tell you what I know. Your father Alec, he was born into a prominent family of gods, his power was renowned for its immense magical capabilities and extraordinary cunning- more than any other god at the time, at any time in fact." Freyja began, she then started weaving a tale of Probetor's childhood adventures and mischievous escapades.

"He was frequently in trouble in his younger days, never for anything of great note, he was cheekier more than he was bad. He possessed incredible magical powers of which he had to be trained to use, he did not know he was in possession of them and when he did, he did not know the power he was capable of, none of us did nor could have done. He rose within the ranks and alongside Morpheus, your uncle I guess, they defended the realms better than any had before, or since, despite having the greatest opposition we had ever seen."

Freyja sat herself down as if preparing to get comfortable and set in for a much more protracted story, Hypnos it would seem would of course remain bolt upright and on guard, if he was capable of relaxing or not Alec was unsure.

"He was always jealous of his brother, Morpheus was indeed older and noticeably had much more physical strength, however he was not as smart as Probetor and did not possess magical prowess. In fact, although Probetor was technically second place in ranking, they were very much seen by all as equals." Freyja paused thinking deeply as if to avoid errors within her tales, "the majority of the remainder you know, how he went to Earth and fell in love, and it would appear that this would have been with your mother and it would appear from all of this, came you.

We now comprehend the rationale for your election—you likely harbour the formidable, unheard-of amalgamation of three bloodlines: Probetor, your Father endows you with the blood of an Erobian God, your mother, she holds the capacities of the Alerion people, she would have been bestowed this honour after acceptance. It is remarkably unusual for a lone individual to possess two bloodlines from distinct worlds, but you magnify this extraordinary feat by adorning a third: human. With the blood of a god and the pristine soul of a human welcomed into the Alerion people, you are able to manifest unprecedented might and unsurpassed singularity. All of this pervades you, streaming through your veins like molten fire."

Alec stood there, mesmerised by their stories and revelations and gobsmacked at the apparently amazing heritage he had. Freyja walked over to stand by Hypnos whilst Alec stood motionless trying to contemplating all he had just heard.

"He is much more special than we could have realised Hypnos, we need him to be ready, they are after him and now we know why." Freyja whispered to her friend.

Hypnos acknowledged Freyja's words, he knew that the war they were preparing for had just moved a step closer to the fight, they had now entered the lands of Sofpavel, and had managed to do so in some numbers whilst remaining undetected, they also know Alec is here.

He looked over at Alec and motioned towards the door, "Come with us, it is time for you to begin your training if we are to unlock this potential you have within you. It would seem you may well yet prove to be the key that will turn this war in our favour after all!"

Freyja stepped forward as if ready in anticipation for Hypnos words, "Agreed, we must teach you how to access and use the power that runs through your veins, and just in case you happen to not have any hidden within you, we must also provide you a weapon!"

Freyja and Hypnos guided Alec out of the chamber through a door that opened to a long tunnel underground. The corridor snaked underneath the castle, its length leading them to a vast area filled with relics from many worlds scattered throughout history, it seemed like an extension of Freyja's own room and collection however these were mostly much larger items and would simply not fit within her walls.

At first Alec was overwhelmed by everything around him, grand statues carved into walls, mysterious items and all manner of strange objects alive with energy. As he watched Freyja and Hypnos move around the room his mind began to settle and his curiosity grew.

Hypnos motioned towards one of the artifacts in particular, "This here is an orb of knowledge," he said pointing at a glowing sphere that floated atop a large pillar in the centre of the room.

"It contains within it all kinds of secrets from ancient times, information that had been lost for centuries before we recovered it frum under the Huug sea." Alec stepped closer to get a better look at the orb as mysterious swirls of smoke moved around inside its giant body, but as he did so Hypnos held up a hand to stop him.

"Just be careful," He warned, "lest you find yourself entrapped within its secrets forever." Freyja nodded her head in agreement fully aware of the power many of these objects held.

"Even I cannot use many of these items, most are kept here for training or teaching, unusable by all, Hypnos teases, we do not believe this Orb still serves any purpose and is simply dormant. Many secrets would still lay within but they are inaccessible and the orb itself is no longer of any danger. Few items here really are, as I say, this is essentially a classroom after all!" She smiled mischievously as she finished off this sentence, it was nice for Alec to see the playful side in them both through all of the seriousness. With this she moved them on through another doorway at the back of the room and into yet another chamber.

This one had several small platforms scattered throughout it along with several weapons mounted on stands in each corner. It was obvious they were preparing Alec for battle as Freyja began explaining how each weapon could be used in different scenarios against different enemies, depending on how that creature or foe was best vanquished.

"You must acquire the knowledge of how to use one of these weapons if you would ever hope to stand a chance against our adversaries. You will sense a certain weapon calling out to you without hearing its voice; only upon wielding the instrument will it make its presence known to you," She said before turning her attention back to Alec, "Now let us begin your training."

She began teaching him how to wield swords and bows as well as other various weapons such as spears and axes before settling on a staff. It was a simple oak staff that had a green, dried vine winding around it like a braided rope. However, when she commanded him to hold it, he found that it gripped his palm like a glove and he could feel a warmth pass from her hands into his. As he held the weapon in his hands, he could feel that it was solid but light as a feather in comparison with many of the other weapons she had placed before him, he felt it was much easier for him to handle than a top-heavy axe for example.

Alec's gaze trailed timidly around the room, taking in the vast array of ornately fashioned weaponry; their glittering blades and razor-sharp edges alluringly beckoned him to pick a weapon that could inflict maximum carnage on the battlefield. But what he held in his hands was a rather dull-looking staff, which seemed to render him utterly dejected. Freyja detects Alec's morose expression and comes to his rescue. She reaches for a staff lying nearby and taps it playfully against Alec's.

"It may not seem like it," she began with an air of provocation, "but this staff can become a most formidable weapon if you have the right tools within yourself. Even if you don't, it is still hard enough to inflict bruises!" All through her words, Hypnos continued watching them both with a quiet amusement.

His own weapon of course would indeed provide the appearance that Alec was hoping for within his own.

Freyja began to diligently drill Alec in the fundamentals of staff combat lightly sparring with him using her own weapon of choice which happened to be a staff of her own. Hypnos silently circled around them, studying his form. He noticed minor mistakes in balance and stance that needed correcting, pushing him to adjust and improve upon his technique.

Gradually, she increased the intensity, teaching more intricate techniques that taxed his strength and agility beyond what he had ever imagined. If Alec was going to have any chance against a real adversary, he had to learn how to manipulate the weapon with speed and precision. These lessons continued on day after day, week after week.

Tension was thick in the air as Alec heard of sporadic clashes between the opposing armies on Midjun. With both sides ready to wage war, they stood their ground and glared at each other on either side of the border, waiting for one wrong move that would spark an intense all-out conflict. It was a matter of time before this powder keg was lit.

As Alec grew more accustomed to wielding his weapon over these weeks, Freyja felt he had much more to give, to reveal within himself. She began to provoke him, to push him harder. Gripping his weapon, Alec raised it to the ready. The first time he had sparred against Freyja, he had become accustomed to its weight and length, and despite some early awkwardness, found his footing. She was not a passive opponent who would wait for him to attack her; she moved swiftly with each different strike he tried and relentlessly parried every move. Eyes burning hot, heart beating hard, Alec increased the pace of their exchanges and Freyja stepped right alongside him.

An iron taste filled Alec's mouth as he grunted frantically, his staff swiped through the air to be deftly redirected by a quick twist of her shield edge as she rarely needed to even raise her weapon. Sweat trickled into his eyes and he could feel them beginning to sting as Hypnos shouted encouragement off to the side and urged him forward. Suddenly, Freyja lunged forward and brought her shield smashing against his shoulder like an angry bear, she was not holding back.

Despite the heavy blow Alec kept moving towards her, knowing that should he falter now in retreat once again he would lose everything he had gained over the last month of training with her. As Alec attacked, Freyja planted one foot forcefully on the ground and released a powerful spell from her staff, sending a wild blue blast of magic that collided with Alec like a runaway bucking stallion. He hit the ground flailing, He was stunned, body paralyzed with surprise; he had never expected Freyja to use magic against him. She had never wanted to do this, but desperation spurred her on. She was determined to unleash the depths of his soul and reveal what he truly hid inside. She needed to get inside his head and prod him until he fought meaningfully.

"You have been improving quickly Alec, but I still feel like you're fighting me with one hand tied behind your back. You need to push yourself and show me what you can do. Stop being afraid of failure, and start realizing your worth! You are capable of so much more than this, do not settle for being mediocre!"

With each strike, she was pushing him further into exhaustion, tapping into his inner strength and revealing it layer by layer. Sweat trailed down Alec's face as he became more and more frustrated with himself for not being able to keep up with Freyja's movements.

He lay there after being knocked down once again, exhausted and frustrated as the feelings of unease built gradually. He was used to this feeling, the one that told him danger was near, surely he was in no danger here, right?

Freyja's staff sent waves of energy, each pounded into Alec with every new blow, sending shockwaves of pain through his body. He was getting more and more dejected each time she hit him, but he refused to show it. Hypnos shouted at him to fight harder, and Freyja's voice echoed in the back of his mind that he was stronger than he seemed. All of a sudden, memories flooded into his head through the pain – his parent's abandonment, his grandparents' love, Jennie's deception, Josh's lies. All the weight of responsibility on his shoulders weighing heavy. It was then he realized a flood of emotions were taking over his body as he felt himself letting it all go.

He closed his eyes and slowly stood up determinedly.

Freyja gaped, her expression a perplexed mixture of surprise and confusion as Alec inhaled and exhaled deeply, almost as if he was in some sort of trance. Believing that Alec had been crippled by fear, she lunged at him with her staff. Shockingly, he effortlessly swayed aside each strike while his eyes remained sealed shut. Somehow Alec was accessing his intrinsic sense to identify the source of the danger.

Hypnos grinned in astonishment as Alec remained motionless, eyes still closed, continuing to manage his breathing. This was the first of her assaults he had stood up against and Hypnos was now hoping to see a glimpse of what Alec may be able to do.

Freyja lunged towards Alec with renewed vigour, her staff slashing through the air in quick and precise movements. Despite her efforts, his parries foiled each attack and deflected every force of energy she launched in his direction. In one final attempt, a flurry of strikes sent him staggering backwards, seemingly dazed. Seizing the opportunity, Freyja shot a concentrated beam of pure magic at an undefended Alec. Instead of dodging it like before, he raised his staff and held it up to meet the strike head-on. In that split second, dark green energy surged around him as the bolt collided against the staff's glowing surface. Achieving remarkable speed, Alec released a changed bolt of energy into the far wall causing the stone to crack as a smoking black mark embedded deep into its surface. As he stood there motionless, not a single thought crossed his mind, his eyes unreadable and face emotionless.

He had been victorious in this sparring match with Freyja and she had not held back a great deal, he seemed to have in an instance, begun to transform into the person he could be. He remained in a trance temporarily as his breathing slowed and he sleepily opened his eyes as if waking up for the first time.

Freyja and Hypnos again looked at each other, it would appear that Alec did indeed have some magic within him after all, and they may well have just unlocked a glimpse of it.

"Well well young Alec," Hypnos said, "I think you may well be nearly ready to join this fight."

Alec remained silent, now seeming a little shocked at the realisation of all he had just done. He looked over to Freyja who was, despite the fight she had just had, looking as beautiful as ever even though a little battle weary.

"Sorry" Alec said, " I do not know what came over me." Freyja smiled.

"The real you Alec, that's what came over you."

9) Let the journey commence

Alec was still trying to make sense of what had just happened. His ability to sense danger had always been with him and was a constant joke between him and Josh in the past. Now it seems as though it is a source of power. But what exactly was the power he had just discovered within himself? How did he do those things and could it be of any use in the coming fight? These questions raced through his mind as he made his way towards to the infirmary.

He arrived to find Josh standing outside the entrance looking quite frail. He had been released today after weeks of medical care following his attack. It had turned out the he had been ambushed by quite a few people and it was in fact Alec's arrival that had made them stop. They were unaware of his being there and when they heard the sound of someone else approaching, they had feared it could be some Nyx.

They did not wish for that fight at that moment, they had come looking for Alec after all.

Josh had heard all about the sparring and training that Alec had been undertaking from the people who had been looking after him, the stories were doing their rounds as the people of Sofpavel all hoped Alec truly was the one and were fascinated by everything he did in his time there.

Alec had not seen Josh at all during this time, not because he did not want to but due to his needing many answers and Josh needing to recover, he felt it was a visit best left for a while. He needed to get over Josh's revelations and besides, Alec had been so busy he had little time for worrying about it.

Josh smiled at Alec as he approached and greeted him with immediate congratulations, "Congrat's Àlec, I hear you have started to become quite the fighter these past few weeks." He hoped that his friendly and playful approach to their reintroduction would to break the tension around them.

"Indeed, but do not believe all the hype, I've still an awful lot to learn before being seen as a 'fighter'" Alec replied modestly, "In fact I even beat Freyja today, admittedly I am sure she was probably holding back quite a lot! I have some magical powers in these fingers myself it would seem!" He informed him in a voice still highlighting plenty of surprise.

Josh seemed impressed by Alec's new found talents as he raised his eyebrows and pursed his lips to display as such, but a little sceptical; after all, in their time together Alec had never shown an affinity for magic or displayed any kind of extraordinary skill like this before, he had always in fact avoiding confrontation at all cost. However, the knowledge of his parents did make it seem a little more plausible.

"It's true," Alec said, feeling a bit embarrassed "I mean I don't know exactly how I did it, but something inside me just... let go."

Josh smiled his understanding smile and nodded knowingly; "Well if you can do that in combat, then you're gonna be one helluva asset in this fight!".

Alec smiled at the thought; what an incredible feeling it would be for that to be true!

As the talk of Alec's new found talents came to an end they found themselves in an awkward position of silence, they had been friends for an incredibly long time but the events that had happened still loomed large in the memory and cast a shadow over them. The knowledge that the entire time Josh was not who he claimed to be was a mountain to climb over that Alec was struggling to peak.

Before he could say anything further, Josh spoke up taking the lead in what he knew could be a difficult conversation, "Look Alec I'm sorry," he said, his gaze never faltering from Alec's face. "I understand the hurt this must have all caused you - the truth about your parents, Jenny any my lying to you all those years. It wasn't something I wanted to do, but it was a decision of necessity. I am Alerion this is true, but I was sent here by your mother- they wanted you to be safe. So, they arranged for you to have an unseen guardian - one who could sense any presence that didn't belong. Jenny, whilst I knew I disliked her for some reason I could never put my finger on, slipped through without me knowing who she really was. Again, for that I'm sorry, too."

Alec listened intently as Josh continued on and revealed his secrets; he realized now why Josh had lied for all these years even though they had been best friends since childhood, it must have been equally as hard for him to do as it was for Alec to discover.

He felt a deep sympathy for his friend - being forced to keep such a burden of guilt and deception secret must have been difficult beyond belief; Alec understood why Josh had done what he did and he appreciated his honesty for confessing it now.

"What else can you tell me, about my parents, about me?" Alec asked Josh, hoping to finally be addressing someone he hoped would no longer be hiding anything from him.

Josh looked at his friend with sympathy, he knew the answers he longed for he could not provide, "I never really knew your mother that well, I'm sorry. I was young myself at the time, but in need of a family. I had been born to Alerion guardians and my destiny was to at some point be appointed as such. Usually to our own, royalty and such but on this occasion, it turned out slightly differently! I wish I could tell you everything there was to know about your mother but I am sorry, I am simply unable." Alec looked to the ground and nodded, he had guessed this himself but had hoped for something, anything.

Josh stood silently across from Alec as he looked at his friend sympathetically. He knew from all of his time with Alec how much he had already yearned to know more about his parents. The room was filled with tension as each of them searched for the right words, and in that time, Josh could feel the questions were building up preparing to burst free from Alec's mouth in a desperate pitch to find out as much as he could.

"What of my occasion, purpose here? How it all really works? Do you know much about Erobus? What of Jenny? Do you know anything about any of this?" All of these questions were ready to be freed from his mouth, but Josh couldn't find it in him to allow them to flow freely; he understood what it must have meant to have them hanging over his head without knowing any answers and he had no desire to subject his friend to that torture. It was like an open wound that couldn't heal as long as the pieces were missing and had always been something hanging above Alec's head, none knew this better than Josh.

Josh looked at Alec, who wanted nothing more than a story or two, some wisdom, or even a good laugh. What Alec didn't want was something akin to what Josh would have settled for just moments prior; awkwardness and uncertainty weighing down his heart like a lead ball. Fortunately, he did now a few things that may appease his friend a little.

"I have done some research myself and had some interesting conversations with people during my couple of weeks bedridden, I did not have much else to do to be fair!" said Josh, bowing his head slightly, "incredible the amount of time you find on your hands when you stay in bed for that amount of time."

Alec looked up with intrigue not having expected any saliant answers at all, however he was now hoping that what Josh may divulge having learnt through this answered some of his recent questions. Josh looked at Alec expectantly.

"Well, Jenny, she's an interesting one." Josh said nervously. Alec knew Josh was leading up to something but wasn't sure what. "I feel we may still need that holiday when we get back, but not to get away from her anymore at least!" Josh joked.

Alec's eyes widened further still as he anticipated what may come next hoping that Josh would move along and stop hesitating.

"She has long been a general in the Koschei army, in fact she is the right-hand woman of a being named Gree, he's kind of her boss and is now himself the right-hand man to Probetor. If you believe Probetor still serves The Jinn I guess this technically makes her fourth in command." Josh paused again as he quickly did the math's in his head and nodded in confirmation at his own sums.

Alec nodded, signalling for him to continue. "Gree assumed leadership after The Probetor disappeared and the Jinn was detained, constructing their empire from its ruins. A few citizens rallied behind him while he endeavoured to reinstate Probetor as ruler, before vanishing for a period of time. Abruptly, he resurfaced alongside his cohort, including Jenny. Honestly, I don't know much more about him, he keeps himself quite secretive." Josh shrugged again. "The only thing I've heard about him other than this is that he's powerful, and dangerous, but we could have guessed that was probably the case."

Alec coiled back whilst taking this in, a little shocked and disgusted that not only had he had a relationship with a Koschei but passionately genuinely loved her, or at least loved who she had pretended to be.

"You know how sometimes when you're around someone you can just tell they're lying and ingenuous just because it feels so off?" Josh asked and waited for Alec's nod before continuing, "Yeah, so I could always sense something about her but figured she was just an unpleasant person, not for a second did I gauge that she was not human, that is oddly something I can usually sniff out quite quickly. The relevance of this, the magic that got her to you, that hid her identity, this would have been some serious magic and they must have really wanted her close to you." Josh seemed very disheartened and frustrated with himself following this comment, he clearly felt he was to blame for all that had happened since and felt as though he had failed in his task to protect him from exactly that kind of scenario.

As they spoke Hypnos and Freyja approached them with some pace. It was fairly obvious that they were seeking them, Alec could see from the look on Freyja's face that she had some bad news and this served to cause a well-timed distraction for him. Despite the look of concern etched across her face she managed a weary, tired smile for Alec as she approached them both. The days were long for her at the moment and taking their toll.

"We have bad news I am afraid Alec." She positioned herself between the two of them and turned her back to Josh showing an even deeper distain for him than previously. The animosity she felt toward him had not eased off in the knowledge of who he was.

"You may recall that Hypnos sent trackers to the location in which the sword was spotted moving across Midjun." Her voice was soft as she spoke again, a hint of remorse for lost lives colouring each word. "Unfortunately, they have been killed," she continued. "We had wondered why they hadn't returned, and we just found out ourselves, a messenger arrived from the tower a little while ago informing us that their bodies were seen at Maredrom. We are acting to recover them now as we speak"

Alec tilted his head downward in sorrow. He knew that they were at war and that its dangers were getting closer each day.

As every new piece of information came in it became ever more real for him and this was the first death he had knowledge of since this all began. He looked sympathetically at Hypnos—his own soldiers had died after all—and marvelled again at how one could be so different on the outside compared to what must lay within.

His expression and toned body did not change, but inside the Spectre did indeed mourn his fallen soldiers, losing men was nothing new for him but it was never any easier.

"We need now to join the Nyx who are stationed on the coast of Midjun, we must provide a presence, the enemy are becoming too bold" he said to Freyja. She nodded before turning back to Alec who stood wondering what the next course of action for himself may be.

"I still do not know how exactly you fit into all of this and what your purpose is," Freyja said taking Alec by the hand "I can't believe you are here to lead the fight, even with your tremendous progress in training, a world beating warrior is something you're not, I hope the decision I have made to take you to the fight this early on is correct, I pray that it is."

Freyja seemed to drift off as if speaking solely to herself as she finished speaking, as much as she knew that Alec was integral to all of this, she still didn't know why nor where he needed to be. Her initial thought process had been to keep him safe at the castle until this became clear, however, the war had entered a new stage and time was not on their side. The sword was by now clearly in Maredrom and she feared in the hands of Probetor. The sea that divided the far end of Midjun from Maredrom was blocked by the camping enemy forces and the only way there without a fight would be an attempt to take the long sea voyage to the south of Midjun. They could no longer afford to sit guard and see what happened; they were losing; they may not realize it but they were.

Freyja wheeled around to face Josh, jabbing her long white finger in his direction. "This applies to you too, now that I understand your intent and plan. However, you must be straightforward with us and we will keep tabs on you. We should have been able to locate you and your purpose much sooner. How you managed to blend in is beyond me. You Alerion's always seem to have difficulty being honest!"

Josh had a slight reaction, feeling a bit self-conscious for not being sincere with his Erobian counterparts. He was aware that he hadn't been very transparent.

Hypnos inserted himself now and took the lead on this expedition discussion, seeming to come to life knowing he would now be assuming control.

"We should make haste then - it is best if we join up with the Nyx stationed there using the cover of darkness. It is early AM now, if we are quick and go via horseback, we should make it just after sun down," Freyja agreed; they had already lost too much time and now was their chance to make a difference and attempt to make some of this back.

Alec watched as Hypnos, Freyja, Josh and then he himself gathered supplies – checked the location of the sun and the wind and reviewed their lists of provisions. As they worked with haste, Hypnos held a long conversation with Freyja in a language that Alec could not understand. Even more surprising for him was that occasionally, Josh would add to the discussion.

The ground was heavy with rocks and the air thick became hotter as they travelled. They rode in silence, but for the sound of heavy breathing from the horses and of their hoofs beating into the ground, which echoed like a thousand hammers on an anvil. Even though Alec was not himself riding, merely a passenger to an accompanying Soldier mainly due to the luxury of using the Celeris horses, a rare privilege that Hypnos felt necessary, his admiration and wonder at how fast these horses were blinded him with a mixture of excitement and fear. He watched its powerful muscles ripple under its grey coat as the wings lightly wafted alongside adding to the increase in speed. The steady pounding of the Celeris strides was hypnotic, he felt like he was travelling down the motorway at breakneck speed in one of the fastest cars he had ever encountered.

They stumbled upon the edge of the cliffs that Morpheus had once surveyed his forces depart for battle from, and Hypnos fervently jabbed at a thin path leading to the shore, clearly recollecting that fateful day. The others trudged down the winding pathways until they arrived at the water's edge.

In the distance, Nyx's fleet of boats and ships could be seen dotting the horizon, waiting patiently. They walked along the shoreline until they found themselves standing amongst the impressive array of boats.

Hypnos scanned his armada, searching for something small enough to go unnoticed yet strong enough to survive long voyages. At last, he found what he needed—a ship that blended in with its surroundings perfectly whilst providing all that they needed for the short trip. Hypnos feared there was a chance it could be one way and he worked hard to not show this fear to the others.

It was sleek and angular, not much larger than a fishing boat in truth. But it was precisely what they needed. Hypnos grinned and gestured towards it.

"Perfect," he said.

Freyja nodded in agreement. The boat would do just fine.

And so, they surged away, a band of drifting silhouettes vanishing into the night. With a palpable tautness felt on board as they stealthily boarded in hushed tones, they hurtled off into the obscure nocturnal ocean; a mission from Sofpavel over the sea towards Midjun where a formidable battalion of Nyx were garrisoned at its shoreline, fervently seeking comrades in this fight against Probetor.

The journey was uneventful at first as they sailed amongst calm waters under a clear star lit sky, the moon reflected off the waters around them providing small glimmers of light as the glowing dream Orbs could be faintly seen shining across the bottom of the sea as they themselves made their way steadily between the islands on their way towards Lemuri.

The evening breeze wove itself around Alec's taut form, his anxiety taking flight as the horizon unveiled the majestic presence of Midjun.

Freyja stood by his side, her small stature belying her deep wisdom and understanding; with a gentle voice, she spoke to him, "Do not fear, for fate has chosen this path and in Lemuri we are blessed and guided. You must learn to trust your own strength and courage; though the storm ahead is daunting, you must remain steadfast. Look upon the stars above us and allow them to fill you with solace. Hypnos stands nearby, as do his soldiers; they are here to guard and protect you."

Alec drank in her words like they were life-giving water, his spirit strengthened by her grace. His heart swelled with gratitude when he felt Hypnos' hand come to rest on his shoulder as if in unison with her words.

As they sailed closer and closer to their destination, he marvelled at the sight before him - the watchtower piercing the night sky even from afar, its peak glowing beneath a thousand twinkling stars. He had read and heard of it but this was the first time he had seen it and he could not help but be impressed by its majesty.

Alec turned to see Josh standing just behind them, his friend looked at him, smiled shyly and shrugged his shoulders before entering the conversation with his own words.

"Well, I'm always here with you, aren't I?" Alec smiled knowing this to be true, despite the hidden secrets he had kept from him. He turned back to face Midjun. The island was growing close enough now to see the small movement of soldiers in the distance within their shoreline camps. The night was coming to a close as the sun now began rising steadily towards the horizon, it had almost created a picturesque scene.

They soon arrived at the camp and Alec was greeted by some of the soldiers as they walked into its depths. Each one seemed to have a story to tell, eyes shining as they relayed their tales of courage and bravery in battle. Hypnos greeted each one with respect and admiration, thanking them for their service and loyalty to Sofpavel. Freyja spoke warm words of comfort to those injured and struggling, reminding them that despite the impending danger, they were all here together working towards a common goal.

Josh stood quietly, taking it all in with reverence while Alec searched the faces of these brave warriors for confirmation that he too could stand strong in this fight; if fate was willing, his own strength and conviction he hoped would be enough.

The group followed Hypnos further inland where larger camps had now been set up since Hypnos sent word of his wish to progress forward. The tents were an array of colours and sizes, soldiers bustling around them like ants on an anthill. As Alec looked around him, he could feel the immense power emanating from these fierce yet noble creatures; he knew that this was a force not to be reckoned with in battle and felt quite reassured to be in their presence. With great respect, some of them leaned down upon one knee before Hypnos and Freyja as they passed, welcoming them to Midjun and offering their assistance should any be needed. Alec watched on with awe at their display of strength, loyalty, and courage - traits he too hoped to embody throughout his journey ahead.

Finally, they arrived at the centre of the camp, where a senior Nyx soldier stood in conversation with some of his men. Freyja and Hypnos stepped forward to introduce Alec and Josh which Alec found unnerving as Freyja referred to him as 'the one' repeatedly. The soldier bowed his head in respect as he welcomed them into his camp before inviting them to sit. Once they had all gathered around, Hypnos informed them that this was Major Araya – one of his Nyx's most experienced warriors and leader of his main battalions. Major Araya nodded again at Alec before began to explain what he knew about the situation on Midjun - the soldiers had been dispersed around the island by this point with strategic locations in order to help protect it from any threats, as well as having sent additional units to the watchtower to assist in protecting the pathway through to Lemuri.

As they talked further, Freyja asked about any new information or sightings that he may have come across; with a serious expression he stated that there has been an increase of activity across Midjun lately, though nothing too concerning as yet. He also recalled hearing tell of a powerful sorcery surrounding Midjun but could not be certain if this was true or rumours being spread amongst the troops.

They had been reporting strange sightings and activities all over and many had been nervous of working in smaller groups.

Freyja listened carefully, she turned to both Araya and Hypnos with clear intent on how she felt they should move forwards with these discussions "We are here today in order to discuss our plans for defending Lemuri against the impending attack that we know will be coming. We have gathered our strongest warriors and are ready to meet our adversaries head-on, but we must also take caution not to underestimate their strength."

Alec listened closely as she spoke and he could sense Josh seated beside him, both of them quivering with anticipation at Freyja's words.

"We must think of a way to reach Maredrom without having to battle our way through the enemy forces," continued Freyja, her gaze fixed on each of their faces. "I propose that Alec and Josh go ahead, accompanied by one of Araya's most highly trained warriors, in order to locate the sword that is believed to now be within the dark lands. Regaining possession of the blade will make all the difference in this fight, if they have indeed found a way to free The Jinn from its clutches it may well be the final act, they require to become unstoppable. Sending you Alec goes against all I should do; however, I feel that they will be expecting you to be here and you may well be the one who can hold and retrieve the sword."

Alec and Josh looked at each other with astonishment - they had never gone on such an adventure before! However, despite his fear Alec knew there was little choice but to accept this challenge if he was going to help protect Midjun and its people from destruction.

He nodded solemnly at Freyja as she continued: "In your absence I shall remain here with Hypnos and his troops to lead the defence against our enemies whilst you are away, we will keep the fighting focused here. This will enable you to travel by land to the far end of Midjun and avoid the treacherous long sea journey south." She glanced around the group leisurely before concluding: "Let us unite together and do all we can, not just for Erobus or Earth but for everyone, everywhere."

Alec had already decided that he was ready to face this challenge even before Freyja had finished her speech, as she reached her final words he stood to declare as such, however before he was able to say anything Hypnos interjected.

"I'm sorry Freyja but I disagree" he said calmly, "whilst he may have learnt a lot, he is far from capable of such a mission, I sent a scouting party of my own soldiers to locate and track the sword and they were all killed, seemingly easily as well. Yet here you are proposing we send this man who is only just not a boy to retrieve said sword from the forces which currently have it. It is a death sentence for him and his accompanying parties and I think a grave error."

Alec had forgotten about the fallen soldiers; Freyja's speech had stirred his emotions but Hypnos's own speech bought him back down to Earth. He looked towards Josh who he could see this whole time had been looking thoughtfully at the ground. He could now sense his good friend looking at him and he in turn raised his head to meet Alec's eyes head on.

"You can do this," said Josh before anyone else had even registered what he had said. His eyes had stayed locked with Alec's own as he nodded slowly before turning to face the others.

"We'll be in danger, sure, but what did you bring Alec here for, did you not know he would face grave danger? Are we not here to protect our people, all people, and to fight for justice? I fear not the darkness and danger that lies ahead - instead I embrace it as an opportunity to prove ourselves and to do what you bought Alec here to do. I'm with you, Alec, if you take on this mission then so will I. Besides you said that we would have a soldier with us, right? And the war will be in full swing and all of the fighting here, so we will possibly not even see anyone!"

Alec was overwhelmed by his friend's sentiment and beamed at him gratefully. They both realized the peril that lurked ahead, yet Alec still held onto a glimmer of faith that they could triumph in their mission. This wasn't just about defending Erobus or Earth anymore - it was about conquering the looming forces of evil everywhere.

He looked back at Freyja who smiled warmly in response before saying: "I think we have a plan then?"

Hypnos however remained firm on his statement, "Freyja I must insist, I feel this is a terrible idea."

Freyja nodded before turning her gaze to Hypnos, "I understand your concerns and I too share them. But I also know the courage and bravery Alec has. He has already made it this far and yes, he will no doubt face whatever comes his way with honour and strength, just as any Nyx would do. He will also have a soldier of your choosing with him as well as Josh who, well, despite the intrusions and lies is capable of his own keeping it would appear. He does also seem sworn to protect Alec and I have no doubt despite all that he will do so" She then smiled at Alec and bowed her head toward Josh."

Without a doubt, I am confident you both can succeed in this mission. Stealth is essential, if they catch sight of us, our chance to foil their plans will be drastically reduced. We cannot underestimate them; they possess the advantage at present, and we mustn't let them know that we challenge that power."

Hypnos inhaled deeply before relenting, he failed to understand Freyja's thinking on this occasion but knew he would have to submit to her will. Sending the one person they wish to have a hold of seemed like the worst plan Hypnos could think of, however he was sure there was some reason as to her thinking.

"Very well...we shall put our faith in you both. May the gods grant you strength on this journey ahead, I fear you will need it and so much more besides."

Alec felt a deep sense of relief wash over him as he watched Hypnos finally accept the plan. Hopefully the focus on keeping the fight with them here on Midjun will provide all the cover Alec may need. Hypnos turned to Araya now looking for his opinion, "who will be your best soldier to not only navigate the way but to protect them?"

Araya responded immediately, "Logan; he's intimately familiar with this terrain. He'll be eager to skirmish but will follow orders and safeguard them as instructed." Hypnos nodded vigorously.

"Then it shall be, we best prepare to start a scene on the frontline here and maintain the focus on us then. You two best get ready too" he said looking towards Alec and Josh.

Alec turned to Freyja, he smiled gratefully at her before nodding confidently and heading off to meet Logan who would be the fine veil of protection on this adventure.

Hypnos turned to Freyja as they began their preparations still perplexed. "Why are we sending our one asset, the one they want into enemy territory?"

Freyja looked back gravely before responding, "I am not sure, Lemuri told me it was the only way, I fear I happen to share your feelings. We can but hope the great falls still know what they are doing."

10) Reunions

Logan set off in the lead with Josh and Alec close behind him, they had a long journey ahead of them as they headed for their destination of Maredrom.

Left behind in Midjun Hypnos and Araya prepared their troops for battle as Freyja returned to Sofpavel to oversee the kingdom praying that she was right in her decisions.

Logan was sure footed and confident in his steps; he knew the land like no other and where there were hazards or potential enemies, he had warned the others. He had been a soldier under Araya for a long time and was quite battle hardened. Logan had the same build of the trained warriors he had already met, tall and imposing with broad shoulders and strong arms. He was clad in armour of the Nyx soldiers, a deep grey with hints of blue in its shine. His face was unshaven, with his steely blue eyes blazing with a sense of rebellion and an almost devil-may-care attitude. He moved with confidence, but it was tempered by a certain looseness around the edges that revealed his lack of discipline.

The sun beat down on them as it gradually began to set over the horizon, leaving the faint glow of dusk to guide their way. He could not believe that yet another day had almost passed them by.

Alec felt his legs start to ache as he and his companions walked, tiredness creeping up on him. He was beginning to tire of not just the journey, but also the circumstances that had brought them here, so far away from their own homes.

He occasionally found himself glancing back at Logan who seemed so calm and capable despite everything that was going on around them all - it reminded Alec of Hypnos' words that if anyone could succeed in this mission it was these two, for that to be true they certainly needed a Logan he felt.

When night fell upon them and the darkness felt thick as the air cooled, they finally stopped to rest, setting up camp for a few hours before they continued on again come morning light.

Logan vigilantly maintained surveillance, and though Alec had volunteered to alternate shifts, he was secretly delighted. Logan could be a bit erratic however, and Alec prayed that they would not find themselves alone due to his having gone off chasing some feral pig!

The terrain they travelled through was treacherous and rugged, but Alec and Josh kept their focus on the task at hand. Logan had an uncanny ability to sense danger before it even appeared, much like Alec's own.

This kept them safe from any obstacles on their travels, like cliffs that threatened to fall on their heads or wild animals that threatened their mission. Luckily Logans reflexes were lightning-fast each time.

As they progressed, Alec observed Logan to be on edge and eager for any possible conflict. His dedication to protect them was unmistakable, filling Alec with comfort and gratitude. Yet he couldn't help but ponder what was driving his desire for battle.

Logan felt a growing sense of unease the closer to Maredrom they got of which he could see reflected equally in the eyes of Alec. Everywhere he looked there were strange symbols carved into the trees or painted onto rocks, some almost menacing in nature while others barely noticeable as if hidden in plain sight. Logan recognised some of them and knew that these would mostly be marking of Koschei forces. How they existed so plentifully outside of Maredrom he had no idea and found it quite surprising. As they made their way closer towards their destination these symbols became more abundant yet still held no meaning to any of them.

Although none of them could comprehend the cryptic symbols, Logan sensed that they were cautionary warnings and his urgency to keep Alec and Josh safe intensified. He regularly glanced back at them, making sure they remained unscathed as he marched onward with equal enthusiasm for what may lay ahead as he did for their security.

After tedious days of trekking, the threesome at last reached the north-western seaboard of Midjun. Glinting off in the North East, Lemuri beamed in the distance, but their destination—the murky vista of Maredrom—loomed to the west. The next stage of the mission required them to traverse an ocean that now stood between them and Maredrom.

Alec wondered what kind of dangers might lie beneath its murky depths, the seas to Maredrom seeming bleaker and more treacherous than those they had traversed days before to reach Midjun.

Logan scoured the shorelines, rubbish and nets lay plentiful alongside shells of what had once been the fishing boats of sea faring folk from all over, eventually he was lucky enough to find a small but sturdy vessel. With some repairs and maintenance, the boat looked like it could still make a journey, although the three of them were unsure what lay ahead and hoped the boat would not be tested.

After some quick repairs of which Alec noted were incredibly durable, they began their travel silently into the unknown brackish waters. During their travels, they noticed strange creatures swimming around them in the depths of the sea, some rising up in curiosity of the travellers in order to take a closer look.

They saw creatures with long tentacled arms and glowing large eyes while Josh saw sleek fish that seemed to glide along effortlessly appearing like arrows as they cut through the water. Even Logan spotted something unusual lurking near his boat - he thought it may have been an octopus as its body changed colour rapidly as if trying to hide itself from view.

The trio found themselves mesmerised by these otherworldly creatures and marvelled at how different and beautiful each one was compared to those on land. They tried not to bother any of them but were also quite curious about who or what lived down below! As they sailed further away from shore however, they soon realised that these mysterious creatures weren't out here alone - there were other life forms in this dark abyss too!

As Logan glanced down at the sea floor he placed a firm hand onto the chest of Alec.

"They aren't noticing us," he said.

Josh and Alec peered over the edge of the boat, eyes adjusting to the dim light as they studied the water below for signs of trouble and to see what Logan was referencing. A mass stirred on the seafloor seeming like a large moving swarm moving in unison. They weren't too far from Maredrom now; the water had begun to shallow and you could just about make out the objects below.

With strained eyes, Alec realized what he was looking at: hordes of Koschei's undead soldiers marching across the seafloor, heading in unison towards Midjun, no doubt preparing for the battle ahead and joining the soldiers already there. They were dressed in shabby armour with plates missing or mismatched, as though scavenged from other corpses. He looked at Josh, who had already noticed what lay beneath them, his face serious and stern. Alec could not help but wonder how the others were fairing back in Midjun, if they had now indeed gone into battle. That may explain why the large number of reinforcements on the way and Alec could not help but be concerned at the numbers he realised they outnumbered the Nyx forces by.

The trio continued on their way hoping the Koschei below would continue to not notice their presence floating above, the closer they drew to Maredrom the more intense the atmosphere became as the reality crept in.

The air seemed to hang heavy with a sense of dread, and the sky was now dark and brooding as if it knew what lay ahead. As they neared the coast, all of them could see that there were no trees or plants here, just jagged rocks and desolate sand dunes. It seemed like an eerie wasteland that had been frozen in time; nothing alive could exist here, not even birds flew through this cursed land.

Even though Logan knew all about Maredrom, this would be only his second ever time here, and a place he could not wish to visit any less. He couldn't help but feel a chill run down even his spine when he saw it with his own eyes and recalled the feelings of dread that came with it. Nothing good could happen in such a place - it was almost like an evil force was present here which no one could escape from. With trepidation, Logan steered the boat towards shore and eventually they all found themselves standing upon its sinister shores.

For a moment, the trio just stood there, taking in the surroundings wondering what had inspired them to take this on. The jagged rocks off the coast with their sharp edges looked menacing and the dark skies looming overhead made Maredrom castle look more sinister than ever as it stood tall in the distance. Dead trees littered the landscape and strange animals could now be seen lurking in shadows, scuttling away from them upon sight, some things did move here after all. They knew that if they were to survive this journey, they would have to be vigilant and on guard at all times; evil lurked here and who knows what kind of danger awaited them further inland?

As they walked away from the beach and made their way into the interior, they soon found themselves gazing down at a deep chasm in front of Maredrom's castle. A huge canyon spanned out before them; its depths shrouded in darkness.

It was even more imposing up close than it had appeared from afar, its walls lined with torches and thick smoke billowing out from the chimneys, its uninhabited appearance from a distance fading the closer you were to its blackened presence. And there below, in the valley of the canyon, they could make out an immense army of Koschei, all standing in formation. They were armed to the teeth and standing battle ready, as still as statues yet somehow alive and dead all at the same time as they stood in their eerie silence. The sheer size of this force was enough to make them quiver and break into cold sweat; how could anyone withstand such power? There were thousands of them standing in formation, looking like a wall of death ready to meet their enemy.

As Josh and Alec glanced down at this formidable force, Logan stood silently but steadfastly behind them - he had seen his fair share of battles before but never anything like this. He had fought in the Nyx armies for centuries and had visited many realms, there were always small sections wanting to break free but there had never been an uprising with such numbers. He had felt a rare mixture between fear and excitement as he stared wide eyed at what lay beneath them. He knew that if it came down to it, he would fight for his new friends until his last breath and that no matter what happened here today - he would not bow down to tyranny or evil, a Nyx warrior would lay on his own sword before doing so.

Whilst they watched on, a figure emerged from a cave buried deep in the cliffs that lay in front of them. Alec immediately recognised the figure, the last time he had seen him he had feared for his life, for the life of his friend and had developed a lot more questions - it was Gree, Jenny's 'keeper'. He stood ominously before the armies below with an air of intimidating power.

He surveyed them but did not address them. As he stood there surrounded by his own, Alec could see him that much more clearly than before. He had horns upon his head that resembled those of a goat, turned inwards in a spiral. He had pale skin and sunken eyes that almost seemed to glow with a hue of red. He appeared crippled as he hunched slightly within his tall frame. He refrained from addressing the armies himself, simply surveyed them and remaining silent. Josh had taken a little longer to get there than Alec having not been able to notice as much detail on their previous encounter, and as the realisation came over him as to who they were looking at he let out a low "oooohhhhh". Alec rolled his eyes as Logan standing behind them seemed none the wiser and perplexed as to how these two foreigners knew who they were looking upon.

"Who is this?" he asked, noting that they had recognised the creature.

"It is Gree" Alec responded. He went to speak further but could see from Logans face that whilst he may not have recognised the physical being but the name he most certainly did.

"Hmmm" Logan huffed "I thought he was nothing more than a fable told to scare young children" he said.

"Oh no, Gree is very much real" Alec said with a knowing look.

Just as they were about to continue their conversation, another figure appeared, this one Logan did recognise. It was Probetor, the leader of the Koschei armies and apparent ruler of Maredrom, someone who Logan had fought alongside personally once before in his own youth, and then again against in the battle with The Jinn. He was a young soldier and new to the Nyx army the first time he encountered him. He had fought under Hypnos himself that day as he led Morpheus's troops out, not that he would have expected Hypnos to remember him given the hordes of soldiers that have travelled through him.

He seemed even more imposing than he remembered him to be and there was an air of dark excitement among the army that seemed to electrify them all in anticipation for what was to come, they clearly felt their time could well be on the horizon. He spoke in a deep booming voice that commanded attention yet he carried himself with an air of power and respect; it was clear why he was so highly regarded by his men and why indeed he had previously had the respect of the Nyx he now fights against.

Probetor paced proudly before his troops and addressed them with a powerful speech that filled each man with courage and unity, ready to face whatever challenge lay ahead. They could not hear his words from high up on the cliff side but they could hear the tone and see the furore created below them.

As Probetor spoke, the skies began to darken and lightning bolts illuminated the sky as if it were nature's way of emphasising his words. The forces below roared in unison at his command and readied themselves for battle; weapons glinting in the light from the torches burning bright on either side of Maredrom's castle walls. Alec looked up at Logan and could see that even this reckless warrior looked nervous.

"God help us all" he muttered under his breath.

Alec's eyes stayed transfixed on the floor, his stomach twisting in knots as he remembered the figure, he was staring at was his own father. He could feel a flare of anger and hatred rising inside of him. As Probetor became increasingly animated, Alec saw it: the hilt of Morpheus' blade clearly visible from beneath his cloak. His gaze shifted to the other members of the group, hoping that they too had noticed the blade - thankfully, they had.

Before they had any time to debate how to retrieve it however Probetor fell silent, the trio looked down towards him as all fell still and whilst they looked upon him, he turned and looked directly back at them. If he had seen them or not was impossible to tell but he seemed to know that he had company. They dove down behind the large rock they had been using to largely disguise their presence.

"What shall we do?" Alec asked of Logan, "Do you think he saw us?"

Logan pondered for a moment, even he knew that they could not face off against their foes, he himself was always happy to run into a battle he could not win but this, this would be suicide for all three of them.

"We need to leave and collect ourselves; we cannot fight here. We have at least gained knowledge of whom possesses the blade." As Logan finished his sentence the group heard a mass movement, they peered back over the rock to see that the armies below had turned, all of them had, most worryingly, to face them.

Alec's pulse raced and his adrenalin spiked as he realised what was about to happen. He scrambled onto his feet and grabbed Logan by the arm

"Come on," He said urgently "we have to go now if we're going to make it out alive". Logan nodded in agreement and followed Alec with Josh in tow as they made a break for their getaway route. However, they were too late. The enemies' forces had caught wind of their escape and were already hot on their heels.

The trio ran faster than ever before as arrows flew past them and spears whizzed by. Alec looked behind him every few moments to check if they were still being followed but it seemed with every glance the numbers had increased. He muttered under his breath "We will never make it" yet somehow kept running; spurred on by Logan and Josh's determination not to give up so easily.

Abruptly, Logan halted the group and thrust his arm out to stop them. He had noticed a miniscule chink in the enemy's defence line, a path that could lead the team to safety.

"Rush ahead," he bellowed, "I'll stay here and hold them back." His sword gleamed as he brandished it, looking at the horde of foes with an unwavering ardour in his eyes; prepared to fight until the bitter end if it meant they'd be able to escape unscathed.

Alec and Josh stood watching in awe of their companion, both feeling powerless as Logan stepped forward preparing to take on the assailants as they arrived. He knew there was no way for all of them to get away without his intervention yet what he proposed seemed like suicide.

Alec reached out and grabbed Logan's shoulder before speaking calmly

"We cannot allow you to do this, there must be another way," but even as he spoke these words, he knew deep down that they had run out of options, their task had fallen into trouble much quicker than they could have anticipated.

Seeing no other path open up before him Alec nodded solemnly at Logan, signalling his acknowledgment of this fact and his agreement for him to go ahead with his plan. The two gave each other one last look before Alec grabbed Josh's ran towards the opening as fast as they could, praying hard that Logan would make it out alive too.

Logan stood tall and proud, facing off against an endless wave of Koschei forces as they charged down upon him. He could feel the blood pounding through his veins as he raised his sword in defiance, ready to do battle. Yet he knew what he was about to face was impossible even though he took it on with a grin. He had seen these creatures move before and knew that even with all his training and experience there was no way he could take them all on at once and survive without a miraculous stroke of fortune; but still he held strong, determined to fight for his friends no matter what it cost himself.

The Koschei charged forward, their roars piercing the air around them as Logan braced himself for impact. He swung his sword wildly from side to side, managing to fend off several of the creatures at a time but never able to break free from their relentless advance. The constant onslaught of creatures seemed never-ending and as Logan began to tire it seemed fate had other plans for him.

With a ferocious shove from one of the gargantuan beasts, Logan catapulted backwards onto the ground, all prospects of survival dissipating as he lay immobilized before them. The monstrosity towered over him, at least twenty feet tall, standing on four thick legs resembling tree trunks and scowling down at Logan. Saliva dripped down onto their valiant hero from rows upon rows of sharp teeth and tusks, the rumbling, savage roar of the creature blasting deafeningly through the atmosphere around him.

As he looked up, he bowed his head almost accepting that this was his time to go.

He raised his blade one last time and prepared for the final strike. Just when all seemed lost however, a loud crack cut through the air like thunder, causing the entire group of Koschei forces to stop in their tracks - stunned by whatever this mysterious sound was, even shocking the snarling creature above.

Alec and Josh had reached a nearby mound, Alec stood there holding his staff aloft, its shaft glowing bright green as he cast a spell across the island. The staff was like the morning sun, so bright it stung Logan's eyes when he looked towards where they stood, casting shadows across the plains and cliffs around them. As the light poured from him and flowed across the plains, Alec held the staff up high and strong, the magic emanating from it still pulsing through. Koschei's forces were blinded by the pure white light that shone brighter than even the noonday sun.

They cried out in pain as they covered their eyes with their hands and tried to blink away the sudden light that filled them with searing heat. Logan blinked away the spots in his own eyes just in time to see Josh standing there in front of him to help him escape himself.

As Alec's grip on the staff relaxed and the magical glow dimmed, he noticed his father, standing in the distance watching the events unfold. He braced himself, expecting a spell or some other attack to come, yet nothing happened—his father turned away and vanished from sight.

Before Alec had time to comprehend what was happening, Josh and Logan had reappeared at his side.

"We have to go," said Josh urgently peering back himself and seeing where Alec's eyes lay, "before they can react."

Without a word, they hurried down the slope of the hill, leaving Alec behind as he gazed into the murky fog, wondering why he wasn't attacked and what his father's intentions could be. The two men turned back to him in urgency as the first of the Koschei began to regain their senses,

"Alec! Now" shouted Logan.

He shook himself and ran after them. As they reached the bottom they ran as fast as they were able, they ran until Alec could feel his lungs burning and wondered if they may well soon collapse. Josh noticing his friends struggle called out to Logan.

"Logan, I think we are well clear, there is no one to be seen following."

Logan slowed and turned to look. He nodded cautiously as his eyes glanced across the vast open plains behind them, they were in the clear for now.

11) Desperate times / Desperate measures

Meanwhile, on the battlefield of Midjun, Hypnos stood strong against a mass force of Koschei forces alongside his Nyx. He had been caught off guard by their sudden and unexpected attack, it had come much quicker than expected and in much greater numbers than what they had seen, but he was determined to protect Midjun from falling into their hands. The Nyx army was strong and powerful, but it was no match for the sheer number of Koschei that were now stood on the battlefield swarming like a pack of locusts. As far as the eye could see there were undead vying for their place on the field of battle. They were not as organised, disciplined or as controlled as the Nyx but at numbers of at least fifty to one they did not need to be.

Hypnos steadied himself for battle and raised his sword in readiness as he charged forward into the eagerly awaiting Koschei. He moved swiftly and skilfully, cutting a path through the enemies with each defiant swing of his blade. The decaying limbs of the Koschei easily tore away leaving a battle field resembling that of a tornado ravaged graveyard. The clashing of steel could be heard echoing across Midjun as both sides fought fiercely for control of the island. Hypnos fought with a bravery and skill unmatched by any other warrior on the battlefield, leading his Nyx army in a valiant effort to protect Midjun from destruction and to ensure they maintained the stranglehold. The Koschei forces were relentless however and it seemed that nothing could stand in their way. The Nyx soldiers fought in strict formation, showing their immense disciplinary skills and fighting prowess, however as hard as they made themselves to damage for every thirty or so Koschei taken down at least one Nyx would fall. This number rendered this fight unwinnable.

The Koschei forces overwhelmed Hypnos' Nyx army and began to capture soldiers and make great advances in area controlled. Camps were set ablaze and rubble filled the plains as the Koschei marched through Midjun, destroying everything in their path. They seemed like a plague, devouring the host bit by bit until there was nothing that remained. Hypnos fought bravely, trying to protect his people and restore order but it was of little use.

The Koschei had come with an unstoppable force, sweeping through Midjun and conquering it with ease. Whenever Hypnos though he may be gaining some ground, he would see in the distance more Koschei arriving, their troops were numberless. Nothing could stand in their way as they took control, step by step, taking whatever, they desired with impunity and leaving destruction in their wake.

Hypnos feared that the watchtower itself may soon fall, he had managed to concentrate them all into the southern part of the island but the battlefield was spreading North, and if so, this would also leave the pathway through to Lemuri unguarded and open.

In a desperate attempt to keep the pathway safe, Hypnos gathered some of his most trusted Nyx soldiers and ordered them to protect the watchtower at all costs. He already had a large quantity of soldiers there accompanying the towers guardians however he now realised, this battle was all but lost, the watchtower would be the last stand. The guardians of the tower themselves were a formidable group. They comprised of twenty warriors, each having to have passed strict and ruthless tasks in order to qualify. Once there they were to never leave other than in death itself.

Even then they were to be buried underneath the tower itself. They were each provided with a sword made from the crystalised feathers of a Phoenix. There were twenty-five of these blades made when the tower was formed. This was the number envisioned for the guardians. Each time a guardian dies and is replaced the blade is handed down. One was buried with the first guardian to give his life for the defence of the tower, one is kept in the towers keep and three are missing, lost over the years.

Once Hypnos had sent these soldiers to their new location, he then sent another lone back to Sofpavel, he needed Freyja to use her powerful magic to find a way to seal off the path to Lemuri, he felt they were going to fail and would be unable to protect it for long themselves. She had to Sofpavel, watching the proceedings and doing all she could to send aid and assistance.

By the time he himself had reached the watchtower he could see that she had already manage to perform her task, forming an impenetrable barrier of energy that would repel any enemy advance, he just hoped she could maintain it long enough for them to have secured the area. The Nyx army had already formed a protective barrier around the watchtower, fourteen lines deep when Hypnos had arrived. He met with the commanding guardian of the watchtower who having watched all of the events from afar was well aware of the position they currently found themselves in.

"It is a grim time Hypnos" the commander said whilst accepting the firm handshake on offer.

Hypnos nodded whilst looking up at the commander. He was every bit as large as Hypnos and stood in full black plated armour. Under his arm he held soundly his blackened helmet which bore the marks of previous fought battles.

"Indeed, it is commander, we are here to help you defend in any way we can," Hypnos gestured.

The commander nodded appreciatively; he knew that they would require all the assistance they could muster. The tower itself was a fortress and not easy to overcome on its own. With the guardianship of themselves also it is something that had never been achieved. However never before had a force of this magnitude tried.

"Thank you" responded the commander, "my men are set in the towers, we have our usual protections in place and usually would not need to leave the towers however I feel we may well be best positioned at ground level with yourselves on this occasion."

Hypnos nodded, the sheer numbers heading their way would indeed require as many men for hand-to-hand combat as they could have. The guardians' usual tactics would generally revolve around the towers sheer size and general impenetrability standing on its own with his men rarely needing to do more than pick off the few that made it through and ensure that the tower did indeed stand its own. Not because they could not fight, but if you do not need to then why would you?

As the Nyx army stood forcibly in unison with the guardians, each watched with unwavering determination. Wave upon wave of Koschei forces charged forward like a wild and chaotic ocean, ready to overwhelm the barrier Freyja had placed across the face of the Lemuri pathways.

Hypnos can see that her spell was waning. With every passing second his army worked harder and harder to hold their position but were no match for the ruthless numbers of Koschei. The clash of war filled Midjun as both sides fought fiercely; yet it was clear that the Koschei forces were gaining momentum and the air hummed with rage and determination. Suddenly, her powerful magic collapsed and the enemy surged forward with newfound ferocity, smashing through all defences as they made their way towards the watchtower. arrows whizzed by while blades clashed in a chaotic dance of death.

Despite fighting with all their might, Nyx army was struggling to withstand the overwhelming force of the Koschei warriors.

Anxiety consumed Hypnos as he saw the carnage ensuing around him, desperately searching for a way to stop them from reaching the tower's entrance and proceeding past the Lemuri pathway. He could feel time slipping away and knew that if he failed to find a solution soon, it would be too late. He frantically searched around for options but nothing seemed to present itself.

Hypnos sprinted with urgency, his mind racing as he tried to formulate a plan that would save his troops and the watchtower. His feet pounded against the ground, leaving a cloud of dust in his wake as he gathered the commander and some of his soldiers around him.

"We need fire," he commanded, his voice echoing through the air.

"It's our best chance at stopping them in larger numbers." He pointed towards the horizon where plumes of smoke were rising from Koschei struggling against an inferno. "We can use it to funnel them down to a smaller area and take them on more evenly."

The commander stared sceptically at Hypnos. "Fire won't stop them," he intoned doubtfully. "They'll still go straight through it."

Hypnos shook his head. "You're right, it won't stop them," he acknowledged. "But it will slow them down and prevent them from getting around us. If we create a line of fire and funnel them down to the front of the watchtower, we stand a chance."

The commander still seemed less than convinced, but he knew that outside of the tower, Hypnos was his superior, and he was compelled to obey. "If this goes wrong," he said reluctantly, "it will be on your head."

Hypnos seemed unfazed by the warning as he barked orders to the soldiers: Set fire to all of the dead trees surrounding the watchtower and across the land as well as anything else flammable that we do not require, we need to create a wall of flames that would block the Koschei and funnel them down towards us at the watchtower.

The troops were hesitant at first, but they agreed to the plan, and began carrying out his orders.

The flames rose high into the night sky creating an almost impenetrable barrier across the barren lands, creating a pathway directly towards and into the awaiting steel of Hypnos and co. The Koschei forces appeared unable to breach Hypnos' wall of fire due to its sheer magnitude of depth. Although they had little sensation of pain, the intense heat could still cause damage to their decaying body parts. Slowly, it would melt their limbs and disable them from taking any further action.

As such they began to either retreat aimlessly back into Midjun or go the one clear passageway forwards. As they charged forwards they were easily defeated by Hypnos' and his ingenious plan. one on one they were no match for a Nyx soldier.

However, for days on end the Koschei forces returned, amassing a menacing battalion with them. What truly shocked Hypnos was the sudden appearance of their hulking, armour-clad creatures. Through walls of orange smoke, he watched as their snarling jaws emerged and pushed through his wall of fire. He knew it was a matter of time before they would force him into another bloody skirmish. Despite killing off a great number of foes with his plan, he realized the odds were stacked against them and all they had done was buy a bit of time and even the playing field slightly.

His Nyx army stood tall and brave yet quite deflated after having believed themselves to be on the precipice of victory in the wake of Hypnos plan. He could feel them waning ever so slightly and he reminded them all of why they were here, that their bravery and courage was what kept the realms safe and that no matter what happened each one of them should be proud of what they'd achieved thus far.

The Nyx steeled themselves for another battle as the Koschei forces began to breach the wall of fire, prepared to face whatever may come their way in defence of Midjun. As the beasts forced their way through, the giant feet and large dragging tails dampened out the remaining flames leaving just a smouldering wasteland around.

The Nyx charged forward with ferocity and rage towards the Koschei forces, using the heavy weight and mass of their own bodies as an advantage in close combat against the giant Koschei creatures. Whilst they were not immune to the piercing weapons of the Nyx soldiers, they seemed to take no real harm or damage from them whatsoever and their thick skin made any blow ineffective. Their sheer size and weight made them seem invincible, like some sort of unstoppable force that was in fact quite the opposite. It took all of the Nyx soldiers combined strength to bring down one of the beasts, even so they managed to defeat a handful of them in thanks to their brute force. Though, the sheer numbers were beginning to tell and soon the soldiers were losing ground steadily.

The Koschei seemed to have no fear of death, and continued to charge forward themselves, determined to reach the watchtower and their prize beyond.

Abruptly a loud crack sounded out over the battlefield, causing the soldiers to pause in surprise. A colossal piece of rock had broken free of the cliff side behind the charging beasts and fallen right on top of one of the beasts. The creature was unable to stop under the mass of his own weight and crashed down hard, becoming crushed beneath the falling rock. There was a collective gasp and cheer amongst the Nyx forces as they realized that Freyja's magic had saved them once again as the faint blue mist that usually accompanied her spells could be seen around the cliffs edge, she was watching, helping where she could and this knowledge spurred the soldiers on further. Her magic was being blocked from the battlefield by the opposition but she appeared to have snuck one through their barriers, and it could not have come at a better time.

"Quickly, kill the beast before it wakes!" cried out one of the guards. The others nodded and rapidly dispatched the beast before it regained consciousness.

The soldiers' spirits lifted, happy to have survived the onslaught of the beasts supporting the Koschei as they now all lay defeated or wounded, and grateful for the timely intervention of Freyja. But there was still much work to be done and many of them had fallen themselves under this onslaught.

Hypnos turned to face the cliff which the rocks had once been safely part of, not too far to the East and saw something that shocked him.

On the edge of the cliff sat a figure wrapped in white robes. The figure raised their hands in the air and fired a single blast of bright light at the cliffs edge. The sound of the explosion could be heard echoing across the battlefield however amidst the chaos few seemed to notice the addition. When the dust settled, the rubble was gone and in its place, stood a stone staircase leading down into darkness.

A smile spread across Hypnos' face as he saw what emerged. He knew what he had to do next despite a short moment of hesitance, it had not been Freyja after all it would seem.

He called for the commander who was nearby to follow him and together they charged towards the cliff slicing their way through the Koschei hoards and finally reaching the staircase of which they instantly begun to descend.

They emerged from the stairs below and found themselves in a dark tunnel. The walls were smooth and seamless, almost appearing to be made of marble and the floor was flat and even. It appeared incredibly well constructed. The tunnel stretched further into the earth in both directions and went much further than their eyes could see. The commander looked up and down the tunnel before turning back to Hypnos.

"What exactly are we doing down here?" asked the commander obviously confused.

"I do not know, but that figure clearly aided us, there must be a purpose to this and we are not in a position to argue." Hypnos replied with a sound of desperation within his voice.

"But the watchtower is now unguarded and we have no way of knowing this figure was on our side, this could be a trap." replied the commander.

"No" Hypnos replied, our soldiers can remain behind, they will hold it for as long as they can, with or without us the tower is looking likely to fall, we would make little difference."

There was a roar from above with the accompanying clash of metal as he spoke as if to reinforce this comment.

The commander looked doubtful. "You want me to abandon my men and descend into the depths of the earth with you? Are you mad?"

"If you wish to return to the watchtower and die with your men that strongly without at least having tried to take whatever opportunity this may present, then by all means, go ahead, I will respect your decision to fight alongside them. However, we may be able to save many, we do not know but I would rather take that slim chance."

The commander paused for a moment, he knew Hypnos was right, they were losing the battle above and the defensive wall kept slipping. His fire trick had done well and plenty of Koschei had been defeated but it had not made them any ground, they seemed unable to make any.

When your enemy reanimates the dead there is never a shortage of troop availability.

The commander reluctantly nodded and together with Hypnos proceeded to run through the tunnel. The further they went down the colder it got, as if they were heading into the depths of winter. Eventually after a few turns and twists in the tunnel the shadows revealed a second staircase going back up to the surface.

As they ascended the towering staircase, both men trembled with trepidation at what awaited them on the other side - serenity or violence? Despite their fear, they agreed that whatever lay ahead of them was worth venturing into for it could potentially offer salvation in this war. Steeling themselves with swords raised high in defence, they approached cautiously; recognizing that while this may be hope, it could just as easily be a snare waiting to ensnare and harm.

The sight that lay before them as they reached the summit was absolutely breathtaking and something neither had been prepared for.

As Hypnos, who had been leading the way, peaked first he could not believe what lay in front of him. Standing in all its splendour before him the sun glinted off the majestic Lemuri Falls, its silver waters gushing over bright red rock, tumbling deep into a vibrant pool surrounded by lush foliage. A kaleidoscope of rainbow colours sparkled in the sunlight as it crashed over the falls, and vibrant flowers filled the green grass surrounding the tranquil pool. The peak of these great falls could not be seen and above a certain point there was just empty space. Lemuri, it appeared flowed from nowhere, seemingly falling from the sky itself.

Hypnos and the commander looked at each other in astonishment and then around, searching for any signs of life or combat that would indicate they were still under threat. But to their relief all seemed peaceful and there were no enemy in sight.

Hypnos began to make his way towards the waterfall and beckoned for his companion to follow. As they reached the base of Lemuri Falls and watched as it cascaded into a large pool below them, it felt as though they had stepped into another realm entirely—one untouched by war and destruction.

The water from the falls glittered in a mesmerizing array of colours while small fish swam lazily around them in the fresh clear water below.

Far beneath the swimming fish, you could discern the whirlpools of movement and barely make out the orbs far, far below completing their voyage. You couldn't perceive the safeguards blocking access to this spot; the tremendous pressures built to shield and bar entry, or the portals they traversed before streaming up through the cascades.

Hypnos could not help but ponder this briefly and wonder how it may have been accessed previously. The air all around them was filled with sweet smells from flowers blooming on either side with butterflies fluttering about everywhere. It truly felt like they had found a utopian world that did not belong in an are facing such destruction.

They both stood there looking around at the dazzling beauty until finally Hypnos broke out of his trance-like state and motioned for his companion to follow him as they looked around for anything that may be able to help them.

Hypnos turned to face south, there in the far distance was the watchtower in all its might, smoke could still be seen rising from the last few remains of the flames previously blazing on the island. The spray of battle was still visible as it continued with General Araya hopefully keeping them back long enough to prevent the inevitable outcome as long as possible. The vision to the south was a stark reminder that indeed this was connected to their own lands, in fact it was the place they were trying so hard to protect.

He then developed an idea, one as unorthodox as his previous, if he could destroy the pathway from this end and make access to Lemuri that much more difficult than it would be better protected from any future incursions. He spoke the idea aloud to his companion who failed to hear him over the roar of the falls. The commander glanced up one last time at the falls as he walked away back over to Hypnos who stood firm, still gazing into the distance with his arms solidly crossed.

"Apologies Hypnos" the commander said in a raised voice in order to ensure he was heard, "could you repeat that?"

Hypnos looked at him for a second before turning his gaze back towards the tower,

"They will beat us there commander, we must prevent them from reaching this point at all costs," the commander now looked to toward the tower himself, he could see the dust raising from the warring troops had now engulfed the tower itself and knew that Hypnos was correct, their troops were being pushed further and further back and his tower was all but lost.

"So, what do you suggest we do?" the commander questions.

"We destroy their way here," Hypnos responds in a very matter of fact fashion. The commander looked at him quizzically and Hypnos could tell he did not understand. "We need to destroy this pathway commander."

The commander looked confused. The path stretches out as far as the eye can see, winding through vast fields and forests. The ground is solid and wide, not easily destroyed. The path narrows to a mere few yards at points, but even then, it's still fortified and sturdy. It's no rickety bridge—it will take a lot of effort to break it.

"How do we destroy it Hypnos? And even if we manage to destroy the connection, we know they can cross in the waters themselves," Hypnos smiled, "Are you forgetting commander, they walk the waterways to the East and West but not the North or South," the commander went to speak but had indeed then recalled, the Orbs travel through the waters to the North and South in larger numbers and also, especially in the North, rise higher and move faster. Anything entering these waters would be torn apart if they attempted going much deeper than the surface.

Hypnos continued, "The only way to make sure they cannot reach Lemuri is to destroy the pathway from this end and to reseal the passageway we just travelled through."

The commander paused for a moment, his eyes scanning the vast expanse of the falls before him. Above, the sky was painted with shades of orange and grey as the few remaining flames collided with the rising ash. He nodded in agreement, his mind already racing to work out how to go about the practicality of actually destroying it. Beside him, Hypnos stood firm, determination etched onto his face, ready to take on the task at hand. They both turned one last time towards Midjun and sighed heavily.

The silence hung heavy in the air as neither Hypnos nor the Commander could think of a way to destroy all this land. But they knew what had to be done if they wanted to protect Lemuri.

The white robed figure had returned just as silently and mysteriously as they had first arrived. The figure glided towards them as if floating on the air itself, stopping before them like a ghostly apparition. Its presence was palpable as if it had been watching their every move from far away.

The mysterious figure was adorned in a drooping hood, which hid them from view. Their voice rang out like a bell, but it was soft and kind and most of the tension Hypnos felt towards this character fell away in an instance.

"I am here to aid you in keeping what is important to us all safe," they declared. Hypnos moved forward with curiosity.

"Who are you? What do you want us to do? And why have you come?"

The figure raised a hand towards the pathway leading from Midjun to Lemuri and whispered something incomprehensible under their breath which sent shivers down both Hypnos and the Commander's backs as a cool strong breeze accompanied the words. In an instant they felt an immense energy emanating from the falls and without warning it became almost as though the falls were alive with life itself - thousands upon thousands of tiny droplets of water began to rise up into the air from its surface and gradually began forming together until each droplet had become one single entity - a large swirling ball of clear crystal-like liquid hung high above the ground for all to see. Hypnos stared, as if in a trance, at the beautiful swirling pool of liquid hanging in the air. The mysterious being put one hand into the water; the other hand on the tip of Hypnos's sword, and drew them towards each other.

The light running down their robed arm attracted Hypnos' gaze as he watched the water flow from one hand down to the other as if using their arms like a riverbed. The water gathered around the blade, seeming almost to enter it. Each droplet had become a tiny mirror, reflecting not only itself but also its surroundings: dancing tree shadows flitted across the being's face and myriad flashes of colour sparkled in the folds of the white robe. Hypnos stared at his blade with wonderment, knowing that something incredible had just happened. The commander stepped forward into the frame, breaking Hypnos's concentration. He put his helmet on his head as if fearing the sword may explode under the power surging through it and faced Hypnos directly, looking intently at both him and the strange figure in turn, however Hypnos was unsure of where all of this was leading.

The being seemed to sense his confusion, and stepped forward placing their hands on both sides of Hypnos's head and looking into his eyes with an expression of infinite compassion. Hypnos at that point noted that the being was female and, in appearance at least, human. Before he had time to think much further though she spoke to him, ""You know what to do with this blade now," she said. "The power of this sword will render the land bridge all but impassable. Make it so, and you will have done your duty."

Hypnos nodded slowly, looking down at the shimmering metal in his hand. "The power within this blade is great," she said. "It will create a barrier between the two lands, preventing war from reaching its shores. It may not be an end to conflict, but it is a start, a shield for those who are innocent."

Hypnos understood; he had been given a powerful weapon to wield against injustice and division. Without hesitation he turned away and walked over to where Lemuri met the land bridge that had connected it so solidly to the remaining world.

The battle was still clear and present in the distance, with even more smoke rising from the remains of the earlier blaze as more and more earth was disturbed in the commotion. The tower now seemed all but gone as he could see it falling to one side and precariously leaning at an impossible angle. A moment of despair came over him as he thought of how many soldiers may have been lost at this point, the needless death was never one that sat easy with him, even under such circumstances.

He hoisted the colossal blade aloft, veins bulging as he exerted himself. Finally, with a thunderous clang, the sword slammed into the earth, tearing it in two halves that snaked towards the sea. The hilt vibrated from the strike and Hypnos grunted as he seized it for another blow.

But before he could act, a tremor pulsed through the ground and it began to give way beneath him as he stumbled backwards. The land bridge fell away into the ocean below, and as it did so, a bright light bored through the waters—seemingly emanating from his mighty sword. The sea surged upwards in a massive wave of churning water, towering at least twenty feet in front of him.

Hypnos was awestruck. Before him, an imposing wall of glimmering water towered into the air, blocking his path in both directions. He could feel the current pushing against his palm as he dipped it into the roiling depths. It wasn't completely impassable, but the strength of the waves hinted at a difficult journey through and created an additional level of protection for the falls, much to his delight.

Hypnos turned to address the mysterious woman who had assisted them, he had many a question to ask. However, as he did, she was not to be seen. All that stood there was the commander who had watched the events unfold completely dumbstruck. His mouth gaped open and his helmet lay on the floor next to his own weapon.

"Where is she?" Hypnos questioned looking around. The commander took a second to realise he was being spoken to, he then looked around himself and shrugged.

"I do not know; she was standing right here." The commander continued looking around himself but it was to no avail, she had clearly gone. "Who was she?" He asked Hypnos.

Hypnos shook his head, he wished he knew.

"I do not know, but I hope to soon find out," he responded.

12) Brief sanctuary

Logan, Alec and Josh had all made it safely back to a cave Logan had been made aware of before they had departed for their trip.

General Araya had informed him of its existence, it was well located buried deep within an intricate collection of rocks and rubble high up on a mountainside. The Nyx had even hidden its presence further with a few large boulders conveniently placed over and around the narrow entrance. In fact, it was so well hidden that Logan had difficulty locating the narrow entrance himself, even with his enhanced vision. Once he had managed to find it, he began shifting the boulders aside one-by-one so that he and Alec and Josh could fit through.

They had used it regularly when monitoring activities on Maredrom, something not done since the age of Morpheus himself.

As they stepped inside the cavernous chamber, their eyes widened in amazement at the expansive space before them. Stalactites hung from the ceiling like giant icicles, glistening under the faint light filtering in from outside. Pools of water were scattered around the floor, and there was a dampness in the air that made Alec feel almost as if they'd stumbled upon an underground spring. Along one wall were several torches, centuries old, which Alec wondered if there was any way to still light them. On one side of the cave there was a large bedroll with supplies gathered around it - long lived food, medical supplies, weapons and other items necessary for survival in such an environment.

Logan immediately set about tending his wounds from the fight with the Koschei while Alec decided to try and light a fire so that they could warm up after their long journey back from Midjun. Josh rummaged through some of the supplies trying to find something useful like maps or clues as to what they should do whilst sniffing the long-life food wondering if he could begin to eat some of the more appealing looking items.

Once Logan had attended to his wounds, an invigorating burst of energy surged through his veins as a flicker of warm orange light illuminated the side of his face. Alec had succeeded in kindling a fire which cast captivating shadows across the walls of this open space.

Logan glanced around the cave, taking stock of their situation. He was not happy to have lost his fight and as impressed with the stunt that Alec had pulled off to save his life. In a strange way, even though he knew he would have succumbed to the ravenous hordes of Koschei he could not pretend there was no enjoyment in the fight.

Josh had meanwhile found some useful information in the supplies – hand drawn maps of Maredrom showing previous expeditions and intentions left behind by hiding soldiers, as well as several books they had written during their times there, some factual and some more of legends filled with tales of things they have seen and strange and wonderful creatures they had encountered including fire breathing reptiles and mermaids in the deep.

Logan decided this was a good start — a better understanding of what they may come up against could serve to help, whilst they are taking stock and hiding it would certainly not hurt.

He grabbed one of the books and threw it over to Alec, "here start with this, I understand you like to read," he stated whilst walking around the area swinging his arms in an arc around his body trying to loosen up some painful areas.

As Alec read, he learned all sorts of interesting facts about Maredrom and the surrounding areas of which had not been covered in the Sofpavelian libraries — although he couldn't quite make sense of them yet nor did he know how factually accurate they may be seeming more like the writings of scared soldiers. There were tales amongst the pages speaking of powerful ancient creatures that used to roam the lands, although most seemed to have dispersed or died out long ago. He also learned that many believed Midjun itself was cursed by its past inhabitants – a belief that looked quite strong within the scripts he now read.

Midjun was a place of serenity and solidarity to its inhabitants - Midjuns sprawling shores echoed with the laughter of children, while fishermen talked stories and sang songs. But on that fateful day Maredrom arrived with a dragon, destroying everything in its path. Fiercely burning down homes, incinerating entire villages - nothing could stand in its way as it wreaked havoc and carnage across the island. Until there were none left alive save but a few who managed to escape. As they fled, Chronos' rage rose up and so did his own dragon. The battle was fierce between the two beasts, until an ancient curse was cast over Midjun, damning all those who dared venture there.

As Alec continued reading, captivated with each and every word, Logan called him over. He reluctantly set aside the book and joined them around the supplies where Josh had scraped together some of the more edible of the food rations. They sat and ate their tasteless meal in silence as they all thought about the events that had unfolded. Alec looked at Logan, he was visibly hurt with blood still seeping through some of the bandages he had placed around his torso. He wondered if he felt pain, if he did, he hid it incredibly well.

Suddenly, Alec had a thought, realising the neglect for the main element of progress of which they had made, or they certainly had not discussed it.

"Did you see the blade? The one that Probetor had? That was the one we are searching for, I am sure?" he asked. Logan sighed heavily, obviously caught off guard by the question and looked up to meet Alec's gaze.

"Yes, I did see it." He nodded before continuing, "I know it quite well, it was some kind of magical weapon, far beyond what I could understand or use — and far too powerful for us to use. The Jinn can be felt within it, trying to wield it can darken your mind, they say the Jinn himself enters into your soul". He paused as if in deep thought before adding "But I'm certain I saw it in his grasp, so at least now we know with certainty who has it."

Alec nodded solemnly and gazed into the fire that cast its light upon them all. It seemed that with this confirmation at least they could determine their next move – but what would that be?

Alec knew that if they were going to find the blade and Probetor, they would need to be creative. He thought of the maps Josh had found earlier and began piecing together a plan.

He suggested they look for Probetor near the canyons around the castle, since it was the closest point on the map to the place where they'd last seen him.

With any luck, they could track him down from there and gain access to his whereabouts. One map in particular was quite detailed and clearly showed many of the areas they had already passed, to Alec it seemed quite navigable.

"Surely these maps combined with your tracking abilities gives us a great advantage, right?" Alec asked of Logan.

"Hmmm" Logan retorted, "I would imagine the extremely large army he seems to be accompanied by should give the location away." Logan seemed frustrated, almost annoyed at Alec's suggestions. He knew his planning may not be the best but he felt a little perplexed as to Logans reluctance to entertain his thoughts.

"How about heading back to the boat, navigating around the exterior of the island until we spot them," Alec tried again. This time Logan looked even more annoyed.

"Alec, what are you suggesting we do once located? We can find him of that I have no doubt. However, we are unable to obtain the blade from him. He can see us coming from some distance and we cannot fight off the extent of the army. Your newly discovered trickery is great for a speedy escape but it will not defeat hordes of undead." Logan sat down looking almost defeated. Even this brave and reckless warrior losing some faith wore heavily on the Alec.

Alec took a deep breath and looked away from Logan, he thought for ways they could gain the blade without conflict and it was then he had an idea. He knew it was a risky plan but if done well, they could succeed.

"What if," he began cautiously, "you and Josh lead the armies away whilst I sneak in and steals the blade from Probetor? If he was distracted and his armies not by his side, I can try to get the blade from him before he is any the wiser." It was a foolish plan but one that Alec believed could work, if done correctly.

Alec looked around for the reaction, his friends sat wide-eyed as he explained his idea. Alec knew this plan was highly ambitious but if successful it could be their chance at getting the blade back in their possession. Josh and Logan were dubious but after a few tense moments agreed that this was their best course of action given the absence of any other ideas coming forward. Josh was relatively quick to volunteer himself for distraction, eager to throw off some of the enemies while Logan still had reservations about leaving Alec alone with such a powerful weapon, such a powerful being so close at hand. But eventually he grudgingly agreed to join forces with Josh's task of leading away the armies. If anything, he probably secretly longed for a chance to have his revenge on any Koschei surviving who had caused his injuries.

It wasn't ideal, in fact far from, but it seemed like their only option. so, they all nodded without any certainty that this was to be the method they attempted. Logan seemed to have a new lease on the mission, the frustration dropping from his face.

"I must say Alec, they call me mad and reckless, but this, I think this would take the crown firmly from me in the mad stakes!"

He sat for a while looking down at a rock he had picked up as he rolled it around in his hand, gazing at it every now and then letting out a deep chuckle and shaking his head. Every third or fourth roll he quietly uttered under his breath "mad man" and raised his eyes, appearing quite mad himself whilst doing so. Suddenly Logan stopped rolling the rock and looked up, a wry smile growing on his face "well, I don't know about you two but I think we should get some rest and attempt this plan in the morning" he stood tall and Alec could see the determination behind his words. Though a risky plan, it appeared they were all willing to give it a go.

Alec dragged the camping bed out from beneath a dusty tarp and opened it up, careful not to let any dust escape from above in his haste.

He could feel the metal frame through the worn leather base as he lay down and knew he'd be lucky to get a few hours of sleep on its hard surface that night. Josh pulled another over nearby, as he sat on its edge Alec could tell that he was not overly impressed with the feeling of his temporary sleeping place.

"Well, it is better than the floor I guess" Alec joked quietly. Josh smiled and tactfully nodded; he was not so sure that it was. Logan however did not join them. He lay on a hard, flat rock near the entrance to their temporary home, his back propped up against the caves wall. He firmly kept his sword grasped closed to his chest. The blade was streaked with dark grey, and one touch of it revealed it was constantly rinsed it off in sea water for many years but never fully cleaned it. The salty water had worn groves into it and it felt rough to the touch. He leaned against the boulder behind him for support and thought of also trying to sleep, but his eyes were wide and alert. He could not allow himself to relax, they may be quite well hidden but they were in Maredrom after all and the enemy knew it. Logan had no doubt that although they felt safe at present they most certainly were not. They would be being hunted.

It had been a long day and as Alec lay down on his uncomfortable bed, he wondered what tomorrow may bring, or if they would even make it through the night without being discovered.

He realised that this was the first time he had contemplated the possibility of not surviving here.

Alec drifted off just as the sound of footsteps and whispered voices appeared outside. He was just on the edge of sleep as the disturbance materialised and he realized that Logan was also very much awake, standing in front of the mouth of their shelter with his sword drawn, listening intently for any sounds as he studied their surroundings.

Alec lay perfectly still, hoping Logan would not notice he was watching.

Logan's face was set in a grim expression, and his gaze never wavered from the direction of the sound. His tall form concealed the small pieces of light that came from the cracks towards the caves hidden entrance and cast a shadow over where Alec and Josh lay.

He turned back to them after a couple minutes aware that Alec lay awake watching, shaking his head to reassure him that there was nothing to be concerned about. But his fingers gripped tightly around the hilt of his sword; if danger appeared, he would be ready to fight without hesitation.

After Logan sat down again, grunting in irritation at the hardness of the ground in disapproval, they both tried to rest once again. After that moment of tension, the night was surprisingly calm. Although Logan didn't lie down until after making sure they were safe from harm, Alec couldn't help wondering if what happened was an illusion or real. But either way, he knew they were safe for now and eventually sleep claimed him again.

13) Faulted boldness

Alec awoke with a feeling of having finally, after many hours, been able to rest his eyes effectively. The old battered bed had served him well in the end despite the original uncomfortableness of it.

The trees outside swayed gently in the morning breeze, and he could just about hear bird song coming from above, filtering down through the cracks in the rocks that had protected them all so well that night. Even the sounds of the birds that flew here sounded terrifying he thought to himself.

He stretched till he cracked all along his back and tilted his head this way and that way to free any kinks that may have developed whilst he slept. As he did so his gaze fell on Logan. He was still sitting bolt upright against the walls. Long streaks of dried sweat ran down his chest and face. His head leaned forward onto the tip of his sword handle as he gripped the blade in front of him. His mouth was set in an expressionless line, and though he appeared to be at rest, Alec doubted very much that this was so.

He looked over then to Josh, he lay in the most uncomfortable looking of positions yet sound asleep. A small low snore could be heard emanating from in between his lips as his head lay at the oddest of angles, one thing that had always been true of Josh was his ability to sleep in any way you can possibly imagine. Alec recalled in this moment all of those times when they were younger where he would awaken to find Josh fast asleep with his lower half on the bed and his head on the floor. He chuckled to himself whilst recollecting these events, briefly forgetting the situation they had currently found themselves in.

For as much as the cave they were currently in provided them, for the short term at least, some shelter as well as basic supplies and safety, they were still deep within enemy territory and hiding from an army of undead soldiers. It sounded like a video game that he and Josh had played all those years ago on the nights in question. He also recalled at around this time that today he was to set off with a task that would put him potentially face to face with his father for the first time in his life. Albeit this also being the man who could well today end that life.

"What's on your mind Alec?" Logan spoke up, breaking the silence that had descended in the cave since he had awoken. His voice was steady and strong but at the same time it had a hint of unease to it. As if he knew what Alec was thinking about and was preparing himself for whatever response may come his way.

Alec looked up at him feeling comforted by the question and show of concern. He thought to himself for a few moments before letting out a long sigh and answering "I'm scared Logan... I'm scared of what I might have to face today. I know it was my idea, I still believe the best one, but I am scared."

He paused, looking away from Logan as his hands gripped tightly onto his own arms as if trying to calm himself down from the sudden rush of emotions that had flooded through him. After he had collected himself again, he looked back up at Logan and asked softly "What do you think will happen?"

Just then, Josh stirred and tiredly opened his eyes. His vision was still blurry from the deep slumber he had just come out of as he blinked a few times trying to focus on the two figures standing before him. As he began to wake up, his mind filled with memories of the day before and why they were there in the first place. He jumped up unexpectedly, almost knocking Alec off his bed.

"What's going on?" he asked with an air of confusion as he tried to remember what was happening around him.

Logan smiled at Josh before turning back to Alec and answering his question from earlier. "I think you will find that we are going to have to face our fears today, the result of which I cannot determine." he said solemnly, but with a certain sense of determination in his voice as if speaking these words aloud helped to further solidify them in the minds of both Alec's and Josh.

"Your father is no doubt out there somewhere waiting for us and it won't be long before we find ourselves standing face to face with him."

Josh shuddered involuntarily at these words, not only did it sound like a daunting task but Logan's tone made it sound all the more serious than it already was. Despite this however, Alec didn't flinch. He knew and understood the task at hand and despite the concern for his own safety understood that what they were doing was for the good of all, that there was a much bigger play at hand. Logan recognised these feelings in Alec's steadfast and determined eyes. It was a sight he had a lot of admiration for. He had seen Nyx soldiers themselves seem less confident, and these were beings much larger, stronger and battle ready than Alec could ever be.

"You'd make a great soldier Alec" Logan stated, "maybe when all of this is over, we have a chat with Hypnos about keeping you on hey?" he winked, receiving an appreciative smile in return.

Josh, who had remained standing still and silent since his initially sharp jump to life, jolted back into life. He was not so willing to send his friend into such a dangerous situation but knew he needed to remain buoyant for his sake.

"Okay let's do this," he said finally, less eager to start their journey but hopeful to end this suspense once and for all.

With that, Alec quickly gathered all of their belongings, stuffing them into makeshift backpacks and hoisted it over his shoulder. He went around the cave one final time, making sure he had everything they needed for the journey ahead feeling more like he was preparing for a casual day trip.

When he was done, the three of them stepped out from the safety of the cave one by one, Logan stepped out first and briskly surveyed the area, all seemed clear enough and so he beckoned out the others. The air was crisp and cool as they ventured out into the sunlight, the dead trees around them casting shadows onto the red rock around them. Every now and then Alec could hear or see something moving in the shadows but none appeared hostile enough for Logan to intervene as random insects and reptiles scuttered around.

As they continued on their way, Alec kept his eyes peeled for anything that might provide a clue as to his father's whereabouts; what he was looking for he did not know, as Logan had mocked earlier a big army might be a good clue! He didn't find anything though no matter how hard he looked so instead his mind wandered onto other things such as what would happen when they found him?

These thoughts were quickly banished though by Josh who interrupted his thought process. "Have you thought much about after Alec?" he questioned.

"After all this, I mean everything has changed now." He glanced at him with a hint of sympathy in his eyes as he finished his own thought process, "This is not what was wanted for you you know."

Alec slowed and turned to look at Josh who was walking beside him. He still showed some weakness from the earlier attack on him, a slight limp as a he walked made him a little slower than the others and he strongly guarded his left side, he plainly still felt some discomfort.

Alec felt this an odd moment to choose a conversation of this fashion, last night for example in the sanctity of the cave may have been the better choice!

"After?" Alec responded. "No, I cannot say I have. The current task kind of takes over, no?" Alec said this in a way that highlighted his thoughts at the oddity of Josh choosing this conversation now. Logan obviously felt the same way.

"Now is not the time for a heart-to-heart gentleman" he interrupted, "stay focused on the task at hand, we cannot afford to miss anything.

Think about after, after." Josh nodded to Logan apologetically but Alec wondered what was on Josh's mind that led him to ask the question, he felt it had not been asked as a conversation starter. Never the less, in the same vein later was a more appropriate time to question this.

This thought solidified as Logan had now seen something. He stopped abruptly and placed his hands out to either side to prevent the others from passing him by. With his hands stretched out Alec could not help but be a little alarmed at just how much larger his frame became in that instance. He wondered for a moment if all Nyx soldiers were derived from some fairytale giants of old. They were back to where the encounters with the Koschei had started, facing down into the canyon by the castle. Yet again also, were the Koschei forces. Half as many as last time but still very much there.

"This must be where they are generally stationed," Logan said in a lowered voice, "the others are probably out searching for us, or they have been called into battle. Either way the depleted numbers here may serve us well."

Josh looked at Alec and then down at the numbers Logan mentioned, depleted yes, low no he thought. Alec could tell what Josh was thinking, whilst he agreed he also could see Logans point, rather be chased by a thousand than tens of thousands.

"Do we just wait here until we see Probetor arrive?" Questioned Josh. "He is quite integral to all of this working of course."

Logan looked stern as he considered Josh's words. He clearly wished to charge into the fray, obviously wanting to fight. His impatience and wish for a little revenge weighed heavily on him as he thought it over.

"Indeed, we do need him here, perhaps attacking will lure the armies away and draw him out."

Alec still felt they should wait at least a while; Probetor may have been down there already and he had no idea what could be waiting for them. Even though he could feel the anticipation growing inside him, he knew they had no choice but to stay put until Probetor arrived. Just as he was about to say something though he heard Josh's voice calling behind him.

"Wait!"

Everyone turned their eyes towards where Josh stood, his own eyes fixed on one point deep in the canyon. Alec followed his gaze and squinted into the distance until he could make out what Josh had seen. Alec watched the tiny silhouette of Probetor emerge from over the horizon. His cloaked figure seemed to float across the dark terrain, like a shadow cutting through the moonlight. On closer inspection, Alec noticed someone else following Probetor; his heart skipped a beat as he realised it was Gree, accompanied by Jenny!

The others took in this new arrival also and Logan quickly sprang into action.

"Him having company does us no favours, let's find some cover and see where they go before, we make our move", they all nodded in agreement and looked around frantically for anything big enough that might hide them from possible searching eyes.

Alec spotted a large boulder nearby and pointed it out to the others, it was situated close enough to the entrance of the canyon so that Probetor could be seen passing through without being too far away from them, nor will it make them close enough to be easily spotted. An overhang of rocks hung around it like a spider's web nearly covering it completely and creating the perfect hiding space.

They tumbled down from the ledge and landed on the ground nearby. The group balanced their way up onto the boulder silently, careful not to alert anyone to their presence. From this position, Alec could see Gree leading Jenny toward a walled area deep inside the bottom of the canyon behind the standing Koschei forces. Probetor however remained lingering behind instead of entering with them.

A solid mass of stone lay before him, a thick sheet of black granite gleamed beneath his feet, he was assessing the troops and Alec was feeling a strong sense of Deja vu. Alec looked down upon Probetor, each time he saw him he found it harder to believe that this being was his father, even harder to believe he had once been a good man and very much in love, this creature that does not appear capable of such an emotion. He now oozes nothing but evil and the idea of good having once existed within was unfathomable.

Probetor seemed to be searching for something, as if looking for an answer to a question not spoken before entering. His eyes scanned the area for any signs of treachery, and his troops stood ready at a moment's notice should the answer be revealed.

Gree and Jenny had already disappeared inside the walled area yet Probetor still seemed unable to move on from where he stood. It seemed like a stand-off between him and the wall, as if he knew something or someone was waiting for him behind it - something that only he could unlock or understand. Maybe he knew that something was afoot, either way for some reason he was hesitant to move.

Alec wanted desperately to tell Logan what he thought or ask him what they should do next but before he could get any words out Josh stepped up beside him with a plan of action already in mind.

"We have no choice," he urgently spurted out, "we need to make our move now before Probetor has a chance to do anything, he's alone and he knows something is not right, you can see it in the way he is acting."

Alec could sense the nervousness in Josh's voice which he felt strongly influenced his words however he knew he was correct in what he said. Logan likewise knew that Josh was right.

"Ok" Logan sighed, "Alec we will cause the distraction and lead the Koschei away, they all followed previously so I see no reason why they will not repeat this. But first, if you make your way to the West I can see a well-hidden pathway besides the castle, it appears to lead to the canyon floor and near where he currently stands. Once you are near the base I will be able to see you and we will begin."

Logan paused looking down at the amassing troops, whilst he himself may enjoy the fight and relish in the battle he was concerned for Alec's welfare, he still did not believe that this was the right way to proceed and he had been tasked first and foremost with protecting him. However, Alec had been tasked with locating and retrieving the blade, one could not achieve their task without the other potentially failing in their own.

It was an impossibility that Logan had come to realise but not one he was incredibly pleased with.

"Alec be careful, once we have led the troops away, I will attempt to double back as quickly as possible, if you become in trouble I will be coming, use any power you have for any needed defence that may arise, do not, I repeat do not go on the attack yourself, you will not be able to stand toe to toe with Probetor, In and out. Do you understand!?" Logans voice turned from concerned to extremely stern as he finished his point and Alec appreciated this. He believed the concern was genuine and not just due to the consequences that Logan may face should Alec become lost. He nodded as Logan patted him on the back, his hand seemed to almost cover the entirety of it and the force that came with what Logan quite possibly perceived as a gentle tap was quite something.

Josh stepped forward and placed a hand on Alec's shoulder. He looked him in the eye as he simply said, "Good luck old friend, your mother would be very proud of your bravery."

These words struck a chord with Alec as he smiled and embraced his friend, "Thank you" Alec said softly as he stepped to one side and proceeded to walk towards his target.

He proceeded to cautiously weave his way down the western pathway, careful not to alert any of the Koschei troops to his presence.

Being discovered at this stage would throw the entire mission. He carefully made his way to the canyon floor, carefully stepping over rocks and branches so as not to make too much noise.

The overlooking castle was much larger than he had realised, with dark stone set into its façade and long windows of stained glass reflecting a hazy smudge overhead. As he stared up at it, holding onto one of the horizontal pillars for stability, Alec wondered about this people's initial motivations for building such a monolith and keeping it running.

Finally, he arrived at the bottom of the canyon and peered out from behind a rocky outcrop. He saw Probetor standing there with a group of Koschei warriors, their numbers seemed to have doubled since he initially spotted them from on high. He could hardly believe that this was happening and all he could think about was getting back up there safely with the blade in hand.

He had no idea what Probetor was thinking nor why he was acting in such a suspicious manner, he only knew that something was amiss. Alec took a moment to compose himself, waiting for the commotion that would come once Logan and Josh showed themselves and caused the distraction intended. The concern with this plan at present was the sudden realisation that Probetor may well go himself.

Suddenly, his distraction took their mark and emerged from behind a rock formation further up the canyon. Alec had to take a second to adjust his eyes in uncertainty at what appeared before him. They had both adorned themselves in traditional Koschei armour though their faces were still clearly visible, showing that they had no intention of blending in with the oncoming army. They quickly made their way towards the troops who equally appeared confused, shouting orders in a commanding voice and waving their swords wildly about them. The distraction worked perfectly however as it caught the attention of every soldier present and they one by one began to follow the two warriors away from Alec's position and towards the opposite end of the canyon. Some at first thinking they were genuine others very aware they were imposters.

Probetor himself was no fool and immediately realised that they were imposters as he slammed his staff to the floor which sent out a signal to the nearest troops to attack. Josh turned to flee however Logan temporarily took a differing stance, throwing off his lame disguise in one swoop and brandishing his sword. He stepped forward into the charging forces and with one swipe of his blade instantly put pay to maybe ten charging soldiers. Alec could see the smile form on Logans face as he did so with great pleasure, this was enough to now allow him to turn and flee, taking the army of soldiers with him.

Probetor seemed to hesitate briefly before turning around and now heading into the walled area himself, he had decided against joining his troops in following the imposters, presenting Alec the opportunity required. He could see they were making progress as the chasing army began to vanish into the distance, only a handful remaining behind. With this he stepped out from his hiding place, quietly making his way towards the entrance of the walled area intent on following Probetor to wherever he may be heading.

He was aware that this was also where Gree and Jenny had disappeared to and he could feel his heart race as he prayed they would not be rejoining their leader.

As he moved closer, he felt himself begin to sweat as an all-too-common feeling swept over him, something was wrong. He stopped and debated turning back but as he looked around, he could see that whilst the majority of Koschei had left there were still some around and he would need to go through them as they moved locations ever so slightly.

As he tried to move, he discovered a new horror - he was paralyzed. His muscles were rigid and refused to obey his commands. He could feel an invisible force drawing him forward, as if some invisible puppet-strings pulled on every limb in turn. As his feet left the ground, panic set in and Alec felt powerless against the mysterious force that now possessed him. It guided him towards the walled-up entrance, turning his body with an unnatural strength until he faced the direction of the doorway. He felt as though something had invaded his body, ripping him apart from the inside. As he hung there, he wondered with fear what on earth was happening to him fearing the obvious answer. Then from the darkness he now faces he saw the dark figure of Probetor appear.

He smiled menacingly at him as he eyed his catch and uttered three simple words, "Hello my boy." Alec was struck with a fear he had never felt, every sense in his body told him to flee but there was nothing he could do, he just hung there around a foot off the ground unable to move or speak. From behind his father, he noticed two more figures appearing and did not need to see them fully to know it would be Gree and Jenny.

Jenny walked up to Alec and grabbed his face between her hands, she laughed menacingly as she poked fun at him, "Poor poor Alec, I told you that you wouldn't be able to escape me".

The force that had been holding him captive seemed to leave his body in an instant, allowing him a brief moment of respite. He looked at the trio before him knowing he was trapped, Probetor looking smug and Gree stood beside him, eager for whatever plan he had concocted.

Jenny stepped closer to Alec now, her eyes staring directly into his own. She seemed so much more beautiful than he had recalled but in a very dark fashion. She had always betrayed a rather dull and plain appearance but now she seemed different. Alec found himself extremely confused by her presence, even now knowing all he did, to him this was still the person he had loved and suffered so greatly from losing. She placed one hand on his cheek and said with a voice full of malice, "Now you are coming with us".

14) The bigger they are

The commander and Hypnos were now racing back down the tunnel, their feet pounding against the dirt as they made their way with haste to rejoin the troops. The land bridge to Lemuri was destroyed and this was now the only feasible way between the two islands, they must return to help their troops but also destroy the entrance to this tunnel before it is discovered. Hypnos could not help but wonder as he continued his fast-paced trip back about the mysterious robed woman, who was she and why had she assisted them so greatly, how did she do what she did and where on did she go?

He had so many questions but at this moment not the time to look into answers. The further they travelled, the more intense the battle appeared to be becoming as screams of agony and pain in the distance filled their senses with dread. They knew that the tower must now be taken, they clearly saw that it had become consumed by the battle and must have indeed fallen.

They soon reached the end of the tunnel, making their way up the stairs to see what faced them. It was chaos.

Probetor's forces had managed to push through the Nyx defences and were now advancing in any way they could, cutting off any escape routes or reinforcements from arriving and completely occupying what remained of the land bridge from Midjuns side. In desperation, General Araya had ordered his troops to abandon their position and called a partial retreat in an attempt to regroup away from enemy territory.

The commander stepped forward and shouted orders for his own army to join in with this retreat, despite the strong unwillingness to let Probetor's forces take over without a fight. Hypnos followed closely behind him, feeling determined but uncharacteristically scared; he had realised that this battle was lost but at least for now Lemuri was as safe as he could have possibly made it, but for the tunnel still being open it had been completely cut off.

He had found it odd that no Koschei had made their way towards the tunnel, he could only surmise that the entrance was a little out of the way of the general fighting and within the cliffs themselves so not visible enough to very sight driven warriors; equally, they weren't known for having any kind of tactical genius. Before he could action any destruction of the cliffs to prevent access however, he heard from behind him an almighty crash that reverberated around the surrounding landscape. He turned back towards the cliff and saw a mound of dirt and rubble obscure what was left of the entrance.

It looked like someone had scooped out part of it with a giant hand. He looked on baffled as to how he had such good fortune in having to have a land-slide come to the rescue until he glanced up and saw her again – the robbed woman, she stood atop the cliffs. She held her hands high above her head, running them along something only she could see. A wall of rocks fell onto the entrance from atop the rise. It was at least two dozen metres deep as she almost danced in her footsteps giving the appearance of enjoyment.

He looked on with disbelief until he saw movement at the top of the peak. This time a large shape appeared on top, which glistened in the moonlight – another one?

A bird with long thick legs unfolded its wings before beating them against gravity to take flight and with it the mysterious woman who had proven to be Hypnos saviour in this battle more than once. His curiosity was driving him wild; he was not a man who liked mystery nor did he like not knowing the answers. He hoped that once he made it back to Sofpavel, to Freyja, that she would at least be able to ease his mind with those answers. As he thought this however his attention turned back to the battle and for a brief moment his thought process changed from not when he returns to Sofpavel, but if.

He heard the loud sound of cracking and saw that the watchtower had been engulfed, with no sign of General Araya or his men attempting to hold them off any longer.

The tower swayed as Hypnos watched on in dismay, slowly it started to crumble down piece-by-piece until it gave way under the pressure, sending a huge cloud of dust into the air. Hypnos's heart sank as he watched what was left of the tower come crumbling down and a loud crash echoed throughout the land before him.

With a sense of despair, he realised that Probetor had finally cemented his win in this battle now without a shadow of a doubt, their work at protecting Lemuri though had hopefully provided them much needed resistance in the war itself. As the ancient tower crumbled into dust, a great cloud of stone and mortar floated upward out of its guts. The lofty eye perched on top of the battlement had for thousands of years provided protection and had watched over these lands. It was the first warning sign that disaster would soon come to the realms. As it crumbled into a heap in the sodden earth, it felt like the ground beneath their feet shifted with rough juts and cracks running erratic patterns through the land as old settled ideas broke down and unsettled reality came to be.

But before Hypnos could fully register the impact of this new reality, he heard a loud and deep voice echoing from an area just past the ruins. His heart leapt as he knew it to be General Araya, rallying his men back together despite their odds.

With a renewed vigour, Hypnos ran toward the source of this voice and soon enough saw an array of his comrades in that opening. General Araya stood tall and proud, hands held high above his head as he shouted words of encouragement and conviction for all to hear. He was joined by several of his most trusted advisors, holding flags aloft in defiance against Probetor's forces.

From atop a steep rock, Hypnos gazed down at the sight before him with awe. He marvelled at the pure triumph of this moment, which had been hard-won through an incredibly difficult battle of which was lost. The warriors moved into position with precision and purpose, executing their orders flawlessly. They were far from done.

Peering down from their lofty perch, they scrutinized the remaining Koschei and surveyed the tattered land bridge that stretched towards Lemuri. Araya realized with a jolt that the bottleneck entrance was ripe for ambush - Probetor's flimsy forces would crumble just as they did when pinned against the fire wall! The danger ahead was too great to risk moving forward, they would not survive the waters, yet retreating led to a wall of sharp steel. The narrow width of the land bridge was an inevitable chokepoint that gave the warriors a strategic advantage in battle.

The men stared up at Hypnos, the flickering firelight casting a warm glow on his face. A newfound sense of hope and optimism filled their hearts. After their beloved general had pulled them back from the brink of despair, seeing the legend that is Hypnos beside them gave them an unshakable feeling of courage and hope.

Likewise for the commander - though he was still grieving the loss of his home, he could feel a wave of passion radiating through his men like a wild fire. A roar erupted from them as they rushed down towards Probetor's army in a powerful display of might; swords gleaming above their heads and shields held high to challenge any who stood in their way. The ground trembled beneath them with each thunderous step, hundreds of Nyx against thousands of

Koschei soldiers who thought they had already won, until the might of the ever-resilient Nyx descended upon them like a ferocious storm wreathed in glory.

The sound of clashing swords echoed through the valley, mingling with the grunts, shouts and cries of wounded soldiers, filling Hypnos' ears with a jarring symphony of violence. The smell of blood hung heavy in the air, mixing with sweat to create a pungent aroma that was both sickening and alluring. For a moment, he closed his eyes to savour the sweet taste of victory despite the horrors it may cause as though it had already happened.

The Nyx forces made their way to the land bridge, determined to secure its expanse and ensure that Probetor's followers could not pass.

General Araya and Hypnos led the charge with courage and vigour, inspiring their allies every step of the way. The men moved with swiftness and agility, outmanoeuvring Probetor's army at every turn. Soon enough they had managed to take control at the mouth of the land bridge, having slayed a good portion of soldiers along the way and pushing many others into the small space.

The Koschei soldiers at the front now fought back however found themselves running into blades and their own dead forces laying upon the ground. The bodies began to pile up and the Koschei found themselves in disarray not able to fight effectively against the mighty Nyx soldiers, virtually having to go one on one. The Nyx advanced steadily with the three great leaders of Hypnos, Araya and the commander leading the line. They continued to move forward, one unstoppable moving machine as Koschei forces at the other end found themselves being pushed into the surrounding waters.

Before long Hypnos swung his sword once more and stopped, there were no longer bodies running towards him, the clashes of metal had stopped and the ground around fell silent, if only for a second before an almighty cheer erupted. From the brink of defeat, they had been victorious, not in the war no but within this battle.

The watchtower had been lost, as the land bridge to Lemuri, but it was secured and their hold on Lemuri kept safe. For now, at least.

Hypnos surveyed the carnage around him and sighed in sadness. He was a warrior, trained to fight and to kill, but he could not help but feel sorrow for the lives lost here today. Though their cause had been just, he could not shake the thought that so many had needlessly been taken from this world, either by his sword or another's. His gaze fell upon the mangled body of a fallen soldier who had no doubt fought bravely in this battle. Hypnos knelt beside him and closed his eyes in silent prayer before moving on.

The scene around him seemed almost dreamlike, as if it were all some kind of strange nightmare that would end when he awoke. He saw fellow soldiers carrying away bodies of those who had fallen in battle, their faces stoic yet solemn as they moved from person to person with respect and reverence for those who gave their lives for the cause. Along with them came medics carrying wounded allies back to safety while others searched for survivors among the dead and dying; Hypnos drank it all in with a heavy heart.

As he looked up into the darkening dusk sky, Hypnos' mind wandered back to something else entirely - the woman who had been hugely influential in this victory, one who had helped to hold back Probetor's tyranny.

Where she had come from and the identity of this person remained a mystery and one that Hypnos was eager to uncover. He saw Araya standing nearby. He was looking around himself, lifting soldiers who were kneeling or otherwise struggling and assisting the arriving medics. He paused himself as he looked around and Hypnos had no doubt that he was having similar thoughts to his own.

"Araya" Hypnos called out. He saw Araya slowly turn; he held his arms in front of himself as he looked upon Hypnos as if to question the mess around them.

"Where does this madness end Hypnos?" He questioned. "Was all of this worth it?" Hypnos immediately responded with sympathetic frustration.

"Of course. Death is never worth it however the lives lost here today were to ensure the protection and security of the billions throughout the realms. Even if we lose the war, we can at least say we fought." Araya nodded, he knew this all too well, Nyx laid their lives down when needed and indeed dying in battle was an honour. However, his frustration at the levels this was reaching showed through.

"Sorry Hypnos, I know, I know" he responded solemnly.

"It is ok old friend" Hypnos said laying a hand on his shoulder. "Let's get the injured back to Sofpavel and set up a new camp here with those who remain, we need to ensure the island now remain secured. They will return with a new wave soon enough."

Hypnos could not shake the feeling that he must return to Freyja, to find out more about the mysterious woman. He needed to know also if the others were making progress, there had been no word back to his knowledge.

With a heavy heart he decided to travel back with the injured currently being transported away from Midjun. He bid farewell to Araya and the others who were to remain behind, wishing them luck in their mission and hoping that his decision would not come at a cost. There was much still to be done before they could declare victory in this conflict, but Hypnos was determined that the cause remain just and that they should take some pleasure from this win.

He assisted the wounded onto the various carts and horses being used to carry those who could not make their own way back on this trip. He raised his sword preparing to sheathe it, pausing as he noticed a light still running its way around the blade.

Lemuri's magic still lingered on within the sword it seemed, as his mind cast back again to the woman who placed it there. He rolled it around in his hand a few times secretly hoping that this power would remain, he liked the look it created along the blade and enjoyed the extra power he felt whilst utilising it.

He turned once more to check on those he left behind, he knew in the hands of Araya and the commander that they were well catered for but he could not help but feel a small amount of guilt in departing, even if it was only to be temporary.

15) Family ties

Alec awoke with a start, for a second, he thought he had done so from a nightmare. He felt he had dreamt he had just been captured, that Jenny had been taunting him and worst of all that he had failed in his mission.

But alas, it took all of a few seconds for him to realise that it had been no dream but instead stark reality. The room was round with curved walls that met the dome-shaped ceiling in a seamless connection. The ceiling itself had a small opening that let in a dim light and howling wind, accompanied by occasional lightning flashes. Dust, or greenery, it was hard to tell, fell lightly like snowflakes through the dimness and the silence.

He scooted up higher on his bed and took in his surroundings. He was in a relatively comfortable bed that looked like something you'd find in a farmer's house; the kind of bed where children would hide underneath if they didn't want their parents to find them because it was so big and squishy and they knew no one would find them there unless they wanted to be found. Surprisingly he felt quite refreshed. A kerosene lamp sat on a small unsteady wooden table to his left with a chair that looked like it may collapse should he try to sit on it, cobwebs had gathered around its legs over the years and made it seem all that more uninviting.

He noticed movement and jumped before becoming slightly embarrassed with himself, realising it was just a rat scurrying from one corner to the other in search of food. He sighed and looked around for clues as to his whereabouts.

He soon heard the sound of footsteps on the stone path outside, someone had come by to check on him, he thought. As the door creaked opened, he braced himself for whoever may come through, but much to his surprise Probetor himself walked in carrying a tray containing something to eat and drink.

He was pleased to see Alec awake as he smiled with a sinister warmth at Alec before saying "It is so nice to finally meet you my son".

His voice was oddly normal and not what Alec had recalled hearing previously.

The sentence itself almost seeming sincere and throwing Alec into a zone he felt uncomfortable.

Probetor placed the tray down on the chair before stepping calmly away, Alec looked at it for a second increasingly aware of his own hunger. He was however reluctant to eat anything provided at this moment and felt concerned that the spider who had worked so diligently creating the webbed chair may set up home within this food before he would have the chance to eat it. Probetor walked over to the bed and sat himself down slowly, he sighed as though he was letting himself relax for the first time in quite a while.

He gestured towards the tray, "eat please, you will be hungry and I promise you the food is safe." Alec looked again at the tray reluctantly. He decided against taking any of the offerings no matter how tempting they may be.

"What is going on here?" Alec begun feeling slightly bolder due to Probetor's lightened demeanour, "This is not a reunion and we are not friends."

Probetor laughed and nodded in acknowledgment whilst Alec slinked back, again feeling a little embarrassed, the words seemed adequate in his head but sounded much less so spoken aloud.

The truth was undeniable - you had every right to question my intent. I brought you here to this place, hoping to protect you from the wicked forces rapidly encroaching upon us all; they were unavoidable and imminent. I saw in your eyes that you wanted me dead as soon as I arrived, yet I resisted. I knew that the dark forces which have haunted me for years, and sought to manipulate and control our realm, posed themselves as something 'good'. It was my aim to eradicate this falsehood and liberate our world - what could possibly be wrong with that?"

Probetor's voice was serious as he spoke, his eyes searching Alec's hoping for him to believe.

"It may be hard for you to understand now but there will come a time where these events, no matter how painful they may feel will make sense. I knew you existed and I tried to reach out to you. I had Jenny sent to you to watch over you and to try to convince you to come here. Her developing a relationship with you was her own doing and a cruel twist I shan't lie and I apologise for this. Just remember Alec that these people who you think are good, they tore our family apart. They are not the good they claim to be. I knew they would bring you here and I give them credit for how well they have guarded you from the truth, they played their part so very well."

Alec's thoughts were a jumble, but instead of speaking he resolved to stay quiet and let his father finish before pressing him for more answers. He knew there must be something more than what Probetor let on, something far more sinister than just protecting him from what he is calling the 'dark forces', especially when this whole time he believed him to be just this. However, he knew that darkness was subjective and two opposing sides will often both see themselves as the ones in the right. Sometimes the evil does not know that it is so.

Probetor saw the confusion in Alec's eyes and sighed.

"I know that this is a lot to take in for you. But please, trust me on this. Let me guess what you have heard, what you have read in the books they have written. You are told that the forces I speak of are not just a group of people with differing opinions. That we are a cult that seek to enslave humanity and bring about the end of the world as we know it. That we have infiltrated every aspect of society and have been manipulating events for centuries. We are masters of deception and will stop at nothing to achieve our goals. Is this about right? Do I really seem this way?"

He couldn't believe what he was hearing. Was his father trying to tell him that he was not the bad side of this fight? He was very convincing and every bit as manipulative as he had been warned. Did he think that Alec would think he was telling the truth or was this all some elaborate delusion and he believed this to be true? He decided to take a chance and speak up.

"How do you plan to fight them? What can you do to stop them?"

Probetor smiled.

"It won't be easy. But we do have a plan. We have been gathering a group of like-minded individuals who share our beliefs and are willing to fight for what is right. We have also been studying the enemy and have discovered their weaknesses. With your help, we can strike a decisive blow and put an end to their reign of terror."

He stood up and pushed his dark heavy cloak across his shoulders, revealing what drew Alec into this situation to start with – the sword of Morpheus.

The blackened blade was unmistakable in its darkness as he twisted the scorched metal within his fingers. As Alec looked upon it, he could see movement down the blade itself, like a river being drawn out from an ocean of molten blackness. Alec couldn't take his eyes off the sword. It seemed to hold a power never seen before. He found it mesmerising and yet disturbing at the same time.

Probetor pulled his cloak back into position hiding the blade from sight once again. Alec noticed as he did so that his fingers themselves had blackened from where he touches the sword, clearly leaving a mark on him bit by bit.

"I have no doubt within my mind that you know what this is, yet what you know of it may not be quite true," Probetor continued now having risen to his feet and walking around the room in circles, looking down towards the floor, his arms folded neatly behind his back. "This is the Sword of Morpheus, although named after him as the last holder I feel, as I always knew it under the name Angurvagal," Probetor continued. "It's a powerful weapon that had been passed down in our family for generations. It has the power to cut through anything, even magical beings themselves. I was next in line for it originally, it should be mine."

He seemed to grow more resentful as he spoke about it, not having been bestowed with this weapon and missing what he felt was his birth right cut deep. "My teacher, nay, my saviour the Jinn bought me back here, and he is trapped within this blade. Again, a tale I am sure you are familiar with. It is not just the magic of the sword itself that holds him in here but also the will of Lemuri. In order to free him I must plunge the sword into the having falls themselves. Something you may not be as aware of however, behind the falls lies a room and within its walls stands what is known as the Drasal tree."

Alec had in fact seen this name written in some of the text he had read however it was barely given any real credence and written about flippantly, it appeared all of those who mentioned it seemed to feel it did not exist.

"Within the Drasal tree lies a hidden power. It is believed that upon placing Angurvagal within its trunk, your wish for transport to any realm of your desire will be granted. This is how the elders used to transmit through the realms and access remained free until Lemuri decided no more. Not only that but it also grants you greater control over time and space as well. Gaining control of this tree, and with this sword, we will be able to move throughout the lands of this realm and beyond easily, allowing us to spread our message." He paused now looking directly back at Alec as if he was waiting for his response. "I want you to help me free my people from the clutches of those who have wronged them, and I wish for you to be by my side in doing so."

Alec stood struggling to grasp all that he was hearing. His father sounded convincing however Alec had seen enough to know this cannot all be true. He knew within his heart that his father was lying, what he could not be sure of was if his father himself knew this.

Alec responded by shaking his head, unable to accept this proposition. He stepped back, his feet moving towards the door in an attempt to escape.

His father's expression hardened and he called out for Alec to stop. "If you leave now then I cannot guarantee your safety, Gree feels you a liability, as do the others and they wish for me to kill you" he said solemnly in a voice that held a deep resonance of power and truth. Despite the warning Alec was determined to flee and continued his path towards the door.

As he grabbed at the handle, he soon found it would not turn - it had been sealed shut from within. As he pulled harder at the door a shock was sent up his arm that jolted him back a few feet.

"It appears you have no choice but to help me", Probetor said with a hint of spite in his voice. The atmosphere was tense as Alec thought about what to do next - stay and help Probetor or risk trying to break through the door and face an almost certain demise? Struggling against this decision he looked towards Probetor who stood waiting for him to make up his mind with a look of anticipation on his face.

Alec turned away from his captor and began searching around the room for any other possible escape route that could potentially find him free whilst Probetor stood watching him, growing ever more frustrated. As Alec continued searching for options, he wished he had his staff, he had recently realised he no longer had in it his possession and wondered at what point he either lost it or had it taken from him. He felt without it he could not possibly channel enough power to do anything, his power thus far having been used via this conduit.

He sensed the room darkening, it was as if a cloud was filling the air around him.

"Why Alec can you not just listen to reason?" He heard Probetor question, "I thought you may even be pleased to see me, reunited with your lost father." His hands raised up next to himself in frustration, "you must understand, if it was not for these people and their rules, their judgements and their punishments, you me and Gaia would still be together"

A sharp pain threw itself at Alec's heart, stopping it dead in his chest like a knife as Probetor spoke his mother's name.

A gust of icy air billowed from Probetor's mouth as he became more and more energized, with a black fire swirling around him and a radiant aura radiating from his raised figure. Alec felt pressured against the wall as he widened his eyes, their luminescence brilliantly piercing through the bleak darkness - it was like a sun rising in a night sky.

"Together we could have it all, we would be unstoppable." Air rushed around Alec as if sucked from his body by an invisible vacuum cleaner. He gasped for breath; his heart beat faster; blood coursed through him like a flash flood storming over dry land. Stillness—then sudden fury—broke over him. He felt the anger swelling inside himself as Probetor spoke and managed to take a gulp of this air before screaming back.

"NO!" At this moment Probetor lowered himself back to the ground and a deathly calm overcame the room.

"Very well" he said, his voice tinged with sadness for a moment before returning to normalcy and control, cool in its monotone disregard for human suffering or emotion. "I tried, I hoped you would join me, instead you will have to remain here. I will tell you when it is done, when those you have conspired with are gone, although given the shift it shall make across the realms, I feel you will know."

With this Alec felt two metal bracelets take hold of his wrists and pull him back towards the bed, at this moment he realised he was essentially now bound, chained, a real prisoner in its truest sense.

No matter how much he struggled, the bracelets could not be removed, and it was then that he knew that these were not for aesthetics. He had been trapped in this room by Probetor's spell, and all of his efforts served to confirm it. There was nothing left but to accept his fate; he would remain here until Probetor chose otherwise.

Alec knew now that even if he could somehow manage to escape the confines of this chamber, the bracelets would keep him there - unable to cast any spells of any kind without his staff and realising that even with it these bracelets were designed to prevent escape He could feel the electricity buzzing through them each time he thought of fighting, they were designed to hold you back in every way. The realization hit him; all hope seemed lost as the truth gradually sunk in. With a deep sigh Alec resigned himself to his new reality, knowing full well that there was no escaping from Probetor's lair.

16) Into the fire

"Where is he?" Josh exclaimed.

They had shaken off the chasing Koschei soldiers, all bar the few that Logan felt an incredible urge to cut down. He had no need to, in fact it would have been simpler for their part of the plan if he had not, he simply could not help himself.

They had now circled back and were once again staring down into the great canyon before them. There was little movement down there now, the majority of Koschei had given chase and were still hunting. A few hundred of their forces still loomed, however this seemed but a small speck compared to the numbers before. More concerning for them was the lack of Alec of Probetor. They assumed Alec had followed him somewhere but he knew this left him vulnerable and in an unknown state.

Logan began to pace, the frustration and worry for this man he had grown quite fond of was beginning to show. He could not help but focus on the fact that he had agreed to this plan despite knowing it was unsafe. Failing in a mission, especially one of such gravity was a pain that Logan could not bear.

"No! We have to go down there and find him!" He shouted turning towards Josh who was struggling to accept the reality that his friend could well be in a lot of trouble, his eyes remained focused intently upon the canyon before them – searching for any sign of their missing friend hoping in vain that he may be there, somewhere.

Logan's almost aggressive response was enough to quieten Josh as he was secretly always a little concerned by his unbalanced nature. Logan himself however even knew this was not wise, even with their combined forces and his proclivity for the fight they would be greatly outnumbered here and especially vulnerable. He felt panicked, but he knew they had to keep going. He glanced at Josh, who was willing to take action to find his friend yet still appeared reluctant. Taking a deep breath, he realized there was no turning back.

"Alright, let's do this." Logan spoke in a gentle tone, barely louder than a whisper. Josh nodded and they both started walking down the canyon towards where Probetor was sighted last.

As they descended into the deep canyon below, the air seemed to become thicker, almost oppressive. It felt as though each step brought them closer to something dangerous but they could not turn back now. They continued on, treading carefully as their feet stepped over stones and brush alike. All around them the walls of the canyon seemed to close in further – each one trying to push them away from their destination yet neither of them willing or able to abandon Alec.

The entrance of the old temple looms before Logan and Josh, its dark entranceway casting an intimidating shadow. The ancient stone walls are marred by rusting brackets marking where grand gates once stood. Stepping through reveals a surprisingly large chamber, illuminated by a few torches that flicker with magical light against an otherwise engulfing darkness.

The room was deathly still aside from some scuttling noises coming from the corner. Josh was the first to spot it, a long wooden staff leaning against the far wall – Alec's staff! Its presence had been lost in the dull torchlight but Josh recognised it instantly. He instinctually reached for his weapon as alarm flooded within him, they were definitely too late – Alec must have already been here and he had no doubt been taken prisoner. Logan however seemed unfazed by what he saw, instead turning his attention towards some faint steps at the back of the chamber that led down into an underground passageway. There was one way to go now and Logan knew they had to take it; if they didn't find Alec there then this mission would be considered a failure and worse still could result in something more sinister happening to their lost friend. The staff was great as confirmation that his instincts were correct as they usually were but the goal here was to find Alec and he remained focused solely on that task alone.

So, they collected Alec's staff and Josh stowed it upon himself, they then carefully made their way down the stairs. As they walked, an unusual chill ran down Logan's spine as he felt the immense pressure of the situation. He had not really felt fear before as he usually enjoyed throwing himself into dangerous situations but something felt off here - like there was an unknown force deep in this place that could put them all at risk if disturbed or even worse, if released.

The darkness seemed to grow thicker as they continued further down the corridor with very little light and Logan wondered how long it would take for his eyes to adjust should he need to rely on his vision. After what seemed like an eternity of walking, a faint glimmer of light emerged from around a corner ahead of them and with increasing curiosity the two ventured forward while still remaining vigilant of their surroundings.

As they rounded the corner, a gasp escaped both their mouths as what lay before them was unlike anything either had ever seen before – a vast chamber filled with ancient symbols and artefacts, lit by hundreds upon hundreds of glowing candles that lined each wall creating shimmering reflections along every surface in sight – it was breathtakingly beautiful yet incredibly eerie at the same time.

Josh spotted an upwards stairwell to the left and summoned to logan alerting him of its presence, they both made their way in that direction careful not to disturb anything.

As they approached the stairwell Josh noticed Logan had dropped back, he turned to see him staring into the darkness, sword held aloft. The far end of this chamber was not visible, it was not possible to see how far it went and no light lit the way. It symbolised to Josh the kind of darkness that would create the fear of dark in a child's eyes. However, something within had caught Logans attention.

"Logan, what's wrong?" Josh whispered. Logan raised a hand to Josh, indicating a wish for him to wait before slowly beckoning him over with that same hand.

"There is something in there," Logan whispered, "Something I am not familiar with."

Josh peered into the vast expanse of inky blackness before him, and felt a presence like something was watching them. He stared harder into the darkness, desperately willing his eyes to adjust so he could see what was hidden within. Creeping out from the dark a thin tendril of smoke appeared from the abyss and coiled towards them, accompanied by an ominous trembling beneath their feet. He knew there was danger lurking in the shadows, but he couldn't help but be drawn forward despite knowing he should turn away.

"Whatever it is it is not engaging, let's move on," Josh said, tugging on Logans arm to make his wish clear.

Logan reluctantly agreed and began to head towards the stairwell with him, he never turned his back to the dark and kept his sword aloft but other than that puff of smoke nothing materialised.

They made their way up the open sided concrete staircase, each step echoing around the chamber as if trying to have them caught. Once Logan and his companion have ascended the steps, they come upon a door that Logan gazes at for some time before pushing it open.

A glimmer of light trickles through the crack penetrating into the dark chambers behind them. Logan looks through before opening the door and stepping through entering into a tall dark large room filled with ancient stone walls and an ornate throne sitting at its centre. It was as if time had stopped in this place, nothing was disturbed or had moved in what must have been hundreds of years, frescoes and tapestries adorned each wall so thick in dust they were barely visible, intricate patterns carved majestically into the ceilings above them watched them with intrigue as they carefully made their way deeper into the room.

Logan lets out a huff as he turns to Josh with eyes wide open, "This is it!" he exclaims, "I suspected it would lead here."

Josh did not need Logan to elaborate, he knew they had entered Maredrom's castle.

It was obvious that they had arrived in the throne room of Maredrom, as it existed long ago when it was ruled by royalty. Although Maredrom functioned independently, its presence acted as a necessary counterbalance to other more tyrannical nations.

Circling the throne were strange ornate statues, their faces stern and hidden away from view. A creepy light illuminated through a window at the back of the chamber whilst shadows danced from unnaturally placed candles that looked as though they had been lit for centuries.

Logan moved to the throne itself and places his hand on its arm rest before turning to Josh with a snarl, "This is where he must have sat, where Probetor no doubt seats himself now...." His words are soon broken by a sudden flurry of movement in shadows behind them. Both Logan and Josh spin around quickly, yet all they find is a raven scurrying through some debris on the ground. Josh chuckles to himself feeling how tense he currently was. Josh felt uncomfortable as he looked upon the throne, it was an imposing and sinister structure that seemed to radiate darkness from its every corner. He could feel the ancient powers that laced this room.

"Come" Logan summoned, "We must continue, I feel Alec's presence within these walls, I do not believe him to be far."

Just as Logan finished his sentence, they both heard a sound of footsteps coming from an adjoining hallway. Knowing that this was not their own doing Logan grabbed Josh and pulled him behind one of the statues. He then motioned for silence and ensured that they were hidden from view.

The footsteps outside the door were getting closer with every heart-stop-ping second. Logan and Josh held their breath as they heard the grating of met-al against stone, warning them of Probetor's impending arrival. With a deafen-ing roar, the doorway was flung open and in stepped Probetor, his face fixed with grim determination as Gree followed closely behind him. The two men moved slowly but surely towards the throne, speaking in raspy tones that filled the air with an ominous feeling.

Probetor took a brief seat on the throne before rising again as he began pac-ing around the room as if looking for something. He was agitated and Logan could not help but be curious as to what was causing such a cold calculated per-son to be acting in such a way. He appeared distracted as if deep in thought, he then raised his hands above him as if feeling some unseen force pressing down upon him.

Probetor then turns his gaze towards Logan and Josh's hiding place, almost as if he knew they were there all along. He stood still for a second before con-tinuing his pacing, if he was aware of their presence, he chose to ignore it.

Gree moved closer towards him and began to whisper something into Pro-betor's ear which caused him to smile before responding with an affirmative nod. They both then began to walk back out of the chamber in the opposing direction to the one they had arrived from, talking quietly amongst themselves until their voices were gone and all was silent again.

Logan heaved a sigh of relief, bewildered by the near-miss they had just ex-perienced. For a split second his mind began to fantasize about taking Probetor in an epic battle, but he knew that if he did there would be no chance of finding Alec.

Steeling himself, Logan glanced at Josh, who mirrored the same mixture of elation and fear. Without delay they both rose from their hiding spot looking around for which way to head next.

Logan stopped and turned towards the hallway Probetor had emerged from, he knew that if they were to find Alec then this was their only current lead. He looked at Josh who seemed to agree with him before making their way down the corridor. They both walked forward, cautiously peering into each room as they made their way further and further into the castle until eventually coming to the base of a flight of stairs. Looking upwards it was clear that this was one of the castles many towers. The first step however appeared to be surrounded by some kind of magical barrier preventing entry. Clearly, they were hiding something up there.

Logan felt drawn towards this place, it called out to him as if beckoning him closer.

After taking a few steps he turned around with determination on his face - he had made up his mind, this is where Alec has been taken and now it was time for him and Josh to find a way to reach him. The thought of being this close created a new will and they knew that they now could not turn back without Alec in tow. However, there was no time to think of a way to reach him, as the second they stepped a few more feet forward Probetor and Gree emerged from the shadows behind them.

Logan and Josh were shocked and stood still in fear, they had been so close to laying eyes on Alec but now their focus was on the two figures standing before them.

Logan instantly flung his sword toward Probetor, but the blade spun in a wide arc. It was as if Logan wasn't controlling it at all. A gust of wind knocked him off his feet as he fell back with a resounding thump. He struggled to lift himself from the ground, but he was unable to move with any huge purpose. The strength within Logan showed as Probetor struggled to hold together the spell that kept him there and felt himself having to concentrate more of his energy on this task than he would have wished, the strain starting to show on his face.

Josh fought against his own invisible force, trying desperately to untangle himself from the supernatural rope that held him prisoner but he was not strong in physicality and could not put up much of a fight. Gree seemed to be more intrigued by their presence and less willing to become involved, as if he could sense something about the two of them that others could not - something that even Probetor was possibly unaware of. He continued to survey them as if expecting something more, but after a few moments he seemed satisfied with what he saw and began speaking in a deep yet calming voice.

"You have come here looking for someone have you not? I could help you find him if you are willing to listen," he said with an authoritative tone. "But first we must find out exactly who you are."

Logan was unable to speak such was the force that Probetor was having to use on him, Josh however could and shared a look of confusion before he spoke up tentatively. "We are searching for our friend Alec, I know the answer to this question already but have you seen him?"

Gree smiled at this; he knew that indeed he did already know the answer.

"Yes, I have seen your friend Alec," he said calmly. "He is one of us now however, maybe you should return home?" He said looking at Josh "Your big friend here however we will have to dispose of I am afraid, he seems too much of a liability to have running around."

Josh looked at Gree horrified and unsure of what to believe or take from what had just been said, he cannot agree to Logan being killed in order to free himself but what else could he do? Die with him? He also did not believe that Alec had turned, he knew Alec, they had grown together and he was always determined to do what was right.

"You lie" Josh replied, " Alec would not abandon us, he would die first, he was prepared to do so."

Gree smiled pleased to have provoked an apparently rather emotional response. "You are right, he nearly did choose to die for you but this was his father he was speaking to and he saw sense, he saw the reality of what the world truly was rather than the story he had been fed by you and yours. I can offer you a way out though Josh, just agree to one simple task and I will set you free."

With this Gree walked over to Josh before raising his hands in front of him and muttering words so low that Josh could not hear them – a faint glow emitting from Gree's hands as he spoke.

The spell seemed to unravel with each syllable spoken and soon Josh stood freely – although surprised by what had just happened – giving Gree an inquisitive glance.

With this Gree beckoned to Josh to follow before turning away and heading back into the throne room. Josh followed on reluctantly leaving Logan writhing in pain on the floor yet feeling relieved to no longer be trapped himself. He thought whilst walking about whether he should fight back or try to run but he knew there was little he could do. As he walked away, he could hear Logan scream and stopped, he wished to turn back and help but Gree spoke in a calm and quiet tone.

"Head back into that room and you all die. Follow me, and you may well yet live." Josh knew he had no choice as the sound of Logans screams pierced his ears and filled him with an anger and frustration that he felt heightened by his inability to act on. Gree led Josh through the throne room and back down the stairs towards the large opening below the castle by which they had earlier entered.

Gree then motioned towards the darkness and Josh looked deeply into it seeing nothing but black. "To earn this freedom Josh," He instructed, "slay what lay in the shadows and I shall set you free". He handed him a blade and stepped back smiling.

Josh looked into the darkness to where the smoke had been seen earlier and he saw glowing back in the dark a deep set of red eyes looking back at him. It was a giant beast with four legs, scales that shimmered like rubies and razor-sharp claws on its feet that showed numerous scars from battles long past.

Although fearful, Josh knew he had no choice but to face this beast of legend or else perish alongside Logan. He had read stories but thought these creatures long extinct, lost to the history books and the tales of old. He raised his blade, took a deep breath and then ran towards it screaming as loud as he could – hoping that sheer force of will would help him win but he knew he could not. He was simply running to his death but he knew that nobody had ever before slayed a dragon.

17) Lucky escape

The dragon swiped at Josh with its claws and knocked him down, seemingly playing with him like a kitten with a ball of yarn. He was sent sprawling across the ground, barely able to keep his grip on the blade as he tumbled backwards.

Utterly terrified, Josh tried to scramble back onto his feet, readying himself for another attack. The dragon lumbered forward with a mighty roar and spread its wings wide. Its scales glimmered in the dim light from the surrounding torches and its eyes burned brightly like embers from a fire. Josh knew he had no chance of defeating such a beast and instead desperately searched for some way to flee. But it was too late; the dragon's clawed talons were already reaching out towards him, ready to deliver death's embrace. He stood prepared to fight but as the glow could be seen building in the beasts' throat Gree shouted a few incoherent words and the dragon stopped, it slunk back into the darkness and settled. Josh was confused, he stood panting for a second, his earlier wounds had largely been reopened as the blood glimmered next to a few fresh ones he now had. Gree laughed menacingly as he walked down the last few steps to the cold stone floor below.

"I do not intend for you to die here if truth be told, I did wish for you to see what we have. This delightful fellow listens to me and me alone."

He walked over and patted the beast on the snout as though he had arrived home after a day of work to be greeted by his Labrador.

"Hypnos seems to feel he has won the battle on Midjun, I guess he did. However, in the war ahead he stands no chance, none of you do. However, I wish to offer you all the chance to stand aside." Josh listened intently, he knew if Gree released this dragon, it would destroy everything and kill them all. They had no way of possibly winning this war. What already seemed like a mountainous task had now become an impossibility surely.

"I want for you to return back to Sofpavel and to tell them of what you have discovered, that Alec is lost along with Logan and if they do not surrender the dragon will be let loose. They must stand aside or else they and those who follow shall face the same fate. I am sure this creature will be more than capable of destroying any army sent against us with joy."

He stepped back and began to head back up the stairs, "Good luck," he said a smirk spreading across his face as Josh looked at him in disbelief.

Gree had just given an ultimatum, either surrender the realms to Maredrom's will or risk facing certain death. Either way it seemed like Gree would end up victorious.

Josh knew he had no choice but to accept Gree's offer and play messenger boy, turning away from the beast he had almost become a victim of and slowly heading away to make the difficult trip alone. As Josh realises, he must leave he hears a commotion from above as Probetor throws Logan down the stairs. Josh looked back in horror as Gree lifted Logan off the ground with ease, seemingly unaware of his size compared to what lay before him. He then threw Logan into the darkness towards the blood thirsty creature in its depths.

Gree laughed once again before continuing on "You now know your fate Josh should you fail, make sure Sofpavel knows too."

Logan had managed to stand despite his many injuries, ready to fight an enemy much larger and stronger than himself. He leaned on a stone pillar as blood seeped from his side, seemingly a stab wound along with other various cuts that were too numerous to count. Josh felt distressed looking at this great warrior standing so bloodied and bruised. Logan looked back at Josh and winked, his fearlessness more stupidity than bravery. He held a small sword in his hand, his own weapon had been taken away, but it seemed pitifully inadequate against the sheer size of the dragon. Josh felt helpless; there was nothing he could do except wait and watch for the inevitable outcome of this battle.

He watched on as Logan stood tall and proud against the dragon as the first few swings wildly began to be cast. He had expected Logan to be killed instantly but as time went on it became clear that Logan was not going to go down without a fight. He parried the dragon's claws away expertly with his sword and avoided its breath of fire with some incredible agility.

The dragon seemed annoyed by this show of courage and seemed to realize that it would take more than brute strength to defeat this man. It began to circle around Logan, trying to outmanoeuvre him and gain the advantage. But no matter what it did, Logan seemed prepared for it, always staying one step ahead of its moves.

Eventually the dragon grew tired of the game and decided to end it quickly. It reared up on its hind legs before lunging forward with its mouth wide open ready to consume Logan in one bite. But just before it reached him, Logan jumped aside and rolled behind a large rock for safety.

The beast took the unprecedented decision to begin smashing its head against the rock in an attempt to break it open. But try as it might, the rock was too strong and did not move an inch despite all of its efforts.

Meanwhile Josh had been watching all of this from afar, feeling quite helpless in this situation. He looked around hoping to find some way of helping Logan but knew there was none, he was a complete bystander in this situation and just had to hope with all he had that Logan could do something, anything.

Neither Gree nor Probetor had noticed Josh still even standing there such was the level of concentration they both currently had towards the ensuing conflict, their bloodthirsty eyes longing for the final blow that took Logan's life but both equally happy to watch as the dragon almost played with its new toy.

With one final powerful swing of its long tail, the dragon knocked Logan onto his back and reared up for a killing blow. As the dragon begun its lunge downwards to finish the task Logan managed to push himself using his feet off one of the nearby pillars, as he slid across the floor, he thrust the blade upwards with all of his might, yet despite striking the dragon aggressively he could barely make much more than a sharp scratch yet causing the dragon some discomfort in his attempts.

The dragon unleashed its fury upon the castle, shaking the foundations to their core. Gree watched in horror as it hammered on the ground beneath them with enough force to shatter the pillars and send debris raining down from above. He yelled at the beast in frustration, demanding that it cease, but his words had no effect - the dragon was now consumed with blind rage and there seemed little he could do to stop it, he had lost control.

Gree did not wish for the castle to fall in order to achieve his goal and had indeed expected the beast to quickly dispose of Logan. He stood frustrated as the dragon paid no attention to his commands now with genuine concern that the plan they had set in place was now crumbling with the foundations of the castle itself. Their eagerness to smugly dispose of Logan and show their strength was now turning against them.

Probetor stepped in front of the enraged beast, staring it down with a ferocity that Gree had not expected, nor was very fond of. The dragon was his to control and he did not appreciate the interference. For a moment the creature seemed to consider Probetor's command before relenting and stepping back. It pounded the ground once more, this time creating an abyssal void beneath them in what had now become a very weak and unstable floor. An angry river surged below, beckoning Logan towards freedom.

It was now or never and seizing this opportunity for freedom, Logan grabbed hold of Josh and together they ran towards the edge of the pit that had opened up beneath them. In one last, desperate move Logan pushed off with all his strength, propelling them both through the air towards the raging waters below before either Probetor or Gree had an opportunity to react.

As they plummeted towards the river they began to brace for impact, but instead of hitting the icy cold water that awaited them they were caught by a large branch that had somehow managed to latch onto a nearby wall.

It slowed their descent, giving Logan enough time to grab a mental map of their current location and plan out their escape route before they eventually fell into the raging waters below.

The river flowed hard and fast around them, pulling at both of them as it raced towards its destination. The current was strong and neither Logan nor Josh had either the strength or will to fight against it; all they could do was let it take them where it may.

Josh noticed far beneath them that the river darkened and looked almost tar like, the nightmare orbs that Lemuri drew from these lands flowed fast through its darkness. For what felt like an eternity they floated down stream until eventually coming to rest a few miles from the castle, not incredibly far from where their journey began when they made landfall here.

Logan wasted no time dragging Josh out of the water and onto dry land before collapsing himself. His body felt heavy and his mind felt foggy, but he knew that if he was going to survive this ordeal then he needed to keep moving – there were still many miles between him and safety and no time for rest or recovery. He held onto the small blade he now had in one hand while using his other arm to help steady Josh. Logan himself was injured greatly, the dragon had failed to kill him but had given it a good attempt. Josh himself was quite injured in the fall, his old wounds having already reopened and he seemed to be taking some time to clear his mind and be entirely aware of their current situation.

Logan looked at them both and then at their surroundings. They were both unable to fight on and they were now in a much worse position than they could have imagined. Logan looked to the floor extremely disheartened, whilst he may have a tendency for the reckless, he was still a warrior, still wise and had not become one of the most recognisable Nyx soldiers by being a fool. He looked at Josh who did now seem to have returned to his senses and became one again in touch with reality.

"Josh we are defeated, we need to return to Midjun and tell of what has happened, we may return with reinforcements but for now we must leave." Josh looked at Logan with distain, he could not fathom the idea of leaving Alec, defeat he could live with but the desolation of his good friend he could not.

"No," Josh replied "We cannot leave Alec behind, we have not completed our mission. Did you take in their lies? Alec would not have turned on us!"

Logan shook his head "No of course I do not believe that but we cannot stay, we are injured, we cannot fight effectively, we know where Alec is but we know we cannot reach him. We most probably have the whole of the Koschei army looking for us with two incredibly powerful beings and it would appear now a dragon even though they are extinct! We can return to gather back up, even I can admit when we need help."

He finished with a sympathetic dip of his head, he looked at the ground and with one leg up on a rock he leant heavily upon it resembling a picture from a lumberjack's weekly magazine. Whilst he could admit that they required the help it was not an admission that came easily.

Logan wished to die in battle yes, but this did not mean bowing to a meaningless death.

"We cannot back down now" Josh continued still staunch in his unwillingness to leave, "We need to get Alec back and we need to get that blade, if we fail in our ...."

"Enough!" Logan shouted at Josh stopping him mid-flow, " I appreciate why you wish to fight on but we cannot, I am here to guide you and keep you safe, we return now. With support we may still get a result here, without we cannot."

Josh stood for a second with a look of near petulance etched across his face. At this point he was feeling pretty sure that Logan may be right, he understood warfare much better than he ever could.

He looked up towards the massive, dark tower that stood in the distance. Rain fell in sheets over it, causing the strange stone to glow with a silvery sheen from the fog and moisture. It loomed above him, as large as ever, suffocating and dark. The storm clouds gathered behind it like a cloak; lightning snaked through the sky and seemed to find refuge within those walls. A sense of fore-boding washed over him.

Little did he comprehend that within the eastern tower he surveyed, Alec gawked outwardly ignorant that he was gazing right toward his comrades. He was also oblivious that the trembling and quivering of the edifice, the ones he had recently endured; ones spawned by these same friends' rescue exploits and near fatalities, were caused by the breakdown of some of the castle's pillars, ones that made this eastern tower remarkably lower now than previously. He stood there feeling disheartened, perplexed and terribly uncertain if he would ever again peer out from these walls.

Josh glanced away from the imposing structure, feeling his heart sink as he conceded to Logan's decision. He nodded in agreement, knowing that Logan was wise.

They started walking away from the castle and a mixture of relief and guilt filled them both. Although they had no proof that Alec was kept captive within the walls, they both felt that he was there, yet hoped irrationally that he wasn't. Josh refused to turn back even once—beside the sense of relief, he felt immense shame. On the other hand, Logan, who usually didn't fear death in battle, at this moment felt angry and embarrassed about what seemed like a surrender.

The two made their way across the dry lands as swiftly as possible not want-ing to stay in any one place too long lest they be discovered by the enemy forces and ultimately led into death's cold embrace. The Koschei were out in numbers looking for them and Probetor was enraged at their escape, an escape of which he blamed entirely on Gree.

They continued on without rest, pushing forward ensuring no time was wasted in order to get back to Midjun as soon as possible. However even the lands of Midjun with its formally standing tower no longer felt like the safe haven it once had and on arrival to Midjuns shores, after what seemed an eter-nity of travel, Logan could but wonder how safe even the great lands of Sof-pavel were themselves at this moment.

They trudged through the remnants of battle, their boots crunching over shattered stones and scattered bits of debris. The smoky sky was a reminder of what had transpired here as they passed charred towers that still emitted an or-ange glow.

After a period of time, they arrived at the camps where they could see makeshift shelters lined up in rows and hear the hushed murmurings of survivors gathering around fires for warmth.

Logan and Josh were escorted to the main camp where they were met by Major Araya, who was overjoyed to see them both alive despite the clear concern of them being not only alone but without the sword they so desperately required. He warmly placed his hand onto Logans shoulder as he sat there being tended to, he fully understood the frustration and inner turmoil that his soldier would be feeling in these moments.

Logan recapped his journey in an orderly fashion, delivering the details as articulately and accurately as he could. He began by telling Araya of their discovery that Alec was still alive and being held captive, even though they had heard words indicating otherwise. Logan revealed the informant of this information as Gree, a very real being who worked for Probetor. Graphic descriptions of the troops, lands and castle quickly came to life in Logan's story detailing how many were there, where they were located and what kind of weapons they carried. His tale almost finished; Logan drew a deep breath before uttered the most dangerous words: "They have something incredible. Something terrifying. I fear Major this may be our undoing - they have a dragon."

The news left Araya dumbstruck; although dragons had been spoken about since ancient times and skeletal remains offered evidence of their existence, he never thought he would be placed in a situation to face one himself, these creatures were thought to have been extinct for centuries. Peering around the camp, Araya could see people exchanging glances full of fear and doubt as they overheard these words being spoken. With a solemn nod, Araya dismissed them all from his presence.

Logan then went on to explain that he himself had fought the dragon, or rather been thrown to it for slaughter, and whilst it appeared under Gree's control there were moments when it showed signs of unpredictability which could make it even more dangerous than they could possibly imagine.

The dragon was immense, towering over anything Logan had ever seen before. Its scales were the same deep red as a roaring flame, with a brightness that seemed to outshine even the dim light of the cave. Its eyes were golden and blazed with an unearthly anger beneath its brows. It seemed like a demon rising from the depths of hell, an unstoppable force of destruction and power.

He explained how the dragon had lost control and fortunately created the opening by which they could make their escape.

"I fear without this good fortune I would have died," Logan finished, with a look of shame across his face at this admission. Araya placed a hand on Logan's shoulder and patted him strongly, he stood in silence for a moment still trying to comprehend the existence of their enemies' secret weapon firmly holding onto Logan for such a duration of time it began to almost feel uncomfortable.

"There is no shame in defeat Logan, and there would be no shame in having your life ended at the hands of such a creature," he reassuringly said after the silence had passed. "The question now is what we do about this." Logan stood, he looked at Araya and pushed out his chest, peacocking in such a manor showed how his dipping confidence was being backed and surviving by his general bravado alone.

"We must return Major, with all the forces Sofpavel has to offer and any we can gather from elsewhere. We must reign our own fire onto them and rescue Alec to boot. We must stop sitting back and defending, the time has come for us to go on the offensive."

Araya chuckled, pleased to see that the fire in Logan that had led to him being sent on this mission to begin with was still very much alive.

"Agreed we must do something, I will have word sent to Hypnos to return as soon as possible with every man that can be spared, his trip to see Freyja has hopefully been fruitful, we need to gather everyone here. Once this dragon has been released it may well be too late, and given what they know about us at this point, it may already be so."

18) Heroes return

Breathless, Hypnos stumbled back into Sofpavel after the long journey home. The scent of sweet green grass filled the air and he glanced around at the picturesque vista that stretched out before him.

The lush greenery brought him solace and comfort as it reminded him that this was his home - a place where he could regain pause amidst life's chaotic storms and admire the beauty of its tranquil landscape. On this occasion he may not have the time to take that pause, but he knew it could be there if he wished.

As Hypnos helped to lay a soldier onto one of many makeshift beds, the smell of blood and sweat filled his nostrils detracting from the beauty that had welcomed him home, a member of the medical team approached him. Although his features were pale and worn, his face showed that he wanted to do good and help people in need. His hair was shoulder length and dark brown, and with rosy cheeks and dark blue eyes, he wore the green clothing that identified him as part of the medical staff. Hypnos could see in his eyes his trepidation at being there, none of these medical staff had ever been in a war zone before, and the current affairs of this filled them with great fear and realised horrors.

"Sir do you need help? I can see that you are wounded," the medic asked pointing towards the blood-stained garment around Hypnos midriff. He looked down at his injured body and shook his head.

"No, I am fine thank you, please attend to those more needing." Hypnos said gesturing towards the soldier he had just laid down. "You could direct me to the next group travelling to the capital however as I wish to accompany them."

The medic pointed towards a group not far from where they currently stood, around thirty or so men, all bar four of those being injured parties.

"That group there are just about to set off I believe."

Hypnos nodded his head in appreciation and began to make his way towards the group. He was welcomed with open arms as they knew who he was, and as he set foot amongst them a feeling of relief set in amongst the guarding soldiers, they were more than capable of supervising the procession however the number of injured meant that each group travelling had a small number of able-bodied men than they would have wished.

The sight of him alone had an effect on those that were wounded also - giving them a sense of hope or purpose that they may not have otherwise had.

As the group set off along the path back to the capital, Hypnos decided that he would take in the sights around him, he had been away for some time now and the beauty of his homelands was never lost on him.

The sound of birds chirping provided a calming backdrop and it almost felt like nature itself was trying to comfort them on their journey - washing away any fear or anxiety that may have been present. For miles upon miles they travelled, observing the beauty of nature in all its forms; lakes shimmering in the sun, fields full of wild flowers and trees budding with new life. With each passing marvel that nature showed, Hypnos became more concerned about what could soon be coming to these lands, the horror of war and the darkness that could follow could destroy all of this.

And then, as if it had been placed there to comfort them further, the group arrived back at Sofpavel's capital as the fortress above came into view first, standing tall above the city. The spectacle was always mesmerizing and a sense of awe filled those who looked upon it no matter how often it had been seen; its gleaming white walls reflecting off of the sun's rays and casting an ethereal glow over all that surrounded it. A beacon of hope in times of darkness - this is what Hypnos needed to help him stay focused on his task. He was determined to do anything he could to protect his home from destruction. As they entered the city, cheers could be heard from far away as people recognised Hypnos amongst their returning heroes, unaware of the fact that they were actually losing this fight.

Hypnos knew what he had to do next. He needed to find Freyja, he had no doubt that she was already aware of this, he was less certain however that she would this time have the answers. He thanked the men for their company on the trip and bid them farewell before setting off on his own.

The entrance to Freyja's chamber were heavily guarded, much more so than usual at this current time, however the guards of course recognised Hypnos and allowed him entry, standing to attention as he passed them by. As soon as he stepped inside, he could tell that she had been expecting him - her eyes sparkled with anticipation as if she'd known all along that he would be coming to her - no matter what odds they faced or how many obstacles stood in his way. However, they were also sunken and dark, the toil of this war taking hold and her knowledge base a wear on her soul. Her chambers were decorated with tapestries depicting scenes from the past, a reminder of their shared heritage and culture even in such trying times. Hypnos saw the open case that had for so long protected the blade still sitting open, its emptiness glared obviously and clearly, highlighting its absence in a way that screamed despair.

Candles flickered around the room, casting a warm glow over everything. But then Hypnos noticed something else - a figure cloaked in shadows standing in the corner of the room. He hadn't seen her enter and yet she seemed to have been there for some time - the presence that had been keeping watch and helping Hypnos was now here.

She spoke first sensing Hypnos confusion - a voice like honey dripping from her lips as she looked up at him and stepped out from the shadows.

"Hello Hypnos, it is nice to meet you in a more," she stepped closer towards Hypnos, her boots clicking on the polished floor. She clasped her hands behind her back as she took one further step forwards, his giant frame towering over hers as she looked up at him "pleasant setting."

Hypnos did not respond immediately, taking a step back and glancing at Freyja, he ignored this woman's polite introduction to herself and gentle appearance and instead turned towards Freyja herself for with his question.

"Who is this?" He gestured towards the cloaked woman, side stepping her and moving towards Freyja. He did not tend to be fond of the unknown, nor the secrets that may be around them.

Freyja sighed softly, her eyes still heavy with the weight of the world and its duties. She knew that Hypnos was not one to trust easily and his suspicions had been warranted in recent times although she had hoped after all these years that he would have more faith in her, even if the rare moment of doubt was indeed just that, very rare. She looked up at him, her gaze softening as she spoke.

"Hypnos," she said gently, "this is a friend who has come to our aid. She has come from a faraway land to help us protect our home and our people from any danger that may arise, I feel she has shown herself to be on our side here, do you not?" Her voice was calm yet firm, conveying strength and conviction as she continued to speak. "I ask you to trust me on this one - I can assure you that she is here for no other purpose than to help us fight for our cause."

The cloaked woman stepped forward, her face still shrouded by darkness but a gentle smile playing across her lips as she looked at Hypnos and said, "It's true. I am here to help."

Hypnos nodded for a second, the silence ringing in his ears in the strangeness of the situation. The smile on her face was intoxicating, but he had little time to acknowledge it before she continued.

"Name?" he asked.

With a delicate chuckle she responded, "I guess you could call me your 'saviour' so maybe Savi for short..." She paused, pursing her lips into a serious expression as her eyes lost their playful warmth and she held up a finger to him to interject. "... when all is said and done." Then added with a grin of course," For now I will be happy just to make your acquaintance."

Hypnos rolled his eyes, this woman was irritating to him, peppy and enthusiastic in a way that annoyed him. He knew that patience was not his forte and felt that as useful as she may have been, and may continue to be, she had as much potential to make it wear thin. He sighed and reluctantly accepted her presence.

"Savi it is I guess for it does not really matter," he responded very matter-of-factly. For indeed it did not. "I came to ask about the identity of," he paused, "Savi here, as well as to discuss what has happened. We are losing this war, Freyja; the tower has fallen and our troops are depleting. It seems that we have secured Midjun for now and thanks to 'the Savi' here, who seems to possess power rivalling your own we have managed to protect Lemuri for the time being, however I fear this is temporary."

Hypnos seemed to wish to for a reaction as he questioned who the more powerful of these two may be but if he had indeed stirred any emotion with this it was not revealed. He turned his attention back to Midjun.

"We are restocking ourselves and the soldiers are setting up camps on Midjun; we should be able to hold it for a time but I do fear that their numbers will break us down eventually," he became thoughtful in this moment, concerned and bordering on confused by the enemies new found strength, "we must pray that Alec and the others have been successful in their part of this."

Freyja looked at Hypnos with a sense of dread in her heart, knowing that he was right and they were losing the war, she had also picked up on the scent that something was not right with Alec. She knew that they had to act quickly if they were to have any chance of winning this fight. Her mind raced as she thought through the possible solutions, trying to find one that would be most effective yet still safe for her people. This war was in danger of arriving on the shores of Sofpavel, something that none had ever seen. Worse still if they lose this war then all would perish regardless. After what seemed like an eternity of contemplation, Freyja finally spoke up.

"I think it best if we all three travel back to Midjun and make our plans there," she said assertively but calmly, her gaze steady as she looked at Hypnos and then at Savi. "I'm not sure how much time we have left before they return, so we need to move." She paused for a moment before continuing, her voice growing more serious with each word as she continued. "We must prepare ourselves for battle; I fear this may be our last stand, especially if Alec has failed."

Hypnos nodded solemnly, although he had not truly believed in Alec from the start he would not wish for anything ill to fall upon him, he knew that failure meant captured, or worse still, death.

"Once we arrive you must make plans with your generals, we need to defend our people." Hypnos nodded, even though he did not know at this point all that was transpiring in Midjun and beyond he was an incredible leader. He knew within himself that defence was most likely no longer the best option.

As Hypnos stood momentarily contemplating this he was interrupted by a commotion from outside the tower. He moved quickly to see what was happening and gazed out of the window. At the gates stood a Nyx messenger from Midjun, but his face was dark and troubled, the toils of this war etched into every fibre. The applause that accompanied the Nyx from the Sofpavelian people filled his ears now as if it were water being poured into a bucket too small for the amount of liquid.

Hypnos raced down the stairs, his heart pounding in his chest as he heard the soldier waiting for him in the courtyard. He grabbed his cloak and flung it around his shoulders on his way out the door. With each step closer to the soldier, Hypnos could feel time slipping away from him until they were face-to-face, and he felt as if every nerve in his body was on fire. The soldier reached out and grabbed Hypnos' hand in a grip hard as iron, and their eyes met, neither one letting go.

"I have come with haste Sir, there is great urgency in Midjun and General Araya wishes your return immediately," the soldier blurted out rapidly, his voice tired from the journey yet strong and unwavering. Hypnos' mind raced as he realized the gravity of this message. He composed himself though and looked at the soldier determinedly.

"Yes," he said firmly, steeling himself for what was to come next. "I will come with you at once."

Freyja and Savi witnessed Hypnos striding down to greet the messenger, sensing a palpable foreboding that swirled around them. Freyja glanced at Savi and nodded, confirming her resolve to join him on this harrowing mission without pause. Savi returned a warm smile, then hastened their preparations for the voyage. Soon, they were suitably attired for travel and had descended the tower steps, arriving just in time to witness Hypnos standing ready.

"We are ready," Freyja said as they walked up behind him, her voice strong despite her apprehension.

Hypnos nodded in acknowledgement and turned to the Nyx messenger who had brought the news from Midjun. He motioned for his horse to be brought forth and mounted it quickly before addressing his companions one last time. "We must move swiftly if we are to make it back in good time," he said gravely. Freyja again silently nodded and awaited Hypnos command.

"Let us go then," he eagerly added, leading the way towards the gleaming gates of the capital.

They moved rapidly through the streets, their feet pounding against the cobblestones as they went. He glanced over at Freyja and Savi, both resolute in their determination despite the uneasiness in the air.

Eventually they reached a small port on the outskirts of town where some local ships were still docked, waiting to depart. The small boat the messenger had arrived on could not carry much more than just himself and they required their own passage.

Whilst the battles had been kept away from Sofpavel the ships that left for any means had steered clear of Midjun for a while, perfectly aware of the battles that had been taking place there and most were reluctant to change this. Fortunately, they found one that would assist and as they approached Hypnos could see that some sort of argument was taking place on board but it soon abated as he climbed aboard and addressed them directly.

The captain took one look at him before nodding in agreement and offering them shelter for the night as well as a safe passage to Midjun. Nobody would have said no to Hypnos in reality; however, Hypnos thanked him for his hospitality before motioning for Freyja and Savi to follow him below deck.

Hypnos filled them in on the situation; General Araya had asked for their immediate return due to pressing news. They'd already figured that much out. Savi had spent quite a bit of time and fought on the island with Hypnos, but even they weren't aware of what was happening entirely. All they could do was guess until they got there the next morning.

They passed a restless night at sea, Hypnos himself never settling or spending much time below deck. The seagulls and the creaking of the boards were his only companions as he swept through the waves on a wide stretch of ocean, surrounded by nothing but water and sky. Eventually morning came and with it the first sight of Midjun in the near distance, the smoke still rose in the air clouding the sunrise that appeared just passed the island and it was clear that the fires Hypnos had left behind had raged on for some time.

The ship came to a halt a little distance away, they were unwilling to travel too close to the island and its turmoil. The captain provided them a small row boat with which to complete their journey and wished them luck. The mood was sombre as Freyja and Savi climbed into the boat with Hypnos, their faces grim with the realization of what could be waiting for them at the end of this journey. They said nothing as they rowed, each of them lost in their own thoughts until finally they arrived on the shoreline.

It was then that they got their first glimpse of Midjun since departing it earlier; a sprawling panorama of devastation and ruin. A continuous flow of soldiers scrambled towards the camp with supplies and weapons in tow.

By the time they arrived on the ground Hypnos' gaze settled on one particular figure standing atop a hill surveying it all - General Araya himself, observing the wreckage. Just by his side Hypnos noticed a figure that sent his heart plummeting, Logan sat there beside him, crestfallen and battle-worn. In that instant he knew that things had truly failed.

Araya's face lit up as soon as he saw Hypnos, his expression turning from one of worry to mild relief in a matter of seconds. He quickly made his way down the hill towards them, his steps light and fast despite the weight on his shoulders. As he drew closer, Hypnos could see that he appeared to have aged dramatically from the stress and it was clear they had much to discuss.

Araya grasped Hypnos's shoulders, his face filled with a deep and desperate worry. He moved to his side and draped an arm around him, the fabric of his jacket crinkling against his own. A gruffness crept into his voice as he spoke, "Let's go then."

19) This way or that

Alec was like a caged bird in the dank room, his wrists bound by heavy metal bracelets that glimmered with darkly magical energy. Each time he attempted to wriggle free of them, a fierce jolt of electricity surged through his body, as if warning him not to try again. He felt a cold weight against his skin, and it seemed no matter how hard he pulled, the bracelets stayed uncomfortably in place.

The walls of the cell were made of grey stone and were cracked from age. A thin layer of moisture glistened on the floor and the corners were filled with cobwebs. The air was heavy and still, filled with an oppressive feeling that seemed to seep into Alec's bones. The only sound was a faint dripping somewhere in the shadows, and a sense of dread hung over the room like a thick fog.

The room was different to the one had originally awoken to and he found it a cruel clever trick for it to now be made so uninhabitable.

He kept his thoughts focused on his friends, hoping and praying that they had been successful in their fight and won the battles on Midjun. If so, they would now surely be preparing to launch an attack here on Maredrom. He remembered their last moments together on Midjun, the determination in their faces and the sense of camaraderie as they prepared for battle. Alec wished he could have been there with them, to fight by their side and help secure victory for their people. But instead, here he was, locked away with no way of knowing if they had succeeded or failed, only the knowledge of his own failure existed. His heart tightened with worry as he imagined all the possible outcomes of this battle; what if they hadn't been able to stop them? What if they had been defeated? What if his friends had been killed in the fighting?

The door to his cell creaked open and Alec winced, expecting the worst. But instead of Probetor he saw Jenny standing there, her eyes twinkling with amusement as she took in Alec's state. She stepped into the room and began to mock him, her voice dripping with sarcasm as she accused him of cowardice. He tried to speak but found himself tongue-tied; what could he say that would make her understand how he felt? His mind raced for something suitable but all he could muster was a feeble attempt at an apology

"I'm sorry if our time together was so bad for you that I turned you this way, I'm sorry I was not who you wished me to be," Jenny just laughed off his words and continued to mock him, her laughter ringing out like bells through the airless chamber.

"Oh Alec, you really do not understand. I never cared for you and you did not turn me into this wonderful creature that I am. I was always this, great actress, aren't I?!"

"The tower of Midjun has fallen by the way," she declared loudly, her eyes filled with joy. "Your friends are losing the war and there is nothing you can do."

Alec's heart plummeted as Jenny's words pierced through him like a razor blade. His face drained of all colour and emotion as his former friend jeered in delight at his misery. The sound of her laughter stabbed into his soul, inducing an unbearable ache of loneliness that was sinking further and further into the depths of despair. As she left, he could feel the emptiness of her malicious victory, knowing that it had come at too great a cost for him and his companions alike. Behind him he heard the door creak back open once more.

"No, I don't want to hear it Jenny," he said as he spun around to face her. But as the open doorway came into view, Alec could tell it was not Jenny standing there; it was Probetor.

A small smirk spread across Probetor's face before he uttered his words in a calm yet intimidating manner. "Good thing, for I certainly do not wish to say it! It is time for us leave now, Alec - we have a little trip to make."

Hesitatingly, Alec raised an eyebrow and gestured towards his wrists with the bracelets on them.

"Do I at least get these removed for this?"

Probetor shook his head, "I do not believe us to be at that level of trust just yet, do you?"

Alec had no response; he knew that if given the opportunity, he would surely try to escape...and his father was no fool.

With a wave of his hand, Probetor commanded: "Come now. We will leave immediately." Reluctantly, Alec followed him out the door - knowing full well there was no other choice.

The two of them carefully navigated their way down the levels of the castle tower, the darkness illuminated by a few sconces on the walls.

When they finally reached the bottom, Alec was overwhelmed with shock and surprised at the different view of the castle he had had previously seen. Everywhere he looked, he saw destruction - charred remnants, broken walls, crumbling floors and holes in roofs were all that remained from what used to be a grand and intimidating castle. He could almost smell the despair in the air as the castle now seemed to feel very sorry for itself.

The sheer destruction that lay in front of them seemed closer to the castle ruins he had visited as a child as opposed to a currently operating fortress pressing for control of all the realms in the known universe.

He couldn't help but wonder what kind of force could have wreaked such havoc. Was it possible that the Nyx had launched a rescue attempt?

A glimmer of hope flickered inside him at the idea, but it was snuffed out by the grim expression on Probetor's face. He didn't seem keen on commenting on the scene before them, and instead opted for a subtle shake of his head. Alec took this as a signal to remain silent about their surroundings, and they hurriedly made their way out of the ruined castle.

The normally unflappable Probetor seemed unusually irked by whatever had caused such destruction - not enraged like one who had been attacked, but annoyed, like a parent whose child had scribbled on freshly painted walls.

Alec inhaled the sweet scent of cold air as they exited through the giant doors that guarded the threshold, after hours of being stuck in the oppressive tower. The sensation was pure bliss and brought a wave of relief to his body as he stepped away from the destroyed ruins. As he looked up at the sky, the wind slapped him in the face, causing some strands of hair to stick to his sweaty forehead. Although Alec wasn't free yet, the removal of walls around him made him feel more liberated with every breath he took.

Probetor pointed a finger westward, across the vast expanse of Maredrom. Alec felt a silent dread wash over him as he looked in that direction and, somehow, knew what to expect from the journey ahead.

"We must make haste to the cliffs - our journey awaits us there!" Probetor muttered with an air of urgency.

Alec nodded, not trusting himself to speak, and took in a deep breath before following his captor. The two were forced into silence for most of the journey, as Probetor seemed lost in thought and consumed by whatever task lay ahead of them. Alec used this time to take in his surroundings, noting details which he had not noticed before - the moonlight glinting off of cliff tops coated in frosty ice and the odd cries of unfamiliar animals echoing from all directions. He could even hear the distant howling wind; it made him feel utterly insignificant in comparison to nature's grandeur.

The air was growing chillier with each passing mile, and a fine mist rose from Alec's lips with every exhale. He watched as it dissipated in front of him, like a thin wisp of smoke, until the cold became unbearable and he had to pull his cloak tighter around himself.

After hours of trekking up steep hills and rocky paths, they arrived at their destination: The Cliffs of Maredrom. The sheer size of them was breathtaking; they seemed so high that Alec could hardly make out the stars beyond them.

But beyond these cliffs lurked something else, an alluring enticement that kept pulling his attention to the narrow opening that seemed to almost cleave this colossal mountain in half.

They stood directly in front of the entrance, just wide enough for someone of slight stature to slink through yet no one knew where it would lead or how far this path stretched on for, only the unspoken promise of what lay beyond its abyss. Despite the unknown danger that lay ahead, Alec felt inexplicably drawn towards this gap, as if bewitched by an unseen force.

Probetor announced his presence at the entrance of the crack, beckoning Alec to follow. He hesitated as Probetor impatiently motioned with a wave of his hands and a roll of his eyes. The bracelets on Alec's wrists began to light up, a dim purple hue engulfing the jewels as they pulled him forward. He struggled against the force but it was no use. His body was determined to continue forth into the unknown.

Taking a deep breath, he stepped in, feeling his stomach knot up and his heart pound loudly. Shadows dance around him like fiends waiting for their prey. He puts his hands out in front of him and feels cold stone walls surround him.

The walls of the passage are dark and damp, illuminated by small sporadic patches of light that creep from the winding path ahead. The stone walls are rough and jagged, as though they have been carved by a giant's hand. They seem to close in as one walks further into the passage, creating an oppressing feeling of isolation.

The sound of their footsteps echoes off the walls, creating a haunting chant-like melody with a mysterious unknown origin. Above, the path is a tangle of branches and turns that split and meld together like an ancient maze. Probetor moves through with swiftness and assurance - like he knows this place by heart - leaving Alec to feel both curious and apprehensive.

A spark of hope ignited in Alec as a gentle, soothing light began to filter through from somewhere further down the path. He felt himself be drawn forward, feeling that the tight confines and suffocating sensation of claustrophobia would soon come to an end. He could only wish so, as he had been struggling with his discomfort for far too long now.

Finally, after what seemed like hours, they reached their destination; an expansive cavern with ceilings as high as a skyscraper. The contrast between this place and the dark tunnels before it was incredible; here the air was fresh and brimming with potential. Alec looked upon the cave ahead of him - its unique shape carved out by invisible hands. Its entrance hung deep in darkness, concealing any chance of seeing what lay beyond. It was clear that they would be proceeding further into the unknown at this point, much to Alec's dismay.

But before they dared to move an inch, a thunderous sound echoed through the depths of the cavern as Alec felt the ground quake beneath him. Whatever was coming for them, it was big and it seemed that Probetor was not fazed. He motioned for Alec to keep still and be quiet as he crept away out of sight. The beast grew nearer with each passing second and soon enough Alec could make out a giant form silhouetted against the faint light of the cave - a two headed serpent!

The two heads of the beast are wide and menacing, with sharp teeth and a long-forked tongue. Its scales glimmer and shine like molten gold, giving off an intimidating aura. Its eyes are like pools of inky darkness, watching the two of them intently as if it could see into their souls. The beast gives off an air of unafraidness, as if it's not bothered by the intruders and is instead curious about this new encounter.

It snarled fiercely at them as if trying to scare them off but Probetor stood tall and unafraid. He stretched out his hand towards the creature's face and spoke softly in a language unknown to Alec - reassuringly comforting words that seemed to have an effect on the giant behemoth. The two heads of the beast relaxed as Probetor spoke, the fierce snarl on its face softening to a calmer expression. Its eyes changed from pitch black to a gentle white, almost as if it understood the words Probetor was speaking. Its fiery scales dimmed to a warm glow, and its body seemed to sink into a more relaxed position.

Probetor spoke in a whisper, now addressing Alec, "This old girl had been charged with protecting the entrance way to this precipice from any unwelcome guests. Punishment after it went on a rampage, although what else you would expect from such a creature I do not know. She has stood here for thousands of years and only ever encountered the very few who have managed to navigate their way here. Usually by chance or accident. The dark magic I learnt from The Jinn enabled me to speak in its tongue and I can reason with it just enough to calm it down for a while." With a final nod from Probetor, the guardian stepped aside and allowed them entry into the cave beyond.

Alec breathed a sigh of relief as they passed by without incident but he couldn't help but feel an overwhelming sense of amazement as he looked upon the giant creature one last time before it faded out of sight.

The cave was pitch black and the single source of light was from Probetor's hand. He held it out and a flame erupted from his palm, scattering an orange hue that lit up their path. The orange glow was mysterious and captivating, casting an eerie feeling in the air. With the flame leading the way, they ventured deeper into the unknown.

The walls of this place were covered in ancient runes that seemed to tell an untold story - one that Alec knew he would never understand but couldn't help but be enthralled by.

As they moved forward further, more chambers opened up around them - some filled with treasures and trinkets, others with strange contraptions and devices long forgotten. It felt like a never-ending journey through time as each new chamber revealed something more wondrous than the last, each revealing its secrets as if it had been waiting for someone to discover it all along.

Alec couldn't believe what he was seeing; a world so old yet so alive at the same time. Clearly it had been forgotten, perhaps never even known about by those outside and Probetor seemed to have little interest in any of its wonders as he sped through chamber by chamber.

Finally, they came to one that was different from the rest. It was larger, much grander than the others and the walls were illuminated by a bright blue light. In the centre of this chamber was a glowing wall of water - a portal which led somewhere else entirely. Probetor stepped forward and gestured for Alec to stay back as he recited a short spell in his mysterious language. As soon as he finished, the wall of water parted ways like curtains, revealing an even more breathtaking world beyond. As Alec steps through the glowing wall of water, he finds himself in a rocky crevice. He can feel the dampness of the walls around him and the cool breeze coming through. The crevice gradually opens up to a vast green expanse beyond. The sky is light blue in the distance, with tufts of white clouds in the air. He stands looking out in astonishment, taking in the expanse before him. Alec gasped in amazement as his eyes adjusted to the bright light - before him was a cascading waterfall that seemed to stretch on for eternity.

The water crashed down from high above, spilling over into a crystal-clear pool at its base. Alec couldn't believe his eyes as he realised what he was looking at; this had taken them straight to the base of Lemuri Falls! Alec's eyes widened in amazement as he took in the breathtaking view before him—from the cascading waterfall, to the vibrant greenery, to the clear pool at the base of Lemuri Falls. He was in awe of the beauty, and couldn't believe that no amount of reading could have prepared him for this experience. However, before he could take it all in, his moment of wonder was interrupted.

He realised that Probetor had bought him here and whilst in possession of Morpheus blade, what this meant he was not sure but he knew this was exactly what they had been trying to prevent.

Confused, he pondered as to why he had not accessed these passageways from the start, when it had been clear that they had been blocking him from getting there via conventional means. Probetor Alec thought had also been here before; so why all the deception? All of the fighting to gain control of this area seems to have been for nothing. Why had he not just completed his target from the start?

The more he thought about it, the more he realised that nothing made sense! All of this felt pointless and frustrating. What exactly were they trying to prevent? And why hadn't he completed his mission without all of this rigmarole? His mind spun with questions.

Probetor sneered, knowing Alecs confusion. His voice dropped as he began to explain; the war had merely been a ruse for him, a way of distracting the rest while he got his hands on Alec and made Lemuri less accessible for all other than himself. After all, he needed someone with Erobian God blood coursing through their veins, someone who could unlock and control Lemuri.

Someone powerful enough to survive the ominous might that lies within the sword whilst equally not being blocked due to stature - none other than an unblemished demi-god. For Lemuri was impossible to access absolutely by any god or anyone from Erobus; it was designed that way to ensure no one ever gained too much power, or the ability to wander through the realms unchecked. But Alec held this gift, able to use Morpheus blade to unlock

Lemuri and gain access to the Drasal tree, to travel through these hidden passageways without fear of detection or risk of danger. Suddenly it all made perfect sense, his mind turning over all the pieces of Probetor's plan - distract and mislead, using powers to gain access unhindered, preventing aid from coming too easily...most eerily however, realisation struck him like a lightning bolt - Probetor wanted Alec as a sacrifice!

"Lemuri can also unlock the Jinn from within this blade" Probetor explained, "However the cost would be high for this, Morpheus himself died locking away, a death would happen to the holder unlocking I am afraid."

Alecs jaw dropped in horror. His throat was tight with fear and the taste of bile welled up inside him. He had known Probetor's purpose would not be good, but he had not imagined this. The realisation that he was this close to winning it all froze his heart solid, and he felt the warm blood stop pumping in his veins. The recognition he had a way to release the Jinn and that Alec himself was about to be sacrificed made him feel sick to his stomach as he stood there, powerless, watching the grin on Probetor spread wider across his face.

20) Great loses

Hypnos' shock was palpable as Araya spoke, struggling to take in the magnitude of their enemy's plans. The weight of Alec's capture, the sheer number of Koschei's and the terrifying existence of a dragon caused his mind to spin out of control. Freyja and Savi watched him with a mix of worry and dread, desperate for him to break the oppressive silence that had descended between them.

The thought of losing Alec made Hypnos feel sick and his stomach twisted in knots. He had grown surprisingly fond of his friend regardless of if he was the one or not. He looked over at Logan who sat there with a look of shame on his face during all of this and shook his head. Despite knowing that he would have done his best if push came to shove a Nyx soldier would fall on their sword for someone in their protection and he felt Logans temperament had made him fall far short of this. Logan could feel the eyes on him, burning into him, and the shame grew more intensely within himself.

"And what of Josh?" Hypnos asked, "Where is he?"

"He's in the infirmary, he collapsed not long after coming back and has not awoken since." Araya responded sounding exhausted from his previous tales.

"Hmmm" Hypnos snarled, "at least his excuse for failure is valid," he said, aiming a shot at Logan.

Freyja tenderly placed her hand on Hypnos' chest, and gave him a meaningful look that spoke volumes. In that brief moment, she made it clear to him that he needed to calm down.

Hypnos sighed heavily and acknowledged her request with a firm nod.

"So, what now, do you already have any actions taking place?" he asked, defiantly.

"We need to mobilise our forces." Araya said, looking into the distance as if he was already planning the battle ahead. "I will send word to the Nyx camp that lay ahead of us and we can march together. They sent disturbing word that the Koschei's have regrouped and are gathering on the far side of Midjun, this time with Gree at their head - we have to be ready for when they come."

The group nodded in agreement. Hypnos looked towards Logan, who had remained silent throughout this discussion. He wanted to say something but held back.

With continued disappointment, Hypnos turned away from Logan and faced Araya again.

"Let's get ready," he said with determination in his voice, "We have a camp to reach and an army to fight."

Hypnos stood calmly, appearing almost emotionless as always, and reviewed the situation.

In the past, Hypnos had been in control of armies that stretched throughout the entire universe and knew things no one else did. He ultimately broke down these armies into separate groups, with Araya emerging as one of the strongest generals -second only to Hypnos himself. Hypnos was often accused of working to be the next Morpheus, a remark he found very offensive, not to himself but to the great leader.

But much more importantly, the fact that he technically outranked Araya was never a factor. Whenever they made decisions, they decided that whilst Araya was himself a feared and strongly admired leader, the sheer presence of Hypnos had a tendency to pull the best out of the men around him. He was a legend beyond compare when it came to war on this plane of existence; his presence could benefit them in their quest against evil. This was shown instantly as he gave a rousing speech to the troops assembled at the base.

Araya steeled himself for the difficult fight ahead, knowing his mission was to protect Midjun. He gladly gave the reins of power over to Hypnos in order to do so.

The group marched onward amidst the silence that filled the air like a thunderous roar. The bright sun shined down upon them once more like an oppressive weight, each step they took feeling harder and heavier than the last.

As they carried on through the monotonous landscape, they passed by the dishevelled remains of recent battles—ruins of former glory and destruction-filled trenches scattered throughout. In the far distance, the glimmering wall of water could be seen clearly such was its magnitude - protecting Lemuri and concealing what laid beyond it from view.

Nearby lay the corpses of the undead Koschei, with some heads still swaying and limbs still crawling despite being slain long ago.

As they arrived at camp two, the Nyx troops that had been awaiting their arrival greeted them with a proud salute. Their faces showed signs of fatigue, black circles under bloodshot eyes, skin pulled tight over bones, but this made them appear more determined and courageous. This was the first time all of the

Nyx troops that were able bodied had been in one place since the day they over-threw the Jinn, providing a rare insight into the powerful force that they had grown to be. Hypnos fully aware of this hoped that this time they could be successful without need for a sacrifice of their own.

The sky above was now a vast canvas of glittering stars, pinpoints of light shimmering like tiny beacons of hope. The constellations were laid out like a map, each one twinkling and glittering brighter than the last. A slight breeze stirred through the air, carrying with it whispers of stories from years gone by - tales of courage and glory that would never be forgotten. The rustling leaves sounded like an ancient song, harmonizing with the soft cries of night creatures. It was as if the universe itself was telling them to have faith, to keep moving forward, no matter what.

Hypnos maneuvered through the sea of soldiers, the tiredness after a full days trek showing heavily as they fought against the sleep that preyed on them so heavily.

He continued surveying the plethora of men searching out for one in particular, his eyes falling upon the Commander of the old watchtower. The few remaining guards under his command now fought alongside the armies here, but their hearts were heavy with the feelings of loss. For many, the fallen tower had been home for longer than they could remember, and they had pledged their lives to defend it - forsaking all else, including families. Now that the tower was gone, their unity rested on seeking vengeance against the ones who had taken everything from them. Hypnos couldn't help but wonder: what else did they have left to cling to in this world?

The Commander stepped forward and reached out his hand. "It is good to see you again, Hypnos," he said in a deep voice as they shook hands. "Tell me how you are."

"I am well," he answered, his eyes searching the commander's face. "How have you been since I saw you last?" He hesitated for a moment before asking, "By any chance did we ever settle on one name between us?"

They both laughed a little.

The commander replied, "No more `Commander this,' and `Commander that.' My friends called me Nero long ago. Please call me by my first name again now."

Hypnos nodded. "Thank you, Nero. I'm glad to call you by your name now and equally pleased to fight alongside you again."

As they spoke, Nero noticed a familiar looking figure in the corner of his eye. He squinted and saw Savi standing near the back of the camp. She had her hood up and was looking at them from afar. Hypnos sensed that Nero had seen her, and he paused for a moment before asking, "You are wondering if she can be trusted, aren't you?" Nero nodded a little sheepishly.

"Do you now know of her identity Hypnos; I mean I know she proved an ally before but we very well know that this does not mean she is one of us." Hypnos nodded; he understood the uncertainty.

"She has called herself Savi, a joke of being a 'saviour'" Hypnos informed Nero, still not pleased with this. "Can she be trusted? I do not know with certainty however Freyja believes in her it seems and she has so far helped us. I see no reason not to."

Nero nodded appearing happy with this response.

The camp was coming together bit by bit with the troops setting up tents and fires. Food was passed around as some of the soldiers even lifted spirits singing some songs of old, their voices echoing off the vast terrain.

Hypnos sits in the centre of the camp while Araya and Freyja flanking him on either side. They are intently discussing the strategies to be implemented during the coming battles while Savi and Nero join in on the conversations at the fires around them with the other soldiers. The flames from the camp fires flicker and sparkle, creating an atmosphere of camaraderie and readiness.

Logan stands alone on the edge of the camp, hunched over with a heavy heart. His head hangs down low and his shoulders sag. His hands are clenched tightly together and his eyes scan for somewhere to belong. He feels isolated and unwelcome, an outcast in his own group, no matter how many people are around him. All he can feel is the disapproval from Hypnos and the judgement of the others for his supposed failure in losing Alec.

Hypnos notices him standing off in the shadows, his face hidden by darkness. He wanted to motion for him to join them at the fire but chose not to and turned his attention away. He feels some guilt over the way he had previously handled his own feelings. He knew that Logan would have given his all but equally knows that the guilt in Logans heart was his own being carried.

As the night sky fades to an inky black, the stars and moon shimmer and twinkle, painting the camp in a soft blue light. All around, tents are pitched and blankets draped over figures resting peacefully. The air is still with settled contentment and a feeling of security as Hypnos and Nero say their goodnights and the others drift off to sleep until the horizon slowly begins to turn pink as the sun starts to rise once again.

Savi stirs from her sleep and opens her eyes to see Hypnos still looking into the distance, his face pensive and his body tensed. She quietly walks up towards him and stands beside the towering presence. He looks down at her, a slight crease between his eyebrows as if he is troubled by something. "What's wrong?" she whispers softly, it soon becoming clear that he has at no point rested during the early hours.

"Listen" Hypnos replies.

Savi listens, his ears searching through the silence until they fell towards the sound of thunder rolling in.

The sky is lit up with a greyish-orange glow as a cloud of dust rises from the horizon. Savi sees a glimmer of movement at its heart. Her eyes narrow as she squints into the haze, trying to discern patterns in the chaos. An army is making its way across the desert towards them with great speed and it is clear it is not overly friendly in nature.

Hypnos stood in all of his majesty, a tall and regal figure watching over his loyal troops. He called out with a powerful voice, the echo reverberating off the walls of the encampment. Instantly his warriors awoke from their slumber, grabbing their weapons as they formed ranks orderly and with purpose. A ray of light shone down on Nyx's leader, Araya, as he emerged from his tent and ran to Hypnos side.

"Prepare them Araya, i fear we do not have long," the great warrior bleakly requested.

Araya fell back towards his troops and looked upon the army before him. His piercing gaze seemed to drill each soldier into place and fill them with courage for what lay ahead. One by one the men fell quiet at his command, eager to hear what he had to say about why they were here - not just to protect their own lives, but also to ensure freedom for those who may suffer if they failed. Araya spoke with conviction and power, his message resounding in every corner of the camp.

The dust cloud grows larger and closer until its presence is undeniable - an army of Koschei marching towards them with intent to destroy everything in their path. The Nyx army stands firm; courage fills every heart and the fear of death no longer matters.

Freyja joined Savi and stepped up on the opposing side of Hypnos, their eyes all fixed on the armies that had gathered behind them, forming a formidable looking force under Araya's order. Freyja's face was set in stone, reflecting the fierce determination that burned within her.

As Hypnos surveyed his troops, he caught sight of Nero standing just a short distance away, he had gathered in with the troops whilst Araya stood proud and tall at the front of his men. The two friends exchanged a silent nod - there would be time for words later, but right now they both knew what they had to do.

"The men are ready at your command Hypnos," Araya informs him.

Hypnos raised his sword high above his head, its gleaming blade catching the early morning sun. He let out a deafening battle cry, and the sound echoed across the vast desert wasteland where they stood.

As one, the army behind him roared in response - the battle that lay ahead would be like nothing many of them had ever faced before.

The Nyx surged forward, their weapons flashing blindingly in the early morning sun and their rallying shouts louder than Koschei's own despite the gulf in numbers that once again proved dramatic in their difference.

The sky was alive with the intensity of battle as both armies clashed together in a ferocious skirmish. Arrows whizzed through the air, swords clanged and twirled against one another in an intense flurry, and cries of distress echoed throughout the battlefield as warriors fought for what they believed to be right or simply for the control they wished to gain.

Despite facing insurmountable odds, the Nyx soldiers stood strong in their footing and refused to back down.

Through the fighting Hypnos realised one thing - Probetor was not on the battlefield. He looked towards where Freyja stood and it was clear she noticed the absence. Hypnos's eyes were drawn to the ground, looking for some clue as to his location. Around them bodies fell and swords slashed through the air like a spray of bullets as shields were used for makeshift cover but he saw none of it, every ounce of his focus went into finding Probetor. They needed him to be here to end this either way, and wherever he may be would surely also be the location of Alec.

Suddenly in the distance lightning cracked loudly above Lemuri as a dark cloud appeared, sending a chill of fear through the Nyx's ranks.

Freyja fell to her knees as the lightning tore through the sky, appearing to have been hit hard by some unseen force. As Hypnos bent down to assist, she looked up at him with a glaze in her eyes displaying a fear within her that he had never bore witness to before.

"Lemuri, she is in trouble!" The panicked words left Freyja's mouth in a single breath, as she tightly gripped the warrior's arm. Hypnos looked up at the clouds gathering over Lemuri as he realised, Probetor was not here for a very good reason, this battle was a distraction!

Savi arrived next to Freyja providing assistance in supporting her, the sweat across her brow mixed with the dirt of the floor and the deep red liquid oozing from a cut to her head. Hypnos looked down at the two and for the first time felt complete hopelessness.

Hypnos's voice trembled, not with fear but with frustration as he stared out in hopelessness at the incredible storm brewing.

"Savi, are you able to get us there?"

Without hesitation, Savi rose to her feet without a word. She grasped her weapon with both hands before she dropped it beside her and sprinted toward the Lemuri pathway.

"SAVI!" Hypnos bellowed after her.

Freyja strained against the agony throbbing in her head as she pulled herself to stand using Hypnos body as support. Despite the pain, it faded away gradually.

With a heavy sigh, Freyja uttered, "Leave her. We must trust she knows what she is doing."

Though his heart was filled with doubt, Hypnos had no time to respond before they heard soft footsteps creeping up behind them. Out of nowhere a Koschei soldier appeared with their sword raised above them. Instinctively Freyja raised her arm and shot out a ball of energy towards the attacker in an effort to protect them both from harm. "We must focus the fight here, whatever you may believe is happening elsewhere, this fight is of importance" Freyja said in a calming voice.

The air was heavy with dread as everyone stopped what they were doing and looked to the sky as a piercing shriek broke through the clouds and an immense creature descended from the heavens, its wingspan casting a shadow over everything below it.

The enormous dragon circled in the sky above, removing any doubt about its existence and spreading alarm and surprise throughout all below, many who would have believed the tales of this beast to be nothing but myth. It let out one more deafening roar before swooping down and landing out of sight behind the wall of water that remained standing tall.

Hypnos and Freyja shared a look of deep concern before they heard a voice in the distance bellowing out over the crowds, "Araya, come forth!"

It was Gree, standing confidently on the battlefield calling out the leader of the army who he could see fighting not far from where he stood. He knew that taking Araya down would have a massive impact on the moral of the troops and in an unusual display of bravado he eagerly wished to see it happen.

Araya stepped forward with his head held high, slightly limp from the fight and exhausted but allowing a smile to creep onto his face at the thought of taking down such a powerful enemy.

Hypnos watched helplessly as Gree drew his sword and readied for battle. He attempted to fly over to Araya in a desperate attempt to help, but any time he dared take off the air was filled with arrows raining down upon him, keeping him grounded. In a flash Gree was face-to-face with Araya and their swords clashed in a brilliant shower of sparks. Hypnos held his breath, knowing full well Araya's skill as a fighter, yet not believing he could defeat such an ageless magical creature.

The fight was a tangled mess of clashing weapons and skills. Araya was agile like quicksilver, darting around Gree's powerful swings. His sword darted in to deliver blows only to quickly retreat from Gree's counterattack. Despite his impressive effort, Araya was pushed back by Gree's relentless onslaught of combined force and magic.

Hypnos looked on in terror as Araya continuously fought back against the increasing pressure until finally, he succumbed to the force and stumbled backwards, unable to stand against Gree's incredible strength. With one final powerful blow, Gree sent Araya flying off his feet and crashing to the ground below, his armour rattling from the impact.

Gree's smirk widened as he stood looming over Araya. His cold gaze shifted towards Hypnos, and with a cruel relish he lifted his sword high into the air like a glinting guillotine. Every muscle in Hypnos' body tensed in terror as he watched the blade descend on Araya, who knelt defeated but proud, giving one final nod towards Hypnos before being swallowed by death's embrace. The sound of steel hitting flesh echoed through the silence as Hypnos could do nothing but watch him die as he continued his charge forward, now filled with anger and wishing vengeance, once again on this field of battle a great leader is lost to a villain of Maredrom.

With a cry of rage, Hypnos charged at Gree head on, to be met with a powerful swing of his sword. He barely managed to avoid the strike and instead used it as momentum to close the distance between them and launch himself into a flurry of attacks.

Gree was not taken off guard however, parrying every blow with ease and retaliating with his own strikes that threatened to break through Hypnos' defence. Still, Hypnos kept pushing forward and dodging around Gree's swings until he found an opening in his defence and thrust forward with all his strength.

Gree stumbled back from the sudden force, barely managing to keep his footing while Hypnos kept pressing forward, the smugness falling from Gree's face as he realised, he may have overshot on his own abilities.

Their swords clashed again and again as they fought for control of the fight, each trying to end on top. Sparks flew in every direction as their blades collided in what seemed like an endless battle before finally both combatants stepped back from each other. They both stood there breathing heavily, sweat dripping down their faces as they waited for who would make the next move.

Gree sprang into action with the speed of an attacking panther, quickly closing the distance between him and Hypnos as he sent powerful blasts of energy forward. Hypnos stumbled backward as Gree pushed him to the ground, pressing his blade against his throat. His words were cold and precise as he commanded Hypnos to turn and face Lemuri. The pressure from the sharp edge of his sword made it impossible for Hypnos to ignore Gree's command.

Every slow rotation of his head dug the icy blade deeper into his flesh. His eyes drifted up to Lemuri as commanded as he saw Gree's dragon diving in and disappear amidst a sea of fire.

The flames spread from one edge of the water wall to the next, engulfing it so quickly that all Hypnos could see were bright orange flashes as the wall of water evaporated into the surrounding air. When the wall fell away, he saw what Gree had wanted him to see.

It was a long way away from where they stood but Hypnos could see clear enough, there stood Probetor and alongside him, Alec.

21) Blazing wings

Hypnos stared out at the battlefield; the battle raged on all around as all around him good men and bad fell alike, all are equal at the end of a sword after all. For all of his super-human strength and skill, it was becoming increasingly clear that defeat was inevitable.

Despite the growing anger and frustration, he felt, guilt started to replace those emotions as he realized his mission to protect the realms was all but failed. He thought of Alec, who had been dragged into this fight by no fault of his own, and then remembered Morpheus – a loyal friend who gave up his life to save them all, yet here he was potentially losing his own and changing nothing except for supervising over all of Morpheus work being undone.

"You should be grateful" Gree gloated, "At least I will end your life for you before you can see the realms change, you will at least not witness our rule and become enslaved. You're welcome."

Gree raised his blade, determined to bring Hypnos down with a powerful crash. He steeled himself against what was to come and locked eyes with Gree - he would not cower away in death, but meet it bravely with open gaze. Despite achieving the warrior's ideal of dying on the battlefield in glory, no triumph graced Hypnos' heart as he faced his impending death.

Gree held his sword aloft, the blade glinting with malicious intent in the moonlight. He brought it down in a single swift motion, but before it could reach its intended target, Freyja had materialized from nowhere, her battle cry cut through the air, reverberating off the surrounding landscape as she thrust her hands outwards and summoned a glimmering shield around Hypnos in a brilliant flash of light. Gree's blade struck the barrier and ricocheted back up into the air, throwing him off balance and forcing Freyja to stumble backwards as she felt the force of the impact herself, thankfully without the sharpness of the blade itself attached.

An enraged growl escaped from Gree's lips as he raised his blade again for another attack. But before he could complete his swing, he froze mid-stride. His eyes widened in shock as Hypnos saw a bloody sword erupt from Gree's chest in a spray of crimson, rending through flesh and bone like an unstoppable force. He tumbled forward onto his knees with a thud, life spilling from him like water from a broken dam.

As Gree crumpled to the ground in an anguished heap, Logan stood triumphant behind him. His weapon still firmly held in his grasp, and a stern look upon face. He had obtained the atonement that he sought.

Hypnos and Logan locked eyes in a moment of intense understanding. The look conveyed their shared suffering and pain, but also the respect between two warriors who had experienced the same trials and tribulations.

Hypnos felt a rush of guilt surge through him for how he had treated Logan, yet was still partial to feeling that this chaotic situation was born from Logans recklessness instead of controlled Nyx soldier conduct. In that moment, time seemed to stand still as they silently acknowledged all that they had endured together and what lay ahead.

As Hypnos helped Freyja back to her feet, Logan remaining at arm's length, they watched as the Koschei army seemed to rampage in the absence of their fallen commander -it was time to end this battle once and for all.

"We need to end this, before he does," Hypnos said pointing towards Probetor, his voice unusually shaky.

Freyja nodded as she steadied herself, the blow she had taken had been hard and she had hit the ground with such force that her outline could be seen temporarily embedded into the dirt. As she regained herself, she looked up into the sky, the darkness and clouds that had developed over Lemuri spread as Probetor's attack grew closer and closer to completion, each moment of suffering Lemuri felt seemed to spill over into Freyja's own being as the feelings of doom became more obvious with each passing moment.

"He is using Alec's body as a conduit" Freyja replied despairingly, "He cannot take the full force himself if he wishes to unlock Lemuri and release the Jinn, it all makes sense now what he had planned, he is sacrificing Alec in order to release The Jinn!" Freyja finished speaking in a quietened voice, almost as if berating herself for not having had seen such an obvious plan.

The breath of a reprieve was barely out of Hypnos' lungs before the full weight of their situation settled on his shoulders. With no time to savour the moment, he launched away from the battlefield with powerful strokes of his wings, heading towards Araya and recklessly cutting through any Koschei soldiers that got in his way as the arrows flew around him, only seeming to miss his outstretched wings thanks to the poor aim of Koschei forces. He descended close by and danced around them, his sword tearing them apart as if they were paper dolls before coming to a stop in front of Nero.

"Nero," Hypnos bellows out over the noise and between swipes of the sword to fend of the enemy, "We need to be moving in that direction" he says pointing towards Lemuri. "We need to move the fight that way." Nero glances in the direction of Lemuri and nods.

"Towards the dragon?" He responds eagerly, "I thought you'd never ask!"

Hypnos smiled as briefly as the moment allowed, Nero's eagerness to fight a dragon was commendably entertaining. He calls out Hypnos orders across the field and in unity every Nyx soldier changed formation and angle to begin pushing the direction of the fight northwards. It worked, and before they knew it the fight was heading that way.

Hypnos did not know what they would achieve once there, in fact he feared that being in the vicinity of the beast could alone wipe out all of his men as well as all of the Koschei, however he also knew nothing could be achieved from their current position, especially with Probetor over there finalising his end plan.

Hypnos eyes the air around him warily, as arrows and other weapons are thrown in all directions he decides not to take to the air once again deciding he was exceptionally luck to have not been bought down previously. He moves steadily, a sword in one hand and a shield in the other. His feet are firmly plant-ed on the ground, as if he is heavily rooted to it and is determined to stay in one place. His gaze is focused and determined on Freyja's form, not wavering for a second as he begins to move forward one step at a time until he is once again by her side.

The Nyx soldiers fight fiercely against the Koschei forces, their weapons of light and wings of feathers a stark contrast to the darkness of the enemy. The dragon roars and smokes in the distance, its wings stretching out as if it were an eagle ready to swoop down upon them. Hypnos voice carries across the field commanding his men to push forward, a reminder that they must continue fighting with everything they have in order to prevent Probetor from unlock-ing Lemuri.

Each Nyx soldier fights with determination and courage, knowing that this could be their last battle before freedom is truly achieved. The sound of battle echoed through the air and could be heard for miles around.

Freyja's fear was palpable as Probetor walked up and down anxiously, sens-ing victory with each passing moment whilst fully aware of the loss of Gree.

He longed for The Jinn to be released, a more than adequate replacement for a right-hand man he had grown to not be overly fond of.

Freyja stared in despair as she witnessed the Lemuri pools fading away into nothing before their eyes. The impending thunder clouds boiled with ferocity and the waters of Lemuri had an eerie dark hue to them of which was a far cry from the usual clarity and beauty. All around, dream orbs floated away from the pools, desperately trying to find another way but in vain as the underground passageways dried up. The rivers and lakes of Lemuri wilted as blackened skies cast a heavy darkness throughout Earth and beyond, instilling a sense of dread deep within, all that remained was a blanket of darkness, spreading over all the realms equally. The days for harmony were quickly fading.

Alec was illuminated in the night sky, his matted hair providing the only indication of his identity. With a flared nostril and bulging veins, he gripped the blade of Morpheus with both hands, plunging it deep into the waters of Lemuri. His body quaked with effort as sparks flew from contact between the blade and what seemed like solidified water. The current cascading over the blade appeared more like jelly than liquid, then crystallizing before their eyes. The life force drained away from Alec's frame as he sustains himself solely on sheer will, harnessing the power within the blade due to his Demi-God status. He poured energy out from himself like steam from a boiling teapot, Probetor stayed in control of Alec's hands, he knew he could not free himself from his father's grip, his last thoughts before his body became lifeless was that of those he had left behind.

Power crackled over the Probetor's hands as he worked his magic on Lemuri, and the black smoke emitting from the charred sword attested to his success. The Jinn was being released after millennia of imprisonment; it was sucking life-force from Alec's body, feeding off him. He no longer held consciousness or even knew what was happening, his mind was no longer with him and his body an empty vessel, he was one step away from being a standing corpse, a vessel now being used by Probetor, no more than a Koschei soldier.

Freyja looked desperately at Hypnos who had realised the same as her. They knew that everything they could be doing was being done, alas they also knew it was not enough to save his life. They were making ground towards Alec's position, they were despite their lacking numbers winning the battle against the Koschei who continued to attack in a mindless, illogical and poorly calculated fashion. Hypnos and Freyja continued to fight alongside all of the Nyx soldiers as they pushed further and further. The dragon was becoming closer to them with each continued step, it eagerly awaited their arrival feeling the very real possibility of being able to slaughter in extreme numbers, the beast had a large appetite after all. The dragon now stood within the vast expanse of water that lay between Midjun and Lemuri, the land bridge no longer in passable fashion created issues for Hypnos, one that Probetor had planned all along. He had successfully created the perfect scenario for his plan, and had them enact most of the actions for him.

As the dragon became within reaching distance the Koschei with their backs to it and without the ability to fear, seemed unusually scared. They began trying to back up in alternate directions trying in vain to alter the path from one which would bring them into direct contact with the beast, it seemed that even they were afraid of some things.

It was too late; the dragon had sensed his chance and Probetor had instructed it to not allow them to attempt access to Lemuri.

With a deafening roar and an extreme level of ferocity, the beast began to breath fire, torching many Koschei and Nyx alike. Freyja repeatedly put-up magical barriers but they could not cover everyone and were beaten down with each breath the dragon took, each time knocking her back in equal measure.

The flames licked at the sky as their screams echoed across the battlefield. Hypnos and Freyja debated the logic of their plan, they could do nothing from here and the dragon would surely slay them all, they knew however they had to be there to do anything, but even so, what could they do?

The sounds of burning flesh and despair filled the air as both allies and foes alike were engulfed by the flames. Those that weren't consumed by the dragon's fire retreated in panic or remained in an attempt to fight on against such a powerful adversary. Freyja sent out telepathic messages for those that had survived to run while she continued her attempts to shield them from further harm. Nero and Logan fought on despite being surrounded by flames, both men helping others along the way and showing their true leadership qualities.

Hypnos felt insignificant in the shadow of the colossal dragon looming before him. Its enormous scales glimmered like rubies, and its imperious gaze seemed to mock Hypnos' helplessness as it reared up, flames flaring around its monstrous face. Its wingspan was like a mountain range, casting a pall of despair as the beast prepared to unleash its fury upon Hypnos. Fear coursed through his veins as he faced sure death once again. He has no intention of backing down as he braces with sword raised, the battle around him continues to rage on amongst those who have not fled or been killed already, the concern of the dragon seeming to dissipate as they turn their attention onto one another once more.

Freyja's hands trembled as she poured her magic into holding back the beast, desperately trying to subdue it. But Probetor's strength had grown too great, and all of Freyja's power could not make much of a dent in his control. The air around Freyja fizzed with sandy energy as she tried to plant her feet. Alongside controlling Alec's bracelets and commanding Lemuri how much control could he hold Freyja wondered to herself. Surely his grip would slip soon, surely?

However, he was not simply controlling Lemuri's waters but at this time successfully drawing power as well. With the blade plunged into the waters the full power of Lemuri coursed through Alec's body and Probetor channelled this through the bracelets around his wrists. Lemuri was broken but still held the power of the realms, even the smallest drop of this made Probetor, even if only temporarily, the most powerful being alive.

From out of nowhere a heroic figure appeared on Lemuri. In the midst of chaos and the broken landscape, he had masterfully fashioned a makeshift raft from what was left around him, and with an unwavering determination, he prepared to do battle with Probetor having incredibly now made his way across the waters. With an unyielding gaze, he stepped forth between Probetor and the dragon, raising his sword in defiance. His skilled manoeuvres parried each attack that Probetor threw at him, unwavering in his resolution despite the great danger he faced against such a foe.

Probetor bore down on him with relentless might and fury, seemingly annoyed that he had dared to present himself as a competitor. All the while, Nero had reached Freyja and Hypnos, providing them with much needed support as he held off any Koschei trying to charge them down.

"Is that, Logan?" He questioned. Hypnos nodded; indeed, it was.

Freyja spread her shield like a curtain, protecting Hypnos and Nero from the fiery blasts of the dragon as if it were an exploding volcano. The creature's skin was thick and tough, like steel. They had no real means by which to attack, and all they could do was throw items from where they stood. They could not reach the beast and even if they could penetrate its thick hide with their most powerful weapons, they would not be able to kill it. Freyja struggled and buckled under the weight of pressure flying from the beast's mouth at them, they seemed like ants in the eyes of a man wielding a flamethrower.

"We cannot just stand here," Nero shouted at Hypnos observing that they were achieving nothing.

Hypnos looked around, each moment leading to this point seemed like a struggle and now here they were at a point with no way forwards nor back. He first glanced at Freyja who was now down on one knee struggling to hold back to force of the dragon, then to his friend Nero whom stood nearby bewildered and lost as to what to do. He glanced across the waters where he could see Logan attacking Probetor looking like a small child trying to fight a man whilst Alec stood lifelessly in the backdrop stuck to the blade sucking his life. Araya lay dead at the hands of Gree and the battle behind him raged on, soldiers of both sides seemingly a little surer of their own in fighting with the dragon occupied by the others in front of him.

Hypnos closed his eyes and took a deep breath, trying to calm himself amidst the chaos surrounding him. He knew he had to think of something fast, before the dragon's fiery breath consumed them all. As he was lost in thought, he heard a faint whisper in his ear. It was a voice he had heard before; however, he could not place it, the voice seemed to appear in his head which at first led him to believe it was Freyja herself attempting to communicate with him.

"Hypnos," the voice said. "I can help you. I am now here." He turned to face where he thought was the source of the voice, but he saw no one.

"Who are you?" he asked.

"You know who I am. and I have continued watching over you, Hypnos. You are a force to be reckoned with, but you cannot defeat the dragon. Let me help you, allow me to place you on Lemuri."

Hypnos was hesitant, but he was equally desperate. As he debated the sincerity of the mysterious voice in his head another much more recognisable entered also; the voice of Freyja reverberated in Hypnos' head like a hammer driving a nail.

"Trust it, the only way to defeat this fire is with fire in return". He knew there was no room to reason or argue and he placed all his trust in her.

Across the waters Logan's strength was waning as Probetor's relentless onslaught grew ever more ferocious. Inching closer to certain death with each passing moment, Logan was no real match for what stood in front of him; unless something miraculous happened and neither was Hypnos for the beast in front of him. Taking all into account. His thoughts drifted for what seemed like hours before his body yielded to the wisdom of Freyja and he murmured in solemn acceptance: "Ok."

With that one singular word the darkness of the hills around the valley were broken by a blinding light that illuminated everything. All those present beheld a sight more beautiful than any they had ever seen before - molten orange lightning split the sky, and thunder rolled like drums beating out a call of warning. The grey clouds were torn apart and rain cascaded from the heavens in liquid gold.

As if sent from the gods themselves, a phoenix descended from on high and hovered delicately above Hypnos. Its wings spread wide as ripples of light began to travel down from the skies, transforming the ground into a golden sea with each passing moment. Like pebbles thrown into a lake, waves of light echoed outwards from the bird, slowly filling all with its glow.

Hypnos felt a warmth fall over him as the giant bird hovered above.

He felt a sudden surge of energy course through him like never before. His own wings, which had been white as snow, suddenly began to shimmer with gold as the Phoenix gifted upon him a taste of its own great power.

He lifted himself to the height of the phoenix and stared into its ancient eyes - the power radiating from it was undeniable as it shared a knowing nod with Hypnos, he could not help but feel a connection with the bird as he looked into its eyes. Then with a loud caw, the Phoenix burst into flames and flew off towards the dragon. Hypnos followed suit, he knew now what he needed to do as he himself headed off to be by logans side, his wings now glowing in golden brilliance as he ascended higher and higher above his friends below. His wing beats created an incredible wind that blew outwards at great speed.

Hypnos surged above the glassy waters, his wings beating like the drums of war in the sky. His newfound strength sent a wave like a whirlpool in his wake. When he reached the far shore Probetor was there, waiting for him and unimpressed. The ruthless figure remained still, his face betraying neither fear nor shock. Yet, he knew he could not escape the airborne warrior's wrath. Hypnos, emboldened by courage, pounced forward with an almighty roar and collided with Probetor head-on, their bodies clashing upon the sprawling, once lush pastures of Lemuri.

Probetor's grip on both Alec and the dragon slip as he tumbles to the floor, a roar of anger and frustration leave Probetor as he turns his attention to now defeating the two men standing tall against him.

22) Savi's surprise

Hypnos and Logan stood as one, their combined strength now showing as a force much more trying of Probetor. With their weapons raised, ready to battle for the freedom of Lemuri they close in on him from either side as he stands ominously awaiting them.

Probetor stands in front of them, his cloak billowing around him. His hands held in front of his body, black fire licks out from his palms as he fires off a barrage of flames, the air crackles and sizzles as they reach Hypnos and Logan. The men stand their ground, exchanging blows with the powerful figure and the ground shakes with each impact. The duo are pushed to their limits but remain relentless in their fight for freedom, the flames licking around them as they take every hit. Despite the danger they continue to fight, determination etched on their faces. The force of his fireballs impacts them, though despite their injuries both press onward with determination.

The Phoenix itself soars high above the dragon, its wings shining in the light as they catch fire with each flap. It screeches as it darts around the larger beast, dipping and dodging while it claws and bites with its sharp talons and beak. The dragon roars in retaliation, spewing fire from its gaping jaws as it attempts to catch the Phoenix with its powerful wings. The two battle fiercely in a clash of light and fire, their scales and feathers shimmering as they move. Neither seems to get the upper hand as they continue to battle, each determined to come out victorious. The dragon's wings beat ferociously as it defends against the Phoenix's attack, its own claws and teeth gnashing as fire roars from its mouth. The scales of the dragon and feathers of the Phoenix sparkle and shimmer in the sunlight, twinkling brightly as they move swiftly around each other. The dragon's wings are a brilliant gold and its scales a deep emerald, while the Phoenix's feathers glint with hues of fiery orange and red. Both glimmer in the light as they weave around each other, a magnificent display of power and beauty as they battle.

Freyja had now been helped to her feet by a near standing soldier, the battle between the Nyx and the Koschei forces continuing as they clashed in a storm of light and darkness.

Freyja stands still with her hands at her sides, her eyes wide and cautious as she looks outwards upon the chaotic battleground. Her mouth downturned in a moment of sadness as she takes in the destruction and violence before her. Tears stream down her face as she watches the creatures clash, feeling a deep sense of sorrow for the struggle and loss.

Her sorrow morphed into rage as she swivelled to face Lemuri and the savage battle transpiring there. Through the fray of the Phoenix and dragon, Logan and Hypnos could be seen yet facing Probetor; however, it was decisively clear that Probetor held dominance as both men fought desperately to keep their turf, now only in defence.

Freyja turned to the soldier besides her "What is your name?" She requests with urgency.

"Gram, ma'am," the soldier responded with a bow.

"I appreciate the courtesies, however there is no time for that, you are now with me," she informs him with a steely-eyed resolve. "We must discover a way over there!" She demanded with finger pointed squarely at Lemuri.

She was certain that victory would evade them, yet her conviction persisted that attempting was their only choice. Gram jerked his head in comprehension and feverishly surveyed the area for any sign of how they could reach Lemuri.

Suddenly a roar echoed from just behind them, startled, all faces twisted around to find Nero panting heavily, racing up to them. He had heard Freyja's desperate plea and rushed to her side. "It can be done!" he declared assuredly, "Hypnos and I found a way earlier. Savi gave us a door, a passageway, though it has been sealed off by the landslide we evoked to shield it."

Nero indicated towards a colossal heap of rubble and dirt scattered in front of the looming mountainside. Freyja had heard tales about a mysterious network of tunnels; indeed, they were written about in the many historical and magical books that adorned her walls in her vast, seemingly never-ending collection.

Freyja and Nero locked eyes, conveying a silent understanding. Freyja then spun towards Gram with absolute resolve. Drawing in a deep breath, she mustered all her waning energy and let loose an immense ray of light aimed at the rubble. The force made the earth tremble and shifted mountains of dirt. With overwhelming strength, a blast of fire struck the mountain, carving out a small pathway into the passageway beyond that had been barricaded before.

As the gap opened, she collapsed to the ground, utterly spent. Gram and Nero hoisted her up, "Hurry Freyja," Nero snapped as Gram blocked any approaching assailants.

The Phoenix and the Dragon continued their aerial dance, neither willing to yield in their tussle for supremacy. They fought against one another with ferocity, each seeking victory over their foe. The dragon belched forth more flames from its maw while its wings beat in powerful gusts of wind that threatened to tear apart anything that came too close. Sparks flew from the Phoenix's feathers as it launched itself bravely forward in an attempt to overpower its adversary.

Both creatures temporarily succumbed to the others power as they found themselves tumbling to the ground, crashing heavily into Lemuri and sending a shockwave that sent the occupants of the island tumbling.

Hypnos and Logan took advantage of this momentary distraction, using it to gain some much-needed distance between themselves and Probetor as they shielded their injuries. As the two creatures retook to the air the men regained their footing, Probetor looked menacingly at the two warriors who had distanced themselves and laughed, this was the best of the opposition and he had barely broken a sweat in not just repelling them both but in having the upper hand.

As he stretched his arms outward, obsidian flames whipped around his wrists and climbed up to his forearms. The warriors gawked at his ominous figure suspended in the air as formidable energy surged from within him, a menacing aura radiating from his core. His immense power permeating the atmosphere.

Hypnos yanked Logan up, his body convulsing as he fought against the agony. His earlier injuries still inflicted a deep pain, and the current combat he was losing intensely was worsening his condition. Yet, he stood firm with an unflinching fortitude; ready to take on another round despite all the adversity.

Hypnos furiously rocketed straight towards Probetor, wings blazing with Phoenix power as he flew in a circular fashion as if having just left the chamber of a gun. He was enveloped in a fiery cocoon as he flew like a projectile to his target. Probetor was preoccupied with his own triumphant crowing and only noticed Hypnos' attack when it was too late.

He had no chance to react before Hypnos clutched onto him and slammed him to the surface, snuffing out the flames and sending him crashing back down to earth. Probetor thudded down to earth not far from where Logan now stood, he was livid at having been distracted and caught off guard as he turned his attention to the nearer man to enact his vengeance.

He leaped to his feet just as Freyja careened out of the Lemuri end of the tunnel, Gram and Nero at her side. They burst onto the island with a deafening roar, their battle cry reverberating off the walls.

Freyja veered away from Probetor however whilst the others intended target remained Probetor himself and joining Hypnos and Logan, she made her way for Alec instead; a sinister black smoke still leaked from his sword, concealing him in writhing shadows as his body continued to weaken further and further. A pair of eyes could be seen looming in the depths of the smoke—The Jinn was almost free, and this filled Freyja with dread for what was to come.

However, as Logan whirled around to face his incoming comrades, the scattered throbs of agony throughout his body vanished into one brilliant jolt through his chest. Nero's expression told him that he was already too late, for Probetor had already yanked the sword from his chest. The sharp point inched out from behind Logan and he felt the sting as it slid back into Probetor's grasp.

Logan's weakened body soon succumbed to his injury as he fell momentarily onto his knees before finally to the side, the last thing he saw before all went dark was Hypnos rushing to his aide in vain, for the damage was already done and irreversible. He had in the end died the Nyx way as he'd wished, in battle trying to protect Lemuri, rescue his friend and keep them from harm. As Logan closed his eyes, a single tear rolled down his cheek as he thought of himself however as a failure.

The Jinn erupted into an ear-splitting wail as he drew nearer to his liberation, and Freyja sprinted towards it terrified that it was nearing completion.

A thunderous boom shook the earth, and Freyja stopped dead in her tracks. Her eyes widened in terror as an incandescent beam blazed from the blade. In that instant, she realized Lemuri had lost and split open and the Drasal tree now lay exposed, just beyond Probetor's reach.

The tree was a majestic sight to behold. Its branches danced in the wind and glowed with their own magical power. The bark seemed alive and glittered with a million stars, while its leaves emitted an enchanting melody as they swayed back and forth.

Probetor made for the tree, his hands trembling with anticipation as a brief display of excitement came across him. He knew that if he could get control of this ancient and powerful energy source, he would be unstoppable. He was so close to achieving his long sought-after goal: absolute power over all of Lemuri and beyond, for him and his master.

He hurriedly moved past his near-freed master and into the chamber beyond Lemuri, his destination being the tree.

Freyja reached the area surrounding the falls, the waters that lay before it frozen in a solid crystal, the waters still ebbing out and flowing but like broken glass compounding and building around them, all else from below evaporating as she watched the dreams of all the realms float away on the wind. She could progress no further; Alec lay within reach but she could not penetrate the surrounding cloud. As she tried in vain The Jinn's wispy incomplete presence glided up to the edge of the cloud and stood mockingly in front of Freyja, a voice whispered on the wind quietly but equally intimidatingly.

"Hello old foe" it said sinisterly as Freyja froze, the voice was one that she had not heard for millennia, after all this time and after all the loss that long ago, had it all been in vain?

Probetor now stood next to the tree, seeming almost tearful in his joy, his grip tightened around his sword as an insidious grin spread across his face. With a single thrust, Probetor sent the blade into the trunk of the Drasal Tree releasing years of energy. The light vanished and a strange stillness filled the air as all eyes turned to Probetor in disbelief.

He had done it; as the wispy breath of the tree swirled around him, they could all see, he had managed to gain control of its power.

A surge of energy radiated from within him as his immense power increased exponentially, radiating menacingly through the atmosphere like a dark cloud hovering over Lemuri as all of the realms plunged into darkness, panic reigned supreme across all the lands as it seemed the end of days had arrived. Probetor's sinister plan was almost complete - with one swift move he now held all of Lemuri in his grasp, a simple click of his fingers bringing him any request he wished for.

The waters of Lemuri now ceased flowing entirely as Alec fell lifeless to the ground. The cloud around him had gone and so it appeared had the Jinn's presence. All onlookers stood still and in shock not able to contemplate what had just happened. The fight in the air continued with the Phoenix and the dragon as did the battle over on Midjun, but here in this moment time stood still as Probetor now possessed the full power of Lemuri and of the realms themselves.

Freyja reached Alecs side, tears streaming down her face as she caressed his limp body.

She bowed her head in sorrow, but when a sudden chill raced down her spine, she knew something was terribly wrong. The Jinn had broken free from its prison and now possessed Alecs body, its malevolent energy pulsing through her veins like ice. Though it hadn't manifested itself yet, the oppressive dread of its presence was almost tangible in the air.

Freyja's eyes widened with horror as the truth hit her - Alec had willingly sacrificed himself for Lemuri and in doing so, he had become the vessel of one of the most powerful forces in existence.

Probetor had now taken full control, using his newfound power to manipulate all of the realms and its inhabitants with an iron fist. He grew increasingly powerful at an incredible rate as he began to use the magical properties of Lemuri to bend the boundaries between individual worlds. He built an intricate network of portals throughout each realm allowing him to travel freely between them and become even more powerful in a split second.

He used his immense power to cause great destruction across the lands, all the other realms suffered in the immediate aftermath as a darkness shrouded them all and creatures of the dark came to life; nothing was safe from his grasp as he created intense storms, summoned beasts from other realms, and turned everyday objects into living nightmares, he insured they all knew there was a new order before he turned his attentions back to his home realm of Erobus. He let out a deep breath as his mental being came back to Lemuri before snapping his eyes open and staring out from behind the no longer flowing falls.

Freyja now glared in the opposite direction surrounded by her comrades who were now filled with wrath, anguish and misery. They stood together shoulder to shoulder, a powerful-looking group but of no true threat to what loomed before them.

Probetor strode out of the darkness and rested his hand on Alec's body. As he did so he rose up, and stood confidently side by side with Probetor.

"It's good to behold you again master," Probetor exulted. As the others gazed on it was all too clear that although the body was Alec's, his spirit was nowhere to be seen.

The Phoenix above glared in anguish, its heart aching as Alec dissolved before its eyes. Until now, it had fought vigorously against the Dragon, but lacked the force to bring it down. Now though, fuelled by its sorrow and rage, flames leapt from its body and swept towards the dragon's weakened form.

The creature screeched in agony as the Phoenix swooped and circled around it, each dive bringing on another wave of blazing feathers that forced it ever closer to defeat. Time seemed to stand still as the fire billowed outwards, consuming everything under its heat, until with one last cry of victory the Phoenix sent an inferno of flame that wiped away the Dragon completely.

The Phoenix, liberated from the destruction of the dragon, dived furiously towards Probetor.

He had witnessed the demise of his Dragon and primed himself for this cataclysmic event, hurling a torrent of jagged rocks at the blazing bird with a single flick of his wrist. The onslaught of missiles pierced the diving creature and ripped through its wings, hurling it to the ground. All those observing were astounded as the bird transformed mid-air into a human form - much to their amazement they realised, it was Savi.

23) The Jinns return

As they gawked at Savi's ravaged, gasping body, they all shared a shocked silence. Hypnos surveyed Freyja in bewilderment, expecting her to be knowledgeable of the situation, yet even the cognizant and sage Freyja was unaware.

The Phoenix was an awe-inspiring symbol; at any given time, only one ever existed and as one perished another emerged to claim its spot. It combatted on behalf of justice, serving as an emblem of goodness. Freyja like every being knew of the Phoenix, a symbol of virtue that continuously reincarnated after death and one they would read about as children, and even as adults within the pages of literature provided to Sofpavelians. Nowhere within these writings however, not even within the fabled pages nor the theorised had it been suggested that the phoenix was of another being at its heart.

Freyja gazed at Probetor, who was obviously astounded by the revelation himself. His expression shifted from haughtiness to genuine shock and surprise as his eyes glared at the person now sprawled in front of him. It appeared that this wasn't just a normal reaction to the Phoenix manifesting however, but something more profound stirring within him.

The others couldn't help but think that Probetor had made a miscalculation, one that he hadn't foreseen in his plan.

In the beginning, he had thought that he could use the dragon to defeat any of the last standing show of strength that stood in his way and truly conquer Erobus, the people of his homelands would after all be the true possible contenders to stop him and he can easily vanquish all obstacles from the other realms quite quickly, as he had shown. Yet all of a sudden, the show of strength became a greater force than even he had anticipated. The Dragon felled which he had not anticipated happening and the forces he knew of being joined by one that he did not.

From out of nowhere Savi's body began to heal, her wounds miraculously mending themselves and becoming whole once more as phoenix energy coursed through her veins. She rose up from the ground and stood tall before them all, her eyes blazing with an orange fire that lit up those around her. Her power however at this point left and it was clear for all to see - she was something different, Hypnos looked to Freyja seemingly speechless until he managed to utter a word.

"Freyja?" He queried uncertainly.

"No clue," she responded in a delightedly perplexed tone.

It was rare that anything could elude her understanding, let alone something as enchanting and mysterious as this. She ruminated on how this individual had escaped Lemuri's notice for so long in its vast longevity, or failing that why Lemuri would not have shared this knowledge within all of its advice and instructions provided in the past. Questioning the magical waters is not something she would do lightly in their omnipotent nature as it were but still, she could not help but wonder.

The others looked on in bewilderment, unable to comprehend why or how Savi had been chosen as the Phoenix. But one thing was undeniably true - Savi had been imbued with a power that could match even the mightiest of foes.

As she stared, the Phoenix had done what it was meant to do: her body healed, she dropped to her knees. They watched the spirit of the incredible bird leave her and fly off, probably making its way back to the heart of Lemuri in the aftermath of its death - ready to be reborn once more.

Probetor and his cohorts would be wise to think twice before standing against her, surely, they thought, something inexplicable would still live within her depths. As if drawn by a cosmic force, all those present converged in solidarity around Savi, offering their strength and courage to boost hers. Hypnos, Freyja, Nero and Gram stood steadfastly beside her in an impressive display of unwavering camaraderie.

Probetor, although momentarily stunned by the situation could only admire such power, but knew he must not take lightly this new alliance formed before him or any of its members. He stepped back allowing space between them beaming with respect yet holding stubbornly to his desires to conquer Erobus at any cost necessary.

He was surrounded by equally powerful entities, and Jenny had moved next to him from her place in the fight. Her prowess as a warrior had been on display in the battle that continued to rage around them. Her form had dramatically changed, even since Alec last saw her. The beauty that he once fell in love with was long past.

Jenny's presence was now formidable, her frame tall and lanky. Her face revealed no emotion, yet her delicate features were striking in their uniqueness. Her complexion resembled a midnight sky, a lick of navy dancing on her skin like stars caught in the void of space. Her head seemed disproportionately small for the length of her limbs which seemed ever so slightly too long. Her movements seemed almost otherworldly as she swayed, each action offset by an unsettling asymmetry.

Within Alec's body the Jinn had comfortably set up home and now possessed nearly all of the power he had once had. Alec's new form is intimidating, a stark contrast to his former self. His skin is pale and ethereal, and his eyes now devoid of colour.

He moves with a new confidence, exuding power and control. The intense darkness that surrounds him can be seen in the intense manner he carries himself. Behind him are at least fifty of the Koschei forces, many tall and strong warriors. They are dressed in dark armour and stand back prepared to join the fighting at any sign from their superiors. The Jinn's voice is loud and imposing as it cuts through the air as though revealing in its long-awaited freedom, Freyja recognizing it immediately. It has an eerie, disturbing quality that draws attention to itself and she had no fond memories of its sound.

The sword from which he had liberated himself lay on the ground nearby, its demeanour having been as dusky as the Jinn's essence during his years of imprisonment within its frigid metal now shone brightly once again as it had in its years of glory in the firm hands of Morpheus.

Lemuri's waters should have cascaded onto it as they streamed, yet the waters no longer trickled and the once liquid waves stayed an impenetrable solid object. The orbs had been entirely destroyed by this point, no longer flowing at all even in the empty state they had found themselves. Probetor had now severed the realms, no longer bestowing them with the blessing Erobus for so long had provided.

He stepped towards his brother's sword and reached out, wanting to feel its power for himself. He felt an inexplicable force pushing him back as if he were not worthy of wielding such a weapon. He pressed forward, determined to take control of the weapon that had once been so powerful in the hands of his ancestors before him. However, no matter how hard he tried, he was unable to move even an inch closer and eventually his efforts were exhausted. He withdrew from the sword defeated and frustrated - it seemed that some unseen force prevented him from grasping the handle, ensuring that he could not harness its power despite his lineage meaning he would currently by the rightful owner. Back in its true form it could now resist him with much more force whereas whilst holding the Jinn within itself it simply could not.

He forsook the blade, its power now futile to him. The thought left him seething with revulsion. He had always imagined himself to be the rightful heir of this formidable weapon following the death of Morpheus; he felt that his birth right entitled him to be the one capable of wielding it in its entirety and he was well aware of the fact that it would be a useful and impressive weapon to carry forward. Yet here he was, unable to even lay his hands upon it which he found a cruel twist of fate.

He surveyed the small brigade that blocked his path, precisely as he had envisioned it—save for one revealing detail. His gaze rested on Savi, an unexpected complication, and a look of vexation crossed his features. He swivelled to address her alone in an astoundingly courteous manner.

"Hello Gaia, it has been quite a while, I understood you to be Alerion in hiding, i would have also thought long passed? It appears that is not the case!"

Freyja was astounded; she recognized this name but could not comprehend how she had arrived here in this form. Before Savi had a chance to respond to him, Freyja stepped between them and looked at her imploringly.

"Gaia? You are Alec's mother?!" Freyja whispered in disbelief, her voice trembling with a perplexing concoction of emotions.

Savi nodded solemnly, in acknowledgement of Freyja's deduction. Freyja was stunned; this woman standing before her was Gaia, the mother of Alec, the previous love interest of Probetor who fled Earth and sought refuge on Alerion. Despite her acceptance and presence in Alerion she was still Human and therefore dead with presumed age, however, as he said this was not true. Her heart sank as she recognized the truth -

Savi had been hiding in the shadows, watching and protecting her son from afar for years.

But now Alec was gone - possessed by The Jinn - and all that remained was a hollow replica of the boy who once filled the room with life. Freyja felt her heart breaking as she looked at Savi, tears streaming down her cheeks, and whispered, "I'm so sorry." She knew there was nothing she could do to make things right as her grief-stricken demeanour reflected the pain of a mother who had once suffered in the same way.

"Yes, I am Gaia" Savi exhaled heavily, confirming her identity with a sense of relief and finality. The two women clasped each other's hands in a firm grip, and Freyja could feel the intense grief that coursed through Savi.

It was clear that she felt like she had failed Alec, and her sorrow was over-whelming.

"You're right," she uttered in a reverent voice.

Freyja placed her slender hand under Savi's chin and raised her head, her eyes shimmering with discovery. "You are Gaia, and undoubtedly this great power had chosen you for a reason." Her look of wonder revealed the magnitude of what was at stake.

Probetor cast a steely glare between the two women, his voice cutting like a blade. "Enough of these foolish sentimentals! We have an imperative to fulfil!" His words warped as he took on a crueller inflection, "No escape this time Gaia! You shall pay for your betrayal to me, what a day this has turned out to be!"

He advanced with purpose, preparing for the confrontation ahead as his gaze was fixed upon Savi.

The air filled with tension as Probetor stood before them; all eyes were drawn to him at this moment as he marched forth, fearing the transformation he had wrought as he controlled the universe like pieces on a chessboard.

The hush was deafening, the roar of Lemuri Falls no longer reverberated off the mountainside as it previously would have. The battle across the waters had stilled slightly as many survivors had either yielded through exhaustion or fled back home as the realms could be seen collapsing in the heavens above drawing everyone's look northwards with a feeling that nothing but doom awaited both sides now in this war. Only a few hundred remained fighting on either side.

All of a sudden the ground beneath them began to tremble and groan as if it was coming alive with power, Probetor's energy intensified as he began to re-alise his full potential. His black hair moved with the wind that seemed to have been summoned solely by his presence, and a powerful red light radiated from his body, engulfing him in an aura of unbridled power. He had transformed in-to an emanation of pure energy, and the impact of his presence was enough to leave even hardened warriors trembling.

The Jinn was now encircled by this blanket of energy that seemed deter-mined to annihilate anything that stood against it; he could feel its intensity burning through his skin and knew that their enemy would have no chance of survival if Probetor succeeded. A small concern crept into his thoughts as he considered the loyalty that Probetor may still have towards him, this insecurity being enough to show an obvious insecurity within his own movements as he paced behind the being that had released him, watching his every movement and allowing him for now to take centre stage, after all if his loyalty was true then soon The Jinn would rule over the entire cosmos.

The others braced themselves for battle, knowing this fight would be unlike any other before it and would ultimately be the final stand- one where one side alone could emerge victorious. Probetor's voice boomed throughout the entire area like thunder itself, reverberating off the mountaintops as he declared his will - "Surrender now and I will allow you to all live, or stand in my way and perish where you are!" All of a sudden, a giant wall of energy began to form around him, and it quickly gained strength as it flew off in all directions.

The air around them crackled with unseen forces; trees quivered as if they were about to snap under its force. Even the rocks seemed to cower away from it.

As the energy built, it seemed to expand beyond its boundaries, reaching further and further into the sky. It grew taller and wider until it encapsulated the entirety of Erobus.

The inhabitants of Sofpavel had already seen with their own eyes that their utopian life was rapidly unravelling. The skies were alight with a purplish hue from Probetor's overpowering surge, painting the night sky an unearthly colour as their neighbouring realms crumbled before their eyes in the skies above.

Probetor was encased in a nearly impenetrable force field that was pulsing and glowing an even brighter purple than the sky around them. His body had grown in size and was bulging, as if his power was pushing him to the point of explosion. His clothing had been ripped away, exposing the menacing purple glow that was running all over his body.

The Jinn's eyes widened with surprise at the immense potential of Probetor, a power he could never have imagined, was this the same creature that he taught and moulded into a master of the dark arts? He had expected loyalty and unquestioned obedience from the being he had created and nurtured, but now doubt clouded his thoughts - had this powerful entity been unleashed with plans to dominate? Threatened by the prospect of a power greater than his own, the Jinn felt his ancient dread engulf him like an ocean wave. His long incarceration within the world beyond served as a plan for dominance, not servitude.

As Probetor strutted and preened in his newfound prominence, the Jinn witnessed what he feared most - a rival ascendant who could challenge him for supremacy.

Gratitude was unknown to such dark forces, and for Probetor he would face an enemy more determined than ever before. The Jinn felt a pang of frustration as he saw, with absolute clarity, the nature of how their new relationship would evolve: no longer master and servant, but rivals locked in battle. It may not be there as of yet but he had no doubt, once Probetor had finished the final stage of his takeover, once all who stood in his way here were vanquished, he would not be planning on stepping to one side and allowing the Jinn his place at the head of it all.

As Probetor continued to bask in his newfound power, the Jinn retreated to the shadows, plotting his next move. Probetor had created a scenario where they could indeed win, however at what potential cost to himself he was unable to see. He knew that he needed to find a way to regain control over his former protégé before it was too late. The Jinn had always prided himself on his ability to manipulate and control those around him, but he had not seen anyone as powerful as this, not even Morpheus himself.

He weighed his options as he contemplated what to do next.

Even if he managed to defeat Probetor, he knew there would still be a task at hand and he was in reality still coming to full strength himself. It was one that Probetor himself had prepared the stage for and that would potentially enable him to complete it successfully without the orchestrator. The Jinn's arrogance however left him feeling more than confident in his ability to handle whatever came next.

That is when Freyja stepped forward, standing tall and confident alongside her friends Hypnos and Savi. She looked at Probetor with a sense of unwavering determination.

"Probetor," she began, "we know that this power you have gained must feel intoxicating, but I urge you to take a different path." Freyja gestured to the wall of energy that held them all prisoner, "These are powerful forces which you now control. You have the capability of altering the destiny of Erobus, indeed of all the realms that exist. But I ask you to consider what will happen if you insist on using your newly acquired strength for evil? We all understand how much pain and destruction it could bring." Freyja paused briefly here, allowing her words to sink in before continuing. "You have been lost to the dark for so long now, but I beg you to think of who you once were, Probetor, brother of Morpheus, rightful heir to the throne. Father of Alec and once loving partner of Savi, look at them now. look at all you have done, is this really what you seek?"

At that moment, Probetor's rage seemed to boil over and he screamed out in a voice filled with hatred, his usual cold calm demeanour slipping slightly.

"I have been nothing but betrayed. I was betrayed by Morpheus! Betrayed by Erobus! And then finally betrayed by Gaia who then took Alec from me!" Probetor's eyes glowed with such intensity and hatred that the walls of energy surrounding them all began to quake and tremble.

Freyja realised it was not as simple as him having been turned towards the dark by The Jinn, he had a genuine belief in his conviction for vengeance and in turn welcomed it in. He continued his tirade as he unleashed a wave of dark energy which caused everyone present to take several steps back.

The Jinn's eyes blazed with determination as he approached Morpheus' blade unseen by all others as their focus lay elsewhere. Despite the danger, he reached out and grasped it by the blade without hesitation. The blade did not repel him, but allowed him to wield its power.

As he raised it high, he felt a tug in his gut that threatened to tear him apart. But the Jinn refused to be denied - he had come too far to give up now. With all his strength, he swung the blade at Probetor, determined to end his enemy's life once and for all knowing it was the only weapon at this moment that could stand defeat him. Suddenly, the force pulling on him became too much to bear, and everything went black.

He paused mid-air unable to finish his swing as the mysterious force grew stronger still, yanking him back until he was almost torn in two.

He felt himself rip away from Alec's body, coarse matter slipping through his fingers like dust. As he twisted, his astral form hovered outside of Alecs body, looking on in despair as the sword stayed stubbornly clasped in Alec's own hands. White-hot rage pulsed through his veins as the connection between them was broken and amazingly, he had regained a body all his own. Unshackled from captivity, he stood independently on his two feet and scowled down at Alec and the figure he had inhabited. Understanding he was now truly free; a tsunami of euphoria engulfed him despite the loss of the weapon he had wished to utilise.

Almost immediately, the Jinn began to recover his full power as Alecs body fell limply to the floor with a thud, sword still grasped in hand.

The Jinn seethed in his fury at no longer being able to wield its weapon. The fleeting pleasure he felt while grasping it evaporated in the knowledge that Alec's physical form not only allowed him to lift it, but also ripped him from his body. As a descendant of Morpheus, endowed with a pure heart and immeasurable courage, Alec was a rightful owner of the blade.

Acknowledging this, it cast away the nefarious being inside of him.

"It matters not," The Jinn hissed turning away in disgust to now face Probetor. "You have done well in my absence but you need to remember your place next to me as I rule, I fear you are forgetting this?" He questioned.

As Probetor watched on, The Jinn seemed to grow exponentially in size and stature. A dark mist surrounded him and he hovered menacingly in the air before Probetor, a living embodiment of evil and darkness.

Now Probetor truly confronted a far more daunting challenge than he had foreseen. He stood resolutely, his assurance matching the magnitude of power now before him. He realized that the might he wielded in this instance could surpass even the formidable Jinn. The defiant look upon his face spoke volumes amongst the lack of words forthcoming. As he looked on, he noticed that those who had stood next to him now waned and stood by The Jinn, Jenny and all of the accompanying Koschei forces now stood with him and left Probetor standing alone.

"No loyalty amongst them then, that is a surprise," Nero jokingly pipped up breaking the complete silence that had remained for some time now amongst the others as they watched on.

Probetor scowled as he looked at all of his troops moving, "more betrayal," he said whilst looking at Jenny in particular.

She looked him in the eyes however, unashamed as she stated boldly, "Our mission was always in servitude to the dark lord Probetor, you knew this."

"You fool," The Jinn spat. With an outstretched arm, he hurled a bolt of energy straight towards Probetor. Instinctively, Probetor jumped aside and with one fluid motion created a blockade in front of himself.

He raised it defensively just as the blast made contact causing an explosion of light that lit up the area like daybreak, temporarily blinding everyone present.

When their vision cleared, they saw that Probetor stood now facing off against the Jinn and that the dynamics of the unfolding events around them were changing, and fast.

24) The power within

Freyja nudged Hypnos as she looked at the air around them, the purple hue was fading and the protective field Probetor had placed around himself was shrinking and becoming much more localised to just his person. She saw this as an opportunity, an opening to do something, anything to turn the tables.

Hypnos, just as aware as Freyja of the dwindling protective shield and energy surrounding Probetor, slowly crept towards Alec's body hoping to see signs of life. He was now well away from all others and the force field had moved away leaving Alec's body lying in the open looking lonely and forgotten. As he moved closer, he could see that the he lay lifeless, drained and burnt from the immense force that had torn his body apart in freeing the Jinn and opening Lemuri.

He bowed his head in mourning for the fallen, another victim of this unending battle. He noticed however that the blade still clung solidly to his hand, and despite his best attempts, it was beyond Hypnos' strength to pry it away from him. Frustrated and confused by this he questioned his worth, he had certainly been able to hold it in the past, to utilise its power no, but to hold it yes.

Savi trudged over to Alec's body and dropped to her knees beside him, crying in anguish at the sight of her son, lifeless on the ground. She raised a quivering hand and carefully swept away a few locks from his face as salty tears cascaded down her cheeks. She had kept an eye on him from a distance for many years, wishing and praying that she would be able to embrace him once more, but now as she did exactly that, she desired nothing more than to return to keeping watch of him from afar.

Freyja strode closer and pressed a compassionate hand onto her shoulder before murmuring in a hushed tone," We must take action now, we can ensure his life was not sacrificed for nothing."

Savi reluctantly nodded, her porcelain face showing a single tear glistening down its cheek and onto Alec's hand. The sword was still firmly in his grasp; its gleaming gold shone brighter as the tear seeped through his fingers and coursed along its blade like molten liquid responding to the pull of the moon.

The two women stared at each other as the blade vibrated, now radiating with a celestial golden brilliance. Savi felt a wave of warmth course through her son's formerly frigid fingers. She gawked downward in astonishment before gazing upwards to the stilled waters of Lemuri, almost imploring the gods to restore life to him.

Freyja backed away as she saw the shimmering energy surrounding them, it felt alive, a resurgence of life and a reminder of hope. She felt inexplicably drawn to the blade and moved closer, extending her arm towards it. As if in response to her gesture, the blade released a surge of energy outwards with such force that they were both pushed backwards as she gasped in surprise.

The two women stared at each other, conscious that something else was observing them - they could feel a mysterious energy directing them without anyone else's knowledge, beside the Jinn who brusquely uttered the word "No" in defiant response.

As the two women edged in closer Freyja was the first to comprehend what was occurring, the first to recognize her ancient companion as they heard a faint murmur from the sword:

"Stand young Alec".

Freyja's mouth grew a faint smile as she understood why The Jinn answered as he had, he too could sense it, "Morpheus" she breathed out.

An unseen force divinely lifted Alec's body off the ground as Savi and Freyja looked on in shock. Slowly, his body hovered higher and higher until he was level with Freyja and Savi's eyes.

As they watched, a faint glow started to appear around him, beginning at his feet and spreading up until it reached the very tip of his head. It was like witnessing a warm light embracing him with its protection.

The two women stared in wonderment for what seemed like hours but in reality, was mere seconds before Alec blinked open his eyes. He felt invigorated and alive, fully restored again. The sword still held firmly in his grip emitted a faint purr as if delighted that it had played its part.

Lemuri handpicked Alec as its champion and with Morpheus's divine intervention, resurrected him from within the sword, blessing him with a virtually supernatural power beyond anything any of them had ever witnessed. As a direct descendant of Morpheus, he naturally possessed the necessary bloodline. Freyja never considered that Morpheus would remain alive in the sword from beyond the grave. Combined with Lemuri's strength and Savi's love, Alec was triumphantly brought back to life.

It was all so obvious to her now why Lemuri had called upon Alec.

Alec plummeted back to the earth, his body blazing a molten gold as the blade he grasped had ignited.

He regained his footing and studied the sword now in his grip, its gleam coursing through his arm before softening away. He brandished the blade outward while examining himself, realising that he was alive again with an unwavering assurance that emanated outwards. Alec seemed to have grown a few inches taller as an exuding air of confidence shone from his body. His muscles were more defined and he stood with a proud, warrior-like stance that showed off every inch of his strength. He held the sword tightly, its gleam illuminating him from within and giving him an otherworldly aura.

Savi approached Alec, affectionately reaching out her hand to softly rest on his cheek. She smiled softly, a brief moment of joy in the midst of all this horror. "Hello Alec, it is so very good to see you."

Alec smiled back at her, his eyes searching her face for an answer to the questions that had been dancing in his mind for such a long time.

"Are you really my mother?", he asked, looking deep into her eyes.

Savi nodded, tears welling up in her eyes. "Yes Alec, I'm your mother." She raised her other hand and cradled his face within her palms.

Freyja watched on, a proud smile tugging at the corners of her lips as she realized that they now had an incredible reinforcement.

Freyja's mind was heavy with a strange blend of emotions as she watched on. Especially since having heard Morpheus's voice. Elation, sadness, and nostalgia filled the air and for a moment, time seemed to stand still. But she knew their respite was fleeting; they had more work to do.

The interaction and events happening with Alec seemed unnoticed on the other side of this standoff. They were much more distracted with each other at this point. As Probetor and The Jinn began to duel with a fury unmatched, Jenny and the Koschei forces charged at Hypnos, Nero and Gram. They moved with incredible speed; their weapons raised in the air ready for battle. They had no mercy in their eyes as they moved closer and closer, forming a semi-circle around them.

Hypnos grabbed his blade tightly in his hands as he readied himself for battle alongside his allies impressed by all he had seen from Freyja's new sidekick in Gram.

Freyja turned to see the commotion as the trio of warriors stood off against the incoming forces. Her eyes then shifted to Probetor as he steeled himself against the might of The Jinn. He now had a two-pronged attack on his hands and now faced off alone, however with the power obtained even this was not an impossible fight for him to win.

She stared into Alec's eyes and sternly declared, "the time has come for you; I can perceive him in you now you know." Alec looked back in shock, he believed after all of this he had demonstrated he was nothing like his father. Freyja smiled cryptically, "I detect Morpheus in you" she continued "You are not your father, you are your uncle, Morpheus is in you, I can sense it."

In an instant, Probetor unleashed a tremendous explosion by extending the reach of his formidable capabilities. He had acquired some energy from The Jinn and thus was able to erect an impenetrable force field that could fend off even metaphysical strikes by enabling energy entry but not releasing it externally onto his adversaries. It was clear he now had a predicament: although he had secured dominance over all realms, the ultimate confrontation at Erobus had become a struggle to recover control over his army—a mission he was losing.

Freyja and Savi left Alec's side and joined the others in their fight as he tried to ready himself, a moment was required after his awakening to gain any composure, they were heavily outnumbered and gradually grouping together within a small circle.

Nero had been the furthest outside of them however he had now stepped forward fearlessly to join them, his axe held aloft in his hands as he shouted out a battle cry that echoed through the air. His confidence was unparalleled, despite the odds stacked up against him he seemed unperturbed and ready for anything. He still felt the need for some vengeance over his lost post, and with no armies to now command of his own a certain sense of freedom washed over him leaving him acting much more freely and less controlled in his actions.

Gram clutched onto Freyja's arm fiercely, dragging her closer to the inner circle and away from the dangers, "Stay back!" he shouted gruffly as she readied herself alongside Hypnos. Freyja scowled in disbelief as she let loose a ferocious burst of energy, obliterating three Koschei soldiers into nothingness. She glared back at Gram who briskly averted his gaze.

"Alright," he muttered sheepishly.

The Jinn took advantage of all the commotion and focused back on Probetor. He let out a loud roar, flaring up his energies to its most powerful level before pointing his long finger in Probetor's direction.

"You are nothing more than a mere being, you who thinks he has gained such power over us powerful beings!" The Jinn said with a stern voice as he continued to let loose an array of powerful spells and attacks towards Probetor. "It is time for you to remember that you serve me, and I will not allow your delusions of grandeur to cloud your judgement any longer."

The Jinn seethed with resentment at Probetor's impudence, struggling to reconcile how his pride had burgeoned to the point that he thought himself worthy of enslaving The Jinn.

Probetor kept quiet throughout this, fixated on the reality that he had to battle both his allies and adversaries. His agitation amplified as the seemingly simple task ahead became increasingly difficult and he desperately sought an escape. He strove to vanquish The Jinn with his own dark magic, but they were equally equipped in this arena. Even with all of Probetor's newfound power, The Jinn still reigned supreme in a one-on-one showdown.

Then, Probetor espied the Drasal Tree in the far distance, and with haste he bounded towards it realising he had no other option but to flee and regroup. His only hope of escape was from this tree that he now controlled.

Arriving at it, he cast a spell and the branches erupted into a golden fountain of light as they opened up a portal into another plane. The Jinn followed closely behind, but could not match Probetor's speed as he sprinted forward. As Probetor abandoned Erobus for the other realm, he had no control over where he would end up in his haste and hurdled through blindly. He felt the viscous air beating at his face as The Jinn's furious jeers resounded through his head.

"You may have eluded me for now," The Jinn roared with rage "but I will find you and I will not forget your disloyalty."

As Probetor disappeared out of sight falling to a realm unknown, Nero breathed a heavy sigh of relief. He was happy to be rid of the tyrant, his presence had brought a direness to Erobus that had not been felt in a long time.

He smiled at Hypnos as he spoke aloud, "Gone is the tyrant Probetor, now we at least only have the original one to face! Let them keep on removing themselves from this."

To which Hypnos retorted sternly, "but The Jinn is not a good replacement for him... trust me, I have been here before".

The Jinn seethed, his frustration boiling over. He pivoted to face the group behind him and charged toward them, eager to unleash his wrath. With Probetor's groundwork laid down for him, he felt he could finish what he had started all those years ago. He radiated with an otherworldly energy, conjuring black flames from his fingertips as a tempest roared overhead.

Although magic was not his forte, the Jinn relished the prospect of an intense battle having always considered himself an incredible warlord. Jinn was a formidable hand-to-hand fighter and he relished the fight ahead of him as he looked towards Hypnos, a foe he recalled well from the battlefield.

The pleasure he gained from feeling a life slipping away between his hands was far greater to him than any satisfaction he could muster from afar. Such were the thoughts of his depraved mind.

Hypnos shuddered as he met The Jinn's gaze, feeling a prickling sense of fear. Even though he had battled many foes before, this was the first time he would be confronting The Jinn face to face, and it made even him uneasy.

He had been on the field of battle when he fought Morpheus, he had seen the power he held and was aware he now held even more. How could he hope to defeat an enemy that even the great Morpheus had to sacrifice himself to defeat?

He stood tall on the edge of his unwavering determination, but the thought of a fearsome enemy converging on Erobus still made him tremble. Fear was to be expected and he accepted it, yet he knew that he must stay strong even in the face of it. For when one could accept the courage that comes with facing fear head on and not backing down, could they truly be an invincible warrior.

He knew that if the oppressive tyranny Probetor had opened the doors on was to truly be ended, then they must first stop The Jinn from wreaking havoc on the one world that still stood. The idea of two tyrannical forces pulling the realms into a never-ending battle of evil minds was as close a thought of eternal hell as could be.

Hypnos inhaled sharply and braced for battle before advancing on The Jinn. Breaking away from the melee he was engaged in, he marched deliberately towards his adversary.

The Nyx troops had broken through the walls and were now heading down the passageway to join forces against the Koschei. The battle would surely be over soon enough however it was a first for Lemuri to turn into the battlefield she had become.

Hypnos threw himself into battle against The Jinn, knowing full well that his life depended on it. His training and reflexes were pushed to their absolute limits as he worked to gain any advantage over the Jinn.

He attacked with a ferocity that was born of desperation, never allowing his enemy a moment's peace as he sought desperately to survive. But even with all of his skill and determination, Hypnos was unable to withstand the onslaught being thrown at him by The Jinn. Every attack seemed to bring an icy chill of pain and brutality from The Jinn; every defence Hypnos threw up was met with unrelenting fury and ruthlessness.

In the end, the sheer power of The Jinn's onslaught forced Hypnos back until he had no more ground left to give, and he could do nothing but accept his fate.

His body flew through the air, propelled by The Jinn's powerful blows. He felt his strength ebbing away with every hit, desperation setting in as he struggled to defend himself against the overwhelming force.

With a thunderous roar, The Jinn charged forward and Hypnos could do nothing but brace himself for the onslaught. Miraculously, at the last second, The Jinn halted mid-swing, standing tall over him with an arrogant smirk on his face.

"No magic was even needed here; you are so feeble and without any strategy to turn the battle in your favour. Even Morpheus had an idea of how to take me down." His taunts rang through the air like thunder and Hypnos could not help but almost amuse at the ironic number of times he had stared death in the face in recent time.

As Hypnos sank to his knees, searing lightning seared through the air and blasted The Jinn with a white-hot fury. Vicious flames ripped through the sky as Alec stepped forward – a corona of liquid gold emanating from him like a living sun. He tightly clutched the sword of Morpheus and his eyes sparked with unyielding determination as he shouted" I won't sacrifice Erobus to darkness; I won't let Earth suffer; and I absolutely won't let you or my father have your way!"

The Jinn's eyes widened in terror as Alec closed in on him, rage contorting his face. Despite his best efforts to defend himself, he was no match for the overwhelming force of Alec's advances. His glowing golden blade twirled majestically through the air as Alec struck repeatedly, and The Jinn raised his arms weakly in a futile attempt to protect himself. Fear coursed through The Jinn like electricity.

Hypnos grabbed his chance and attacked, in tandem with Alec. The pair fought like a raging fire against The Jinn's ice-cold fury and soon the two of them had him pinned to the floor, unable to move as they continued their flurry of attacks.

The battle was intense and unrelenting, it seemed that no matter how hard The Jinn fought, the combined strength of Hypnos and Alec was more than he could handle.

Eventually, after what felt like hours of relentless combat, Hypnos and Alec managed to overpower The Jinn once and for all. In a final act of desperation - the only time they witnessed any true display of fear from him - he released all of his power into a blazing wave that threatened to consume them all.

However, despite the devastating onslaught that ripped apart Alec's skin, leaving gashes of glistening red where it had clawed at him, he endured the force with equal power. With a tremendous swing of his sword, the world around them lit up in a brilliant golden hue as he drove the Jinn to the ground.

Overwhelmed, he glanced up in disbelief as the familiar feeling of being pulled into the blade took hold once more.

The Jinn thrashed and clawed at the ground while Alec braced for impact. All of a sudden, Hypnos materialized out of thin air, defying the strong air currents created by the sword's pull.

With a resounding crash, Hypnos' sword fell upon the Jinn, shattering his grip on reality and sending him hurtling back into his centuries-old prison with a gigantic display of flashing lights and thunderous crashes that overwhelmed the senses and froze all of those within the surrounding vicinity.

As the smoke cleared and Hypnos regained his senses he could see Alec in front of him, the glow diminishing and, on his knees, handle of the sword still in hand with the blade digging deep into the earth below. The Jinn was gone, defeated and imprisoned once more.

The landscape of Lemuri stilled as the clouds parted, unveiling a magnificent sky above the foreboding blackness that had been hanging over them all.

Alec is standing upright but his body is shaking as dirt falls off of him. His face is flushed with determined exhaustion and his clothes are ripped and torn from the battle. The handle of the sword is still gripped in his hand, the blade embedded in the ground beneath him.

Hypnos rushed to his side and steadied him as he wobbled precariously. He beamed with pride at Alec's achievement before uttering fervently, "Well done Alec, well done!"

The tumultuous war abruptly ceased, as the Koschei forces realized that their leaders were all exiled. Only Jenny still had any standing among Maredrom's ranks of warriors, and they felt liberated from the pervasive tyranny. They dispersed back to Maredrom, eagerly resuming their aimless wandering. Many collapsed where they had stood, having been invigorated by the sorcerer's enchantment.

Freyja, Savi, Nero and Gram surveyed each other with satisfaction, having successfully repelled the onslaught as a cheer arose from the surrounding Nyx soldiers who remained. Nero and Gram clapped each other's shoulders in a sombre celebration as Freyja and Savi advanced towards the motionless lake that had once harboured Lemuri's lively waters.

Without uttering a word, they stretched their arms outwards and placed their palms on the solid surface. Shutting their eyes tightly, they concentrated fervently; suddenly there was a rumble signifying possible recovery of the falls—yet they remained broken and still.

They slumped up from their knees, desolate. Lemuri was the beacon of the realms – it held all hopes and dreams of its citizens throughout all of the realms. To fail to restore it would take them into a bleak period, doomed to be without luck. A harsh reminder of how they may have won the battle but not all their liberties and beliefs.

The couple spun around, eyes wide with surprise at the sight of the ruby radiance beneath the icy surface. It was moving closer to them, shimmering brighter with each passing second. Just as it threatened to break through, there was a deafening crack like thunder and shards of ice flew in all directions. A burst of flame exploded outward, dazzling them both.

As the spirit of the Phoenix bellowed its way back from beyond the veil, time seemed to stand still. Its thick wings spread wide, shimmering with diamond-like flecks that danced in every corner of the sky. The Phoenix's presence electrified the frosty air, painting a beautiful arc of light and colour across the lake below. A deafening roar accompanied its ascension as it flew higher and higher until its powerful form faded from sight. An immense, thunderous boom echoed through the valley as a cascade of energy was released.

Lemuri, ignited by the power of its cosmic parent, was reborn.

25) Reawakening

The group gaped as the effervescent waters of Lemuri cascaded down around them once again, the rain showering them in a fog as Alec and Hypnos alighted next to Freyja and Savi.

The Drasal tree returned to being invisible from view as the waters flowed and the churning waters soon became as invigorated as they once had been sending it back safely to its secure place behind the great falls.

Savi clutched Alec as she released a breathy sigh, " My darling Alec, I have been dreaming of seeing you in the flesh again for so long. You have become such an extraordinary person and I am so proud of you. I have always been watching and I have always been with you, but now you understand why I had to go away from you and I am so so sorry for this. I would like to cherish this special time together before I must return back to Alerion. We will make the journey to Sofpavel side by side, if you are happy to do so of course?"

"Leave?" Alec stammered. "But why? I have only just- got you back."

Savi caressed his face tenderly, her smile lingering as she spoke with a tear in her eyes.

"You don't need me here however much you may feel you do; you've found yourself and you have found me. I may not be here but we will find a way to maintain communication. To be truthful, when I was adopted into the Alerion world, I befriended some powerful beings there. They allowed me to use their magic and blessed me with these gifts that you have seen. But in exchange for them, I'm now obligated to watch over their people. I made a promise. When I left to assist you, it was beneficial to all realms and the one catch I always had was that if you needed me that I would leave until you no longer did. The threat now comes from your father - wherever he may be - and you are as safe as you can be with your new allies. And sadly, I no longer have the Phoenix within me; I must help guard Alerion without my second-best present."

"Second?" Alec inquired curiously.

"Of course," Savi said, her smile still on her lips. "You'll always be my first."

Alec smiled in response and nodded in acceptance of her words before he whipped around to face Freyja, the sword still glowing hot in his palm.

"This is yours I believe," he declared, the blade cooling and darkening as the Jinn's spirit receded back into its depths. Freyja gave a nod of comprehension, gesturing for Hypnos to accept it from Alec's grasp.

"I knew you'd be able to do this," she said with a sly wink. "We can lock it up in a secure place again now and ensure it remains that way."

The group now turned towards Sofpavel, eager to return to their homelands and begin the rebuilding that would be required, forgetting for now that with Probetor still out there somewhere the fight was in truth never over.

Along the way they paused for a day at the camp in Midjun, where troops were busy celebrating the party's success briefly before preparing for whatever came next.

The villagers welcomed the warriors with open arms, and none was more thrilled to see Alec than Josh. Although a bit disoriented and flustered, he leapt to his feet in glee.

And so, the heroes continued on their journey, Josh alongside them. The cool air of Sofpavel met their faces like a soothing balm after the perilous journeys they had in days passed. Nearby, amidst the woodlands was a pleasant village, that they stopped in to rest and gather themselves. All along each path, each respite and destination brought joy, as well as a sense of accomplishment to their quest.

The woodland folks had experienced a great deal in their lives, as they were naturally peaceful yet apprehensive of the unfamiliar. As the first populated area someone encountered when coming into Sofpavel, they held a certain dread for all that was on its way, and were grateful to the group they currently welcomed. Before sending them off on their journey, they gave them food and supplies and ensured they were sufficiently rested.

As they returned to their trek, Freyja scrutinized her surroundings and gaped at the marvel of nature reminiscing the grandeur of her homeland – from sumptuous meadows to copious woods, it was a spellbinding sight that she never became weary of. With a fresh gust in her sails, she carried onward while Nero hopped beside her, offering comic relief and dialogue along her journey of which she enjoyed far more than she let on. Now that he had relinquished his tower he would be searching for a new mission, and Freyja sensed that a new robust settlement would be necessary on Midjun, the decisive leader for such being right here in the sad absence of Araya.

Alec walked along talking to Josh, their friendship had been through a lot but had survived unscathed if not a little different. Josh who had been a part of Alec's life since before he could recall, ever-present with a helpful hand and an eager smile.

As Savi had said, he was as much their family as anyone else, and Freyja was certain, even though her earlier feelings towards him, that he could be of help in more ways than one and would be a crucial asset for Alec going forwards. She knew the path ahead for him was a long one and he would need his friend by his side. Josh himself had equally seemed to found a new lease of life, he provided assistance throughout the trek like a beacon of hope amongst the weary travellers, revelling in no longer hiding his true identity.

When times were tough, he gave encouraging words to spur forward those who had grown tired or disheartened and when everyone else needed cheering up he always had a funny joke or two up his sleeve that got them all laughing no matter what. His infectious enthusiasm was matched only by the unwavering loyalty shown towards Savi in his protection of Alec.

The group forged on, travelling through rolling hills and lush forests until reaching the city walls of Sofpavel; a sight so grand it brought tears to some of their eyes, especially those who feared never seeing it again.

After such a long period away from home, there it lay before them - a reminder that they had stood united against all odds with no force too great for them to resist. They made their way inside the gates and were then greeted by an outpouring of joyous cheers and celebration – finally they had arrived home safe and sound!

For Hypnos, this was all too familiar. He had experienced a near-identical welcome home many years before, and as he surveyed the area, he remembered the comrades lost during his journey. A heavy burden weighed upon him; last time it was guilt for letting down his leader Morpheus, now it was the great Major who served under him in Araya combined with his shame for having being so unkind to Logan. He had vowed and ensured that Logan's body would be returned with them alongside Araya's, and he'd arrange a grand send-off, one of a Nyx warrior—it was the least he could do and he knew Logan would be proud to receive such a sendoff.

Now that they had arrived back at Sofpavel's grand capital, Savi began to contemplate Alec's future. She sensed an intense beckoning from Alerion and knew it was time to go home; she had been away for far too long and her people needed her guidance. Although the realm could not be seen in its entirety from Erobus, she realized that only by returning would she get a full view of all that had transpired. Yet, she decided to spend this final day with her son and enjoy his company for the first time since he was a small child.

She was unsure if Josh would be accompanying her on the journey back however. Thinking back over the years since she first sent Josh to Alec's side, Savi was grateful for all of the help Josh had provided and the comfort and protection he had offered Alec when things got tough.

She felt it was right that Josh should stay with Alec and continue with his recovery, and their strong friendship instead of travelling back to Alerion with her. Savi knew that Josh would be grateful of the opportunity to remain here. His relationship with Alec was after all something he had known for much longer than anything else, given his true family were long gone he did not have anything to return to Alerion for, it made sense for all for him to stay wherever Alec chose to be.

Freyja beamed as she surveyed the merry-making around her and gazed upon the motley crew that stood before her. Despite their tumultuous beginnings, they had come together to form a strong and formidable team that would do a grand job in safeguarding the realms. Even though she knew they'd be tested soon enough, Freyja decided to rejoice in the festivities alongside them for now.

Nero reunited with his former watchmen, who revelled in his presence and honoured him with the utmost respect.

Freyja spied Nero rejoicing in the distance, he appeared joyous but had a desolate look within his eyes. He had provided reliable support to her during the journey back and been a remarkable asset on the battlefield. All of his former comrades who fought so daringly with him in the tower had now joined the Nyx forces, the days of the watchmen were truly gone but as she had previously supposed, it was necessary to establish a new settlement somewhere in Midjun.

Freyja sidled up to Nero and put her arm around him, asking, "So what's next?"

"Ah Freyja, who knows? Maybe I'll find a place to call home and get me a wife. Care to join me for the next few hundred years or so?" he replied with a laugh.

Freyja smiled; she found his arrogance amusing, but most definately not husband material. Then she offered her suggestion.

"It is to be debated but I believe we are going to set up a settlement in Mid-jun, almost like a mini-city. We'll need someone strong to keep Maredrom in check. Fancy spending the next few hundred years there?" She winked at him, showing that she had been paying attention to his earlier joke.

Nero nodded his consent and asked if he could be king of this new settlement.

Freyja laughed again and said, "Call yourself whatever you like—we won't recognize you as such." With a gentle nudge of her elbow, she began to walk away from him before calling over her shoulder that they would discuss it more another time.

As the night drew to a close and people made their way back to their individual homes safe in the temporary peace they had found, the group looked around at each other with a certain melancholy that had come over them all. It had been a long hard painful journey to reach this point with painful loses along the way.

Finally for Alec the worst of those was about to come, it was time for Savi to say her goodbyes.

Alec felt the warmth of her embrace as she held him tightly. She told him that he could call upon her at any time, that no matter what happened she would be there for him. Her presence enveloped him like a blanket, providing an intense surge of emotion coursing through his veins, filling him with the assurance that she was always watching over him.

As she walked away from the settlement with Freyja and Nero following behind her, she glanced one last time at Alec who was standing tall in the moonlight—waving farewell.

Freyja stood in front of Savi preparing to send her back almost a little saddened to see her new friend depart. She stood standing tall with a confident grin across her face.

"So how are you so sure you can do this?" Savi questioned with doubt oozing out from every word. Freyja chuckled then replied slyly,

"I have a few new tricks." She reached into her pocket and pulled out a rather suspicious looking stick.

"Erm ok, I'm not sure what you are planning on doing with that," Savi queried pointing at the stick, "did you take a hit on the head at some point?"

Freyja ignored the comment and with that she held the stick up high, singing happy songs as she twirled it around. Eventually a portal opened up around its path like a sparkler at bonfire night.

"No way!" Savi exclaimed in astonishment. "Did you steal that from the Drasal?!"

Freyja shrugged innocently and without words simply gave a mischievous wink.

Savi gave a knowing grin back, "naughty naughty" she said, wagging her finger before stepping through the portal and back into Alerion.

Freyja then turned to Alec and Josh and asked where they plan to be.

"You can go back to Earth if you wish, only a few minutes have passed there you can carry on and nobody would know you had been missing, or you can stay here in Erobus and carry on the good fight," she said, looking from Josh to Alec for confirmation.

Alec thought it over for a moment before responding.

"I think staying here in Erobus is the right thing to do. We have already come so far and I don't want to stop now. Besides, I'd miss you all now."

He said this jokingly with a little laugh as he looking at Freyja expectantly, waiting for her response as Josh nodded along in agreement. Whilst said in jest there was a lot of truth in those words, he now felt more like he belonged than he had for a long time.

Freyja smiled as she assessed the spiritedness of her two companions, "Excellent choice," she said sagely before continuing on with the plans they had made earlier that evening.

"Looks like it's time to get started". She placed the Drasal stick back into her inner pocket, a formidable tool that now lay within her arsenal.

"Before we put it away, I'd like to go back and say goodbye to my grandparents, if that's alright?" Freyja beamed as she opened a portal to Earth for Alec.

"Of course, take your time." She responded with a smile. He stepped through and was met with the look of astonishment on his grandparents' faces. Freyja quietly shut the portal behind him, letting him have his precious moment of farewell in privacy.

She turned to Hypnos and the two agreed that they would survey their situation and start rebuilding the next day; all the hardships they had gone through bore many newfound advantages as well as problems that require resolving.

But for now, they needed to make sure that the threat of Probetor was shielded against with until he could be located and dealt with.

With a wave of her hand and a few whispered words Freyja cast a powerful spell, creating a barrier around Earth and Erobus, the two planets they could be sure he did not current reside within.

A great wall in the sky stood tall and firm with no way for Probetor to cross without an invitation - it would hopefully be safe until he was found. With their work complete for the time being, Freyja and Hypnos bid each other farewell as they retired for the evening, wishing to enjoy a moment of solitude before beginning the next phase of securing the realms, a never-ending battle in reality.

The night air surrounded them with its chill as the stars twinkled in the sky above. This was their new life for now, although they were partially unaware of just how extensively they were living on borrowed time, especially against such a powerful enemy. But despite all of this and all of the losses incurred, it had been a great day; one of newfound hope and strength for the billions of souls throughout the realms, one that no enemy could take away from them in this moment.

Meanwhile.... Probetor was isolated in a far-flung domain, engulfed in pitch blackness and surrounded by strange beasts of all kinds of which he was already trying to bend to his will. Fortunately for him this world had gone unnoticed by those keeping watch from Erobus, at least for now.

On Alerion, they'd picked up a subtle warning signal of his potential whereabouts within their far advanced control rooms of which cast an even wider net of vision than Erobus own, but, for now, he evaded them also. He had plenty of time to conspire and strategize for his great return.

He may have been knocked down hard but he hadn't been defeated.... yet.

Printed in Great Britain
by Amazon

32237959R00132